The
Stranger
from
the Sea

The Stranger from the Sea

A NOVEL

Paul Binding

THE OVERLOOK PRESS
NEW YORK, NY

This edition first published in hardcover in the United States in 2019 by
The Overlook Press, an imprint of ABRAMS
195 Broadway, 9th floor
New York, NY 10007
www.overlookpress.com

Abrams books are available at special discounts when purchased in quantity
for premiums and promotions as well as fundraising or educational use.
Special editions can also be created to specification. For details, contact
specialsales@abramsbooks.com or the address above.

Cataloging-in-Publication Data is available from the Library of Congress

Book design and typeformatting by Bernard Schleifer
Manufactured in the United States of America

FIRST EDITION

1 3 5 7 9 10 8 6 4 2

ISBN 978-1-4683-1642-1

For Christopher and Deb Sinclair-Stevenson

Contents

PART *One*

I Find a New Home (I Don't Think)

W hen I was given the job on *The Channel Ports Advertiser*, I felt fortune had turned in my favor at last. I had been working on a South London newspaper for three whole years and was still spending far too much time running backwards and forwards between office and printers. I'd been taken on, after all, in the understanding that sooner rather than later I'd be a reporter going out and about in pursuit of stories. And I followed all the latest movements in our press, particularly the activities of W. T. Stead at his *Pall Mall Gazette*, and regularly relayed them to Mr. Burton, my editor. Well, eventually the day came when Burtie called me in to say he'd been chatting with fellow editors in our newspaper group and had learned of a vacancy in *The Advertiser*, down in Dengate, on the south Kent coast. So the very next week—on Thursday, February 19, 1885, to be exact— I took the train down to meet one Mr. Edmund Hough.

"We are expanding here handsomely," this man informed me. "And so have room for another young man on our staff. Provided, of course, that he has the required largeness. Largeness of spirit, that is," he added, his brown eyes twinkling.

Well, if he'd been looking for the other kind, I would not have fitted the bill, being on the short side, and lean and wiry in build. With respect to physical largeness, Mr. Hough, a man in his mid-forties wearing a black velvet jacket and crimson bow-tie, wasn't doing too badly: ruddy face, bull neck, full stomach.

Dengate I already knew from daytrips with friends from my South London paper: crowded beaches, famous white cliffs, long terraces of boardinghouses and hotels. My mates and I had thoroughly enjoyed ourselves here: listening to singers and comedians in the booths, whispering outrageous things to passing girls (well, that was Will Postgate of course, with the rest of us egging him on!), and, naturally, partaking of jellied-eels and winkles. But I'd no more thought of living in Dengate than in the Tower of London or Madame Tussauds. I was only twenty-three—though, to my shame, a few months older than the great W. T. Stead when he took over *The Northern Echo*—and had spent at most half a dozen nights away from London. Could a seaside resort—further from "The Smoke" than I'd realized—truly cater to my needs?

Mr. Edmund Hough was clearly reading my thoughts.

"What goes on in Dengate, Bridges, is as important as what goes on anywhere else in the world. *The Advertiser* is in the vanguard of British papers in giving attention to regional news. When the last of those beastly restrictive taxes went, it became easier for a local paper to be, well, local. As it should be. In the bad old days"—Mr. Hough batted them away with his right hand—"many of our pages were filled with syndicated stuff just like your average London rag. But no longer! Bridges, you'll be able to write all those exciting articles I hear you aspire to without going beyond this goodly borough of ours. Like any other reporter you'll be covering the usual run of civic events, but any high dramas that come our way, you'll be in line for meeting head-on!"

Music to my ears! Edmund Hough's voice, coming though it did from an ample body, was light and breezy, and every so often leaped upwards with excitement into a boyish register.

"For the moment, like every other paper in Kent, *The Advertiser* is a weekly, but I am aiming at twice a week, no less . . . Well, you'll be wanting to know about the outfit here. We are seven, excluding our unwaged apprentice, Peter Frobisher. The rest are seasoned pressmen of various shapes and sizes. Everybody turns his hand to everything; we all sub our own pieces, and usually each other's as well, provide our own headlines, attend to questions of length and space, and jiggle pieces so they fit in 'round the advertisements which—though I says it as shouldn't—are now positively pouring in. This obviously involves discussion with . . ."

I knew it! I said to myself even before he'd finished his sentence. I hadn't done with visits to the printers yet, and those *The Advertiser* used were situated at a convenient distance of three streets, Barrett Brothers, in red-brick premises built to accommodate their new-model rotary machines. Oh well, if I had to, I had to. I was now noticing, as Mr. Hough talked eloquently on, two framed lines of handsomely lettered verse hanging over his none-too-tidy desk:

> *Flesh unto spirit must grow.*
> *Spirit raves not for a goal.*

Shakespeare? Milton? Anyway, I wasn't sure I agreed with this bloke. My spirit did have a goal, even "raved" for it: to be a first-class reporter. And Mr. Hough himself surely had one too: the success of *The Advertiser*.

"Is there anything you'd like to tell me," he was now asking, "about your own approach to a newspaper?"

Here was my opportunity, all right. I spoke—jolly well in the circumstances, but then I'd been rehearsing all train journey down—of the example *Tit-Bits* was setting us all, with its miscellanies of interesting facts, its jokes, its short stories. (I didn't mention that I had gone in for one of its competitions myself, with a humorous story, and had received not, I confess, the "Tit-Bits Villa" promised as first prize but an Honorable Mention!) I expressed my admiration, too, for W. T. Stead's *Pall-Mall Gazette* with its emphasis on interviews, its determination to show readers areas of national life other publications shied away from.

"Capital, capital!" said Mr. Edmund Hough. "You're clearly a man after my own heart." Then he took out a huge crimson handkerchief, which matched his bowtie, mopped his brow twice or thrice, and then said: "I've just one further question for you, Bridges."

My pulse-rate speeded up, my mouth turned dry. Whatever finer points of typography and modern equipment had I coming to me? Or, worse still, elaborate and testing intricacies of costing? Imagine my surprise at being asked: "Would you say you are *cheerful*?"

Dare I reply that both inside the South London office and outside it, folk considered me something of a wag? Will Postgate, no less, had called me this.

I answered: "I believe I am."

"Good!" said Mr. Hough. "Cheerfulness makes the world go 'round."

"I'll say!" I agreed sycophantically, though I'd always heard it was love which did this. I could hold back no longer. "Mr. Hough," I blurted. "Might I be so bold as to ask if I have a chance of this vacancy on *The Advertiser*?"

"My dear Bridges," Edmund Hough sounded positively grieved, "how can you doubt it? The position is yours."

So this then was my great day. I had my feet now on a sturdy rung of exactly the ladder I desired.

Yet almost as soon as I left the *Advertiser*'s premises, I was struck by Dengate's overpowering quietness. I was in the very center of the town, and where was the bustle, the mishmash of diverse, and often intriguing, folk such as any ordinary London borough would provide? On this February afternoon of half-light and clammy sea-fret, the seagulls wheeling whitely under gray clouds were the most active living beings in sight. Then I recalled, *Spirit raves not for a goal*. Which probably meant, *Take any damned opportunity given you and make the most of it*.

A fortnight later I went down to Dengate again, to settle the little matter of where I should live. Mr. Hough, ever helpful, had not only suggested the best date for me to start work, but had recommended lodgings—with "my good friend," Mrs. Fuller, in Castelaniene, St. Ethelberga's Road. I'd therefore written to her. Her house's unusual name—but it was now quite the thing to call your home after some favorite exotic place—ought apparently to be pronounced "Cass-tell-an-yaynay" being "the name of an Italian village very dear to the late Mr. Fuller. But most Dengaters, bless 'em, can't cope with Italian, and call it 'Castle Aneen.' Mrs. Fuller, though, puts up with such ignorance, as, dear soul, she has put up with so much else."

"Dear soul," eh? This friend of my new Editor's would require my best manner, and as much sophistication as I could muster.

All journey down it rained. The train pulled up at stations the very names of which meant nothing to me, and behind which buildings receded into the murk of the day's unrelieved wet weather. Dengate Station, when it arrived, though built to receive jolly crowds burning to spend money, had this day a decidedly forlorn look. I found myself a cab.

"St. Ethelberga's Road? Blimey! I could do without going all the way up there!" said my driver. Understandably, I soon saw, for my street turned out to lie on the western edge of the resort, at the top of a steep hill not at all to the horse's liking in this strong insistent rain.

"A house called Cass-tell-an-yaynay," I reminded the cabbie. "But you may know it as Castle Aneen."

"Don't know it as anything at all, guv," he replied, "got better things to do with my time, thank you very much! If you're so eager to get to Castle Thingamajig, you'd better keep your eyes skinned when we get to St. Ethelberga's Road, had you not?"

In fact, we found it easily enough, one of a row of thin, tall, semi-detached villas from the previous decade, three stories excluding the basement. A monkey-puzzle tree grew (and grows still) in its pocket handkerchief of a front garden. Above the front door I noticed a stained-glass fanlight, the sections of which made up a picture of a Greek temple.

My cabbie didn't wait to see whether anybody greeted me or not, but trotted off downhill, the rain now at his back, as though he couldn't get away fast enough. I gave the bell-pull a few vigorous tugs. Perhaps the "dear soul" had forgotten I was coming, though she had assured me, in flamboyant purple ink, of her "enormous pleasure" at seeing me at precisely this hour.

When the door opened, the lady (or was it maiden?) who stood before me looked—to my raindrop-watery eyes—as though she'd stepped out of the vitreous classical scene above my head. She was wearing a loose, ankle-length, lilac tea-gown with long flowing sleeves. I myself, in deference to the cold day and the comparative formality of the occasion, had on my best Norfolk jacket, nattily belted at the back.

"Mr. Bridges?"

No, no maiden she, I could see the lines of middle years in the graceful neck she was craning toward me. Even so Mrs. Fuller wasn't anything like the age I'd been ascribing her from the respectful yet pitying tone of Mr. Hough's letter: she was in her early forties at most.

"The same, ma'am! I hope I've not come too early."

She was peering beyond me at the watery veils screening her little front garden from the rest of road.

"Early?" she repeated vaguely, as if I'd used some foreign word. "No, of course you're not. I was expecting you at just this time, though I didn't know you would appear right on cue like some young hero in a Shake-spearean romance."

Like a Shakespearean romance, eh? Such a compliment had come far too soon in our dialogue. I might be only twenty-three, but, lacking a proper home for five years, I had abundant experience of landladies.

Indispensable to a chap though they may sometimes be (perforce), they have as a species two attributes that make 'em damned difficult, if not downright impossible, to deal with: first, the power that comes from their unarguably superior position, and second, their incontestable right to be anywhere they want in their own houses. True, some are hoity-toity, others only too bally willing to have a chat; some grumble, some shout, some even use coarse language to you, while others are genteel to a degree. But I couldn't think of one member of the species I wouldn't have been better off not knowing. Mrs. Fuller would be charging me a considerably higher rent than her predecessors, but then I would be earning more here than hitherto. Also, a Channel Port would make fewer claims on the pocket than did the biggest city on earth, the New Babylon into which I'd been born.

Mrs. Fuller shut the door against the miserable afternoon and turning 'round with a swish of her tea-gown, informed me: "I have been greatly looking forward to this moment, Mr. Bridges. Shall I tell you something most interesting? The night after Edmund—Mr. Hough—suggested you as a lodger, I had a dream. I was walking by a little stream in a garden, and was wondering how I could get across it, when the kindest voice issued from the trees, saying: 'Remember, Beatrice, there are bridges, though you cannot see them yet.' Now wasn't that remarkable?"

"Remarkable indeed!" I concurred, though taken aback. "But then my name lends itself to that sort of thing. If I'd been called common-or-garden Smith, you might of dreamed of a forge with horses' hooves!"

Mrs. Fuller gave a fluttery little laugh clearly uncertain how to take my riposte. "Who knows? The mind does work in the most extraordinary way," she assented. "And yours, I can tell, is a very quick one. Exactly what Edmund—Mr. Hough—said."

I, naturally enough, would have liked to have heard more here, but I couldn't ask for this and maintain dignity. As I had gone all out to please Mr. Hough, it wasn't so astonishing he'd been praising me to his friends.

Mrs. Fuller, a tall woman, wore her hair swept up to the crown of her head, and, as I studied it, that sentimental song came into my mind, "Silver threads among the gold." *Beware, Martin!* I told myself. *She may be styled a widow, which makes you picture an aging woman dressed in black weeds like our Queen, but this woman before you ain't no nun-like recluse never giving men a thought. Perhaps she gives the editor of* The Advertiser, *for instance, something more than just a thought. You might have to tread carefully in Castelaniene.* But Mrs. Fuller was telling me something that sounded important . . .

"This, Mr. Bridges, is the real Castelaniene." She was pointing to a gilt-framed photogravure showing houses of Italian appearance like tiled upturned rectangles standing on a mountainside. Apart from dull Latin lessons at school, through which I'd daydreamed (as I had through most other subjects in that horrible realm of chalk-dust and scratched desktops), Italy had scarcely impinged on me.

"Nice-looking spot!" I said.

"Nice!" Mrs. Fuller gave another flutter of laughter. "My husband, George Fuller, called that place *un antícipo di paradiso.*"

"I beg your pardon, Mrs. Fuller?"

"Italian for 'A Foretaste of Heaven'!"

"And that's why he called this house—?"

But Mrs. Fuller obviously felt she'd confided in me enough: "Castle Aneen!" She gave a bitter little smile as she pronounced the name Dengate-fashion. "And I think it's to Castle Aneen we should now give our attention, if you are serious about coming to live here."

Integral to Mrs. Fuller's household, I now learned, was her one resident maid, Sarah, whom at her insistence I met forthwith, a shy, dishevelled woman of perhaps sixty, with a thick unplaceable accent, a wall-eye, and flat feet. Sarah seemed neither surprised nor interested to see me. She did both housework and cooking, but was aided by Mary, a girl who came in every day except Sunday.

"Mary," Mrs. Fuller informed me, "is the most delightful little vehicle." I had never heard this word applied to a person before. Immediately I had an image of this Mary as a human dog-cart, trotting in and out of Castelaniene to do her bit of charring.

I would, continued Mrs. Fuller, be given breakfast and an evening meal every day except Sunday, when the principal meal was luncheon, which, if I ever wanted it, would be an "extra" on my bill, Sarah being a "Roman" who had to go to Mass beforehand. The very words "Sunday luncheon" brought back gloomy memories of my own home-that-was-no-more, the board presided over by my garrulous father who'd already taken aboard a damned sight more drink than was good for him . . .

And now Mrs. Fuller was showing me her two downstairs sitting-rooms, in one of which it might be my privilege to sit on a weekday evening. Here I noticed a copy of *The Channel Ports Advertiser* spread out on one of the occasional tables. In a few weeks' time, I thought, its pages would be carrying articles written by myself. The room itself was extremely, well, *pretty* with rose-patterned wallpaper, chintz-covered sofa, and green felt carpet. Definitely not a place for a fellow to sprawl out comfortably, let alone have a smoke at the end of his working-day.

Time now to go upstairs. On the first floor were a bathroom and two bedrooms, the door of one of which was ajar. Mrs. Fuller's footsteps slowed down as we passed it, as if she half-wanted me to peek into it, which of course I did. It had an unmistakably masculine air, containing a tallboy, at least a dozen prints on the wall of Greek- and Roman-looking subjects, and a dressing table on which different-sized hairbrushes with tortoiseshell backs were neatly arrayed.

"The occupant is absent," Mrs. Fuller explained, without further elaboration. "Now I shall take you up to your room, Mr. Bridges. It will be your sanctuary."

Well, that boded well. With increased enthusiasm for this place becoming my new quarters I followed Mrs. Fuller up a very steep flight of stairs to the top floor. She then opened the door of the room on our left, like some magician performing a favorite trick, and truth to tell I instantly wanted to applaud her. The room she revealed was not large and was furnished very simply—bed, bedside table, wash-stand, chest of drawers, small dressing table, bookcase, desk, two chairs, and on the floor three rag-rugs—but more congenial to an independent bloke like myself than I had dared to hope for.

"I'll really be able to write here to my heart's content!" I exclaimed.

"And it's not cut off from the world outside either!" said Mrs. Fuller.

She pointed toward the dormer window. My eyes followed her, and momentarily I was baffled, even unnerved. Had I not reached the top of the house? Well, you wouldn't think so to look at all the water on the glass panes. This room, so like a ship's cabin in shape and size, might have lain below the Plimsoll Line.

"March is certainly coming in like a lion," Mrs. Fuller said (it was the fifth of March), "but I'll open the window nevertheless . . ."

She suited action to words, and straightaway rain swept into the room in cold anger. Nevertheless, I couldn't stop myself moving closer to the open dormer, and what I saw through the onrush, beyond the tumble of gray roofs, walls and gardens below, made me gasp: the broad, rough, striped back of some primeval monster stretching itself under the sombre, laden sky. Perhaps it was half a minute before I realized I was looking at the sea, at the English Channel here at its narrowest.

"The sea will be your constant companion," Mrs. Fuller was telling me, "as it is mine. To lie at night, when one is full of sorrow, and to listen to it, in all its various moods—that's the most wonderful thing in the world!" An image came to me of this woman in her bed a mere one floor below me—though not directly underneath, thank heavens!—catching the sounds of the sea with the delicate shells of her ears! I must beware of such pictures. "And most days—though sadly not today—you can see from the window the French coast. When people ask me if I've ever been abroad, I say, 'Well, I see France practically every day of my life.'"

How to respond to so arch a remark? "I haven't been abroad, myself," I said. "So seeing France out of my bedroom window will be quite something for me, Mrs. Fuller. I'll be very happy to be your lodger. If you'll have me, that is!"

Mrs. Fuller graciously inclined her Grecian head: "I shall be happy to have you, Mr. Bridges! But I just have one question to ask you."

"Please, ma'am!"

Imagine my astonishment when she inquired: "Are you cheerful?"

Hoping I didn't betray my reaction, I replied, "I truly think I am!"

"Cheerfulness makes the world go 'round, I believe."

"So it is said." *By Mr. Hough at any rate!* I could have added.

"Edmund—Mr. Hough—considers you cheerful, Mr. Bridges."

THE STRANGER FROM THE SEA

"Does he?" I said. "That's most kind of him!"

We had shut the door of "my" room behind us and were back on the landing. This last exchange had disconcerted me; behind it lay something I obviously couldn't yet know about. To change the subject, I pointed at the door on the other side of the landing. "Is that where your other lodger lives?"

"Other lodger?" she repeated sharply. "I have no other lodger. That is my Mercy Room, Mr. Bridges."

My face must have displayed my puzzlement.

"Mercy Room?" Not a term I knew.

"I wonder Edmund—Mr. Hough—didn't tell you, Mr. Bridges. Living on my own—except for dear Sarah, of course—I constantly feel I don't do enough for others. So from time to time I make that room available for somebody in need. I like to think that every now and again I've been the means of easing distress."

What was I expected to say here?

"Oh, I'm sure you have been, Mrs. Fuller!" I managed. Would she often make these demands on me, this woman in lilac resembling some house-bound seabird?

"One simply has done the best one could!" said Mrs. Fuller, apparently disinclined to leave the landing and traipse back down the stairs. "Whatever else can be said of me, I have been merciful. Because of experiences of my own, my heart goes out readily to the sorrowful." I didn't think the time was ripe for me to hear all this. Perhaps I should make some impromptu witticism to change the subject completely, but I couldn't think of one. "George, my husband," she went on, "disappeared—as the good Edmund Hough no doubt told you."

No, the good Edmund Hough most certainly had not told me anything of the sort, had merely written the plain words "the late Mr. Fuller."

"Disappeared?" I repeated interrogatively. Not that disappearance was all that rare an occurrence to a newspaper-man like myself. In London's dockland people disappeared all the time, and, if ever found, turned out to have been dispatched horribly.

"Disappearance is not easy to accept, let me tell you," said Mrs. Fuller, her eyes blazing at me her wish that I should not accept it easily either. "That is why I must have a cheerful person in my house as lodger."

Oh Lord, I exclaimed to myself, *so that's to be my role here, is it?* Perhaps Mrs. Fuller too felt she had struck the personal note rather too loudly, for turning herself 'round to descend the stairs, she said, "Well, there are probably some domestic matters that we should now establish once and for all."

These matters seemed, as I went down the stairs behind her, to proceed from the back of her bent, elegant neck. Perhaps just as well; I wouldn't have wanted to look her in the eye. Not only was she charging me a pretty steep monthly sum, and not only did she expect me unfailingly to pay it in advance, but she required a deposit (two months' rent), which she would not refund me till the end of the calendar year, nine months off! Also she didn't expect me to entertain visitors without her permission, which she reserved her right to refuse.

"I must have a peaceful, uncomplicated life after all I've been through. I have a right to ask for that. Besides, Castelaniene *is* my own house."

Two steps behind her, I had no alternative but to acquiescence. By the time we were once more down in the hall, we had fixed the day I should move in. Easter Monday falling on April 6 that year, Edmund Hough had decided I should start work on the Wednesday of that same week, Wednesday being the paper's publication day. I would therefore take up my residence at Mrs. Fuller's on Tuesday, April 7.

Just as I was debating what manner would be best for saying goodbye—

"Now you've met everybody—or almost!" Mrs. Fuller cried, "There they are! I was hoping you'd see them before you left." She pointed to the stairway leading down to the basement, that region under the wall-eyed Sarah's sway. Two pairs of pricked-up ears showed in the interstices of the banisters; below them narrow green eyes glinted in shadowed pointed heads. "Japheth and Ham," Mrs. Fuller told me. "Their mother—called Mrs. Noah, naturally—must be out catching mice. She is an animal with a very particular part to play in existence. But you'll be friends with all three ere long."

"I'm sure I will," I replied. "I've a way with animals." All my landladies would have agreed on that. Probably nobody cares for animals quite so ardently as someone who has had a lonely childhood. From the mice I rescued out of traps to the jackdaw with an injured wing I found in our backyard, from the variety of half-abandoned dogs who roamed South London to the local organ-grinder's shivering pet monkey, my affections had gone out to them as fellow beings and friends.

I decided I'd walk back to the station, and distance be blowed! After the intensity of my interview with Mrs. Fuller, the continuing rain refreshed rather than discomfited me. As it assailed me, I thought, I'm going to share my new home with two absences—one from that first-floor bedroom with the tallboy and the classical prints, the other from the Mercy Room. What an odd situation to be in!

From the end of St. Ethelberga's Road I saw it again, but now more extensively because of the lower vantage-point: the back of that mighty primeval beast, the sea, flexing its muscles under the still discharging clouds. Gulls wheeled inland, away from its power, crying as they did so.

Inevitably I spent my last weeks in South London finishing things off at the paper and sorting through my stuff at my lodgings. I had accumulated very little in my twenty-three years of existence, having inherited next to nothing when my parents died—separately, but, in my view of events, at a single stroke. I had fewer than forty books, some of them my father's, three postcard-albums, and a cheap leather-framed print of Camberwell Green. Some clothes, some shoes. Ah, well! The way in which my home had come to an end had made me suspicious of putting trust in possessions, and chary about acquiring more of 'em. I suppose I have stayed that way, indeed seen to it that I have.

One afternoon I took a walk, the first in well over a year, to the house at the back of Grove Lane, Camberwell, to which my parents had moved when I was two; we'd left it when I was sixteen for two wretched years of chopping-and-changing. Small trees, still leafless, guarded the buff-bricked façades of the small terrace to which it belonged. In the bay-window of our former parlor a slender girl my own age, her dark hair piled high on her head, was smiling to herself as she watered a potted geranium. Its bright red flowers matched her cheeks. Behind the girl I could see a lamp, a sofa, two deep armchairs, all the paraphernalia of comfortable family life. I never was to learn this sweet-faced flower-tender's name, but the mere sight of her was welcome—made me more *cheerful* as, apparently, I would have to be in Dengate. Inside that very house I had listened to the incessant arguments of my mother and father, and the forlorn attempts of our maid, Doris, to smooth them over.

"Oh, madam," she'd say, "you know what they say about luck. That it always turns. The old sun's got to come out some time."

That night I woke up at 4:00 a.m., something I'd hardly ever done before. Whatever were these extraordinary sounds I was hearing? Increasing in volume they drove sleep from my head. *Be calm*, I told myself, *because if you're not, you won't find out what's going on and so save yourself from possible danger!*

Outside, beating the walls of my lodging-house, hammering at the roof-tiles overhead, a wind was blowing the likes of which the humdrum hugger-mugger of South London had surely never entertained before. Invigorated by its noise rather than fearful, I clambered out of bed, and stumbled over to the window. What a scene of violence! Cry havoc! Trees— planes, birches, beeches, sycamores—rocking frantically to and fro; wooden fences creaking, bending, loosening, splitting; dustbins toppling over, then rolling so helplessly their contents fell out; windows rattling as if their frames were being tugged free of the brick walls. But no people anywhere. Well, what sane human being would be out in this . . . hell? The only living creature I eventually spied was a white cat who shot like a streak of electric snow from behind a fallen dustbin, off into I-couldn't-make-out-where. I've seen him in dreams since. His plight apart, this entire hypnotic show exhilarated me, might even, I felt, have been put on for my benefit. I didn't once think of my current sharp-tongued landlady or her fat, spoilt, middle-aged son. They had stopped being real to me once I'd learned I was to move to Dengate.

The next morning everybody was talking about the storm, which had spent itself out 'round about six o'clock. Its visitation on London, it soon transpired, was as nothing compared to its vehement and continuing harassment of the southern Home Counties, in particular the Kent coast and the ports of Dover and Dengate. Just my luck, I thought, that the Channel Port I'm bound for has its greatest drama in years *before* I arrive there with my journalist's skills.

Down in Dengate the gale proper began about 4.30 a.m. on Friday,

March 27, and didn't abate all day. A brief lull followed in the small hours of Saturday, and then up it flared again, raging for the rest of the night and the whole of the next day. Even for the notorious spring equinox, it was excessively savage. For precedents townsfolk had to scour records and the memories of the aged. At its fiercest the prevailing southwesterly wind roared through the Straits of Dover (at the end of which Dengate stands) at a speed of forty-seven knots per hour, top force on the Beaufort Scale for a "Strong Gale." It whipped the high waves that it created with such strength that their crests became spray which dangerously reduced visibility for all navigators of the Dover Strait, the busiest seaway on the globe. On those two dreadful days of March 1885 many a ship making her way through its narrowest section was in such distress that coastguards were overstretched 'round the clock and had to call for reinforcements.

Though in London the Thames swelled and writhed and splashed its filthy water onto the embankment, we city-folk were unable quite to appreciate the turmoil on the coast. I recalled Mrs. Fuller opening the attic window for me at Castelaniene, and showing me a sea I mistook for a broad-backed prehistoric monster. And now that monster had revealed its innermost terrifying self, even to those who declared themselves familiar with and even fond of it.

Well, eventually my very last evening in London came 'round (as I sometimes thought it never would) and Will Postgate, the fellow at the paper I was closest to, had chosen to play the biggest part in it. Three years and six months older than myself, Will had gone straight from school to the newspaper. He was already that desirable being "a seasoned pressman," and managed all our sports and entertainments features. Printers never intimidated him; his own father being a professional binder and book-designer, Will had, he said, "imbibed printers' ink with my mother's milk." Nor did the trade's well-known radicalism ever scare him. On the contrary, having grown up with politics, he held confidently progressive opinions himself. He also had an enviable ability to draw—amusingly and accurately. Every so often he'd grab a piece of paper, and before you knew where you were, he'd covered it with comical likenesses of the company present. Will was tireless in his endeavors to bring my education up to scratch. My innocence amazed him—about politics, how society worked, and more inti-mate matters too, these last prompting him to arrange a trip to Limehouse I will never be able to forget. But for all my deficiencies Will liked me well enough to introduce me to friends of his outside the paper, some of them reporters elsewhere, a lively, not to say racy bunch, with whom I was proud to associate.

And they all came along for my farewell bash at a restaurant in Dean Street, Soho, for mock-turtle soup and first-class steak-and-kidney pie, with both beer and full-bodied red wine to wash the meal down: Walter Pargeter, Ben Jackson, Lionel Cartwright, Arthur Maltby. They live on now, caught in that moment, so significant to me, me so insignificant to them, in the lightning pencil sketch Will did of us all that evening, myself a stripling by comparison with the others, my mouth agape with admiration.

An invisible guest present might not have realized that my own im-minent departure from London was the occasion for the dinner, so heated was the talk on other matters—on whether MPs should take a religious oath when they weren't believers, on the appropriate role of trade unions, on what the term "socialist" properly denoted . . .

For some quarter of an hour I had not spoken a single word, when Will, flushed with wine and argument, stood up to say: "Gentlemen, we must now put the cut-and-thrust of discourse behind us. I speak, I know, for all of us here when I say that we shall greatly regret our friend Martin Bridges being no longer in our midst, enlivening us with his repartee and comic turns. And I myself shall feel a bit under-employed now I no longer have to supervise his sentimental education. Instead I shall have to let Life—or rather Life as it manifests itself in a certain remote Kent port, Dengate by name—continue my good work. I could end my little speech with a few extra words of wisdom about The Ladies, the pleasures and the perils thereof, but will pass on to Humanity itself, and will recite for all our benefits some stirring lines:

> 'The seed ye sow, another reaps;
> The wealth ye find, another keeps;
> The robes ye weave, another wears;
> The arms ye forge, another bears.
> Sow seed,—but let no tyrant reap;

Find wealth,—let no impostor heap;
Weave robes,—let not the idle wear;
Forge arms,—in your defence to bear.'"

"Doggerel, Postgate, doggerel," said Lionel Cartwright.

"Doggerel by Percy Bysshe Shelley himself," said Will. "I have composed a banjo accompaniment to it but forgot to bring my instrument along."

For my part I felt quite embarrassingly moved by the recitation, though as much by Will's voice, sufficiently loud to make our fellow diners turn 'round, as by the actual words themselves, which struck me, for all their nobility, as a mite impracticable.

After such soul-stirring stuff the actual goodbyes bidden me were a bit anticlimactic.

"Toodle-oo, old bean," Will said. "I'll pop down to Dengate one of these days for a spot of the old sea air if I've nothing better to do!"

In Dengate, not least at *The Advertiser* itself, I found—as so often happens after a disaster—that one particular incident had gripped the public mind above all others: the foundering of a Norwegian ship, *Dronning Margrete*, and the attempts, far from all successful, to rescue all members of her crew. Again and again I would be given details, as if the town felt not just some collective responsibility for these men, but a deeper relationship with them bestowed by the lashing waves they had witnessed themselves in horror and even disbelief.

My entire knowledge of Norwegian shipping was at that time confined to my having met, on a Saturday night excursion with Will to the Port of London, two Norwegian sailors thoroughly and unashamedly drunk. We'd helped them back to their lodgings, ironically the Scandinavian Sailors' Temperance Home, down by West India Dock. Their mates were awaiting them there, strong, blonde, taciturn men with piercingly blue eyes. Norway and Norwegians were becoming decidedly popular in England. Mr. Gladstone himself had recently declared his fondness for the country and had taken a holiday there, in the west coast resort of Molde. And every year of my life ships had been plying between Bergen/Christiania and Halifax/NewYork, navigating the English Channel en route.

This particular vessel, a sailing-ship, was returning from Halifax to Christiania, due to call at Antwerp on the evening of the day she came to grief. Her casualties had been high, though the final count wasn't yet established. Her captain and six of his men had successfully escaped the sinking ship in one longboat, but the sailors who had got into the others had died (or were assumed to have done so, so difficult was the process of recovery). But those seven surviving seamen were sure that, as they climbed down into their longboat, they saw at least three other crew members getting into the dinghy alongside. Impossible for them to make out, in all the obstructive flying spray and with wall-like waves advancing toward them, how these others were coping. Or if they'd coped at all! Nor had any news of these men come through. More likely than not they should, regrettably, be added to the wreck's terrible death toll. The photos of those eventually rescued stumbling ashore in England, hardly able to comprehend that their ordeal was (in a literal, physical sense anyway) over, were much cherished by *The Advertiser* staff, not for printing on the newspaper's pages—in 1885 we were not yet up to that tricky process—but for helping us visualize more clearly the grim events we were presenting to the public.

Childishly, I could not altogether keep back my jealousy of those asked to write up the aftermath of this tragic disaster. Why could not the gale have waited another week-and-a-bit? Fate, which had decided to bring me to Dengate, had then unkindly denied me a presence there at the most important occurrence in the place's history for an entire century.

The strangeness of the workings of Fate did not lie in *that*, of course, I hastened inwardly to add here—to appease The Great Listener, the ever-attentive Judge of Mankind. It lay in the behavior of the sea itself, for such long spells restrained, even manageable, and so often serene and beautiful of aspect, then all of a sudden turning implacably defiant and aggressive. Those first two weeks in Dengate I would look out over the Channel in incredulous wonder, for the weather was calm and mild, if showery.

CHAPTER TWO

At the Mercy of the Mercy Room

I come to Monday, April 27, one calendar month after the storm, another
day of gentle, watery sunshine and light breeze. I was now taking pleasure in my morning walk to the newspaper offices. Below me Dengate harbor sparkled, full of fishing-smacks; as many as two hundred can be moored
together here, making it easy to step from one vessel to another. Nearer
to hand, gardens displayed many splendid blooms: red tulips, cream tulips,
tulips combining red and cream, boldly yellow broom, and wall-flowers of
terracotta shades.

Said two or three voices as I came into *The Advertiser*, "Edmund
wants to see you, Bridges!" Mr. Hough was always called "Edmund" by
everybody, if not to his face.

He was standing by the window when I entered his Editor's office,
and when he swung 'round his face broke into a smile. "Just the man!" he
exclaimed. "I have news you'll welcome."

"Good news for good weather, sir!" (See how eager I was to sound
"cheerful.")

"Yes, and don't we Dengaters deserve it after what we went through?
Bridges, when we first met, you told me of your admiration for the use of
interview."

"It's an A-1 way of making events and people come to life."

"Absolutely. And now you can conduct your own interview for *The
Advertiser*. We'll be up there with Stead's *Pall Mall* before you can say Jack
Robinson, with a truly thrilling affair, jam-packed with adventure and hero-
ism." Who had he in mind for me? An explorer? A general? An audacious
criminal? "And the marvellous thing about it, Bridges—from an editor's
point of view—is that you can conduct it in your very own home."

This was a mite disappointing, but I endeavoured to keep a bright anticipatory smile on my face. Nor did Edmund Hough's next words improve things, spoken as he moved toward me from the window, bringing sunshine with him on pomaded patches of his boyishly thick dark brown hair.

"Beatrice Fuller, your revered landlady, is of the company of saints, I do believe." Hard to know what to say back; nothing these last two-and-a-bit weeks inclined me to think her in the least saintly. "If there is good to be done, Bridges, Beatrice Fuller will be there doing it!"

Really? Like asking an inordinately large sum as deposit from an obviously hard-up young man awaiting his pay-packet? Like charging him for a Sunday lunch he'd never eaten with the excuse that he'd given her insufficient notice he'd be out that day?

"You know about her Mercy Room?"

"Yes, sir, I live right opposite the door to it!" *Kept perpetually locked against my possible intrusion*, I could have truthfully added.

"Only Beatrice Fuller could have conceived such a beautiful idea, only she would have the integrity to convert it into reality." Crikey! Perhaps there really was some hanky-panky going on between the two of them. "Well, the Mercy Room is to have a new occupant. And he will be the subject of your interview."

"Tell me more, sir!"

"Do you remember, Bridges, the names and fates of the individual survivors of the ill-fated Norwegian ship, *Dronning Margrete*? And if you do, can you recall one called Hans Lyngstrand?"

Though I'd recently sub-edited a piece keeping readers up-to-date with the fortunes of the ship's crew, I had not kept their names in my head, in which all foreign words tended to run into one like water-colors on a clumsy boy's art-paper.

"Was he the chap who—?" I bluffed.

"Yes, Hans Lyngstrand was the boy of nineteen," said Edmund, as if I'd made a correct identification, "who paid dearly for his long time in the freezing-cold sea. Developed acute pneumonia, poor lad. For two weeks the doctors at the hospital here doubted he could pull through. But thanks to them, and doubtless to some inner strength of his own, he did. But now, before he goes home to Norway—where he has a generous guardian—he must rest awhile somewhere comfortable and pleasant, somewhere different from a hospital but just as solicitous. Otherwise the journey back might prove too much of a strain. And what better place for recuperation than—"

"The Mercy Room at Castelaniene!"

"Exactly! Dr. Davies at the hospital is a keen supporter of the plan and will visit him regularly. And I'm looking to *you*, Bridges, to talk to Hans on behalf of *The Advertiser*. And you'll be doing him good in the process. After his ghastly ordeal he surely needs a sympathetic as well as a medical ear. He's clearly a likeable youth, they became very fond of him at the hospital. And he's totally fluent in English, the common language on the ship, it seems, so you'll have no problem in communication. I have every confidence, Bridges, you can produce for our readers just the kind of piece Mr. Stead and ourselves so admire."

"It's good of you to have such faith in me!" I said, a-tremble with delight. The task flared up before me like a bright beacon on a hill. Of course, I couldn't help noting that Edmund Hough, though doubtless sincerely sorry for the nineteen-year-old Norwegian, was principally interested in him for the sake of column-inches to attract even greater droves of readers to *The Advertiser*. But might not the same go for myself?

"Good! That's settled then!" said Edmund Hough. "And perhaps as a result of this project, we may at last see something of that cheerfulness to which you once laid claim."

I'd no reply to make. I hadn't fooled my editor after all. I was not showing cheerfulness because I was feeling none.

My fears that Mrs. Fuller might prove an obtrusive landlady with sentimental designs on myself had proved ludicrously wide of the mark. I saw remarkably little of her, which was clearly how she wanted it. Whenever, following her earlier suggestion, I entered the downstairs sitting-room after a day's work with a book or periodical and found her already ensconced there, she immediately got up and left, making me feel so uncomfortable that after a quarter of an hour at most I, too, made an exit. And I didn't *dare* to smoke. So after less than a week I kept to my attic-room. As for mealtimes, she always had her breakfast up in her bedroom while I, at an earlier hour, had mine provided by Sarah in the basement, generous portions (kippers, bacon, eggs fried or lightly boiled with "soldiers" of toast) served with something like reluctance, the taciturn, wall-eyed woman with the West-of-Ireland accent banging plates before me as though I were a greedy schoolboy she'd been ordered, against her judgment, to oblige.

Three times a week Mrs. Fuller took her evening meal at a different hour from myself, so dinner on such days was a repetition of the solitude of breakfast. But that was preferable to when Beatrice Fuller condescended to share the same table as her over-charged lodger. She clearly found conversation an effort she would rather not make. Admire Edmund she might, but she took no interest in those doings at his paper which I chose to relay and often illustrate with mimicry.

"Shouldn't such matters stay in the office where they belong?" she said at the end of one of my narratives. After which I decided I'd relay no more. A subject Mrs. Fuller did introduce, off her own bat, was the need to be useful to others, speaking loftily of various commitments of her own: sewing-bees for her "fallen sisters," afternoon classes where women less educationally fortunate than herself were shown the rich rewards of reading. (She could hardly expect me to join *those*!)

"But I also frequent other circles possibly more appropriate for you, Mr. Bridges, where the interest is, shall we say, metaphysical."

MB: Metaphysical? My goodness!

Mrs. F.: Have you *never* felt inclined to explore the metaphysical, Mr. Bridges? Have you never heard of groups like our Gateway here in Dengate?

MB: I don't believe I've had that pleasure.

Mrs. F.: Pleasure? Well, I suppose, at an exalted level, the Gateway *could* be said to constitute pleasure, though I doubt if either Colonel Walton or Lady Kershaw would take kindly to that word.

MB: I meant it only loosely. Not of course, Mrs. Fuller, that your pleasures could ever be *loose*, ha-ha-ha!

Mrs. F.: I'd already presumed you didn't mean that, Mr. Bridges. Perhaps if you got to know the Gateway, it might make you more aware of that large gap in your life which certainly requires filling. Only through attention to the spiritual dimension can one meaningfully cope with existence even on its humdrum level. That's how the Gateway helped me, you see, after the . . . after the Disappearance.

MB: Disappearance?

MRS. F.: I have already informed you of that tragic event, Mr. Bridges. My husband, George Fuller disappeared three years ago. . . . I really must have a word later with Sarah about cabbage. She will overcook it unless one is firm and vigilant with her. I've told her repeatedly to *steam* the vegetable, or else boil it very lightly, so that one can truly experience all the sweet juice that lies in the green leaves.

Yet there were aspects of my life at Castelaniene that pleased me: above all, my room. Here I'd arranged those books I'd elected to retain from London, my Bulwer-Lyttons and Harrison Ainsworths, my novels by the incomparable Jules Verne. I also put upon my dressing table some photographs of myself and friends on various jaunts we'd made (though not the one to Limehouse), and a merry bunch we looked. Folk were, I'd decided, far harder to get to know outside The Smoke, so much more constrained by family and caste.

As much as the room itself did I relish its view. France was every day now an enticing green line on the other side of which life went on probably not merely paralleling but replicating our own. Somewhere, across the Strait, there must be, I thought, some young reporter like myself who'd exchanged one job for another, and was far from convinced he'd done the right thing. Who didn't know what to do with himself most evenings, and who longed for a friend to talk to. Sometimes, especially weekends at dusk, I'd stand by the window imagining myself back in an earlier period, in, say, the time of the Napoleonic wars when that green line denoted enemy territory.

The cats, too, were a daily source of delight. Mrs. Noah—the last of the house trio I met—kept a certain aloofness from everybody except Sarah. She'd been given her name, I was told, by Mr. Fuller himself, who, out for a stroll one evening, had spotted her, alone and bewildered, on a small abandoned boat right in the middle of Dengate harbor. He'd made his way easily enough from one boat to another—despite the choppy water between them—and scooped her up off her Ark into his arms, to her everlasting gratitude. Probably the cat still missed him, still regretted his "disappearance." Her coat was a deep lavender color. Though a prodigious catcher of mice, shrews, voles, and little birds, she liked to be present at human mealtimes. During my solitary breakfasts she would rub herself against the legs of my chair, and if there were a bit of kipper going, she was happy enough to accept it from my hand. And if it were a kipper morning, her two sons would be close by.

These two cats, whom I'd met on my first visit to Castelaniene, were from the same litter, fifteen months old, and far friendlier than their mother, if jealous and watchful with regard to each other. They had inherited from Mrs. Noah a pointedness of face, but what distinguished them immediately were the long-tufted ears I had first noticed between the banisters. Japheth was less conservative in his habits than his brother, and soon was following me upstairs, exploring the contents of my room (he seemed especially fond of my leather-bound Bulwer-Lytton, along the line of which he ran his purring head), or sitting close to the dormer window (though of course it may have been the swooping gulls visible through its glass which interested him). Ham, on the other hand, preferred to save his high spirits and affection for the ground floor and basement, settling himself, directly after his brother had left the kitchen, possessively in a large orange cushion on a basket-chair by the window. But after any separation the two would greet each other with what looked, to the human eye, very like kisses.

Mrs. Fuller noted with approval my good relations with the cats, but inferred that even here I showed weakness of judgment. Mrs. Noah, not either of her sons, was the noteworthy member of the trio, the one with the highly esteemed "properties"—whatever that might mean.

What about work? My very first morning at the paper I had the definite feeling the staff thought I had been foisted on them, and this feeling hadn't gone away as I hoped it would. Always there seemed to be inquisitive, almost inquisitorial, eyes on me, measuring me up and then coming to unflattering conclusions. I spent as much time as I could with Edmund in his Editor's office and—this will make my readers laugh—it came as a positive relief when he asked if I could kindly go down to the printers for him, there's a good chap.

"Seasoned pressmen" my colleagues certainly all appeared, even Peter Frobisher, two or three years my junior, as composed and competent as some kid at Sunday school intent on impressing his teachers. But Peter wasn't somebody you could object to for long. The team's most senior member, Thomas Betterton, Deputy Editor and Edmund's stand-in when need be, was another matter entirely, fifty-five, big-bearded, an inveterate pipe-smoker, and, I soon learned, a Mason prominent in the Dengate Lodge. His manner was as ponderous, as rhetorical as his stomach was vast and his neck bull-like, and though in literal fact he spoke no louder than the next man, he gave you the impression he was delivering his long convoluted sentences from a great distance, his over-large dew-lapped face turning puce as he expressed his frequent indignation over police and crime, taxes and tariffs, and whippersnappers who thought they knew everything about a newspaper when they patently did not.

Philip Goodenough and Archie Penry were more amiable, I thought, but a club of two. They exchanged knowing grins as they watched me settle to my first task—writing a few sentences about a tedious book by some local historian on the Romans in Thanet.

Terence Hathaway's province was the layout of the paper, though he, too, mucked in with other tasks when needed. He was in his late thirties, had a large family, seven children already. He had a kitchen garden he was proud of and would bring in produce from it for his colleagues, rhubarb being the first sample I saw, the long red stalks glistening with lumps of rich soil and drops of dew. He had the thickest beard of any in the office, and the quietest voice too; indeed, he was mild of manner altogether which, in addition to his expertise, made him the ideal person to deal with the printers. He worked unremittingly. Illustrations were sparse in *The Advertiser*, though Edmund wanted ever more articles accompanied by drawings—photographs we couldn't publish until two years ago at the time of writing—while advertisements improved all the time in appearance and size, brightening up the pages hugely.

Advertisements lead me to name Arthur Forrester, at the time of my arrival mid-forties and unmarried, a Primitive Baptist, who surprised me by bringing in his Bible to read between his many calculations, even sometimes reading passages aloud. If Terence Hathaway's was the thickest beard, Mr. Forrester's was the thinnest, like some mandarin Chinaman's on a vase, and I soon was chuckling to myself when I saw the two talking to each other, two nice men, I early realized, with good hearts.

There was another member of the staff still like me in his twenties, Mr. Betterton's godson: Barton Cunningham. His hair was a dark, dank red, his eyebrows and eyelashes contrastingly fair, his eyes hazel, his skin very white though freckled. Was it his connection to Mr. Betterton that gave him his aura of superiority? But various gestures of his—casting his eyes up to the heavens during some little speech, or muttering some crude monosyllable under his breath after being given verbose instructions— suggested he didn't hold his godfather in unadulterated esteem. And once, understandably irritated by some pomposity of the older man's, he winked at me behind his back. Like Will Postgate in South London, he oversaw the sports and entertainments pages, though without Will's amazing stores of knowledge. On my first day at *The Advertiser* Barton Cunningham was only too obviously trying to size me up. Over a fortnight later he appeared not yet to have done so to his own satisfaction and was consequently unsure how friendly he should be to me. Shortly after the tête-à-tête with Edmund I've recounted, he and I had the following conversation:

BC: I forget what hole you were bunged up in, Bridges?

MB: Hole?

BC: School.

MB: The Thomas Middleton School, Camberwell.

BC: Can't hear you!

MB: THE THOMAS MIDDLETON SCHOOL, CAMBERWELL.

BC: Somebody's got to shout its name, I suppose. Can't say I've ever heard of it.

MB: Well, you haven't missed much.

BC: That's rather what I feel about my place, but you can't *not* have heard of *that*. St. Stephen's, Kingsbarrow. All the sons of local gentry go to it.

MB: Do they now?

BC: I was Victor Ludorum there in '77.

MB: Well, I never was that at mine.

BC: Come to think of it, Bridges, you've got a connection with the Old Hole yourself.

MB: I have?

BC: Yes, your landlady's old man, Mr. George Fuller BA, was a "beak" there, in common parlance, a teacher. Taught classics, Old Fulsome did.

MB: I didn't know Mr. Fuller was a schoolmaster before his disappearance.

BC: *Disappearance?*

MB: Yes, Mr. Fuller disappeared.

BC: What *are* you talking about, man? Old Fulsome's dead. Dead as the proverbial doornail. Didn't snuff it till some years after I'd left the Hole, but they went and had a big funeral for him in this town, and old pupils, like yours truly, were obliged to turn up to it wearing the requisite black tie.

MB: Well, I must have got hold of the wrong end of the stick . . . Did you like the late Mr. Fuller? Nice man?

BC: Let me think! Did I *like* Old Fulsome? Was he nice? No, not particularly. Rum cove, really! Half the time he didn't seem to be living in the same country as the rest of us. Too busy dreaming of temples and statues and pentathlons and nymphs by streams.

MB: Yes, that I can believe from what he's left behind in his house.

BC: None of all that stuff appealed to me much. Except the nymphs by the streams. I like a nymph—well, a pretty one, don't you, Bridges?

MB: I've never put it to myself like that.

BC: Aren't you a bit of a masher then? Aren't you walking out at present with some charming young miss from your London days?

MB: I'm not walking out with anybody.

BC: Well, I expect you've got your work too cut out fitting into an expanding newspaper like ours to go chasing after women . . .

Wouldn't I have been better off staying on at the South London paper, putting up with tasks which, if sometimes tedious, were never unpleasant and were always appreciated? I should have been more mindful of my extreme good fortune in having a friend like Will Postgate and, through him, access to a circle of vigorous, progressive, cosmopolitan young men, cleverer by miles than any in this . . . damned swamp-by-the-sea where a bloke like Barton Cunningham could patronise me.

I arrived back at Castelaniene that afternoon to hear, rising from the basement, voices in earnest-sounding discussion, belonging to Mrs. Fuller and a man I couldn't identify. Rather than become involved I tiptoed through the hall and then up the two flights of stairs to my attic story. But when I reached its landing, I saw that the door of the room opposite mine was ajar. That could mean only one thing: the Mercy Room's new occupant had arrived. Good Lord, Edmund had been speaking not of the impending future but of *today*; Mr. Hans Lyngstrand (there, I'd remembered his outlandish name!) must be established here already.

I could hardly pass the half-open door by, now could I? I gave it three perfunctory knocks before noiselessly easing myself into a room of which I'd had not even the most fleeting glimpse. (I won't pretend I hadn't fruitlessly tried the door handle quite a few times!) I knew the Mercy Room matched my own bedroom in size and shape, but I'd pictured it as more rudimentarily furnished than mine, as Mrs. Fuller was not using it for any money-making purpose.

How wrong I'd been! What I saw when, after so long, I had both feet on the other side of its door made my jaw drop.

From the rafters of the ceiling two model ships, old Spanish galleons, swung on either side of a big, long-tailed kite sporting the British red, white, and blue. On the walls various items of sporting equipment were suspended from pegs: a squash racket, boxing-gloves, a fencing helmet. On the floor, resting against the walls, were a cricket-bat, stumps, a ball for soccer, and one for rugby. The walls themselves were painted duck-egg blue; curtains and rugs, chair-cushions, and bedspread were bolder hued than their counterparts in my own room, crimson and Navy-blue predominating. On the table a magnificent stuffed Golden Eagle perched; a bookcase offered a whole set of Chambers Encyclopaedia.

I'd entered a boy's treasure-trove, a Chums' Ideal Den.

And now in the midst of all this a real boy lay, looking younger than his given nineteen years, fair head propped against a bank of pillows, and the rest of him obscured by a bright-colored patchwork quilt. There were cavernous hollows in his cheeks, and the sockets from which his eyes looked out, eyes so blue they resembled drops of water from the deepest ocean, were cavernous also.

"Hullo," I said, "I'm Martin Bridges, your neighbor here across the landing. And you must be Hans!" The boy nodded but looked bemused. "Didn't they tell you that you'd be sharing this attic-floor with somebody?" I asked. A shake of the head followed. How typical of Mrs. Fuller that she didn't think me worth even a mention! "I'm very pleased to meet you," I told him. "I've just come back—from the town newspaper."

"*Newspaper?*" The word had an electric effect on the young Norwegian. He immediately hauled himself up into a semi-sitting position.

"Yes, *The Channel Ports Advertiser*—biggest circulation for miles."

"News?" he was gasping out. "Tell me straightaway, please! Don't think you've got to spare me. You have news for me, of *him* after all this time?"

Hans Lyngstrand didn't sound like a foreigner, more like a native of some remoter county of the British Isles which I had not visited. The urgency of his question took me aback. Perhaps a direct denial would be unwise for somebody in his condition . . .

"No," I said. "I don't think I have."

"Not?" The blues in those twin caves of bone were so brilliant they alarmed me.

"You're talking about . . .?" I was, I realized, practicing just the kind of stalling an experienced interviewer has to use.

"About *Johnston*. I've asked after him so many times—asked every-body who ever came to the hospital. But nobody's heard anything."

"Johnston?" Hardly an unusual surname but I knew no one who bore it.

"Yes, the American." This was nothing short of a plea to come up with information I did not have.

"I'm sorry to disappoint you, but I didn't come in here to give you any news at all."

Hans had now manoeuvred himself into a more-or-less normal upright posture, though doing this had brought him a breathlessness not pleasant to hear. He smiled his forgiveness of me with a friendliness that only compounded my discomfiture and sense of incongruity at being with him here in this hidden, unexpected shrine to schoolboy enthusiasms.

After a few painful-sounding gasps he got out, "Johnston, Alfred Johnston, may not be the American's *real* name. Most probably isn't. Perhaps it just came to him when they asked him what he was called. I'm not even sure he's American, though that's what he always said he was. I want so much to know whether he's . . ." I knew immediately what about him he wanted to know, and indeed, after an effortful half-minute he ended his sentence, ". . . alive or dead?"

I saw again, as in actuality I had not, the unbeatable viciousness of the Channel at the spring equinox, wind bullying water into ferocious waves curling upwards only to crash punitively down, destroying whatever was vulnerable in their course. For hour after hour these had been this youth's only physical reality. I stepped a few paces nearer his bed. My very movements would make clear to him I was a well-wisher; I must not stir up the poor young chap any more than I had already. Heavens! Further agitation might *kill* him.

I said, "I'd like to help you with your inquiries, Hans. I happen to work on the most important newspaper in this whole Dover Straits region, and its editor happens to have asked me personally to take an interest in you and your story."

Hard to tell whether these words brought any consolation to Mr. Lyngstrand, because, more to himself than to me, he said, speaking rapidly, "Probably there never *will* be any news. But I think about Alfred Johnston night and day. He's probably gone out of my life as suddenly as he came into it. Six of us went in the longboat with the Captain while he . . ." This time he was unable to complete his sentence.

"I know!" I said, to make it unnecessary for him to do this painful thing. I heard the anguish in his voice, and—as if he'd shot an arrow—I felt this aiming for my own heart. Pain was something a wise fellow avoided, especially if it were another person's.

"I'm pretty sure Johnston was one of the three who climbed into the dinghy. But you couldn't see more than a few inches in front of you with all the sea-spray. Every sailor's worst nightmare. Our Captain called out, 'The bulkhead's gone. We must take our chance now.' But we didn't react immediately; we couldn't believe it was all happening to us! And then Johnston—yes, I'm sure it *was* him!—shouted, 'Stand by the boats! STAND BY THE BOATS!' For a moment I thought it was God himself speaking."

There was no stopping the young Norwegian now. He was no longer in the Mercy Room but out on the tempestuous English Channel.

"The Captain kept me fast by his side; I was his employer's ward, you see, being godson of the ship's owner, and he had a duty to see I survived. And me, I just did as I was told, wherever the Captain went, I went too, what he did I did also. But—yes, I'm pretty certain the three of them went into the dinghy. First Mate, Anders Andersen—Norwegian, like the Captain and me—and after him that young German who was always reading the Bible with Luther's Commentary, Wilhelm, one of the Third Mates who usually kept watch with Andersen—and I could *swear* the other, clambering down after them, was Alfred Johnston!"

He spoke these words so fast and so intently they seemed to twine 'round me like a rope, delivering fleeting images of chaos, panic, death.

"But who *was* this Johnston?" I asked. Didn't I need to understand why the man bothered the youth so?

"*Was?*" He clearly attributed my use of the past tense to my knowing all along that this American was dead.

"I meant, what was his position on board *Dronning Margrete*?"

Hans was still temporarily trapped in the world he was describing; he met my question as one dumbfounded at its having to be asked: "Johnston was our bo'sun. And no ordinary one. He was not like any other bo'sun I've ever come across."

He spoke as if I too would have enough experience of the breed to be able to recognize this man's rare qualities if he were to expand on his statement. Thank goodness I knew from the adventure yarns I so liked to read what a bo'sun (boatswain) was: a nautical non-commissioned-officer under the authority of the First Mate.

"Perhaps," mused Hans, almost imploring me to agree, "the two of them—Johnston and Andersen—made up their differences when they faced Death together. They talked together in Norwegian sometimes; I used to hear them. Johnston must have had a real genius for languages, don't you think?—an American who could even *read* Norwegian. But he was a genius in all respects, I think."

"Genius, a big word! Tell me more!" I begged this unlikely stranger from the sea, so young and yet with so much life behind him. Never had I wanted to hear anything so urgently as I wanted now to hear the story of a man perhaps called Alfred Johnston (but perhaps not), perhaps an American (but perhaps not), but certainly a bo'sun even though unlike any other an experienced sailor had come across, and, it now appeared, a genius as well.

"I might have known it! Yes, I *should* have known!"

These words, spat out in fury, issued from right behind me from that gap in the doorway through which I had edged my way in. I turned around. With the late afternoon light on her high-held, silver-streaked golden head Mrs. Fuller looked more Grecian than ever—like one of the Three Fates. "The very idea!" she exclaimed. "Entering the Mercy Room before you were asked to do so! Before I had time to tell you about Mr. Lyngstrand."

Well, I thought, *it might have been a damned sight politer to me to have done that earlier, instead of leaving me to hear about him from Edmund Hough. But then,* I silently addressed her, *you've preferred to keep so much from me, haven't you, Mrs. Fuller? Not least this astonishing room.*

"Yes, the idea of a young lodger coming into an invalid's quarters before checking up with the lady of the house herself!" came a reproachful half-echo of her words but in a deep male register and emanating from a dark three-piece-suited form behind her. This I rightly took to be Dr. Davies from the Royal Hospital. "Patients, Mrs. Fuller, must simply not be besieged by any Tom, Dick, and Harry unable to curb his curiosity."

To my surprise—and instant, intense gratitude—Hans replied, and in a stronger tone than he'd mustered so far: "But Martin"—there, he'd caught my name!—"has been so friendly, so eager to help me. I am very happy he is up here with me in this room now, and is my neighbor in this house."

· · ·

42

I ate by myself that evening, Sarah bunging down a plate of the predictable stew in front of me, with, I thought, a look more hostile than usual. *Should I stay on at Castleaniene*, I once again asked myself, *where I'm so little appreciated or even liked? But then where else to go?* And now Hans Lyngstrand had arrived in the Mercy Room, there was surely a reason for me to be living in this house.

Beatrice Fuller put her head around the kitchen door. She asked me to join her, when I was ready, for coffee in her sitting-room.

"I feel we have things to talk about, Mr. Bridges."

Aha! Quite a few of her predecessors had "felt" they had "things to talk about" with me, and invariably, only days later, I'd found myself moving on. I gloomily reflected that it'd be far harder to find acceptable new quarters in Dengate than in London. Most landladies here were intent on summer lets for which they could charge high rents, and so were not interested in year-round lodgers at inevitably more modest rates. I should have to conduct myself very carefully during coffee, perhaps be as bright and amusing as the old South London Martin Bridges had been, if I wanted—as I realized I now did—to remain here.

Imagine my amazement when, pouring out coffee into fine china cups, Mrs. Fuller said, "I owe you an apology, Mr. Bridges. You entered my Mercy Room from honorable motives and have done poor Mr. Lyngstrand good already. For that I'm most sincerely grateful."

How to reply with the wind taken out of my sails like that? My hand shook as I took the cup proffered me, and I spilled drops of hot coffee onto the green felt carpet. "Oh, don't mention it!" I said in as warm and hearty a voice as I could manage. "I can see just how it must have looked, me blundering into a private place without so much as a by-your-leave."

I had described Mrs. Fuller's initial view of the situation perhaps too accurately, for she murmured "Exactly!" before saying, but as if still having to convince herself: "I do truly see you meant well, Mr. Bridges."

A winning boyish smile across the occasional table on which the coffee-tray rested might be appropriate. But looking across at her I saw that this would not do so far was she herself from smiling. Oh Lord, apologizing was just her way of beginning some pi-jaw. What would Will Postgate do in my place? Well, he'd surely maintain a level head, be a man with a manly wit. I applied myself to my coffee cup. Receiving its hot steam full in my face, I was thankfully spared the indignity of my blushes as Mrs. Fuller discomposingly continued.

"The thing is, Mr. Bridges, I am finding you a difficult person. Not *cheerful* at all." Her tone suggested a private world of sad disaffection to which I had handsomely contributed, while her words echoed closely those addressed me earlier in the day by Edmund himself. "Which is why, I suppose, I reacted as I did when I saw you with Mr. Lyngstrand, who evidently found your company enjoyable."

As equally evidently you yourself don't, I silently added. *And isn't that what's wrong here, and why I can't be cheerful? Everything about me, even my voice with its South London twang, fails to appeal to you.*

Although I had been in not dissimilar predicaments before, and although her admission was hardly a bolt from the blue, all I could come up with was: "Sorry to hear I'm difficult, Mrs. Fuller, I don't mean to be. I'm too much of a cockney sparrow, I suppose." Mrs. Fuller neither agreed nor disagreed. Maybe a touch of my old inimitable humor was required. "Maybe I should take elocution lessons. There's a lady who advertises in our paper. Which might cough up the money for 'em if it really wants me to become a Dengater and sound like one."

Mrs. Fuller's eyes were brightly glacial with lack of amusement. "I did not mean difficult *linguistically*, Mr. Bridges. Anyway, I've been used to cockney trippers all my life." Well, how about that! For all my self-disparagement just now, I didn't see myself in quite this class, even though, as I have already related, I had once or twice joined it, with Will Postgate and the rest. "No, I was speaking of—personality."

As, of course, I knew. "Well," I breezed, "it takes all sorts, doesn't it? To make a lodging-house, let alone a world."

"Lodging-house? Castelaniene is *not* a lodging-house, Mr. Bridges." I could have hardly said a less tactful thing.

"Except that it's got a lodger in it," I contended, always keen to have the last word in any disagreement. "Two if you count the Norwegian. And one of 'em you've just called 'difficult.' I bet you wouldn't call a purely private visitor that to his face."

I suppose it's enormously to Mrs. Fuller's credit that she didn't give me my marching orders then and there.

"Anyway," I continued, "I'm sorry I come into this unfortunate class."

The look Beatrice Fuller now gave me made me involuntarily lower my head. "Sorry to hear it—yes, I'm sure you are. But are you sorry to *learn* it? Do *my* feelings matter to you at all? I rather doubt it, Mr. Bridges."

Still bending my head over the coffee cup, I said, "I'm not sure I've got your meaning, Mrs. Fuller."

"Oh, come, Mr. Bridges, for a lively young reporter you're showing very slender powers of observation. Which always must include sharp self-observation, wouldn't you agree? In those interviews you're so keen on, hasn't the interviewer to take into consideration his own behavior as well as the character of his subject? Surely you must have *some* awareness of how you yourself behave?" She was obviously going to give me a helping hand here. "Going about as if you were the only person in the world whose wishes and tastes are important. Judging everything and everybody by how much you like them or by how convenient or useful you might find them."

I wanted to hear no more of this. "So are you telling me to leave, Mrs. Fuller?" I asked. "If so"—for, since she herself had spoken of interviews, there was the one I was due to make, right here in Castelaniene with Hans Lyngstrand—"you'll have to give me at least a week's proper notice."

"Of course I'm not telling you to leave, Mr. Bridges. Do you really see me as somebody who chucks people out because I've got a bone or two to pick with them? What insecurity you must suffer from! Besides, you're a protégé of Edmund Hough, and I would be letting him down if I did such a hasty and callous thing."

And perhaps, Mrs. Fuller, you need my rent, I couldn't help inserting here to myself, recollecting the many times I'd seen her poring over bills and household accounts.

"All I ask for is a little more consideration shown to myself—and to the tireless Sarah, and to Mary too, such a sweet and valuable little vehicle. She most certainly should not be obliged to pick up your *inexpressibles*— your undergarments—from the floor; she has her own refinements, ones more developed than your own, I fancy." (This surprised as well as embarrassed me. For my part I had thought Mrs. Fuller treated Mary as a lady-of-the-manor might a girl from a cottage on her estate.) "So dare I hope that Mr. Lyngstrand will be the means of your regeneration."

"Regeneration?"

"Mr. Bridges, I've asked you into my drawing-room"—she pronounced the word proudly, as if she believed its curtains and carpet, sofa and wallpaper were not merely indications of her social status but projections of a soul infinitely loftier than mine—"because I didn't want us to continue in the shallow, unsatisfactory mode of these past weeks. May I be so bold as to say that I regard you"—and she tilted her head up as if miming that boldness—"as an incomplete person. And I believe it is your incompleteness that makes you difficult, so insensitive, willful, selfish, and disappointingly *uncheerful*."

I put the coffee cup down for fear I might spill it. Though I could scarcely be pleased by her unflattering picture of me, I was too big an egoist not to be interested by it. And even more so by what she said next:

"I suspect you have seen more of the dark side of life than many a young man your age, and have had sorrows that have bewildered, as well as pained, you."

Other landladies coming into my mind, I drew back from the possibility of making her a confidante—well, not just yet.

"My advice to you, Mr. Bridges, is quite simply this: open yourself more abundantly to the Forces of Life, do not fend them off with jokes and sallies and plans for petty advancement."

Petty advancement—was that how she saw the stages by which a serious journalist gets on? I wondered.

"Come to the Gateway with me. We are hospitable to everybody, and as a guest of mine you would be received with the greatest consideration. Colonel Walton has a truly distinguished mind, by which you could well profit, Lady Kershaw's is a stern vision of existence, though we are probably none the worse for it. It might be of real help to you."

But why should I need "real help"? Here I was, without home or family, without any financial support—or supporters—behind me, and I hadn't done so very badly for myself, had I?

"We convene in an eminently dignified place," Mrs. Fuller was now telling me, "Banstead Lodge on the Newchurch Road, Colonel Walton's own home. And—I checked this earlier in my diary—we have a meeting there a week on Wednesday, on May 6 at eight o'clock in the evening. A light collation is served after we have done what we came to do."

And whatever, I wondered, *might that be?* I didn't much like the sound of this Gateway nor did I want to meet all these Isle-of-Thanet toffs, not even if a "collation" was on offer. But agreeing to go on Wednesday to Colonel Thingummy's "eminently dignified" house was better by far than being kicked out on the Dengate streets for being "difficult" and lacking in "cheerfulness."

Therefore—"I'd be honored to come along, Mrs. Fuller," I said. "It's extremely generous of you to ask me. Bearing in mind," I couldn't help adding, "my shortcomings."

"We will let those rest awhile now, I think," said Mrs. Fuller with a sudden smile which lightened her pale, tired, bony face, making her look not merely more relaxed but much younger, as young as she'd seemed on our very first encounter that wet March afternoon, and yes, as pretty as then, for all her "silver threads."

"I'm sure after due consideration you can amend, even eradicate them . . . And now we should talk about something else, I think. About Mr. Lyngstrand."

"Yes, indeed." Best temporarily to withhold the already hatched plan for an interview with him. Edmund had clearly told her nothing about it.

"That nice young man is in a grave way; I fear you may not have understood quite how grave, Mr. Bridges. (Let me refill your coffee cup!) Do you realize how long the poor youth spent clinging to his boat in freezing water? That longboat he managed to get into with his Captain capsized at least twice. It was virtually inevitable he developed pneumonia as he did—high temperature, acute respiratory problems—but (and here's a very important thing) Mr. Lyngstrand turned out to have a weakness of the lungs anyway, maybe inherited, maybe the legacy of some childhood illness. Once he's back in Norway he'll undergo another full-scale examination, and further treatment. It is our business to see that he is as comfortable and calm here as possible—for we have to remember even the move to this house may have set him back a little—so that he's well enough to endure the fatigue of the long homeward journey. His patron is coming over for him in person."

"He seems"—surely I was obliged to say this?—"troubled about something. Some*one*, I should say. Someone called Johnston who has either disappeared or died."

"Disappeared or died"—embarrassingly these words applied also to George Fuller, I realized, but happily Mrs. Fuller didn't react.

"A close friend?"

"I'm not sure," I answered. For Hans Lyngstrand had not once described "the American" as any kind of friend, though he had called him a genius. "He was the bo'sun, and therefore vital to the ship. He says he saw him getting into the dinghy alongside his own longboat. After that—the rest is silence . . ."

Mrs. Fuller, rather than look at me as she absorbed my reply, fixed her gaze on an engraving over the mantelpiece of some classical scene, as though its mezzotint could reveal truths about her present guest's problems. "There may be . . ." she began. "Yes, why ever not? . . . There may be ways in which our Gateway could help Mr. Lyngstrand as well as yourself. I think he would be a good subject for its attentions, with a naturally favorable disposition toward it. After all, he's already responded well to Mrs. Noah, says she reminds him of the Ship's Cat, their beloved White One, a favorite of every crew member but particularly of himself, and who, he fears, went down with the vessel, poor creature."

I climbed as stealthily as I could up that steep top flight of stairs, aware that my life in Castelaniene had undergone almost literally a sea-change. By caring for Hans's well-being, I would morally improve both my inner self and my outward standing. And my interview for *The Advertiser* might well flush out the missing Johnston thus alleviating some of the young Norwegian's anxiety—to such an extent that his health could be restored, this old reactivated lung-trouble shaken off.

"Martin? Is that Martin?"

I halted on the landing. "Yes, it's me!" I couldn't but recall those haunted nights of illness that are part of everybody's childhood, when Death feels so close you could put out a hand and stroke it. "Can I help you, Hans?"

The Mercy Room door was still ajar. Beside the young Norwegian's bed was now burning a nightlight, under a little dome representing St. Paul's Cathedral.

"There is so much I'd like to tell you, Martin."

I stepped right inside his room, surely now having *carte blanche* to do so.

"And I'd like to listen!"

"But I can't tell it to you tonight, I'm too tired . . . What a state of things," he grimaced, like a small boy facing up to horrible medicine, "for a sailor to be exhausted by a change of bedroom, me who's been in seas like mountain ranges, and seen schools of killer whales and helped hold down a man gone crazy after drinking too much raw spirits. And, on top of all that, shared a cabin with Johnston"—yes, Johnston!—"when he was *possessed*."

"Possessed" was a term I'd not encountered outside the Bible. I must not press him for more, not now, though how could I fail to be intrigued? I detected fever in the youth's voice as well as in his nightlight-illuminated face—those over-bright eyes, those too flushed cheeks—and recalled Mrs. Fuller's concern that transference from the hospital might have worsened his condition, at least for a while. My eye fell on the Spanish galleon nearest to the bed, swaying on its rope from the rafter, and I suddenly saw its movement as representing Hans's health. *It may improve, it may not! Maybe. Maybe not . . .*

Then, with an abrupt yet clearly deliberate gesture, Hans drew his hands out from under the bedclothes, and placed them, palms down, on the counterpane: "What kind of hands, Martin, would you say these are?" he asked.

For all the fragility of the body of which they were extremities, they looked muscular, sturdy, capable.

"A sailor's hands?" I ventured.

"Well, of course they must be that, I've worked on ships long enough. In fact they recently made me an Able Seaman, and now want me to qualify for Second Mate. But I never will. I have another vocation, and I was wondering if you could tell what that is from looking at my hands." He turned them over, showing me tough-skinned palms with unusually strong lines.

His sickness has disturbed his reason, I thought, and fear accordingly rolled through me. I was no physician or nurse, had no talents for either profession. What had happened to my father and mother had given me a full enough acquaintance with illness and death for one still young, as Mrs. Fuller had divined, and yet I found both of them baffling, terrifying, better banished from thought or talk.

"*You'd* better tell *me*!"

"Would you not say that these were a *sculptor*'s hands?"

"I—I know nothing at all about . . . sculptors," I replied, before I knew what I was saying. Then, unable to keep my stupid fear down, but realizing I must humor, even soothe him, I added, "But yes, I can see that they are."

"I'm so glad, Martin!" said the young Norwegian. "Because I *know* they are. I had so much time in the hospital to reflect. You see, when I was in the water, I saw, just for a few moments, the strangest sight imaginable: my hands suddenly expanding in size above the waves until they appeared far bigger than any human limbs could possibly be. Then there spoke a voice inside my head, saying: 'Yours are hands for making things!' Didn't that mean that, if I were spared, I should work with those hands, and how better than by becoming a sculptor? Because sculptures are the greatest, most timeless things that human hands can create."

Strange as this may sound, no sooner had he made this admission, unlike anything I'd heard spoken before, then my tremulous uneasiness left me. It was as if I partook on the instant of his curious self-confidence. I stood there, a yard from his bed, my feet splayed out on a rag-rug, and told him: "I am sure you are right, Hans."

CHAPTER THREE

Important Information Comes My Way

*B*ack then, when *The Advertiser* came out once a week only, Thursday morning had a special quality; then it was that we put our minds to the next issue—and even to the one after that. On the morning of Thursday, April 30 (Hans Lyngstrand's third complete day at Castelaniene), Edmund summoned me into his office to say: "Bridges, I'd like your interview with Mr. Lyngstrand handed in this coming Monday, May 4. Readers are still interested in the fates of the wrecked Norwegians, and their youngest survivor already has a place in their hearts." And he gave another of his boyish smiles as if already he had in front of him a 1,500-worder to bring tears to our readers' eyes. "But before we know where we are, the gale in the Channel will have been forgotten in favor of Spring: what bird's nesting where, what the latest London fashions are. Folk are fickle, even in Dengate."

As if suddenly illuminated, those framed words above his desk met my gaze:

> *Flesh unto spirit must grow,*
> *Spirit raves not for a goal.*

By now I knew these to be the words of George Meredith, "The Sage of Box Hill," as people apparently called him. Didn't they recommend me to put all diffidence aside and harness my spirit to successful accomplishment of the task ahead? For a disagreeable truth now bothered me as, surprisingly, it had not done before. For all my enthusiasm for interviews, I had myself never actually conducted one, let alone written it up. Nevertheless, "Monday it is, sir!" I promised.

"Bravo! And as a reward for your good work—nay, I jest, I was intending to invite you anyway—I propose that a week this coming Sunday, that's to say the tenth of May, you hie yourself to my family seat—to whit, Furzebank House, my modest Englishman's castle situated at the northern edge of our great borough—to partake of that best of English institutions, the Sunday family luncheon. Susan, my wife, is already planning substantial dishes to put a little more flesh on your protruding bones. My brood will of course be at table with you; I doubt, at twenty-three, that you'll be much interested in the Little Ones. However, the Grown Ones—my son, Cyril, my daughter, Lucinda—are another matter, and they have already expressed a wish to meet you. Your glowing reputation, Bridges, has preceded you."

So Beatrice Fuller had not told him I was insensitive, selfish, and willful. Or was this Sunday luncheon, like my visit to the Gateway in a week's time, a means of improving my morally deficient character?

"And, of course, if he's well enough, Mr. Lyngstrand must come with you. I will see to transportation, so have no cares on that score."

Barton Cunningham, often apt to be close to the office door when I was with Edmund, proposed we walked home together at the end of the afternoon.

"Your idea or his, this interview?" he asked, as we contemplated one of the last April showers that year from *The Advertiser*'s doorway.

"I suppose it was simultaneous," I said. "I mean, on our very first meeting I told Edmund how much I admired W. T. Stead's *Pall Mall* and he said he did too. And here's the perfect opportunity for me to live up to my words."

Barton Cunningham eyed the rain again. "We mustn't let this feeble trickle from the clouds put us off. If you knew Bengal when the rains come, you'd scarcely notice it."

"You do know Bengal, I take it?"

"Well, I've made the comparison, haven't I?"

I was suspicious of Barton's motives for wanting to walk my way when he himself lived on the northeast side of the town, and even more so when he suggested we take "the long way 'round," down by the harbor, up along the Esplanade, through the Royal Gardens. But after the fug of the offices I welcomed exercise on a day of fresh light rain and intermittent sunshine.

We had been scarcely two minutes together before Barton said, a trifle conspiratorially:

"I've got something else to tell you about Old Fulsome. Don't know why I didn't when we first spoke on the subject. And there's me who won a prize for being the Best Cub Reporter in Kent . . . You see Old Fulsome and his missus have a son. He went to the Hole, too—I mean, St. Stephen's College. Named Horace, after the great Latin poet Fulsome was always gassing about, who had a villa in Latium that Fulsome went to visit, and then bored us all with descriptions of. Horace Fuller was a mite younger than Yours Truly."

I was wholly unprepared for this information. Mrs. Fuller, a mother! But then why not? Simply that she'd given me not a single hint of it. Now a new explanation for the Mercy Room's appearance came to mind. Rugby ball, cricket stumps, toy galleons, et al. belonged to a flesh-and-blood boy, child of my landlady and her "disappeared" husband?

"Well I never!" I exclaimed. "And where might Horace Fuller be now?"

"That's the burning question, Bridges my friend. It ain't easy to answer either. Master Fuller was a Black Sheep, you see."

It was pointless to pretend I wasn't curious. "In what sense?"

"In what sense not? No good at schoolwork, always took a low position in form-orders, embarrassing for Old Fulsome with his vast learning. But that's a well-known situation, isn't it? Beak's son turns out a dunce. But Fuller Junior didn't make up for his academic failings in other ways, on the playing fields for example. Unlike Yours Truly, he was no Victor Ludorum."

"That must have been a bitter disappointment!" And there he'd been in a room enviably full of sporting equipment!

"We can only pity him. But what I am trying to tell you, Bridges, is no mere matter of failing to conjugate fifth declension Latin verbs or to run the 440 in the proper time. Fuller Junior was a 'Real Handful' as the popular expression goes, in constant hot water, to use another one, and nobody knew what to do with him. *He* didn't know what should be done either. So he used to run away."

Remembering my own unhappy youth, I felt a pang of sympathy for Horace Fuller of whose very existence I'd been ignorant until a few minutes ago. "Running away! Where to?"

"Not exactly hard to get out of this country from the port of Dengate, is it? More than once he stowed himself on boats just like the ones we can see before us." For we were now above Dengate's famous Royal Harbour, looking down through sun-filtered diagonals of rain to its forest of gently swaying perpendiculars: masts of fishing-smacks and yachts. By the small pier on the far side of the harbor a steamer lay in dock, a gleaming black-and-white, sure temptation to any unhappy daydreamer. "But he was no better at stowing away than at anything else, poor young Horace. He was caught and hauled back home—the house Fulsome had named after one of his favorite places, thinking it would bring them all good fortune."

But inside that house Horace Fuller had had a room to meet many a boy's greediest dreams.

Barton, giving me a mischievous side glance, now said: "Well, Bridges, you haven't asked what means young Horace had for traveling after he'd crawled out of the holds of scrubby boats. How he could support himself, even as a runaway?"

Barton Cunningham had a winning card up his sleeve, I could tell from the glint in his eye. We had now turned southwest and were beginning to ascend the rise to the Esplanade. On our right was the prestigious terrace of houses from the Regency, each with a white-painted façade, each with bay windows overlooking the sea, each (from our present perspective) standing a little higher than its neighbor. On our left, the equally white Kentish cliffs fell away to a beach that increased in sandy breadth with every upward step we took. On the seaward side of the Esplanade there stands a little shelter (it has a part to play later on in this history), built in the Chinese or Japanese manner, with red-tiled roof and curved eaves. Here strollers (or town boys out courting) can take a seat and enjoy the splendid view in either direction (or fail to look at it, too preoccupied with other delights).

"Unfair of me to put questions to you when only *I* know the answers. Sadly, Horace had no means of self-support whatsoever!"

"So how . . . ?"

"Use your reporter's wits, Bridges. We are always meant to be a few jumps ahead of a situation."

"He—he appropriated . . ."

"If you insist on avoiding plain language, yes indeed. Bad Lot Horace *appropriated* money that by no stretch of morality could be thought his. He stole, in other words. He stole from one of Old Fulsome's fellow beaks— a distinguished chap, writer of a famous mathematics textbook, one Mr. Azariah Welbeck. As Azzy is the very nicest of men, he wanted the episode to go no further. But then Horace went and stole from Fulsome himself, who had, as ill luck would have it, already reported the theft. I've always thought that pretty stupid of the young blade, as well as being against the Good Book's prescripts. (Breaks at least two commandments, doesn't it?) The sum was discovered on Horace's person. So behold, Fulsome Junior was in even hotter water than ever."

"But how on earth did Beatrice—Mrs. Fuller—his mother—react to all this?"

"Well, she can't have been exactly *pleased*. What mother would be?"

"What happened? He didn't go to prison or anything, did he?"

"No, they managed to keep it 'in the family,' as they say—though not completely so, otherwise I couldn't be telling you this tale, could I? Nobody in truth wanted the poor lad punished, they just wanted him to mend his ways. Some hope! He was determined never to fit in with anything anybody else wanted of him—and he didn't budge no matter what others said or did. You could say he had guts! He had his nicer sides, I suppose, but he didn't let many people see them. He was very friendly, I remember, to a little girl who acted as a sort of skivvy at the Hole. A natural democrat, I suppose." He didn't make that sound much of a compliment.

"So what happened to him? After the—thefts?"

"The Hole was jolly understanding. The Headmaster and George Fuller joined forces and found some English consul in Rome to take him in for a while. And put him to work. Gardener's boy, stable-boy, something of that lowly sort. The democratic line again! But I know from Mr. Betterton, my godfather, that Horace is not with that official any longer but has preferred to stay 'over the seas and far away.'"

"I couldn't have deduced any of your story from Castelaniene," I said, conceding too much advantage to my informer, "but it does shed light on things there."

But did it? In finding all those distressed occupants for the Mercy Room was Mrs. Fuller seeking to replace the son who'd deserted her? Or was that clutter of boyhood totems her way of preserving the absent Horace in St. Ethelberga's Road?

"Light on *what* things?" By now I appreciated that Barton Cunningham was a thoroughgoing gossip, who took as well as gave, so I judged it wise to hedge. Looking at him, his pale yet inquisitive eyes, his red hair spangled with raindrops shining in the mild damp sunshine, I felt, as I had several times before, that he was someone I should go carefully with, even though he was the only compensation *The Advertiser* offered me for those London mates with whom I'd spent so much time these last years.

"I can't say without giving the subject a lot more thought," I said.

"Well, let me know when you're ready," said Barton sarcastically. "You owe me that much, Bridges. Without my revelations you might have remained ignorant of the whole Horace saga, and could have put your foot in things at Castelaniene."

I have already done that, more than once, I could well have added. Instead I inquired: "And when did all this take place?"

"Well, Old Fulsome died year before last, and I'd reckon Horace exchanged our Scepter'd Isle for foreign parts about ten months before that."

"He wasn't back in Dengate for the funeral?"

"No, he was not. Funny, that!"

As I was digesting all this, two girls in blue bonnets, both about seventeen, passed us; we were now on the highest point of the Esplanade. Automatically both Barton and I had turned 'round to give their trim healthy prettiness a second glance, which indeed confirmed the favorable first. Had either of us been alone, turning 'round could have been followed by a fleet, cunning retracing of footsteps and some inspired sentence of self-introduction. As it was, we were each hampered by the other's presence.

Barton gave a laugh of a distinctly Will Postgate kind. "Now I know a *little* more about your taste in girls, Bridges."

"And me about yours!" I rejoined.

Barton stopped in his tracks and took a deep breath. I was about, I appreciated, to learn his real motive for making this roundabout walk with me. He said, "Didn't I hear Edmund asking you up to his place, for luncheon Sunday-week?"

I longed to reply: "You know darned well you did! Your ears were close enough to the door!" But instead I nodded a yes.

"He's so generous! Asks just about *everybody* to luncheon some time or other. You will enjoy the occasion, I'm sure. I know Furzebank House pretty well, you see."

"Something to look forward to then?"

"Certainly. You'll meet his family. I gather they'll all be at home."

How could he possibly have "gathered" this without eavesdropping? And what bally business was it of his anyway?

"So I understand."

"Lucinda will be there."

"That's what Mr. Hough"—I decided to refer to him formally—"told me when he asked me over." We were now nearing the copious blossoms— almond, pear, cherry—of the Royal Gardens, a place personally dear to the Queen herself as an engraved plaque on its railings proclaims. From the middle of the park tall metal poles of scaffolding reared upwards. A new bandstand, to be ceremonially opened later on in the summer, was under construction, as anyone (everyone) in the town would proudly tell you.

"You will like Lucinda Hough." The words came out of my companion awkwardly, almost reluctantly but, I could tell, as the result of a conscious effort on his part. Then, taking another deep breath, and speaking more rapidly than I'd yet heard him do, Barton continued: "She's a truly remarkable person. She and I have—well, shall we call it an *understanding*?"

"You mean you're beau-ing her about?"

Barton's pale face flushed. "I meant what I just said. We have an understanding. So bear that in mind, my friend. She's not just a lass on the Esplanade for you to fix your greedy lights on."

Barton Cunningham and I said goodbye at the side-entrance into the Royal Gardens. Its flowering cherries shimmered in rain-streaked sunlight like a line of girls in some sweet daydream; by now the town end of St. Ethelberga's Road was within sight. My young colleague had shot his double bolt, and there didn't seem anything further for us to say to each other.

As I had not yet met Lucinda Hough, it seemed foolish and mean-spirited to mind the two of them having this "understanding," but somehow mind I did, as doubtless Barton had intended. One more proof of what a mere incomer to this society I was! Walking "homeward" along St. Ethelberga's Road a dreadful thought seized me. What if Hans Lyngstrand, so chatty this morning as we talked across our attic landing, had, during the day, taken a turn for the worse? What if he'd . . . *died*? The very notion was terrible enough for me to keep my head down for fear I saw drawn curtains or pulled-down blinds in the front bay-windows of Castelaniene.

I couldn't dismiss this as melodramatic fancy. Hans provided daily evidence of the seriousness of his condition. And I knew what it was to return home and find blinds down because of Death: one late November afternoon five years ago I found the familiar Walworth Road windows blanked out because my father's life had come to a sudden end . . . Oh what a relief!—the windows of Castelaniene were no different from when I'd left that morning.

Back inside the house I discovered Mary, that "delightful little vehicle," in the hall busy with a feather-duster.

I had said nothing in letters to London friends about this girl of almost nineteen, whom I found myself unable to call pretty. She had a face like a potato, from which sprouted a button nose, usually raw-red and dripping from a heavy cold, and she invariably had a sty in the eye. She had heavy pendulous breasts not quite commensurate with the rest of her figure. I could well have penned humorous lines about Mary's failure to fit the hackneyed role of tempting servant wench, but did not. What stayed my hand? Not, I fear, her self-containment and her proud kind of humbleness, merely the fact that, with all her defects, I found the sight of her, especially when engaged on her chores, appealing, if not downright alluring, and did not want to give this truth away. At night-time my thoughts strayed to Mary, lingering on her person far more than was good for me.

"You're not usually down here at this time of day, Mary," I observed breezily and truly. She was, as a rule, upstairs at this hour.

"Oh no, Mr. Bridges, but today we have had a real turnabout. On account of that Mr. Longstrand."

My pulse instantly quickened; my forebodings had been justified after all! "Lyngstrand," I corrected her, "has anything happened to him? I don't see any drawn blinds."

"Happened? Well, he was taken badly just after luncheon, *very* badly, Mr. Bridges. Just couldn't get his breath. Gasping for air like a fish pulled out of the water, he was."

"That *is* bad news, Mary!"

"But it isn't all bad, Mr. Bridges," Mary was looking up at me with a half-smile and an extra shine to her sore little nose. "That Dr. Davies from the Royal came 'round here, and he said Mr. Longstrand had got better more quickly-like from this attack than from any of his earlier ones in the hospital. Real pleased Dr. Davies said he was, for all the poor boy's cruel puffing and wheezing. But now he's giving him a thorough going-over just to be on the safe side." She applied the bunched-up red, green and blue feathers of her duster to the banister rail as if miming Dr. Davies's attentions to his patient. "Madam says we should look on Mr. Longstrand like some poor wild creature, a deer or a hare, with an injured limb that we've rescued from a trap or from them wicked hunters' hounds. Treat him kind and gentle, and then he'll be ready to go free, she says. Still, Mr. Bridges"— her small, grayish, sty-afflicted eyes looked soulfully at me—"at one o'clock I felt proper afraid just standing there looking at him. Thought he was about to—*disappear*, if you get my meaning."

Get her meaning. Well, for a second or two I did not. And then— goodness, why had I been so slow on the uptake?

I must dissemble. "I'm not sure I *do* get your meaning, Mary, I'm afraid. However could Mr. Hans *Lyng*strand . . . *disappear*?"

Mary put down the duster and, lowering her gaze, said, "Only too easy, sir. Madam says it's been Dr. Davies's view that Mr. Longstrand may likely have done a lot of damage to hisself that can't be repaired. Through being in the freezing cold sea all that long time."

"Terrible! But I still don't see how he could *disappear* now he's safe in Castelaniene and with Dr. Davies still looking after him."

"Anybody as ill as him can easily disappear, Mr. Bridges." Mary's tone was reproachful.

"Really! Being ill could make him do . . . *what*?" I gave a sophisticated little laugh. "Vanish into Dengate Harbour? Fall off the edge of the world?"

Mary can hardly have cared for the way I was speaking to her, and she glanced up at me with hurt, puffy eyes as if she could scarcely credit such heartless levity. But how else was I going to arrive at the admission I required?

"Tell me, Mary," I continued. "Tell me the names of some other persons who have 'disappeared,' as Mr. Lyngstrand might, if he's unlucky."

Mary's mouth dropped open in protest. "But I couldn't do that, Mr. Bridges. The list would be far too long."

"Well, keep to people you know who've 'disappeared' in the last couple of years. Where is it you live, Mary?"

"Farthing Lane."

"Well, who's disappeared from Farthing Lane?"

Mary looked pleadingly at me, but complied nonetheless. "Well, there was my grandpa last November. And poor Aunt Ada at much the same time. And that sweet little boy who lived next door to us—only six years old he was, and the cleverest, most delightful little chap—name of Samuel. And only six weeks ago Mrs. Price at the Post Office, and—"

No need to listen any further. "Disappeared" was merely a substitute for the hard, disagreeable, frightening word "died." A euphemism! Helpless, uneducated Mary had adopted it under the influence of her more educated but, in this respect, scarcely more honest, employer. It was, I thought, an even worse alternative to the plain-speech term than the more popular "passed away" or "passed over," because it had another quite specific meaning, one denoting an altogether different destiny than death. So Edmund Hough and Barton Cunningham had both been right; George Fuller had not gone missing but was dead, was truly "'the late Mr. Fuller" of Edmund's initial description. Therefore, my landlady's coy rhetoric about his "disappearance" was an affectation used to evade the bleak truth, and to ensure that others evaded it also. Nor, I now knew, thanks to Barton, was this the only truth Beatrice Fuller had evaded during my weeks of living under her roof. There was the matter of her son, Horace.

Indeed, her erratic presentation of her circumstances was enough to vex somebody far less intent on facts than a young journalist such as myself. The woman had had a husband who had died but whom she preferred to describe as "having disappeared." And she had a son who actually *had* disappeared, but whom, by never once alluding to his existence past or present, she was treating as though he were—well, dead!

I was, I realized, standing before the geometrical squares and rectangles of the real Castelaniene's medieval houses in that framed photogravure in the hall. It occurred to me that the Italian scene contained clues to these problems which sooner or later I would understand.

I went upstairs after supper, bound for my room with Mrs. Gatty's famous book on the seashore because I'd been told—by Mr. Thomas Betterton, no less—that, in view of the community our newspaper served I oughtn't to be quite so obviously ignorant about marine life as I was. But just as I was putting my hand on the doorknob, Hans called out to me. His own door was yet again ajar. Well, wasn't he himself "marine life"? The survivor from the sea.

Though the day's attack had plainly wearied him, deepening those hollows in his face, he was, in general aspect, far better than I'd expected, in fact to use Edmund's and Beatrice Fuller's favorite adjective, surprisingly cheerful. Dr. Davies's honest opinion that his system had coped with the weakness in his lungs more vigorously and effectively than before had acted on him like some fast-working tonic. And doubtless he was pleased to be in a proper house (if Castelaniene could be so called) rather than a hospital, and to have a friendly housemate his own age. Now Hans could see health as something to be reached out for and held on to, like boughs laden with golden apples. Until today it had appeared more like one of those apples-on-a-string with which children torment each other at Halloween, something dangled and then withdrawn.

Hans was not as taciturn as traditionally his compatriots were; he positively liked talking—and listening too. And he was interested in me, as nobody else, even Will Postgate, was: in where I'd been born, where I'd grown up, whether I had brothers and sisters, what had made me want to become a newspaper reporter. My answers—which I could not, at this stage, make as full as truthfulness demanded—appeared to chime in with situations and experiences of his own. Yes, he too was an only child, and no, he didn't have parents either. Instead he had this guardian, Herr Strømme, shipping magnate and city philanthropist, and a man universally respected in their native city, Bergen. Apparently the Strømme mansion was situated on the slopes of Mount Fløyen, and looked commandingly down over Mariakirken (a big church), Haakon's Hall, and the Rosenkrantz Tower, and of course over the harbor itself—which invariably had a Strømme-owned ship or two in dock. Very different from the back of Grove Lane, Camberwell, I said to myself, let alone the other houses we'd lived in after perforce leaving that pleasant little terraced villa—and different, too, from Castelaniene. But Herr Strømme resembled "the good Mrs. Fuller and her late husband" in being very fond of pictures and *objets d'art*.

"Why, he has plaster casts of Bertel *Thorvaldsen* sculptures," he told me, lowering his voice as in awe of the information he was imparting, "both in the *salon* and in his private study. One is of 'Jason,' the Argonaut hero—that's my favorite piece—and then there's a larger statue of Our Lord Jesus Christ."

The name of the Dane, greatest sculptor of his age, was wholly unknown to me, but, in the light of Hans's feverish remarks on his very first night in this house I registered Thorvaldsen's calling as significant to the youth in front of me.

About Bergen Hans was even more expansive:

"I doubt there's a port like Bergen in the whole world. Seven great mountains at the back, and the town meeting the long fjord that's wound in from the open sea. And the main harbor always so busy, with Torget at the end of it—that's the name of the open market square with stalls piled with all the fish you could ever want."

He smiled suddenly with a sweetness I found oddly touching, as if he were not a patient in an English Mercy Room but a young Norwegian prepared to guide me through his native town for sheer love of it.

"As a small boy I liked more than anything else just to stand on the quaysides. I'd think of the Vikings who set out on their expeditions from these very quays, my ancestors (and yours too probably; the Vikings conquered England, as you must know, Martin), making expeditions as far east as Byzantium and as far west as—well, America itself. I'd gaze at the ships themselves, of course, and ask myself where I wanted to sail away to most. Often, I'd get into conversation with sailors—as I didn't have company at home, I looked for it outside, talking to whoever looked friendly enough—

and surprisingly often they'd show me 'round their vessels. I'd wonder whether they'd let me join them on their next voyage if I could convince them I was old enough. They never did take me, of course."

I couldn't help thinking of Horace Fuller the stowaway here. So these two youths had not only the Mercy Room in common!

"But perhaps," continued Hans with an almost happy sigh, "I knew even back then that I'd be working on craft like theirs someday, spending far, far more time at sea than on land, seeing it in all weathers, and meeting men who have learned its ways. Men like Johnston."

Ah, Johnston. Him again.

And, predictably, his expression changed. "If only I could know whether he were alive or dead, Martin. I don't suppose you heard any news of him at the paper today . . .?"

"No, there was none—"

"That man connects Life with Death, and Death with Life. It's important for me to know which of them holds him now."

CHAPTER FOUR

The W. T. Stead of Dengate

I carried out my interview with Hans Lyngstrand on the afternoon of Saturday, May 2, a couple of hours after I'd come back from work at *The Advertiser*, the two of us seated in basket-chairs in the walled garden at the back of Castelaniene, blossoms all about us: weeping pear, crabapple, wych-elm, and then bluebells in clumps that released color into the air as a fire does azure smoke. The two cats, Japheth and Ham, kept us almost motionless company throughout.

During my first year on the South London paper I'd successfully set about mastering Pitman's Shorthand, remembering what the young Charles Dickens had done when he was a young reporter. As invariably happens, my final piece used only a small portion of what I took down, and that not the most extraordinary part.

I started off asking Hans about Johnston; for some reason "the American" preyed on my own mind as well as his.

"Have you known him a long time?"

Hans gave a laugh of astonishment. "Not at all! I wasn't aware the man—or anybody like him—existed before February this year."

"Really? February?" I scribbled the name of the month down importantly on my pad.

"Yes, that's when we docked in Halifax, Nova Scotia. You see our usual bo'sun, a Swede by name of Karlsson, was taken ill very suddenly. But . . ."—he broke off, an anxious look on his face—"Martin, I don't think we should be talking about Alfred Johnston, not just now! Shouldn't I tell you how I came to be a sailor and what ships I worked on, and so on?"

"Well, I know how you used to hang about the quays as a kid in Bergen, so I suppose it was love of the sea that—"

"Excuse me, Martin!" Hans interrupted in an almost urgent tone. "*Not* love of the sea. I *don't* love the sea." He paused. "I don't believe any sailor does. Love of adventure—that might be nearer the truth. But most fellows go to sea because—well, they have to."

"Did *you* have to?" Hans had given me the impression that—on land anyway—he was accustomed to a certain affluence, with his patron Herr Strømme owning all those works of art.

I saw myself a mere six years ago, in contrast with such circumstances, wondering how I could possibly "keep body and soul together," as they say, and then coming across that notice in the window of J. B. Spencer, Stationer's, advertising their need for a bright and hardworking lad. I recalled the effort it had taken for me to push open the shop door and present myself. And it was through humble Spencer's that I heard of a young man being wanted at Lewisham-and-Lee's thriving newspaper . . . So Hans too had known something of such difficulties.

Anyway, here follows the edited (though *not* by any means the final published) version of Hans Lyngstrand's story. I interrupted quite a lot, sometimes involuntarily, sometimes in order to be sure that I'd got things right. These, I need hardly say, I have not troubled to set down:

"My mother was ill ever since I can recall. She'd become ill bringing me into the world, and never truly recovered. Mine was a home you had to tiptoe through for fear of causing a disturbance, doctors were always calling, and nurses moving in. Finally, shortly before my thirteenth birthday, Mamma died. Her funeral comes back to me in dreams sometimes or if I am ill: all those solemn faces and lowered voices, the ritual throwing of flowers onto her coffin, and the expression on Pappa's face as he looked at me—as if I was the one remaining obstacle in his life. Did I grieve for my mother? I'm not sure. I'd never properly *known* her after all.

"Pappa was manager of one of the bigger banks in Bergen, a highly-respected citizen, known in all the circles of the town which count. One of his best friends and clients was Herr Strømme who entrusted him with the accounts of his shipping company. I am assured he looked after these very shrewdly. I've told you something about Herr Karsten Strømme and his home on Mount Fløyen already, and honestly I'm surprised you haven't heard of him, his reputation is so high and extensive, here in England too.

His name is so right for him: 'strømme' in Norwegian means 'flow' or 'pour,' and you simply could not find a more generous man. Herr Strømme and his wife were not able to have children of their own, which is one reason why, I suppose, he always made a fuss of me whenever he came to our house for supper or a glass of punch and a game of cards. He'd bring me sweets such as you couldn't get in Bergen, or exotic fruits transported by his ships: persimmons, pomegranates, and unbelievably sweet and juicy dates and figs. He appreciated my interest in voyages and far-off places, and would trace the courses of his own ships on a map. But then Pappa got impatient: 'Karsten, you're giving the boy far more attention than is good for him. Hans, it's time you went to your room.' More than once I overheard him say: 'I confess, Karsten, I don't know what to do with him. I certainly do not want him hanging 'round my house indefinitely. And now that Berthe, rest her soul, is dead, I've my own life to lead for a change! His schoolmasters have made it only too clear Hans is no great shakes as a scholar!'

"Well, as you've probably guessed, the eventual outcome of such conversations was that Herr Strømme proposed I leave school to work for his company. Not as an errand-boy in his Bergen offices (which is what I at first feared—I have no head for figures) but actually *aboard* the ships themselves.

"I started my life at sea no different from any other Norwegian boy who wants employment, a regular pay-packet, and a challenge. In no way did I benefit from being the son of a well-off bank manager on familiar terms with a Bergen shipping magnate. That's how Herr Strømme wanted it, that's how my father wanted it—insofar as he wanted anything for me at all ('It'll shape you up a bit, boy!')—and that's how I wanted it myself. We Norwegians are a very democratic people, we have nothing to do with rank and privilege and deference. From this point on my father departs from the story of my life. His attitude to me was 'Well, I've got that useless son of mine off my hands!' He resigned his position in the bank, while remaining a major shareholder, and then left not just Bergen but Norway altogether—for the South of France—some two years after I first went to sea. I always used to say, when anybody asked me, that he'd *disappeared* as far as I was concerned; that was the truth as I saw it.

"The first ship I was assigned to was bound for Baltimore. She made a smooth Atlantic crossing, beating her own record, and I enjoyed every waking hour of that voyage. I felt free, alive for the first time ever. When my shipmates told me all voyages wouldn't be as straightforward and enjoyable as my maiden one, I hardly believed them. When eventually the ship made her way up past the wooded banks of the Chesapeake, I felt like one of my Viking forebears entering the estuary of the unknown continent with who-knew-what inhabitants and wildlife to confront. But now, after five years of travel, I think no coast can compare with Norway's. I shall be so glad to see it again. There have been times this last month when I didn't think I'd survive to do so.

"I did every kind of job expected of me, from skinning up riggings, and in pretty tough conditions too, to helping the cook down below in the steam of the kitchens. You'll be wondering how a boy from a privileged background with an actual connection to the ship's owner got on with his shipmates, however democratic we Norwegians might be—and anyway many crew-members were *not* Norwegian. Well, naturally there were some pretty rough types and troublemakers, and some real bullies among them. I learned from their lips things that back in Bergen I never dreamed as existing. But I got along, and not all my learning was bad for me, by any means. Of course, rumors spread that I was an important man's son and an even more important man's godson, but for most of the hands I was just plain Hans, and that was that. Things will usually go all right for a lad if he aims to be friendly.

"Anyway, your English expression 'It's all hands on deck!' is a very good one. When trouble comes—a storm brewing, a fault detected in the rigging—you all have so much to do you forget your differences, and become so close it's as if you're parts of the same living body. After the boyhood I'd had, having comradeship 'round the clock was something I welcomed gratefully. The friends I've made, Martin! And the talents I discovered in almost every one of them.

"Think of little Niels from Frederikshavn in Denmark, sixteen years of age. It was a full week before he let on that he played the concertina but hadn't brought one with him. Somehow, somewhere on the ship we found him an instrument, if very old and wheezy. And when Niels put his hands on the key-buttons, he looked like somebody who'd been set alight, mouth grinning, eyes sparkling, and as for the music he made, I've never heard anything so joyful ever, one tune after another, a polka from Poland, a *hambo* from Sweden. Oh, I so hope Niels survived the wreck. It would be a real treat to hear him on the concertina once more . . .

"I've already told you I'm now an Able Seaman. Yes, Able Seaman Lyngstrand. After I'd proved myself on my first two voyages, I moved up from Lower Deck with the idea that I work for a Second Mate's certificate. Herr Strømme spoke of this when we met in Bergen for Christmas. He remains my official guardian, or patron, until my twenty-fifth birthday, and therefore manages the trust my father set up for me. But, Martin, never say this to anyone, not a word in your article, but after all that I have just been through, after all that *everyone* I've been close to has been through, and after the death of *Dronning Margrete* herself, I don't want to be a seaman anymore, of whatever rank. I've already told you what I hope to be . . ."

At this point I wanted to hear no more of his ambitions to be a sculptor and feared they might divert him for too long from his main story. So, a little pointedly, I made no interpolation here.

"But of course you will need more information about Herr Strømme's ships for your piece.

"I wonder how many of your readers being English realize that Norway—such a very small nation, not a million of us yet—has the third, yes, the *third*, biggest merchant navy in the world. But we've been slow to adapt to steam. Almost all the vessels in our fleet are sailing-ships, and I myself have worked on no other kind. Company owners in Norway, even Herr Strømme himself, tend to be very conservative, and as a result we've let you British, and the Americans too, get well ahead of us—and the Age of Steam is here to stay. *Dronning Margrete*, at 480 tons, was the largest ship I'd ever joined, and the most beautiful. In full rig, in the sunshine, she looked as though she could take you to Heaven. And in fact, she *was* taking people to what they thought might be Heaven compared with the poverty they'd known in Norway and Sweden. Yes, she carried 'human cargo,' emigrants bound for a new life in the New World. That was on the outward voyage, alongside Norwegian timber and fish. Then in Halifax these folk disembarked—and on the return trip we had non-human cargo only:

Canadian timber, Canadian fish, Canadian fruit and grain, Canadian arti-facts, as well as ice, which we could store pretty well in our big wooden hold.

"Our plan, once we'd completed the outward voyage, was to dock in Halifax three to four days while loading up the ship. But it was February and our crossing had been very rough indeed. To avoid the worst we changed course with the result we arrived in Nova Scotia two days behind schedule. Every single one of us was pleased to get into port after such weather, and be on firm ground again, and see other faces apart from the familiar ones, and go where you'd find interesting company, bars and cof-feeshops and—certain other establishments also, naturally. But the morn-ing after we'd docked something completely unexpected happened. And now Johnston does enter the story.

"A group of us hands, having an hour to ourselves but not enough time to go into town, was relaxing in one of our larger cabins over a card game—a kind of poker for low stakes, which Toto from Palermo had taught us. I was doing rather well, as it happens. And then into our fun staggers our bo'sun—a long-serving man we considered a permanent fixture, a Swede called Karlsson. We thought he'd come in to say: 'Hell, can't you boys pipe down for a bloody second?'—but the minute we looked up at him, we saw that wasn't why he was there. He'd come for our help! He was doubled up in pain, deathly pale, dripping sweat and shivering even as he moved along, and clutching himself between the legs as if a horse had savagely kicked him in the crutch. He said, in a voice we could hardly rec-ognize: 'Old Nick's got me at last!'

"Judging by his appearance, he might have been right. We all knew that Karlsson, the gravest, soberest man imaginable on board ship, was a wild man on shore, and what we were seeing was likely a consequence of what he'd been up to two nights before. One of us—Niels, the Danish boy who played the concertina—ran to get the First Mate, and it was he—Anders Andersen, level-headed as they come—who insisted Karlsson be taken into Halifax. That took some doing (Karlsson was by now shaking so much three of us hands had to hold him) but they did succeed in getting him to the city hospital. No question whatsoever of him returning with us to Norway. In fact, when we left him, we doubted he'd make it through the rest of that day. But—last thing we heard, he was responding to some treatment; mercury, you know. So it fell to Andersen, the Chief Mate, and to Wilhelm, the Third Mate, the German Bible-reader, to recruit another man to fill his place. For a ship always needs a bo'sun, even in dock. We hadn't time to waste either; we were already well loaded with fruit and salt, though not all the manufactured goods had arrived. So you can see how jolly relieved these two officers were when someone with Alfred Johnston's kind of experience presented himself for Karlsson's post.

"Johnston!—he is (but perhaps I should say 'was') about forty. You could tell just from his face he'd been around a hell of a lot. And, if only half of what he let slip was true, he really had: China, South America, California—add to those Nova Scotia, and you've pretty well covered the globe. The First Mate said he was just the man for the job, and Third Mate Wilhelm agreed.

"We entered him in our ship records as an American because that's what he said he was, though I now have my doubts, and as a bo'sun by trade. But I have my doubts about *that* too. Definitely—100% certain— he'd been a bo'sun on his last ship, which had sailed up the east coast of America, from Charleston, South Carolina, to Halifax. We know that because First Mate Andersen talked to her captain in Halifax who gave Johnston a tremendous recommendation. The only reason why Johnston was leaving his command was his personal need to be back in Europe.

"In case you're thinking Johnston didn't have sufficient experience for the position of bo'sun, then you're thinking wrong. Quite the opposite; he had a great deal too much. He'd clearly dealt with stuff well outside your usual bo'sun's duties. Twice I heard him mutter under his breath something about a certificate he'd studied for, and both times I thought: 'You've been a Mate yourself at some stage!' That's as far as I got in knowing about his past. But I'm telling the truth when I say that I've never met *anybody*—in Norway or in the Americas—with such a store of knowledge."

"Explain!" I asked, intrigued.

Perhaps if I hadn't inquired in that manner, Hans, carried away by his own narration, would have done this. As it was, his face underwent a disquieting change, suggesting to me (who, after all, had known him less than a week) that he was made of steelier stuff than his complaisant manner might suggest. He didn't want—or intend—to say anything more on this matter, not for now.

"Johnston and his knowledge will not be what your newspaper's interested in," he said, and there was no denying the reproof in his voice. "It will want the difficulties of *Dronning Margrete* in the Dover Straits during the worst of the gale. Besides"—to my dismay he sank himself back in the basket-chair, and passed a hand along his brow to mop up perspiration—"I should not tire myself by talking too much of troubling things. Dr. Davies says I shouldn't."

Accordingly, we paused there. Beatrice Fuller and Sarah had astonished me with their attentiveness, and soon Sarah was bringing out a jug of lemonade and a plate of sweet biscuits, which helped Hans regain his earlier energy. But when he and I resumed the interview, I learned, against the birdsong and amid the pear and crabapple blossoms, a truth which subsequent experiences as a pressman have only confirmed.

People are neither at their most articulate or accurate when describing the extreme situations they have endured and survived. You might think they would be, but mostly they are not. The very enormity of their experiences defeats them, and maybe also they are afraid of finding themselves enmeshed in them anew and so refrain from recreating them in any circumstantial detail.

Certainly that is how it was with Hans Lyngstrand. He gave me a bald summary of those weather conditions in the English Channel that *Dronning Margrete* had to face, but it scarcely differed from the versions with which I was already familiar, its language as flat, as matter-of-fact, as any coastguards' report. And when he reached the ship's last hours—which were of course also the last hours of many a shipmate whom he'd worked alongside and known intimately—he started speaking (it seemed to me) almost as though he were in the witness box in court, giving evidence on behalf of his Norwegian Captain, defending him from any ungenerous as well as unjust accusations.

"Once we were in the Strait the headwind was too strong for us. Waves are more dangerous in narrows where you can't escape them, and worse in shallow water than in deep. Our Second Mate told us that if you set St. Paul's

Cathedral down on the seafloor of the Dover Strait, it wouldn't be completely submerged; that's how shallow it is! Oncoming waves put dreadful stress not just on our rigging but on the whole structure of the hull, and so when that cracked and the ship sprang a leak, we were shocked but by then not really surprised. 'The bulkhead's gone! We must all take our chances NOW!' our Captain cried. These are words every sailor has imagined hearing yet has always hoped he never will, especially when coming from a calm, quiet, wise man whose authority was law.

"From that moment existence became one desperate attempt to get the scattered crew into the aft of the ship and from there onto the lifeboats. But it was impossible properly to see what we were doing, the spray was coming at us so furiously like flights of arrows in some olden battle. And the noise of it drowned out almost all of our voice. When Johnston raised his voice: 'Stand by the boats! STAND BY THE BOATS!' it could have been God himself ordering us.

"I have asked myself since, over and over again, whether the Captain should have made a decision earlier to shelter our ship in some French port until the weather improved, rather than take her so exposed further to the northeast. Possibly he should. There are those, I have heard, back in Bergen who think just that. But honestly we had no indication that conditions would turn so hostile so quickly. *Dronning Margrete* was not the only vessel in the Strait that afternoon, not the only one to get into difficulties.

"None of the crew gave way to fear, but some, you could tell, were desperately afraid though resolute in not showing this. For myself I felt fear coming very close to me, but I was able to resist it—somehow! Then 'STAND BY THE BOATS!' came Johnston's voice again. Many of us felt our last moments had arrived, and of course, Martin, they were right to feel that. The last minutes had! Some of us noticed that the ship's White Cat wasn't around anymore; two of the hands tried to look for him but were unable to move on the deck it was tilting so violently one way or the other. Even though we'd been in evil seas before—including on this very voyage—a lot of the sailors couldn't believe what was happening to them. They thought that sooner or later, things would return to normal—as they always had done before. When they saw that this time they were not going

73

to, most of the crew turned strangely calm, and that for me was the worst thing of all. All these lively men and boys, who for weeks on end had taken all manner of risks as a matter of course, were now patiently preparing for the end of the ship—and for the end of themselves, too!"

"And you?" I could not stop myself from asking. "Did *you* believe you would come out of the wreck alive?"

Hans shook his head not so much in denial as in baffled wonderment that he, unlike others, was still among the living. "I did as I was told," he replied. "The Captain said, stay by my side, out of his promise to Herr Strømme—so stay I did. And that put me near Bo'sun Johnston as well, and I thought: 'That man is a survivor if ever anybody is!' But then, to watch him dart and leap about the ship, you'd have said the same about White Cat, and where had *he* gone? It was only when I was in the longboat—getting thrown out into the sea and clambering back—that I doubted I'd come through, and by then I'd stopped having what you might call my normal thoughts and feelings."

Perhaps temporarily, briefly, he returned to this state of being, for he fell silent and I could detect his strong disinclination to continue. I must respect him. In the quiet between us a blackbird sang in the espaliered pear tree. Mrs. Noah was waiting under the wall for a moment of weakness from him that happily never came.

I worked on my piece all next day (Sunday), harder than I'd ever worked at anything in my whole life. Folk like Sarah went to their places of worship, and a great many other Dengaters remembered to keep the Sabbath holy by keeping as unoccupied as possible. I was distinctly impressed by the copiousness of my shorthand notes (Charles Dickens would surely have acknowledged me as a promising junior colleague at the very least!), and only very occasionally supplemented them by going across the landing to Hans with further questions. Just in case I needed them again, particularly before the next issue of the paper went to press, I stacked up my notes in a pile on my desk. That contributed to the effect I desired of mine being a proper journalist's room.

My piece ended:

"Mr. Lyngstrand's happiness at having survived so terrible an ordeal has only one thing marring it: his concern for the whereabouts of the ship's boatswain, Mr. Alfred Johnston. He would welcome news of him as he still devoutly hopes that the dinghy conveyed him to safety, so he can once again employ his remarkable store of knowledge for the benefit of others."

"Shh!" said Philip Goodenough to Archie Penry on Monday morning as I was trying to get on with another piece of work while Edmund perused a further revised version of my piece. "The young prince mustn't be disturbed; he's busy earning his spurs."

"Let's hope once he's earned 'em," said Archie Penry, "he's able to keep 'em; that's the difficult part. Especially if you're a bit wet behind the ears."

They went on in this snide, stupid vein until I felt obliged to look up from my corner, screwing up my eyes to do so, for I was working in a great splash of bright spring sunshine. "I'm glad you both find me so funny," I said. "Perhaps if you like humor so much, you should go to Dengate Pier and watch the clowns."

"Oh, I don't think we need go *there*, Mr. Bridges," said Archie Penry, "when you provide better entertainment free of charge."

Edmund's abilities as an editor, his way of transforming the indifferent into the good, I appreciated from the first. But going in and out of his office for yet another going-over and improvement of my interview piece, under the amused gaze of the others, irked me—especially as I had to keep up a seamless good front. It turned a working-day in which I'd hoped to prove myself no neophyte but a born journalist into something of an anticlimax. But at the end of it Edmund said: "After all your good efforts, you deserve a slice of the afternoon for yourself. So, hop it now, with my blessing."

Well, that did make up for things a bit—though I would far rather have had my copy judged faultless. I would, I decided, walk the long way home last taken with Barton Cunningham. The Channel ahead drew my gaze with its many strong streaks of a rich deep blue; this was a phenomenon I hadn't seen before. Young Peter Frobisher, a local lad who'd hardly ever left Dengate except for football matches in Margate, had told me this was the Spring Outburst, so familiar to me now, quite unknown to me then. The sea fills with plankton, which innumerable other creatures have moved in to feed on—sole, sardines, lobsters, even octopuses. No doubt Hans's Alfred Johnston with his remarkable store of knowledge could have told me far more about it even than Peter.

I passed by the Chinese/Japanese shelter, and the sight of a young courting couple—probably from a shop already closed for the afternoon—spooning on the bench made me remember those two pretty girls whom Barton and I had simultaneously turned 'round to look at. When would I have a chance of meeting their cousins and sisters, or was my life just to be confined to my own sex at the newspaper premises and at the printers'? I really might as well be confined on a ship like the ill-fated *Dronning Margrete*, which had foundered fatally in this very stretch of salt water on which the sun was now so benignly shining.

By this time, I was within sight of the Royal Gardens railings. Beyond them I admired two huge horse-chestnuts—these trees, which don't produce fruit until they are twenty years old, always suggest to me the defiance of time—their white flower-spikes already starting to rear upwards from the boughs. Within a week they would have fully bloomed, but very fine they looked even now against the new greens of the leaves and the gentle blue of the sky. How come, I asked myself once again, I had lived so many years on this earth and yet been so negligent of the wealth of trees, plants, and flowers all around me?

A fair number of Dengaters of all ages were ambling about the Gardens in the warm caresses of the late afternoon, many peering at the progress of the bandstand-to-be, roped off from the over-curious. It was to be a proud octagon, entered via four openings in the delicate wrought-iron tracery running 'round the exterior, and surmounted by a gilded onion-dome.

This particular afternoon (Monday, May 4) I couldn't but be struck by a little group assembled about fifty yards beyond the gates into the park, below the nearer and taller of the two horse-chestnuts. Ten or so ragged-looking children, mostly boys, were standing in a rough semi-circle around a young woman my own age, who was apparently giving them a lecture. It being half past four in the afternoon I doubted this was a teacher with a school class, though she clearly had some kind of authority over her audience, which was attending to her with evident respect and even interest.

Probably my curiosity in this open-air meeting would not have been aroused—to the point of considerably slowing my walking-pace and debating whether to go home through the gardens rather than around them—if the girl's hair had not been so arrestingly beautiful. Appropriately enough its color was chestnut, the very hue of the conkers these great trees would produce in due season. She was wearing a light-gray velvet-trimmed cloak ending just above her waist, below which flowed the pleated dark-gray of her skirt. When her voice became properly audible, it had a bubbly, breathy confidence that quite took my fancy.

"We call the flowers of these chestnuts 'candles,' and you can see why, children, can't you?" Vigorous murmurs of assent followed. "These trees usually grow to between eighty and a hundred feet in height," she now informed them, "this one here being probably about ninety feet tall."

"Yes, miss!" loudly agreed a chubby, pasty-faced little boy close to this young instructress, "ninety feet would be *my* reckoning too."

"When you look at horse-chestnuts now, so strong and huge and so much a part of these gardens, you imagine they have been in England for ever and ever. But in fact they come from Greece and the Balkans, and weren't brought to our country before the sixteenth century. But Shakespeare lived in time to see the trees and admire them."

Really? I feared some of these kids might well not even know who Shakespeare was. At this point I saw the girl's face turn in my direction. *Heavens, she mustn't catch me gawping at her!* Realizing she had an observer in the vicinity, she held onto herself, wordless in mid-speech, for a few moments, like some dancer keeping statue-still in the middle of some arabesque.

Then, somewhat pointedly as it seemed to me, she said: "Come along, children, let's see how well you remember what I told you about the hawthorns!" and moved on several steps deeper into the Royal Gardens, her little troupe following. All except one, one of the oldest of the boys, aged about eleven, who, with a "see you on Wednesday, miss!" bolted off down the drive and through the open gates—to run slap into me.

"Steady on! Look where you're going, young man!" I said, in a friendly enough voice. This near-collision could be useful to me. "Whatever have you just been up to just now in the Gardens?"

"Hearing miss talk about the wonders of nature!" came the straight, unabashed answer. "She does it Mondays, Wednesdays, and Saturdays. Anyone who wants to can come and listen to her. On Saturday she told us about broom. Broom ain't got anything to do with gorse, you know. They're just both yellow. Golden-yellow, if you like."

"Absolutely," I agreed. "And who, may I ask, is she? The cat's mother?"

"Don't know her name, mister. We all just call her miss."

"That's very forward of you," I told him, "when you're so young. And where might she live?"

"Wouldn't you just like to know, mister!"

Clearly a more roundabout way of getting information was required, one that flattered the boy with a sense of his own importance.

"And what is *your* name?" I asked, as though personally interested.

But I'd underestimated him; this urchin was wise to my cunning. "Ain't got one!" he said.

"I can't believe *that*. Everyone's called something."

"Well, what's *your* name then, mister?"

"Martin." I felt justified in holding back my surname.

"Well I never! Martin's *my* name too."

He had won—this round anyway.

"Nice to know we have such an important thing in common!" I said, not challenging him. "Do you live 'round here?"

"No."

"So where *do* you live?"

"I live in Farthing Lane, don't I, mister?"

Farthing Lane. Why, that was where the vehicle Mary lived.

"And where might that be?" I asked after a pause.

But too late! The ragamuffin had taken to his heels with the celerity I myself had possessed at his tender age. Irritated at myself I watched him turn a far corner and pass into invisibility.

A letter was waiting for me in Castelaniene. The bold scrawling hand on the envelope I identified at once as that of my old London pal, William Postgate.

"I promised you a visit." I read . . .

You secretive man you, who has let me know so little about all his do-
ings, doubtless nefarious, down in sleepy old Dengate. I have every in-
tention of coming down in person in the imminent future to wake you
up and hear your account of them, right down to the last naughty de-
tail. I am writing as a man on holiday before he—But whist! Not a
word of what is to befall one William Postgate, Esq. Not until we
meet! Meanwhile I have been tasting the pleasures of the Idle Life
alongside Walter Pargeter and Lionel Cartwright—who send their
regards and remember you as a bit too drunk in Soho to be able to
give a proper reply to the magnificent valedictory speech I delivered—
a-walking the Sussex downs ("mens sana in corpore sano," you know)
and making the most impressive strides as an artist with the old pencil
and paper. Yes, I've executed no end of sketches of scenery, geographical
and human, these last days. Leonardo da Vinci must be my middle
name—or my three middle names if you insist on being pedantic. At
the end of a week I shall bid my comrades a fond farewell (I trust it
will be fond, though we have been argufying something terrible of
late, particularly when one of us talks to a pretty girl who the others
are damned sure they spotted first!) and then I shall make a solitary
contemplative way north-eastward up the Kent Coast. Therefore I will
arrive sometime Sunday afternoon at a certain Channel Port to see a
certain young friend, living in a certain house with a certain prepos-
terous Eye-tie name, (we are talking about Sunday, May 10, I hasten
to make clear)—and I expect to stay that night either in the aforesaid
house or in some palatable nearby hostelry to be found by your good
self. I hope this news fills you with due elation.

Well, if ever there was a man to talk to about a beautiful girl spied in
a park, it was Will Postgate, though he would be contemptuous in the extreme of anybody who had simply walked away from her. Will would have
been up that path, past those horse-chestnuts and accosting the girl as she
addressed her admiring band of guttersnipes, before you could say knife.
But I was no Will Postgate.

Not that I wanted him to give me any more instruction in what he sometimes called *Ars amatoria* (in fact he didn't know any more Latin than I did!). Being taken by him to Limehouse had been a nasty mistake whose poison I could sometimes still feel the effects of—when I was tired, or when I'd just seen a pretty female of the pure breed to which She of the Royal Gardens so evidently belonged.

And no, Will, I was *not* drunk that farewell dinner in Soho. Others of the company might have been, but not myself. Also the day on which he proposed to come was none other than that on which Hans and I had been invited to luncheon with Edmund and his family. The letter bore no address, having been obviously written out on the Open Road, so I had no means of informing him that I might well not be in when he turned up at Castelaniene in Dengate . . . Anyhow I should be able to find him a room somewhere easily enough. "The Wheatsheaf" would probably be the most acceptable nearest "hostelry" for him. If I had a best friend it was surely Will, and I should endeavor to make his brief stay in Dengate a rewarding one.

When I'd reached the attic landing, Hans called out: "Hullo Martin?"

"Hullo to you, Hans!"

"I suppose you have no news of *him*?"

"None, I'm afraid."

"If you can spare the time, I'd like a talk."

So I entered the Mercy Room, to which I was no longer a stranger even though strange was what the place still seemed. Hans was out of bed, fully dressed, seated at the table on which perched the stuffed Golden Eagle. He'd been making sketches of this on sheets of artist's paper. "Is your article finished now?"

"It is, yes!"

"You've handed it into your editor?"

"Yes, and it'll appear on Wednesday."

"So you won't be able to add anything to it?"

"Afraid not!" What if he suddenly had some amazing memory which would change the complexion of what was already written? But—

"Don't be afraid. I'm *glad*. You see, I've been keeping back part of what I experienced on *Dronning Margrete*. I didn't want you to be tempted to put any of it in your paper."

I felt my professional honor had been at least a tad impugned. "About . . . *Johnston?*" I hazarded.

"How did you know?" *Because*, I could have added, *your bo'sun—whom I see as a blonde giant with a bull-like head and massive shoulders—has, thanks to you, taken residence in my own imagination*. But instead I shrugged my shoulders and said, "Well, I'm a newspaper-man, aren't I? But tell me, please! I'm all ears."

"I didn't say much about how Johnston was *after* he'd joined our ship, did I?"

"You said he had a more remarkable store of knowledge than your usual bo'sun."

"Yes, far more! While we were still keeping close to the Canadian coast, we could hear him talking to himself about tidal streams and contours and the slope of the sea-bottom, in a way nobody below the rank of Second Mate ever can. And when we'd got further out into the Atlantic, he turned his attention to the stars and the 'fix' they provided for the ship's course. He knew exactly what star would be where in the night-sky, and he had an old sextant which you could tell had been much used. You know what a sextant is," he added, seeing my blank look. "The instrument with an eye-piece and an angular scale that you hold in the hand to work out latitude and longitude. Johnston would look through its eye-piece every evening to determine the angle of a star to the horizon. And *that's* Captain and Chief Mate's work, Martin. Not the business of the Lower Deck's. Not what a normal bo'sun troubles himself with. And I've no doubt his estimations were accurate every time, come calm come storm.

"But the general information in his head was just as astonishing, and sometimes he unloaded it, and we'd reel back in wonder. He told us, for instance, that whales spend three times as much of their lives playing as they do searching for food, and that dolphins are so fond of their offspring they follow them affectionately long after they've grown up."

"Hans," I interrupted him, "I want to take all this down. Have no fear, nobody at *The Advertiser* or any other newspaper will ever see a sentence of it. But let me get my reporter's pad from my bedroom. Please!"

Hans, if a trifle reluctantly, consented.

So now follows Hans Lyngstrand's story, the secret part, again minus my exclamations for never had I heard a narrative that held me so strongly, and I couldn't prevent myself from commenting or occasionally asking for repetitions. I feel now able to say, from this distance in time, that my life, my development, would have gone entirely differently had I never heard it.

"To give you an example of the astounding knowledge at Johnston's disposal, one afternoon we heard thunder rolling in the distance, and he said, 'Do you know the origin of that sound?' None of us did. 'It began with the mating of Ukko with Akka,' he said. None of us understood him. Then, another time, we were all looking up at the North Star—the Pole Star— and he asked, 'Does the dome of the sky look like anything to you fellows?' We dared not answer for fear of saying something wrong. 'It's like the top half of a great broken egg, isn't it?' We quickly agreed. Then he explained that this was how the ancients in his country saw it; they believed that before our universe came into being, a gigantic water-bird laid an egg which then exploded; this was the origin of everything we know. And half of that egg still revolves around the North Star, but from time to time gets so close to it that it causes a huge whirling in space, and that in turn churns up the sea below. All the time he spoke, he was smiling, though he wasn't a man who smiled much. Then he said: 'Don't worry, boys. If any of you fall overboard, all the white spray on the waves will carry you safely and speedily enough to the Great Quiet Land of the Dead. That's what the spray is for!'

"Soon after he'd taken up his appointment, First Mate Andersen decided I should act as bo'sun's messenger, and also help him with accounts, duty-rosters, etcetera. I had increasingly been doing these things for poor old Karlsson. Johnston was even more efficient than the Swede had been but not so good a task-master, too hard to please, too hard to talk to. But every so often he'd relax and when we heard him on the subject of seals, whales, dolphins, or porpoises, it felt as good as hearing an actual sea-creature speak.

"The third day out of Halifax we ran into shocking bad weather, a low depression bearing down on the sea and whipping it up. Mile-long wave trains collided and clashed, and we'd regularly find ourselves in water troughs four to six meters deep. Hard to believe at times that any ship could climb her way out, but ours did, time and time again—up-up very gingerly, then CRASH! down-down on the other side of the water-wall. But hour after hour, day after day of all that was hell. We used to tell ourselves, well, things can never be as bad again. But two weeks later they were, not just as bad but worse—in your Dover Straits.

"To spare the two of us difficulties in getting 'round the ship when she was pitching and tossing so much, Third Mate Wilhelm suggested I move into Johnston's cabin. This had two berths in it at opposite ends, one biggish one, his; one very narrow one, mine. That was a sound enough plan bearing in mind what occurred next.

"Suddenly our ship made a shuddering lurch forward that took every one completely by surprise, even old Johnston who tripped down the stairs into the Lower Deck and wrenched his foot. Tough as old boots though he was, he cried out in pain if only for a moment. Third Mate then decided he must be spared any further unnecessary movement for a while, but should lie on his bunk with his injured foot raised. So there the two of us were together, Martin, him and me, and then to make things worse—I feel ashamed even now—I became seasick. Me who'd been a sailor the best part of five years! Johnston didn't even try to disguise his contempt. And I went on throwing up until I thought there'd soon be little—or nothing—left of me.

"Johnston was himself a reluctant, foul-tempered patient. He had to be told many times, 'The more you rest the foot, the sooner you will get better enough to resume your duties. The ship *needs* you to improve.'

"'Ach, I'm bored as hell with lying down!' he'd grumble back. 'What do you think I am? I'm a man of action, not some silly girl with the vapors. Or'—looking at me—'a fledgling knocked sideways by a touch of seasickness.' Then he had an inspiration. 'Tell you what, though! I could just about bear passing the time if you gave me that stash of old newspapers from the Captain's room. Good for my Norwegian.'

"Good for his *Norwegian*, eh? He always used English to me, which you might think odd for someone who knew enough of my native language to be able to read papers published in it. In fact I'd already caught him a few times talking Norwegian both to Anders Andersen and to the Captain himself, though his accent was odd—like somebody, I thought, from the very far north, from Finnmark, beyond the Arctic Circle. I suppose he must have worked on some ship that called at Hammerfest and Kirkenes and

picked up hands from there. Whatever, he plainly encountered no difficulties reading his way through this pile of damp-smelling, yellowing old
newspapers, and I could see that they actually were taking his mind off the
pain in his foot, and therefore off all those tasks he was temporarily unable
to carry out.

"The two of us must have made a funny picture, Martin, our cabin
floor tilting first upwards, then downwards, then upwards again, our port-
hole showing one moment nothing but sky, the next nothing but sea, then
nothing but sky again, and him with his swollen foot screwing up his eyes
over newspaper stories about communities several thousand miles away,
and me spewing my guts out into a bucket and trying to divert myself
by making pictures in my head. For some reason I'd found myself all trip
long remembering my grandfather—my mother's father, that is. He'd been
a very accomplished wood-carver up in the mountains to the back of
Åndalsnes on Romsdalsfjord, and I recollected Herr Strømme telling me
that Bertel Thorvaldsen's father, an Icelander, had also been a wood-carver.
If you have sculpture in your blood, perhaps sooner or later, it has to come
out—and I relieved those tedious hours of the storm by imagining carvings
I myself might make, mostly of friends of mine among the crew.

"And then all of a sudden, my daydreaming was broken into by a quite
terrifying sound, less like a human being than an enraged animal at bay,
boar or elk or wolf.

"I hadn't vomited for about a quarter of an hour so felt stable enough
to risk turning my head to look at him. My first thought was that my cab-
inmate must have made an awkward ill-judged movement and started up
the pain in his foot afresh. But no; there he was in precisely the same physical position as when I'd last glanced at him, with the same newspaper in
his hands—the *Romsdals Budsticke*, the local paper of the very part of the
fjordland my grandfather came from. Johnston's hands were trembling to
such a degree that the sheets of newsprint rattled in them, and his face had
turned white as chalk. And then—not caring that I was in the room, or
perhaps not even remembering that I was there—he crumpled the whole
paper up and hurled it on the floor, like some wild ill-behaved boy in a
rage. But that wasn't the end; having done this crumpling, he leaned over,
picked up the sheets, and began in a kind of slow motion to tear them into

small strips. I watched him, horrified, mesmerized; I'd never seen anybody behave like that ever, even though I'd seen hands getting roaring tight in port and picking fights.

"When he'd finished ripping up the entire *Budsticke*, he bent down and pushed all the strips away from him so they formed an untidy heap on the floor, and then said in a low throaty growl—to himself, mind, not me: 'Married. To another man. While I was away.'

"No, I haven't told you that right, Martin. That *isn't* what Johnston said. He said: '*Giftet sig. Med en anden mand. Mens jeg var borte.*' I could not believe my ears, in spite of those brief conversations of his I'd overheard with the Captain and First Mate Andersen. I thought, well, either he's a genius at languages or his friends have taught him exceptionally well, because he said those words exactly as a real Norwegian would.

"Should I now say something, I wondered. If only to remind him he was not alone, that Hans Lyngstrand was right there, close by. But he hadn't finished yet. In that same voice, choking and cracking with passion (that is the only word for it, Martin, I promise you—I've searched for others when telling the story to myself), Johnston went on to say: 'But *mine* she is, and *mine* she shall become. And she shall follow me, if I have to come back home and carry her off as a drowned man from the dark sea.' No, what he actually said was—sounds even more alarming, I think, in Norwegian: '*Men min er hun og min skal hun bli'. Og mig skal hun følge, om jeg så skal komme hjem og hente hende som en druknet mand fra svarte sjøen.*' I felt he was making some solemn sacred vow to the old Gods of the North. It was a threat and a promise at one and the same time. What would *you* think, Martin, if you overheard a man saying something of that sort in that manner? It wouldn't be something you'd forget lightly, would it? Well, *I* haven't either, even though so much else has happened to me since—and to others, so many dreadful, tragic things. You see, I *knew* he meant what he was saying. Knew from his eyes, his voice, his clenched fists.

"Of course working out what I'd just witnessed wasn't too hard: Johnston had come across an announcement in *Romsdals Budsticke* of the marriage of a woman he believed to be his—by love or betrothal, or possibly both. But what was his state of mind when he made that oath? I couldn't decide even as I witnessed it, let alone later. Was it grief? Was it fury? Was

THE STRANGER FROM THE SEA

it disappointment so overwhelming that he felt he couldn't get his own life back until he'd avenged himself? Or else had taken the woman herself back into his possession. The force with which he spoke—I felt I would never be able to rid my mind of his words. And I haven't done so. I am as superstitious, I guess, as any other seaman.

"As I've just said, Johnston appeared unaware of my very presence. Now he reached across his bunk for the heap of torn newspaper-strips and chucked the whole lot into the wastepaper tin in the corner. After that he shuffled all the other old Norwegian newspapers together, saying—in English this time—but still more to himself than to me: 'And to think I was on my way back to her. To think *that* was why I chose to work on this damned ship!' I don't know why he switched languages. Though he'd never once addressed me in my native tongue, he knew I was Norwegian and so must have understood exactly what he'd said in his frenzy. Perhaps he spoke in English because it was the language he'd been using during his absence from this woman he loved so much—who presumably was herself Norwegian.

"I didn't know how I ought to respond to him when eventually our eyes met. Whatever could I say that would be of the least use to him? I almost hoped I'd retch again; that horrible business would at least stop me having to make any comment. But, as it happened, the sea these last minutes had been noticeably calming down, and the ship was steadying. Thank the Lord! Normality had returned. All at once I found myself dozy, because in all the adverse circumstances it hadn't been possible to get any proper sleep. But now we all could. When I woke up, wonderfully free of seasickness, Johnston said in a voice that didn't brook disagreement: 'If you feel up to going about your errands again, I've got one or two things for you to do. Chief of 'em is taking this heap of shitty old Norwegian newspapers back to our Captain's office. They have no interest for me. But if he has some American or English ones, then I might take a peek at them. And don't go forgetting that accounts sheet that you said you'd check. You've wasted too much damned time as it is honking like a baby . . .' Not long after this, Johan, one of the crew most skilled at that sort of business, came in and applied a fresh poultice to Johnston's sprain, so by the next morning he too had improved, and was able to hobble about the decks with a stick. And then the two of us went back, to my enormous relief, to separate quarters.

"But that wasn't quite the end of the matter, Martin. Two evenings later, Johnston and I were once more together in his cabin with nobody in earshot, going over a newly drawn-up job roster. So he caught me off-guard when he said, in the same growl in which he'd spoken of his faithless fiancée: 'Hans Lyngstrand, I don't know if you were too busy spewing to hear what I said when I read that filthy rag, the *Romsdals Budsticke*.' I tried my hardest to look as if I didn't know what he was talking about. 'But if I find you've told others on this ship about it . . .'—I tried not to let my apprehension show—'well, I wouldn't like to be you, that's all.'

"I said, quite truthfully: 'Nobody on this ship has heard a thing about the matter, and nobody *on this ship* ever will!' Of course, with these words I was really admitting that I had heard something. I expressed myself in the way I did because I thought—well, if, *if* I ever do go to Romsdalsfjord, my own grandfather's country, might it not be my duty to tell someone—particularly this woman and her husband, whoever they might be—about Johnston's strange vow? Because he had made it in complete seriousness. And when I looked at him after he'd said he wouldn't like to be me, it came to me in a flash that he *was* capable of killing somebody—and not only that: ten chances to one, he actually had killed somebody already.

"Johnston never referred to the matter again, though, and I have to say from that moment on he was markedly nicer to me. He told me more facts about the whales we saw spouting so spectacularly and the birds which got ever more numerous as we approached Europe. And it came to me: perhaps I'm on his side, really. To be betrayed by someone you really love, that must be terrible, so terrible it'd be impossible to forgive. Perhaps Johnston's love and his need for that woman and his fury at her marriage are all so strong that it doesn't matter if he's alive or dead, because—as he said—he will come back and carry her off *even if he himself were a drowned man from the dark sea . . .?*"

"Well, that's the strangest story I've ever heard," I said, for once not bothering whether I sounded like a "seasoned pressman" or not. "I've never heard anything like it before. And as you talked, I could see him, pretty clearly; Alfred Johnston. I have met men like him in my time, you know. In the London Docks. Tall, strong, with fair hair and fair beards."

Hans looked at me in such wonderment that I was sure a compliment was forthcoming on my telepathic powers.

Instead: "In that case you have *not* met anybody like him," he said. "Johnston was clean-shaven. And a redhead. A darkish sort of red. And then there were his eyes. Black, but their blackness changed—and I wasn't the only chap on board to notice this—changed with the *weather*. Clear when the skies were clear, clouded when the skies were overcast. I don't know in what human race such eyes are characteristic."

That night I dreamed of the Royal Gardens on a day of sea-storm which, strongly though it raged, did not prevent that girl with chestnut tresses from giving one of her talks to children. Among her audience of children, however, I spied Will Postgate armed with a sketchbook even though it was pouring with rain.

"You must never confuse broom and gorse," said the instructress, and Will answered: "I shall bally well confuse them if I want to." The children laughed. Then all of a sudden they turned quiet. Because someone else had entered on the scene. At first as I skulked under the horse-chestnuts, I thought it must be Barton Cunningham because of the red hair. Then I remembered what I had just learned and realized it must be none other than the Bo'sun himself.

"Mine she is," he cried out, making for the young female nature teacher, "and mine she shall become, and she shall follow me, even if I have to . . . carry her off as a drowned man from the dark sea."

CHAPTER FIVE

The Dead Can Speak—Or So it Seems

*M*y (unsigned) interview with Hans appeared in *The Advertiser* of Wednesday, May 6, 1885, and if no colleagues pronounced themselves impressed, Hans himself more than made up for them in enthusiasm. The evening of that day we were engaged to attend a meeting of the Gateway. I'd been half-hoping that somehow Mrs. Fuller would have forgotten about this, but not she. By twenty past seven we were all down in the hall ready—Mrs. Fuller herself, in long skirt of regal purple amplified by bustle and offset by tasseled black shawl, Hans Lyngstrand in a too-loose dark gray suit she'd found for him (the late Mr. Fuller's or her son Horace's?) and myself—awaiting the arrival of Stanley, my landlady's favorite cabbie, "a man more precious than rubies." I was feeling that knot of tension in my stomach associated in earlier years with those few children's parties I'd ever attended. I was certainly not expecting Sarah to clump up from the basement out-of-breath, carrying a large wicker basket inside which was Mrs. Noah.

"Here she is, all set for your gathering!" Sarah said. "I've fed her and given her the milk too, but if them at the Gateway choose to offer her a saucerful more, I don't think she'll be saying no."

"Mrs. Noah is coming *with* us?" I asked.

"But naturally," Beatrice Fuller replied. "She is both respected and loved at the Gateway. She has proved time and again indispensable to our activities."

Had Will Postgate, or any other of my London mates, been with me in the hall, had even Barton Cunningham been present, we would have exchanged looks here, even a wink and a grin. But Hans Lyngstrand, always complaisant, always eager to say or do the appropriate, grateful, kindly thing, took the procedure with the seriousness of his hostess. Maybe, of course, he thought that in famously animal-loving England it was quite usual to take a cat out for a social evening. Mrs. Noah herself certainly behaved as though it were. Contentedly established in her basket, the bottom of which Sarah had lined with a rolled-up blanket, she was sitting there with her legs tucked neatly under herself. Nor when he turned up on the very stroke of half-past seven, red in the face and beaming, did old Stanley exhibit any surprise.

"Evenin', Mrs. Noah, how's tricks?" he said, as, obviously well-practiced, he gently swung the cat-basket onto his own front seat. "We like a little ride side by side above a trotting horse, don't we, my fine missus?"

Banstead Lodge, home of Colonel Walton of the "truly distinguished mind," was situated halfway between West Cliff, which St. Ethelberga's Road straddled, and that northerly residential quarter of the town where Barton Cunningham lived. The house had been built a good thirty years before; the most casual glance up at its creeper-covered, crenellated façade reveals the hand of Augustus Welby Pugin, who had such a personal fondness for Dengate that his architectural influence is everywhere. The pointed arches over the recessed windows and doorways of Colonel Walton's villa are more ecclesiastical than domestic.

Mrs. Fuller's nervousness, after her cabbie had deposited us outside, surprised me. She banged the large dolphin-shaped knocker a little too vigorously against the iron-studded oaken front door, and the elderly maid in black skirt, white blouse, and black-and-white mobcap who answered her looked accordingly irritated.

"You are the very last to arrive!" this grim woman informed the three of us—four, if you count Mrs. Noah, now arching her back and stretching out her front legs in her basket. Almost reprovingly she admitted us first into a large hall so dark that, but for a light under the door immediately to our left, I could have fancied it part of an empty building. Next we were shown into a huge rectangular room which, with its flagged floor and high vaulted ceiling supported by a double row of stone pillars, resembled the nave of a church. Except in color. A deep red, like Burgundy wine, flourished on Turkey carpets, wallpaper, and hangings, on curtains and heavy velvet table-drapes, on sofas and chairs, even in candles under tinted glass domes. I might have stepped inside the maw of some enormous carnivore. About twenty people were assembled here, for the most part standing, not sitting, and conversing in low solemn voices.

A large man well into his sixties, his bearing of a man of some consequence endorsed by silver hair and beard, came up to us.

"Beatrice, what *kindness*!" he exclaimed, in the tones of a public figure who positively expects to be overheard. "the Gate may be hard and obstinate, but the Way is bright and shining."

Mrs. Fuller gave what in a cab-horse would have been a neighing toss of the head. "Colonel Walton, such kindness on *your* part—as always! The Way is bright and shining, however hard and obstinate the Gate. May I please introduce my friends: Mr. Lyngstrand from Norway who is honoring us with his presence in Dengate for some weeks, and Mr. Bridges, a young man of letters from London." Friends, eh? Well, I never! "And Mrs. Noah—"

"But Mrs. Noah needs no introduction, she is the most precious of acolytes," laughed the Colonel. He looked and sounded like one of those tedious public servants who gave out the prizes on Founders' Day at the Thomas Middleton School, Camberwell, exhorting us all, yawning and sniggering down in the Assembly Hall below, to think of our country's unique destiny and our duty to her. Though how many of those men would have gone on to say: "Pray be so good as to take our valued guest to her usual spot on the far table!" and gesture to a cat-basket?

At this point a tall big-boned woman of much the colonel's age, and with equally silver hair, bore formidably down on us. Like Beatrice she was wearing tonight a bustled purple skirt with matching blouse. But just as her height and coiffure eclipsed my landlady's, so did the purple of her dress. She resembled an aging High Priestess from some remote civilization.

"You actually managed to produce them, then?" she inquired in an aggressive, incongruously hoarse voice.

"Indeed I have, Lady Kershaw. May I introduce Mr. Lyngstrand from Norway—"

Hans Lyngstrand gave her ladyship the bow that good manners in Scandinavia require.

Lady Kershaw responded by saying to him: "You're the one who almost *disappeared*, are you not? More than once, I believe. I hope they're keeping a good grip on you now. By the look of you, they'd jolly well better!" She gave a mirthless laugh, which seemed further to strain her larynx.

Hans looked bemused. I, by contrast, was experiencing a moment's sense not so much of illumination as of confirmation. Mary, the other day, had used "disappeared" for "died" or "dead." What I had not known then, obviously, was that this clearly was *Gateway* parlance that she'd picked up from her mistress.

"And you . . .?" Her Ladyship had condescended to address me.

"This is Mr. Martin Bridges, a young man-of-letters from—"

"Man-of-letters fiddlesticks!" said Lady Kershaw, "Mr. Bridges works on that deplorable publication, our local newspaper, as I know perfectly well. And I have only one word to say to anybody who has stooped as low as he. *Mammon!* Nobody can serve two masters, you know—we have that on the best authority—and there is no doubt which master *The Channel Ports Advertiser* is serving."

On hearing this, as though in protest at its high-and-mighty censoriousness, Mrs. Noah, hitherto so peaceful, gave a piercingly loud *miaow*, followed by a second one only very slightly less loud, both causing more than one person to turn around anxiously.

"Well, do the obvious thing, Beatrice!" ordered Lady Kershaw, cross at having her ill-mannered homily interrupted. "Go and take your cat to her usual table, can't you? She desperately wants to be released from her basket, and can you wonder? Rank cruelty on your part I call it, standing there talking away with a poor suffering animal callously confined. That isn't the Gateway approach at all, as you ought to know by now."

Lady Kershaw's is a stern vision of existence. Well, that was one way of putting it! *Lady Kershaw is insufferably rude, even to those she affects to like!* might be another. I couldn't but feel sorry for Beatrice Fuller. Gone now was that self-conscious superiority, those hoity-toity airs. She clearly counted it a great honor to be accepted, on whatever terms, by these people here. All servility and apology, she now hastened toward the big velvet-covered table at the back of the room, heavy cat-basket awkwardly dangling from her hand, Hans and me self-consciously in tow. There was no other young man present; we should clearly have to stick together until this odd social event came to its allotted close.

Though Colonel Walton and Lady Kershaw would appear to be the senior figures of the Gathering, almost all the others we passed on our way to the table were of reasonably advanced years and lofty social standing. Hans, I realized, thanks to his father and his patron, Herr Strømme (with his Thorvaldsen statues), was not unfamiliar with such persons, and this showed now in his demeanor. Besides he was Norwegian, an outsider with a dramatic personal history; everybody here would know about the wrecked ship, and so would want to be friendly to him. I was a different kettle of fish. With my sandy hair, freckled face, snub nose, and buckteeth, to say nothing of my London voice, I surely struck them all as more than a mite "common," just as they struck me as more than a mite "stuck-up." I would have given anything to leave this wretched throng, but here I now was, and what could I do about it? Nothing except take an inward vow never to come to the Gateway again . . .

But Beatrice Fuller was motioning me to undo the clasp of Mrs. Noah's basket. I did this gladly enough, enabling the cat to spring with happy alacrity onto the tabletop. Once there she proceeded, first putting her front right leg into a vertical position, to give her hind quarters the most thorough, if inelegant, of washings. Her intense lavender shade showed to attractive advantage against the Burgundy of the table's velvet drape. She clearly had many admirers here in Banstead Lodge; this was to its guests' credit, and they bestowed on her friendly words and smiles, and stroked her affectionately. These same people also exchanged with Beatrice what were obviously the prescribed ritual phrases:

"What *kindness* that you are here, Beatrice. The Gate may be hard and obstinate, but the Way is bright and shining!"

And Beatrice had to come back with: "Such kindness on *your* part! The Way is bright and shining, however hard and obstinate the Gate."

All that was gauche in me, all that was half-defiantly aware of my unimpressive social origins, and—worst of all—all that refused to be impressed by those who gave themselves airs held sway over me now. I was positively relieved as well as startled when Lady Kershaw clapped her hands with a loud bang which made even the composed Mrs. Noah, for a few seconds, break off from washing herself. Silence ensued.

Then Colonel Walton's gently commanding voice announced: "Time for proceedings to begin. Please, all of you, be so good as to make your way to the table."

Now, as though suddenly wound up by clockwork, all his guests made their several ways, separate or escorted, to join Beatrice Fuller, Hans, and myself around the large table on which Mrs. Noah now sat quite firmly. Some carried chairs or stools with them across the room, so that, within three to four minutes, the entire company, including the Colonel and Lady Kershaw, were seated, hands clasped and placed on the velvet drape. This intensified the room's ominous semi-religious atmosphere, the table becoming a kind of High Altar.

What alternative was there to behaving like everybody else, however awkwardly, however reluctantly, especially as Hans—so much more at ease with these folk than I was—was following the collective example? So I leaned forward as in prayer and encouraged my hands, with fingers interlocked, to relax on the wine-red velvet, to give the rest of my body a lead. As for my eyes, I had them half-closed, with the result that I saw my surroundings from behind a curtain of red-filtered eyelid. And in this unnatural posture I felt a curious change come over me.

No, of course I didn't *like* these members of the Gateway, these friends of Mrs. Fuller's, with their cut-glass voices, snooty manners, and general air of ignorance of what it could be like, say, to serve in a stationer's shop, as I had done for two whole years, on dirty, often disreputable Walworth Road. But sitting in this unnatural attitude as one of them, I felt my dislike of the company physically decrease, ebb away, though no doubt it would eventually return. I simply could not pretend to myself any longer that I didn't know what they were all here for, nor could I pretend it was unimportant. For nothing could be more important than what lurked so palpably behind the whole Gateway, awareness of which animated every member of this oddly assorted community. Why didn't one oneself spend every minute of every day thinking about it—with wonder, curiosity, awe, and (hard to bear but harder indefinitely to stave off) terror?

As maybe Hans already did. He had good reason to, if anybody did.

Perhaps I should make an effort to shut my eyes and keep them shut, just for a few seconds! As I blanked out the room, what I was seeing instead was that miserable little parlor in Crespigny Road, Camberwell, which, with its curtains drawn, had contained my father's coffin until the day of his funeral. Hardly anybody had come to pay their respects, my father having had few relations and fewer friends (but many an enemy and many a creditor). Overripe lilies were standing in alabaster vases like sentinels over the concealed corpse, and I seemed right here to catch a whiff of their sickly-sweet scent. So I opened my eyes again, to rid myself of their presence . . . However long were we to remain thus bound together in silence?

And Hans next to me, what images was he at present seeing? He had surely an extensive tragic gallery to choose from: the hands making their way in sheep-like quiet and dignity toward those longboats which, more likely than not, were to take them out of existence rather than back into it; the boys he'd shared jokes and played games with, cruelly tossed about on the wild March waves of the Strait until they met destruction. Or, just as troubling, those whose deaths he had *not* witnessed: the concertina-playing Niels, White One, the ship's beloved cat, whom Mrs. Noah reminded him of, and then, of course, Johnston, Alfred Johnston of the strange vow and the eerie threat.

Then at last—oh the relief!—Colonel Walton got ponderously up from his chair and, all eyes upon him, spoke up:

"Dear Friends, We of the Gateway are met here tonight as always, because we believe, to use our own words as they have evolved through our mutual sympathies, that though the Gate itself, which we have no alternative to facing, may be hard and obstinate, the Way that extends on its far side is bright and shining. We believe that, limited and erring beings though we are, we have been blessed with the ability to communicate, if fragmentarily, with those fortunate enough—and often after the severest *misfortunes*—to have preceded us on the Way Beyond The Gate, and to be progressing along it, some slowly, some at a happier speed, toward the eventual destination of us all: the source of Everlasting Light, the Nameless, the Ineffable."

I was proved right. Death, and Death alone, had brought these folk to Banstead Lodge, with its constant attendants, Pain and Sorrow, most likely still keenly at work. Lady Kershaw, for instance—what beloved husband or daughter might not this old harridan have agonizedly watched over? Surely, therefore, I should give them the benefit of that quality extolled in their ritual greetings; kindness. I recalled, to my irritation, reading that the great W. T. Stead himself, who held Life, public and private, up to such intense scrutiny, was interested in what lay beyond the frontier-line of Death.

"We have been further blessed," continued the Colonel, "in having, over the years, to aid us in our communications (invariably of unspeakable comfort) truly sympathetic and virtuous human vehicles. Our latest vehicle, the youngest we have yet been privileged to avail ourselves of, is no unworthy addition to those honorable ranks. Friends, the hour has now come for us to invite into our midst our newest vehicle who moves between the world *before* the Great Gate and the world *beyond* it. This I proceed now to do. I PRITHEE ENTER." He gave the table three hefty, booming thumps. And if any man-made sounds could penetrate the hermetic realm of the grave, surely these could.

The door in the wall behind the table now opened, and in came—

Why, Mary.

I could not, as they say, believe my eyes.

Should I have guessed?

Very young, very short, and very pale she looked, but her simple dress of black wool transformed her, displaying becomingly that low-hung bosom and those wide hips of which I had become already only too aware. All the eyes that had played so eagerly on Colonel Walton now focused avidly on this skivvy of Castelaniene, though surely few as amazedly as mine or Hans's. And, on seeing Mary, Mrs. Noah, who after all knew her intimately, got up on all fours and gave vent to a brief peal of loud purrs. Mary was pleased to extend a soothing hand for the cat to rub her head against, before taking up an aloof position about a foot behind the table, her head lowered in the servile attitude of one waiting to be spoken to, even commanded—as always in her life, not least in the naughty *tableaux vivants* inside my head!

"You are most welcome here tonight!" Colonel Walton told her.

"I will be glad to be of use," answered Mary demurely.

"You are a good and trusted vehicle," affirmed Colonel Walton. "We are truly privileged to have you with us again."

General murmur of agreement; Mrs. Noah returned to her former posture. I looked sideways to identify the expression on Hans Lyngstrand's face. He, being at home in Castelaniene all day, had far more dealings with its housemaid than I myself had had, but I could see perfectly well that until this minute he had no idea of any abilities she possessed other than those needed for cleaning a room or changing bed-linen.

For a full minute I thought nobody would ever disturb the silence, so thick was it. Then—

"Mary," the voice was soft and frankly anxious, and emanated from a stout woman in black two seats to my left, "have you tonight any glimpse to give me, from beyond the Gate, of my son Walter. Walter Castle."

Without raising her head and speaking against the throes of her usual bad cold, Mary replied as readily as if she'd been asked about the weather. "Walter is so well and happy, Mrs. Castle. I saw him only a short while ago." Her voice was almost exaggeratedly sing-song, like a sweet little street-urchin who might any moment break out into nursery rhyme. "He was exercising two horses—Arab steeds they were—beautiful dark creatures running through the fields. And Walter, he was running after them, and then jumping on the back of the bigger of the two, and there was a fresh breeze blowing behind them—and all three were enjoying themselves no end. Ooh," and she gave a rapturous little smile, "ooh, they were having such merry romps!"

"Mmm!" went the audience in appreciation. "That could only be Walter Castle."

"That's the boy to a T!"

"Oh, how dear Walter loved horses!" His stout mother gazed upon Mary for a few moments, as at some heavenly messenger, but then, as the description of her late boy struck home—for had she not been hearing about the pleasures of a once flesh-and-blood being now gone from this world?—her face crumpled. She cupped in her hands her large, gentle, face with its folds of fat, and began to sob.

I hope to goodness it's not all going to be like this, I said to myself. Still I couldn't pretend Mary hadn't impressed me; she had completely convinced Walter's nearest and dearest, more indeed than was surely good for the woman.

And Mrs. Castle was followed by one seeker after another, five to be precise, five anguished voices wanting the consolation of hope, no matter in what fragmented form. Mary did not deal with them all alike. "Oh, that's a difficult one, that is," she told an elderly man begging for news of someone to whom he'd once been affianced, and who had died shortly after their troth. "Can you please remind me, kind sir, of where you your-self are living?"

"Hollybrook House, Dover Road; I'm Major Henryson," came the imploring reply, as though this man with the husk of a Scottish accent in his antique voice would be unable to bear any inability on Mary's part to bring him news of his beloved of long ago.

"Oh, Hollybrook House, I know the place—with them two holly trees, one on each side of the gate." A nod confirmed that she had identified his home correctly. "Yes, I think the picture is a-coming now. The lady you was inquiring about has never forgotten those days of beauty and love you shared up in the old country, with all that wonderful heather and pine around you, and the whizz of the birds flying overhead. And she says now—oh, I have to *strain* to catch it, kind sir, I really do . . ." Mary gave her head a shaking rather as if she were trying to rid her ears of tiresome lumps of wax. Then, "*Now* I can hear what that sweet young woman is wanting me to tell you. Look after your pigeons, she says, see that they are well-fed and maybe pay a lad from the town to help you do so now you is getting on—forgive me, kind sir, but those are her words. It's helpful to me, says she, for many years now on the Great Way, to know that my dear one from Scotland tends his birds so lovingly."

The old man looked much moved. "Jeanie . . . Jeanie, my dearest!" he murmured to himself.

And Hans Lyngstrand whispered to me: "How can Mary give these answers? She must be . . . a *genius* like Johnston."

But genius would not have been my own word. Remarkable, yes, but genius surely not! For her offerings about the "disappeared" were monot-onous to the point of tedium, however emotional the reactions they obtained. Favorite dishes, pets doted-on, pipes fondly smoked, gardens and potted flowers once devotedly tended, these were what she plucked out of the ether after all the head-shakings, rubbings of the eyes, and scratchings of her lank, mouse-colored hair. But it did seem that a telepathic sense of some kind was at work in her. And this in itself disquieted me.

How to account for what I did next? Six or seven years of constant self-questioning have brought me no truly satisfactory explanation for what I now consider the most unaccountable, the most significant action of my life, which refuses to submit to the command, "Just put yourself back in time!" However often I try, I simply cannot recapture just how I was immediately before—or even as—I got up onto my feet in the reception room at Banstead Lodge. But I know that, once on them, I could have done nothing else but ask the question I did.

"Mary," and I hardly knew whether the voice was my own or whether I was a ventriloquist's dummy for some external agency. "Have you anything to tell us here about a sailor who has not been seen since Friday, March 27, the bo'sun of the Norwegian ship *Dronning Margrete*, which sank that very day. Two of us in this room would dearly love to know."

No sooner had I delivered myself of these sentences than I felt a curious and far from agreeable lightness in the head, and an almost instantaneous dryness of the mouth, the roof of which soon afterwards began to smart, even to burn. Tremulously and awkwardly I resumed my seat, trusting my movements didn't look too odd to the outward eye, yet inwardly feeling strangely, unwarrantedly satisfied with myself. Hans, his head swiveled to his left, was now looking at me with astonishment in his sea-blue eyes, but also, surely, with some gratitude for what I'd just done.

But what was it I had just done? Seen to it, that, for the first time this evening, maybe for the first time in her Gateway career, Mary the "vehicle" would be at a loss? That, after some frantic dithering, she'd be compelled to declare ignorance, and this in front of a group she'd just been dazzling and dumbfounding with her inexplicable gifts? "I'm sorry, sir," she perhaps would say, "but I don't know of no Norwegians!" She could even break down, her reputation in collapse.

Meanwhile Hans had turned his head away from me and thrust it forward so his eye-beams could play on the girl he had, only three minutes back, pronounced a genius. Unpromisingly, she was dabbing her ever-runny nose with a sleeve of her black-wool dress. And then—breaking the hitherto unmitigated demureness of her performance—Mary raised her head. The shafts from her eyes did not meet those from Hans or mine, but rayed up toward the vaults of the high ceiling, so like the palate of a beast's red mouth, as though up there help in granting my request might be found.

She's not going to come up with anything, I told myself, with a stab of dark pleasure. But on that last silent word of mine, Mary's voice broke:

"Oh, I have quite a few things to tell you of *him*, Mr. Bridges, because that sea-faring gentleman has been a-coming to me all day. And a sad sight he is, I'm sorry to say, though there are them on the Great Way who are comforting him and trying to make him feel better now he's arrived in Eternity. Hours in that freezing heaving water he was, after his dinghy turned over in the terrible wind in the Strait—and him splashing about, desperate-like against them fierce waves, before he went under, to drown to his death."

The assembly collectively gasped at these last words, and I can't vow that I myself didn't gasp along with the others. "*To drown to his* death," *eh?*

Hans Lyngstrand shuffled in his seat and leaned his head against mine, whispering: "Martin, I swear it, I have never breathed a word, *not a single word*, about the bo'sun to Mary," a sentence which the "vehicle" must surely have caught. Her breathless rapidity of speech increased.

"But when he came to, and saw where he was, beyond the Gate, he began to talk. All about some sweetheart of his it was, some woman who'd done him wrong because she'd gone and got married to another man. 'I shall go after her!' he cried, even though he should have been attending to the beautiful shining roadway stretching beyond the Gate—with all them lovely green fields on either side—and orchards too, full of every kind of fruit: apples, pears, plums, peaches, cherries—ooh, just so many kinds. But he isn't enjoying them delicious things, not yet, and doesn't want to, no, not this old foreign seaman. 'Cos his mind is on the dreadful time he's had in this wicked old world down here. And he isn't just thinking of the mighty waves that finished him off neither."

Hans removed his head from my right cheek against which it was temporarily resting, and put his hands firmly on his thighs, gripping them to control the trembling that came over him and made all the seats in our tight-packed row vibrate. "No, no!" he muttered, "this cannot be!"

Whatever would happen next? I fixed my attention on Mary herself, who, after casting her eyes up to the heavens a second time (or rather to that vaulted roof), brought their light to bear, as she had not done once before, directly on her supplicant—in other words, on myself. Horrible, truly horrible. Talk about blushing, I had never experienced quite so fierce a fire in my face before.

She had yet more to say.

"Please, Mr. Bridges, be kind to me for this is very difficult, and I am doing the best I can for 'ee. 'Cos you see I don't rightly know what this sea-faring gentleman is called, he changed his name that many times in his sojourn on earth. But one thing I am sure of, he had a message of friendship he wanted to give to someone down below. 'That boy I shared my cabin when the storm blew up in the Atlantic, he's a good 'un,' he says, 'and I give him my blessing wherever he is. But *her*, she was bad to me, right cruel, and I'll go after and fetch her to where she belongs, by my side! Whether I'm alive or whether I'm dead, that's what I will do! Even as a drowned man!' And that's how he goes on, and not an apple nor a cherry nor even a delicious sweet damson can they tempt him with."

Hans, hectically a-quiver with excitement, managed now to raise himself into a standing position by putting his whole weight on his hands palm-downwards on the tabletop: "Mary, you must give *my* blessing to *him*. I would never have imagined him so kind. Kind enough to . . ."

But what the dead man had been kind enough to do, the Gateway never heard. For the boy about to impart a secret to the Gathering toppled over, falling backwards and knocking his chair onto the floor, with a speed that momentarily perplexed the eyes. My cheeks still burning, I instantly knew that odious softening in the loins which invariably accompanies guilt. *This is all my doing*, I thought, and who could, or would, say I was wrong here? *All my wretched fault, and yet I meant it for the best.*

Really? Had I? The best? If I'd not been a young male in this nineteenth-century England of ours, a member of a genus to whom such conduct is abhorrent, I honestly believe I would have gone on now to scream, to yell out in protest, at the sight of Hans lifeless at my feet. As it was, it fell to Beatrice Fuller to do the screaming, the yelling. Never would I have believed so refined a lady could give vent to such eldritch and ear-piercing screeches.

And Mary? Who knows what temptations to do the same were fighting within her, or whether she was still in a trance-like state, still more "vehicle" than ordinary human being. She did not move even a few inches from the sibylline, statuesque attitude she'd adopted on the other side of the velvet-draped table, though, once more, she wiped her running nose with her sleeve.

I had not bargained for Mrs. Noah, however. That lavender-colored cat, with the little white stripe on her head and the white tip to her tail, now leaped from the tabletop onto the body on the flags of the floor below. With anxious determination she rubbed her thin sharp-eared head against the Norwegian boy's pale cheek, pressing her bones hard against his at least half-a-dozen times, until, bemused, he lifted his head up and thereby proclaimed to the whole tense room that he was still to be counted among the living.

"Yet again," Colonel Walton pronounced a little later, "we are beholden to Mrs. Noah. Yet again a seeker has been restored by the intelligent offices of this virtuous and thoughtful cat."

CHAPTER SIX

What Hath Night to Do with Sleep?

Where had my attic-bedroom gone to, why was there no sound from the English Channel beyond the dormer window? Surely I was in Dengate no longer, and now I looked about me I knew I wasn't, was instead back in Camberwell, in the Fourth Form at the Thomas Middleton School, enduring a "Divinity" lesson from the local vicar. The Reverend Samuel Arkwright was a tired, tetchy, doughy-faced man in early middle age, resentful of the burdens of large family and sprawling parish—which included such schoolboys as myself. Here we all were sitting with our ink-stained Bibles in front of us, apathetically turning over their thin-papered, close-printed pages whenever told to with equally ink-stained hands.

"You see, boys," our teacher told us, "the answers to any question you might want to ask are there in the Greatest of Books."

"I'll bet there are *some* questions it won't answer," said the facetious voice of Robert (Bob) Fairbank from the desk behind me. "Like whether Mary Richardson of Denmark Hill is in love with me. Whether she'll let me give her a kiss. That's something the Book of Deuteronomy won't tell me, I bet."

"Sir, I have a question!" It was myself speaking, and with that uncharacteristic boldness I had just shown at the Gateway. Indeed, now as then, I was rising to my feet. "Why did God make the sea the way it is?"

"He made the waters before He made anything else," said Mr. Arkwright, who sounded as much interested in the subject as in, say, the current price of calico. "And since Bridges has kindly brought the matter up, why don't all you boys take a look at Genesis, Chapter One, Verse Two. After all, some of you may want to join the Navy later, and spend the best part of your years at sea."

"Not on your bleeding life I won't!" said Bob Fairbank.

The noise of the bored turning of pages all the way back to the front of the Good Book sounded, I thought, like the sea itself, breaking on a hull or a pebbly shore.

"Read what it says there, boys," commanded Mr. Arkwright (insofar as somebody so unanimated could be said to command anybody or anything): "'And the earth was without form, and void; and darkness was upon the face of the deep. And the Spirit of God moved upon the face of the waters.'"

"There was sea everywhere then at that time?" I asked, confused.

"*Waters*, Bridges, not sea, waters!" said the Reverend Arkwright, "*they* were what was 'everywhere,' as you put it. God did not separate those of heaven from those of earth until the end of His *second* day. And not till His *third* day did He divide what He now chose to call Seas from Land. Which He now called Earth."

"But He'd called something-or-other 'earth' already!" I objected, pointing with the inkiest of all my fingers to that second verse with which we'd started our re-reading. "'And the *earth* was without form, and void . . .'"

My point, surely a valid one, was lost on poor Mr. Arkwright.

"God liked the sea so much," that put-upon man went on, "as some of you boys will after you've signed on to Her Majesty's ships"—he seemed determined to shove his class into the Navy, though none of us London boys had ever expressed any inclination to serve in it—"that when, on the *fourth* day, He decided to create the creatures, starting with the great whales, it was not to the land that He turned (that was for plants) but to the *sea*: 'And God said, "Let the waters bring forth abundantly the moving creature that hath life, and fowl that may fly above the earth in the open firmament of heaven."'"

Well, it had certainly been out of the sea that Hans Lyngstrand had come to Dengate, and out of it too that Bo'sun Johnston had passed into the realm of the dead. Onto the Great Highway Beyond the Gate, if you were to believe what Mary the "vehicle" had imparted to us a few hours ago.

And it was hard not to believe it when her account was so rich in detail I knew to be wholly accurate. And yet something inside me protested at doing so . . .

Heavy with the odd dream of my school I'd just had, and still spent in body and mind after our visit to the Gateway, I opened blurry eyes onto my bedroom, and felt, as I did so, as if I were dislodging weights from my eyelids—like those coins placed on the eyes of a new dead body. I was not dead myself; on the contrary I was very much awake again. But it did seem to me I had been altered in some strange, maybe indefinable way. Something was not the same about the entire condition of "me." But what? Through the dormer window moonlight was streaming from between the clouds, but the room it illuminated looked (and surely was) exactly the same as when I'd gone to bed: the chair on the back of which I'd arranged my Norfolk jacket and on the seat of which I'd piled my clothes, the bookcase with the long row of Bulwer Lyttons, which the cat Japheth so liked to caress with his head, the desk with its self-importantly neat stacked papers, still including indeed those latest sheets of shorthand-notes taken from Hans's last narrative, all about Johnston. No, nothing had changed in all these. And yet I had a definite intimation that something had happened here while I was asleep and dreaming myself back into Camberwell and the bible study class. It was as though—yes, as though I were no longer alone in this private attic-chamber of mine. As though I had somebody at my side.

Another evening like the one now past must never occur again. I would have to keep the strongest bridle on my willful tongue, otherwise who knew what grave damage I could do in the names of truth and honesty?

Actually Hans Lyngstrand recovered from his "turn" (following Mrs. Noah's ministrations) with wonderful rapidity and completeness. But for a few immeasurable, appalling moments, I, in company with many, if not most, others at the Gathering, had thought the young Norwegian had slumped to the floor to die. In literal terms I doubt he was "out" for more than a minute and a half, yet when we saw him come 'round, we all felt we were witnessing a kind of resurrection. Those not engaged in calming Beatrice Fuller down made the boy the object of attentive concern. They took him over to the largest of the sofas, onto which Mrs. Castle—maybe seeing in him a kinship to the missing Walter—plumped further cushions for him to sink into like some wounded man into a remedial bath. But these attentions Hans soon declared unnecessary, and in a comparatively short while he was sitting up, doing his best to combine politeness with profession of a diminished appetite as plates of food and glasses of drink were brought to him from the collation already set out by the Colonel's servants. "*One* glass of elderflower cordial, sir?"

"Yes, *most* kind!" said Hans.

As for Mary, either its direct cause or its means, according to how you saw things, she appeared, as far as I could tell from my surreptitious glances, to be totally unaffected by the huge to-do her testimony had brought about. Remaining on the far side of the altar table with scarcely a focusing look in our direction, she wore an expression of unconcerned, blank placidity on her child's face. Yet she could hardly be unaware of the disruptive effect of her communications, could she? Or did being a "vehicle" mean that she had such slight relation to her own outpourings that she could not understand the significance of anything she gave out? Yet there were surely too many specifics in her reports from Beyond for this to be the case. She had known while she was speaking that she was dealing with highly inflammable emotional matter.

Hans was adamant he did not want to be rushed back to Castelaniene in some conveyance of Colonel Walton's, as our host proposed. Much better to stay quietly in this magnificent room, which so much reminded him of the Viking halls of Scandinavian history, until the meeting had come to its proper end. Now was the appointed "collation" hour, and Hans assured everybody, many times, that he was perfectly happy to sit and watch them until the appointed time came 'round for that friendly, helpful cabbie to call and take him, with his good friends Beatrice Fuller, Martin Bridges, and Mrs. Noah, home again. He actually referred to Castelaniene as "home." More than I did—or could. Or would.

Beatrice Fuller in the meantime had been restored to herself by "sal volatile" administered by Lady Kershaw. I cannot, I thought, have endeared myself to her through the happenings I have put in train, even though they might well seem to have vindicated her own—and her friends'—spiritual beliefs. And most probably a number of other Gateway members also considered us new arrivals, Beatrice's baggage, as more nuisance than anything else. Probably this is what they were saying to each

other in the low well-bred whispered tones in which many of them conducted conversation.

The journey back to Castelaniene was not, except in the literal sense, an
easy one. Because of all that had happened in its course, I'd assumed the
meeting at Banstead Lodge had lasted a long time. Not at all. As we left
that church-like house, there were some bells in the town still sounding
the half-hour—for half-past nine! The streets through which we clopped
homewards were by no means deserted, and lights burned in the majority
of downstairs windows. I, burdened with an uncomfortable feeling of responsibility for the direction the evening had taken, thought it was up to
Mrs. Fuller to start up a conversation. Who could deny that the idea of
Hans and myself coming to the Gateway had been hers and hers alone,
neither of us young men having so much as heard of the society, or that
she had given us no clue whatsoever about its purpose? I have to say I was
even less cordially disposed toward her than usual.

But Beatrice did eventually raise the subject of the evening, speaking
in an extremely hoarse voice, unsurprising considering the punishment
she'd recently given her throat.

"You are now in a position to appreciate, Mr. Lyngstrand," she said,
"what the Gateway can do for people. It can link us poor mortals with those
who have gone before them into the unknown, like your sea-faring friend.
Of course it is not always easy to accept what we hear, and please understand that everybody at tonight's Gathering will have understood that only
too well. But I think it must have been beautiful for you to have heard that
your Disappeared One sent you his blessing. I found myself greatly moved."

"Oh, yes, very beautiful," Hans agreed. But his immediate use of her
own word made me instantly doubt whether it'd be one he himself would
have chosen. Whatever had his real reaction to what he'd heard from
Mary's lips? "I would never have imagined him [Johnston] so kind," had
been his spoken response to the bo'sun's posthumous blessing, a strange
one really. Truly nothing whatever that he had told me about Johnston had
suggested kindness of any sort.

"I expect you were astonished—both of you," Mrs. Fuller was pleased
to include me now in her remarks, "when you saw Mary at the very center

of our activities. I did not warn you in advance, because, seeing her, as you do every day, in the function of *domestique*, you might have been tempted to doubt her powers. Whereas confronted with them, what could you do but marvel? Marvel and accept. Normally she is able to give me such wonderful news of my husband; it is a joy as well as a sorrow to listen to her."

This sounded almost like a rebuke. For had we not prevented Mary doing this?

"Yes, I marveled at Mary," said Hans. He did not say he accepted, I noted.

"You have conducted yourself tonight, Mr. Lyngstrand, both sensitively and sensibly," she said, "and the Gateway was fortunate to have you as a visitor. Obviously you will need a good night's rest after your shock, but I think—no, I truly believe—that you will look back over this evening as one of the most important and beneficial of your life."

The Royal Gardens now came into sight, the poles of the Bandstand under construction glowing silver in the darkness like upright sticks of mercury. What I would not have given to be returning to my quarters from a convivial, bibulous evening with Will and his pals! Better than being here, even remembering Hans, here in stupid Dengate bound for the even stupider Castelaniene. Will Postgate—he would soon be turning up in Dengate. How glad I would be to see him!

Yes, what or who was it that made my room so unlike its customary self, and me, as it felt, so unlike *my* customary self? A presence of some kind there surely was.

I rolled over in my bed onto my right side, thus moving further toward the wall and away from the rest of the furniture. To realize that near me, on top of the counterpane, was reposing a body swathed in white, a white which shone out from certain folds and patches in the fabric into the bedroom's general murk. It was a young male body lying very still, three-quarters on its back, the remaining quarter resting on its right flank, head turned slightly toward the wall. The body was breathing, gently but regularly, if a mite wheezily.

The body was Hans Lyngstrand's of course, and the whiteness came from his crumpled nightgown. Without my hearing or seeing him, he had walked out of the Mercy Room, opened my door, and clambered onto my very own bed—not itself particularly large—while managing not to rouse me. Or was it his advent that had roused me out of my unexpected dream of Camberwell and "Divinity"?

"Hans?" I asked him in an urgent whisper, "it *is* you? What did you want?"

Had he heard me? Should I repeat my questions? Or simply let him sleep? He was after all a boy still recovering from a "grave" illness, with full recovery by no means certain, and, thanks to me, he'd undergone a further ordeal, and a painful one, this very evening. He should slumber on in peace.

But heard me he had. He moved himself around so that his face confronted mine with brilliant sea-blue eyes gleaming out of the dominant bony paleness. And spoke. What he said astonished me, not least because it was said—if this doesn't sound too contradictory—as a whispered shout.

"'STAND BY THE BOATS! STAND BY THE BOATS!' That's what he said, wasn't it? Johnston! The bo'sun! And he did stand by them. But it didn't do him any good. No wonder I couldn't see him when I was in the longboat with the Captain and those others. He perished. Johnston! In those terrible waters of the Channel."

It seemed an age before I made reply. "We can't know that for certain, Hans," I managed.

"But Martin, didn't you hear the message Mary gave us? He drowned to his death and is now in Eternity. On the beautiful shining roadway near all those fields and fruit—but thinking of the woman he loved who was faithless to him—and, so she said, thinking of me. In a kind way, it sounded like. It wasn't always like that on-board ship . . ."

What to say to this? Or to what Hans said next: "I don't think Alfred Johnston would like the kind of existence Mary described. He was a very active man, he liked danger and difficulty and facing them with his own strong body and mighty will."

Nor was this the last disconcerting remark of Hans's. "Martin," he asked, "*why* did you ask Mary that question tonight?"

Was that what he'd come into the room to find out? His tone suggested that he already had been pondering the problem hard and long.

I replied with what seemed to me the truth. "I needed to know about Johnston." But I then added, more truthfully still: "So I could be of help to you."

Hans shuffled himself a little nearer to me. Now we were contiguously side by side. "You're such a good friend to me!" he said. "I doubt I've ever had a better one. Not in Bergen, not on the high seas, not anywhere."

I knew then that he intended to stay the whole night in my room, to go to sleep next to me. And this he did.

I myself did not sleep—at least not very much. A line of Milton's my mother (who'd suffered from sleeplessness) liked to quote came into my head: "What hath night to do with sleep?" And yet the words retained the innocence they (presumably) possessed for my mother. Strange it was to be lying next to another body at once uniquely itself and yet, in all important details, the same as one's own, to be entering into some unspoken pact of sharing. Yet by the time Dengate bells rang out three o'clock this state had come to seem oddly natural, if that isn't a contradiction, far more so than the uncountable solitary nights that had preceded it. These dark hours united into a milestone in my life, though, in a strict factual sense, nothing happened in them.

As six o'clock pealed out—and yes, I had by now managed a little sleep, full, it seemed to me, of the persistent movement of waters both in the heavens and on the face of earth—I was aware of Hans gently clambering off the bed, so as not to disturb me whom he clearly thought asleep, and then leaving my room as stealthily as he'd entered it.

CHAPTER SEVEN

The Morning After

*A*nother Thursday morning at the newspaper, and this one brought us dramatic news of one of our own. While Stanley's cab was taking Mrs. Fuller, Hans Lyngstrand, Mrs. Noah, and myself back to Castelaniene, Mr. Thomas Betterton, no less, was falling down the steep flight of stone steps connecting Church Lane with High Street. We were without our Deputy Editor.

"We did a piece only three months ago saying His Worship the Mayor ought to have those damned steps seen to," said Archie Penry.

"I think you may find they weren't the principal cause of the mishap!" said Philip Goodenough, with a smile and a wink. "A few drinks too many at the regular Wednesday revelry down at the Masonic Lodge was the culprit, I fancy."

Barton Cunningham, tilting his chair back into the morning sunshine, guffawed disloyally at our club-of-two's exchange. "You may have a point there, Mr. Goodenough," he said. "Anyway, the sawbones has already seen my godfather and told him to put his feet up for a few days."

"Goodness me, the cruelty of some people's lots!" exclaimed Archie.

Young Peter Frobisher chuckled appreciatively from his corner of the room. Nothing made the boy feel more of a man than being privy to such banter. I myself felt definite relief we were to be spared the Dep Ed's bulky inhibitive presence that day. Perhaps he'd be away from the office quite some time.

"Cruel indeed!" grinned Barton Cunningham, relishing being on the opposite side of the divide from his godfather. "But I don't want you to be too disappointed, Mr. Penry. At the end of only a few days, Uncle Tom will indubitably be walking about once more, even if it's only with a stick."

He followed this sentence with words which sounded remarkably like "More's the pity!" and would surely have gone on to break more confidences had not Edmund emerged from his private office, probably having overheard some of the disrespectful talk.

"Gentlemen, please!" Edmund's voice was a virtuous elder brother's reproaching his less-than-kindly siblings. "An injury to the senior member of our team is hardly a subject for amusement, though of course healthy laughter will always go a long way in assisting us through life." This mild reprimand was surely just a mite hypocritical, since Edmund noticeably kept his deputy at a distance, the two men differing so widely in temperament, mode of living, and political allegiance. "Barton, a word with you, if I may."

Barton, who, because of his familial connection with Mr. Betterton, had an aura this morning of unique if lightly-borne connection to the mighty, followed Edmund into his office almost as though he were about to be invested with his godfather's authority. But he came back after barely five minutes, this quite plainly not having happened.

"Here, Bridges," he said, and I could tell he wasn't much pleased at what he was having to relay. "Assuming you're not already engrossed in another earth-shattering interview, I've got two things to pass on to you. First and foremost, you're to help me sub a piece my poor injured godpapa left unrevised."

"I'll be glad to!"

"Me being busy sorting out the thorny problems of Margate's Cricket Club finances doesn't matter a hoot to Edmund, clearly!" grumbled Barton.

Sulkily he sat down at Mr. Betterton's desk, behind its huge Remington. While our printers were still perfectly prepared to receive copy in longhand, journalists increasingly, even dyed-in-the-wool old codgers like Mr. B, favored giving them articles typed beforehand, usually by themselves—though Edmund dictated his to the good Mrs. Carter, who then typed them out at twopence a sheet. The practice of typing has accelerated this last couple of years to a degree I would not have predicted; I approve. It's so much easier to gauge the effect on readers of a piece in finished newsprint if you see it typed-out first!

Barton was a chap who took naturally to machinery, and the sight of his godfather's handsome possession, and the prospect of using it himself, cheered him up, made him feel less of an office-lackey.

"Imagine yourself back in the olden days, Bridges, if someone as wet behind the ears as you can do such a thing," he said, all but caressing the Remington, "when typewriters lacked shift keys. But to fellows like ourselves not moving out of capitals into lowercase seems like Ancient Egyptians having to deal with papyri . . . Shame we can't find Godpapa's last will and testament on this roller, ain't it? The fellow's not short of a bob or two, and when he snuffs it, 'tis rumored Yours Truly will be getting a little something. That'd be most welcome. I could even flee the old parental nest. Still, whoever died of a twisted ankle?"

The accident that had befallen Barton's godfather could not but remind me—why hadn't I thought of it at once?—of Alfred Johnston, who had so painfully injured his foot on board *Dronning Margrete*, and so been holed up in his cabin during foul weather, with Hans and those old Norwegian newspapers for company. Had that not happened Hans would not be the haunted youth he now was.

Oh, would I never get the figure of Johnston, a man I'd never met, out of my mind? Did I really want this pressure on me from Hans Lyngstrand's recent experiences? Or even from Hans as an individual?

I didn't know. But, as I sat beside Barton Cunningham and his godfather's Remington, I realized I required other types of companionship too and right now I was being given Barton Cunningham's and was pretty glad of it.

"Was it his tin that made your parents choose Mr. Betterton as your godfather?" I asked Barton, a touch impertinently, but I knew he wouldn't mind.

"I shouldn't wonder. You see, the Governor and he were great pals when they were both in Bengal," said Barton. Ah, Bengal, where it rained harder even than in spring-time Dengate! Other chaps always had more exotic histories and backgrounds than me. "My father was working in indigo there, y'know, making his own little pile, and Uncle Tom was on a newspaper in the same city. There were no flies on *him*, I can assure you, and he collected lucrative tips from every quarter he could, so when he came back to Kent, he had enough to buy himself handsomely (or so he thought) into *The Advertiser*, hoping one day to run the whole bally thing himself. Sad story, Uncle Tom's, really. A liberal lord came along and bought the group of newspapers up, and appointed as editor a man of his own, Edmund. So, where had the poor old chap to go but the Deputy's desk here, and we all know how influential *that* is. And, of course, along to the Freemasons of an evening also, to drown his sorrows . . . Anyway, let's have a dekko at what the old man's been up to before he toppled over. I can't believe we shan't find it needs an improving drop of Young Blood."

It was not a particularly interesting story we found there, about the bankruptcy of a once-thriving local business (Higginson and Busby), and far from interestingly told.

Barton scoured our Dep Ed's piece twice, then remarked: "Though it goes against the grain to criticize an eminent family-friend who's so sadly in the wars right now, I have to confess I find Uncle Tom just a *trifle* long-winded in the telling of this tangled tale. Would you not agree, Bridges?" I remembered the wink Barton had given me behind Mr. Betterton's back on one of my first days in the office. "Some jigging around is most assuredly called for, in my humble view. You see, I did my training not here but on Maidstone's, our county town's, main rag—a pretty superior affair to this, I don't mind telling you—and I learned a thing or two there . . . I take it, my friend, you're familiar with the term 'inverted pyramid'?"

I was not, I hadn't even heard the term from Will Postgate's lips?

"Did you say . . ." I began unconvincingly, as if I hadn't quite caught what Barton had just said.

"Oh dear!" said Barton, giving a mock-sigh. "I'd have thought the notion would have trickled through from Fleet Street down to Lewisham-and-Lee by now. It's the new way of writing things up, Bridges. Let me explain, as I see I must." I let him do this. "You start with the full story itself, in other words with the broad base of the pyramid, arousing your readers' interest with a bold but succinct presentation of the affair as a whole. As a whole! Then you consequently work your way downwards—this pyramid is *inverted*, remember!—so that you end your piece on a fine point, preferably in the form of a question that will resonate inside your readers' thick skulls for hours, not to say days, afterwards. Let me put it this way!

If we were to take Uncle Tom's injury as our subject—and let us hope and pray we will never have to—we would begin our piece with the broad tragedy of his being indisposed and therefore unable, most regrettably, to come into the office today. And we would *end* with the dramatic incident itself when—*bang! thump! ooh! ouch!*—down Church Steps the old newspaperman tumbles."

"I thought you just said a piece of this type should end with a question."

"Bridges, you are a fast learner," said Barton, "and I am mightily impressed. Yes, of course, you are quite right. '*Has the good man been permanently lamed?*' would be the desirable conclusion to our hypothetical story about Uncle Tom. All so much better, don't you think, so much more *modern*, so much more nineteenth century, than just going plod-plod-plod through something?"

"Plod-plod-plod just about sums *this* piece up!" I agreed sycophantically but sincerely. "Only something like your inverted pyramid could save it from being a right old invitation to yawn."

"One has to be careful, though!" said Barton.

I was the young man of London experience as I answered, "And sometimes one simply has to be bold and decisive."

"Put like that, how can I not concur?"

It was fun, it truly was, greater fun than any I'd had so far in the office, more like what I'd known in South London before all those excursions to the printers had begun to multiply: the two of us tinkering about—well, something more than that, I'm afraid—with Mr. Betterton's work, and knowing that we both should and should not be behaving as we were. We really enjoyed ourselves being (as we saw it) two clever, resourceful young men together, abreast of the times and unwilling to kowtow to outmoded conventions. From having, only hours earlier, been—literally as well as spiritually—closer to Hans Lyngstrand than ever before, I was now—again literally (and possibly the other thing as well)—closer to Barton than I had yet been—him of the red hair and long, well-exercised limbs, the person the nearest to me in the whole outfit in terms of age, position, even (possibly) personality.

"You said there were *two* things Edmund asked you to tell me!"

"Yes, though to tell you the truth the second is something he had asked me first to do myself—for obvious reasons—but which I simply couldn't face."

This didn't bode well. "Which is . . .?"

"To go over to Kingsbarrow, to the Old Hole, St. Stephen's College. Every First of June it holds a Grand Open Day for parents and local big-wigs and gentry to show them all how wonderful the place is, and the Headmaster, the Reverend Richard Whittington, commonly and obviously known as Dick, escorts people 'round and takes the lion's share of the credit. Anyway, this Monday—May 11—a bit prematurely you might say—he wants someone from *The Advertiser* to go over there so this paper can start preparing huge coverage of all the events of the Great Day. As an alumnus of the place—like himself!—Edmund thought of me, naturally enough, but I've had quite enough of the Old Hole for one young lifetime . . ."

"Despite being Victor Ludorum there?"

"Despite even that. The whole place is given over to establishing the sainthood of Dick Whittington and the mighty eminence of the greatest local bigwig, Sir Greeley Donaldson, who makes great gifts and whose sons attend the school. It's enough to make you 'chuck' as the coarse expression is. That got to be what I wanted to do when the bally name of Donaldson came up, as it did at every touch and turn. So it occurred to me that, as one who should be getting to know the region and all the most important places in it, *you*, Bridges, would be the ideal man for the job. And Edmund saw my point!"

"Well, thanks. It certainly would make a day out for me."

"Morning out!" corrected Barton. "Edmund's even found trains for you to catch, so don't build up the outing too much in your imagination."

"It'll be interesting to see St. Stephen's," I said, doubtful this was quite the aptest adjective. But you never know, I might there find out more about George Fuller and his son Horace, and that might well prove interesting.

That night, just as I was wondering whether he would or not, Hans slipped surreptitiously into my room again. He wanted his entrance, I now realize, to be an inextricable part of the nocturnal quiet (he waited until I had extinguished my bedside lamp), with only the *swoosh-swoosh* of the Channel beyond the window for accompaniment.

Eventually he broke the stillness by saying: "Martin, Mary spoke to me today."

"Oh yes?"

"She said she was certain I'd meet the bo'sun again. That he would come back into my life. And she said she knew this not after being in any— what did she call it?—trance, but from her natural sympathy with living people. 'You will see him again, sure as sure! Whether he's alive or dead.'"

"But she told you—he was *dead*?"

"She told me he was beyond the gateway, and on the shining path. Perhaps that isn't the same thing as . . . *dead*?"

"I'd rather we talked about other matters," I said, surprising myself by the intensity with which I spoke, "about Norway, for example. Its fjords, its mountains, how its people live whether on land and on sea."

So Hans obliged, and very vivid were the word-pictures he gave me. This second night he did not merely lie down beside me but lifted up the bedclothes and eased himself underneath them. How night changes its complexion when you share it with somebody. I had not until that moment appreciated just what a solitary business, just how lacking in any of the consolations of closeness, my life had been.

CHAPTER EIGHT

Mercies of One Sort or Another

*F*riday afternoon. "Hullo, hullo!" I called out, once I'd got to the top of the attic-story stairs. No need for any formalities with somebody beside whom you have lain under sheets all the previous night. "Hope you've had a good day!"

As usual the door of the Mercy Room was ajar, with Japheth sitting outside it, his exceptionally long and pointed ears perked for my arrival. On actually seeing me he did as always, quickly padded toward me to rub his head against my right calf while emitting the loud but somehow insect-like purr he'd inherited from his mother. "Hope too you haven't been plagued by too many thoughts of your bo'sun!" And with this rather breezy remark I entered the bedroom—

To see there not the young Norwegian whom by now I thought its rightful occupant, but somebody else entirely. Sitting in a chair underneath the kite patterned with the Union Jack was none other than Mrs. Fuller herself, as still as any specimen of Hans Lyngstrand's beloved sculpture, so still that the strands of its tail, swaying in a gentle breeze from the open window, looked as though they were tickling a marble statue of some Greek goddess.

God, whatever has happened? Whatever is she *doing up here?* Beatrice Fuller's eyes were half-closed, and even when they opened only reluctantly admitted me into focus. I was wondering whether (and how) to address her when this marmoreal figure spoke in a voice of appropriately mineral quality:

"I've seen you, Mr. Bridges, my peace you've already disturbed."

"Is Hans Lyngstrand all right?" It was impossible to disguise the fear now coursing through me. There was never going to be any guaranteeing that Hans was "all right." "Why is he not here?"

"Hans is well enough," said Mrs. Fuller. "That's to say, as well as one in his grave state of health could ever be. The Appleton-Whites—who live at Gulliver House at the end of this road—such hospitable, cultivated people—invited him to take tea with them on his own. Both the Appleton-Whites admire Norway greatly, you see, and visit the country frequently. The three of them will have a great deal to talk about." She somehow implied it was a fault in me, as well as a lack, that I had not been to Norway myself. "You seem surprised, Mr. Bridges, that I am sitting here in the Mercy Room." She gave an acrid little laugh. "But the room does *belong* to me, you know, in common with every other room in this house. The whole of Castelaniene, you do realize, is *mine*."

"I never thought otherwise," I answered, but she didn't appear to hear my rejoinder, though she was no longer holding herself in a lapidary attitude but had relaxed into the contours of her chair.

Then, as much to herself as me, she said: "I speak to him too sharply too often." I could hardly disagree with her judgment. "It is after all little more than a *boy* I'm dealing with." I did not take this as a compliment and was surely not meant to. But what she said next, inclining her elegant head forward, was ever-so-slightly mollifying: "You must understand, Mr. Bridges, that I have many things of my own to think about, things which make huge demands on my feelings and even challenge my principles." This statement promised to be interesting. "Things connected with this very room." And a sweep of her hand indicated the rugby ball, the soccer ball, the fives racket, and the stuffed eagle, all of which had never ceased to attract my puzzled gaze. "It is hard to do justice to all the associations this Mercy Room has for me, independently, I might add, of the various guests I have been kind enough to invite to stay in it."

It's now or never, I said to myself; *nothing ventured, nothing gained*. "Are they associations with . . . with your *son*?" I asked.

The effect of these words—well, of that last word—was electric, Beatrice Fuller was indeed like someone administered a shock current. She jumped out of her chair, knocking her head against the kite as she did so and making its red-white-and-blue tail strands flutter furiously. I thought for a few dreadful seconds she was going to take me by outstretched hands and savagely claw me, an avenging harpy. But in fact she lowered her arms onto her sides with a loud sigh, stopped in her tracks beneath the suspended

Spanish galleons, and said: "How—however—do *you* know about *him*?"

Had she really expected, I have often asked myself since, the whole of Dengate, of which community I was now, you could say, a working member, to be silent on this subject? That pointed to a decided vein of unreality in her. As she herself perhaps dimly saw, for, nervously rubbing the palms of her hands against her skirt, she said: "I suppose Edmund told you. Even though he promised me faithfully never to speak of . . . *him* to my lodger. It was a little condition I made when I agreed to consider your boarding in this house."

"It was not Edmund who told me," I was quick to defend my boss. "It was somebody quite different."

She didn't inquire who that person was, and I didn't want to sneak on Barton. "Well, I suppose *somebody* was going to tell you sooner or later," she conceded begrudgingly.

Exactly! So why all the elaborate secrecy, why even this present drama?

"This was his room?" I might as well get everything clear now, even though I knew the answer.

"Yes, this was his room." Spoken gravely and in a low tone.

"And all this—" It was hard to find the right collective noun for what was so lavishly all about us, and the collective noun I nearly used 'stuff' would obviously never have done, would have only insulted the boy's mother further. "All these," I tactfully changed from singular to plural, "were Horace's?"

Mrs. Fuller's eyes blazed like splinters of ice caught by fiery sun. "So, you even know my son's *name*, Mr. Bridges. Quite a snooper, you've turned out to be, quite a little Mr. Peter Pry. I suppose you fancy your personal brand of ill-bred inquisitiveness to be some sign of your being a master journalist?" She snorted contemptuously at the very notion of such delusion on my part.

"Mrs. Fuller," I said, deciding to marshal what dignity I had, not greatly helped by Japheth intensifying the vigor with which he rubbed his head against my leg. "I called him Horace because that was what he was called by the individual who told me about him. I was asking *no* questions at that time about either you or your family, I'm not in the least a Mr. Peter Pry." I amazed myself by using the absurd term back to her.

A long pause, then—"You must excuse me. It is not a happy subject."

Mrs. Fuller sighed, "Even after all this time it brings me pain. Have I been right, have I been wrong? I ask myself those questions over and over again. But," reverting to her more usual manner, "someone such as yourself who has never known responsibility can scarcely be expected to understand all my various dilemmas."

I could not have this. Annoyance rose from within me and demanded words.

"I assure you," I replied, with what I hoped didn't sound too much like wounded dignity. "I have known very considerable responsibilities, and I'm sorry that's not apparent. You yourself have said—very perceptively, I thought—that I had experienced more of life's sorrows than many my age. My father and mother died in distressing circumstances, and I was the one who had to"—well, why not come out with some of the sordid truth?— "answer to creditors and defend their reputations. And almost as soon as they were both . . . gone, I started earning my own living and in fact made good some of what my parents—well, my father—owed. And I was only seventeen and had been brought up to think of myself as having quite different prospects. And I should add that no employer has found fault with me yet. Quite the opposite, and nobody should know that better than yourself. Edmund Hough hired me thanks to excellent recommendations from my former employer, and then judged me fit to live in your house."

Mrs. Fuller made no acknowledgement, direct or indirect, of this little speech but I could tell straightaway that my words—however impertinent-seeming—were not entirely wasted and would continue to resonate inside her.

"He wasn't contented here," she said, again not so much to me as to herself, or, maybe even more, to some other invisible half-accusatory presence. "In fact, he was in the end *discontented* nearly all the time. Many a boy would have given his eye-teeth to have only a fraction of what you can find in this room, but not Horace. He cared for none of it."

"I'm very sorry to hear that!"

Mrs. Fuller looked at me now with softer eyes. "Yes, I do believe you are, Mr. Bridges. And I can imagine that for all your clumsy attempts to swagger, you were simple and ingenuous enough when younger to enjoy a model galleon or two, or even this Patriots' Kite. Whereas Horace . . . Well, it's too late for regrets now, far too late."

Did this last sentence mean that Horace Fuller was another person who had disappeared—"disappeared," that is, in the Gateway's sense? Surely not! Barton had spoken of Horace Fuller as one alive and flourishing somewhere, if far away. And Mrs. Fuller's own manner, though strained and sorrowful, didn't suggest bereavement, though that shouldn't be used as too much of an index, for I did not find her widow-like either.

This exchange—which was to alter our mutual perceptions of each other—could proceed no further because at that moment we both heard the unmistakable heavy wheezy breathing of Hans Lyngstrand, as slowly he mounted the precipitous stairs. What a far cry his movements were from those brought to mind by all the accoutrements in this room, agility on the footer field, accuracy of aim in the cricket nets, hardy scaling of rigging on the high seas. But no sooner had I thought this than I reflected that this last action Hans had literally carried out hundreds of times, with never a slip, and that it was after more dangerous adventures than even the ideal occupant of this Room would usually have to face that he had come here to receive its Mercy.

The Appleton-Whites of Gulliver House had been kind enough to lend Hans a book, *The Art of Bertel Thorvaldsen*, containing photogravure plates of his work. After supper he took the volume upstairs to his bedroom, and when I looked into the Mercy Room later, I found him engrossed in it, seated below the swaying pendant model galleons.

"So much in common between Herr Thorvaldsen and me, it's astonishing," Hans informed me, his bright eyes an extra deep blue. "Not that I am going to be so great a man as he . . . Impossible!" said Hans with a laugh that maybe disguised a hope that such an ambition might not be unachievable. "There's the woodcarver grandfather, and Thorvaldsen as a boy delighting in the old man's designs and even helping with them. And then his experience as a youth on a frigate-ship (though the ships I've been working on never came in *that* category) and all the dreams he had when young of going south to see the home of the great classical legends—everything I find out about him reminds me of *myself*, Martin. And once he'd got there Thorvaldsen went on to live twenty-three years in Italy—in Rome itself. That's longer than I've been alive. He even used to give himself a Roman birthday, March 8, because he felt his life only truly began when he first arrived in the Eternal City on March 8, 1797. This book is going to be a real inspiration for me."

"You'd better point out which of his stuff you like most," I said, to stem this flow of fervor, which disconcerted me, I don't mind admitting. I had given art scarcely any thought at all my whole life long.

Hans was only too willing to oblige. I appreciated I would more likely than not be a spot bored during the next quarter of an hour or so, but then I'd been bored often enough in my young life and had learned how to cope with this state.

"Well, this is one of my very favorites, here: 'Ganymede and the Eagle'," Hans was saying. "Thorvaldsen gave himself over to the classical masters from his very first days in Rome; he did lots of studies of Ganymede."

The plate to which Hans Lyngstrand was now directing my attention reproduced a marble composition in which an eagle drank from a cup resting on the raised right knee of a strikingly handsome youth with a strong, gentle facial expression. He was completely naked, his skin smooth and hairless, his left buttock reposing its flesh on his left calf. In his right hand he held a jug, presumably containing more water for the great bird to drink. The posture of its subject riveted me like a magnet drawing my eyes to itself.

"And who was Ganymede when he was at home?" I asked.

Hans furrowed his brow in puzzlement, then said: "I don't know exactly where he lived, Martin, not at the time of Thorvaldsen's statue. Later his home was Mount Olympus where he waited on the gods."

I blushed. "I must apologize, Hans. 'When he's at home' is just a silly English expression. All I meant was—whoever *was* Ganymede?"

Hans recited to me, like a keen schoolboy repeating his lesson, "Ganymede was a young man that the god Zeus liked so much he changed himself into an eagle so he could get to know him. Ganymede was a thoughtful, generous sort of boy, so he gave the bird water to drink. Later Zeus—disguising himself as an eagle—took him in his beak and carried him off to Olympus where he became cup-bearer to all the gods but to himself in particular."

"And was that a good thing to happen?"

Hans looked as though unable to make head nor tail of a question both so literal and so facetious. Perhaps indeed only a young unserious Englishman would have asked it.

He made no reply but turned the page of his book: "And here's another of Ganymede, alone this time. And here is an earlier piece, the sculpture that first made Thorvaldsen famous, 'Jason.' All Rome praised it, including the greatest sculptor of the time, Canova. I think I've told you already there's a plaster cast of this work in my patron Herr Strømme's house in Bergen. So I got to know it very well, I even used to have imaginary conversations with it.

"You may think it strange, Martin, but now these classical figures keep reminding me of boys I've known on board ships. Specially ones who are now dead; so often it was them who were the strongest, the bravest, the best. Knut. Jantje. Jakob. Boris . . . Look at *this* page, Martin. This is one of Thorvaldsen's masterpieces—'Shepherd Boy with Dog'; it brings Giacomo into my mind. He came from Italy, from a farm on the hills above Genoa; he would often tell me about it when we were on watches together."

The statue was certainly a beautiful creation, though never could I have brought myself to say so, the boy, seated on a sheepskin on a rock, with his dog below him on his right. Probably many times on the heaving Atlantic Giacomo—or Knut or Jakob or any of the others—would have achieved a similar attitude of sturdy triumphant gracefulness (and perhaps even in the Channel too before the ship went down) . . . But I didn't want to tarry over these works much longer and pointedly shifted in my seat while Hans continued to turn pages. But a picture of a sculpted head, inclined gently downwards above large, muscular, splayed-out arms, caught my attention.

"And who is that?"

"Oh, that is Jesus Christ!" he said with something like embarrassment. "Perhaps we should leave him till later? I am very familiar with Jesus. Karsten Strømme owns a cast of *that* sculpture also."

I could think of nothing to say back. These statues were all like messengers from a world totally unfamiliar to me.

Perhaps that was the reason why I was later able to tell him as I'd told nobody else ever about my own life, my childhood: Father's drunkenness, Mother's tearful ineffectual remonstrations, my desolation and my relief after their deaths, my job at the stationer's, and then at the newspaper. He received it all as if absorbing it into his very being.

Saturday was (indeed it still is, seven years later) a ragged kind of day at the newspaper when many jobs that have been shelved for one reason or another get polished off, often somewhat speedily, in order to begin the week on Monday with clean consciences—and clean worktables. But remembering what that little urchin (the one apparently called Martin, like myself) had told me about Saturday afternoon being the time when the chestnut-haired girl held her outdoor nature classes, I went home after work via the Royal Gardens. Benign sunshine flooded the little park. The candles on the horse-chestnuts looked taller, thicker, firmer, and a few inches nearer the sun, than at the beginning of the week. Courting couples were strolling hand in hand along the pathways of the park, and I decided actually to pass through its wrought-iron gates and join their throng—in the hope, of course, of catching a glimpse of the nature study group if it had, as it should, assembled today.

I must have walked a hundred and fifty yards at the very least when I spied them—and what a pretty sight! Sitting on the far side of the large right-hand lawn, in the center of a collection of about twenty children, was the girl of my thoughts, wearing today a white chiffon scarf which showed the color of her hair to perfect advantage. I stopped dead in my tracks to drink the sight in, and, at the very moment I did so, she raised her head and saw me, catching me in my stationary posture of inquisitive long-distance scrutiny. I was pretty sure she recognized me as the prying young man of Monday—or was I flattering myself? Lowering my head reluctantly, I walked on.

As for the morrow, it'd be quite a day, would it not? Hans and I would go to luncheon at Edmund's, and—yes, why wasn't I thinking about this rather more?—Will Postgate was due to turn up here in Dengate after his Hampshire/Sussex/Cinque Ports walking tour. But that night, alongside a now peacefully sleeping Hans, I dreamed of somebody quite different— Jason, his fleece over his shoulder.

"You've no idea of the dangers of the voyage I made to get hold of this," he said, "and how many times I looked down into the sea, and thought: 'What unknowable life-forms exist down there!' But then, truth to tell, unknowable life-forms exist everywhere . . ."

CHAPTER NINE

Furzebank Ho

*I*n London I had never been as aware of Sunday morning bells as now in Dengate, nor, for that matter, of all the many people who, even in the last quarter of the nineteenth century, obey their summons. I'd watch them all making their way churchwards, their faces transformed into masks by the smart hats surmounting them, hats the men would have to take off once inside church while the women kept theirs on. What a pantomime! I noted the young plodding cheerlessly behind their elders and from time to time exchanging sheepishly conspiratorial grins with each other.

These bells, so busy since daybreak, had just finished ringing out noon when Edmund's eldest, Cyril showed up in his dog-cart outside Castelaniene, as had been arranged, to take Hans and me to Furzebank House. Aglow from his trot through the morning's balmy warmth, he looked like a younger, slimmer Edmund—the same dark curly hair, the same beard running lightly around the jaw instead of covering it, and when he spoke, it was with his father's breeziness.

"Cyril Hough, at your service!" he cried. "Would you fellows appreciate a little jaunt 'round the neighborhood before I deliver you safe and sound to the family manor?"

He obviously expected the enthusiastic answer he got. "That sounds a first-rate idea!" I said.

Then—"Mrs. Fuller," he shouted out, "the Pater sends his greetings. Soon it'll be *you* I'll be fetching for luncheon at Furzebank."

This sentence, though charmingly enough spoken, did not disarm Mrs. Fuller who gave the chilliest and shortest of smiles, and only when the dog-cart was actually moving off down St. Ethelberga's Road did she call out, "Of course, remember me to both your parents."

"Working in the Smoke as I do," Cyril told Hans and me, "Mincing Lane—Blandish and Young, tea-brokers, you probably know 'em?—I really appreciate being down in old Denners of a weekend. You know—trees, flowers, gardens—there ain't many of those particular commodities at my outfit."

The cart turned the corner of our road with a sudden liveliness of motion on the horse's part, Cyril keeping him on a very free rein. Our jaunt around residential Dengate as it climbed toward the downs took in two lookout points from which we had fine views of town, harbor, and shimmering Channel—why, I thought with surprise, this place was somewhere you might actually *like* to live. Even me! Cyril provided a running commentary on many houses and gardens passed.

"That big house belongs to Mr. Howard Iddesleigh. *He's* something colossal in Mincing Lane; they faint there at the very mention of his name . . . Hullo, hullo, do I see drawn blinds at the Gudgeon-Rogers'? One of 'em must have kicked it, I suppose. Probably the old man. Oh, well, in the midst of Life we find Death, or whatever the saying is."

But it was hard to find Death on a morning as kind to the senses as this, even someone who knew the dark history and troubled prospects of the young Norwegian sitting beside him. Laburnum drooped its racemes the other side of walls over which lilacs bent fragrant sprays of purple; hawthorn, with its white scented snows, was everywhere, in the gardens, beside the roads, forming hedges for the fields or the common-land—and then there was, especially on the fringes of the town, the gorse whose yellow the girl in the Royal Gardens had told those kids never to confuse with that of broom, also plentiful here.

"The Pater's got some favorite lines about the gorse, or furze as he likes to call it—that's why our old mansion is called Furzebank Ho," said Cyril, turning his head to address Hans and me behind him. "But as he'll doubtless be spouting 'em to you, I won't quote 'em now! By the way I most sincerely hope you fellows will be getting enough food today, and at a reasonable time, too. Some days you can get pretty darned hungry before the grub comes up, I'd better warn you right off. To be warned is to be forearmed, after all. Mater and Pater don't keep a servant, though there's a maiden who comes in from the Lower Town thrice a week. So we rely on a nice old hag who's a relation of my mother's and lives with us, working her fingers to the bone for her keep. But I'm sorry to say that, for all her excellences, she isn't always as efficient as one might hope, even if we have visitors—or should I say, *'specially* if we have visitors—and as for the Mater herself . . ." I couldn't make out whether it was by accident that this sentence didn't reach completion. At any rate he said no more because the horse had to be gently persuaded to turn down a half-concealed lane, after which, I could see, you left town behind for further down-land. That we had almost arrived I could tell from a rather wonky signpost saying TO FURZEBANK HO, the last three letters of the second word having been scrubbed off by some mischievous urchin; hence Cyril's facetious name for his home.

The dog-cart took us now down a narrow lane with high, thick, tangled gorse-bushes on either side, their scores of gleaming yellow phallus-shaped flowers filling the air with sweet, wine-like scent. Beyond the gorse I could see orchards—nut-orchards, apparently, producing the famous Kentish cobs—and inside these were geese grazing, dazzling white against the green of grass and leaf and the blue of the bright sky. The lane came to an end in a farmhouse, the object of our drive and of many hours' speculation: front wall white clapboard, and side-walls half-timbered, darkish seasoned brick crisscrossed with oaken beams.

When Cyril turned the dog-cart into the yard to the back and side of this, I was taken aback by the untidiness and the shabbiness of what we confronted: outbuildings looking in need of repairs and re-painting, and in front of them a large, unsightly assemblage of discarded bits-and-pieces: spare wheels, broken shafts of earlier carts, chests and boxes crammed with obvious rubbish. As Hans and I prepared to descend from our conveyance, two fiercely hissing huge-seeming birds, necks stretched out, heads bent down like rugby-players about to tackle, came running from the unenclosed orchard to our right.

"Away with the pair of you," Cyril told the geese, standing before them in an attitude mimicking theirs. "Back, *back*! You may once have saved Rome from the Gauls but that's no reason for you to be unfriendly to guests having their first glimpse of Furzebank Ho."

At this little commotion a woman came out of the farmhouse through the back door. Wearing a loose sky-blue smock, she waddled toward us—all too clearly in an advanced state of pregnancy—with a put-out expression on her otherwise pretty, fresh-complexioned face.

She said: "Well, this is a fine time to arrive home and no mistake, Cyril. Whatever have you been doing with our visitors? Taking them to Dover and back?"

"Keep your hair on, Mater," said Cyril. "I've merely been showing Mr. Bridges and Mr. Lyngstrand some of the beauties of our neighborhood."

"I'll say you have!" said the "Mater." "Pausing in front of every single building and jabbering your head off the while, I shouldn't wonder."

I hadn't expected the rusticity of Edmund's wife/Cyril's mother's voice. She had a tumble of copper-colored hair and a shiny face like an apple polished on an apron. She stomped up closer to Hans and me, and, looking at us rather as she might have done at some mangy sheep that had strayed into her orchard, asked: "So which of you two is the Norwegian one?"

Hans bowed and admitted to the identity.

"I thought Norwegians were meant to be tall," she said, and then, to me: "So you're the new boy in Edmund's office."

This was not at all how I wanted to be designated. I put out my hand but it was not taken, not out of impoliteness but because Mrs. Hough's own hands were wet and floury.

"Put the horse and cart away right now, Cyril," she ordered her son. "I don't want any more time wasted than it's been already . . . You two had better come along inside with me."

Perhaps, considering her "interesting condition," which Edmund hadn't mentioned to me, Mrs. Hough hadn't wanted to entertain visitors today. Certainly nothing in her manner suggested she was pleased to see us. Foxgloves were growing against the side-wall of the farmhouse alongside the broom and the crimson valerian, and I noticed that, before passing back through the open back-door, Edmund's wife quickly slipped three of her own fingers into the fingers of the floral "gloves," as though following some rural superstition.

We exchanged the noonday sunshine for a big, oak-beamed, flag-floored kitchen, which, when my eyes adjusted to it, resembled, I thought, in its disorder and its abundance of children, an ill-run baby-farm . . . Not to confuse readers as I myself was confused my first quarter of an hour at Furzebank Ho, I will tell them that Edmund and Susan Hough have eight surviving children: first the quartet of Cyril, Lucinda, Lotty (Charlotte), and George; then, after a sad period when offspring did not survive more than a year (and often not that!) Bella (Isobel), Rose, and Grantley. On August 2 of the year I'm writing about, 1885, Lionel, the child Susan Hough was now carrying, was born.

An elderly woman with straggly white hair and watering brown eyes (but she'd been peeling onions) came up to me: "I bet I know what you are thinking, young man?"

She gave me no time to respond, but recited:

"'There was an old woman who lived in a shoe,

She had só many children she didn't knów what to do!'"

Well, that wasn't far off the mark.

"Except that Susan ain't old, and this house ain't a shoe." And she laughed so hard at her joke, which she must have made many times before, that I found myself laughing too. I rightly surmised that here was "that nice old hag who's a relation of my mother's"—Elsie Woodison. By the time I'd taken in who she was, two little Cairn terriers, tired of being pulled about by infants, had come up to me and started to tug at my trouser turn-ups.

Cyril returned from re-stabling the horse.

"Crumbs!" he exclaimed. "Are you both still in the kitchen in the middle of all this moiling? Where's the Pater?" I had been asking myself this. "He will certainly want to know that his protégé and one of *The Advertiser*'s biggest heroes have arrived."

"About an hour later than was expected," his mother couldn't resist saying, as she carried a large saucepan over from the range to the principal kitchen table. "But that's only to be expected from His Highness the Great Intelligence when he condescends to do a favor for somebody."

"Luncheon doesn't look anything *like* ready," observed Cyril, "so I don't know what you're making such a to-do about? I'll go and seek out the Pater, probably sitting in the drawing-room with a book."

This prediction proved accurate. The drawing-room itself was a large, comfortable, battered-looking room with threadbare patches in both carpets and curtains, and two more children—to be precise the Houghs' youngest-to-date, Grantley, and their youngest nephew, Stephen Woodison. They were playing with Edmund's slippers much as the two Cairns might do. On seeing us Edmund put down his book.

"Up here already?" he said. "Welcome to Furzebank. Hans, *vilkommen*." Hans gave another of his charming bows and broad happy smiles.

"However many children," Cyril asked his father, "did my Aunt Woodison see fit to deposit on us today? The place is positively infested with infants! And where is Lou?"

Edmund said: "Your sister is being her usual thoughtful kind-hearted self and is entertaining two little Woodisons and one little Hough in the garden; she has a magical way with children. Perhaps we should go and find her. Let us proceed through the French windows"—these were, in fact, already open—"and enter the Hough estate."

"Life in England," said Hans, watching the two infants move across the lawn to find their kin with newfound ability and zest, "is so cheerful." He could not, of course, have hit upon a word to please Edmund more.

Edmund said: "Thank you, my friend. We do make rather a virtue of cheerfulness here. And just smell our marvellous gorse! Another name for gorse is 'furze,' you know, hence the name of our house, a very ancient name too."

"Here it comes," Cyril whispered to me, "just as I told you it would."

"Our greatest living writer composed some very fine lines about gorse," Edmund told us, "in his poem 'Juggling Jerry':

'Yonder came smell of the gorse, so nutty,
 Gold-like and warm; it's the prime of May.
Better than mortar, brick and putty,
 Is God's house on a blowing day.
Lean me more up on the mound; now I feel it;
 All the old heath-smells! Ain't it strange?
There's the world laughing, as if to conceal it,
 But he's by us, juggling the change.'"

"The Pater feels as pleased with that poem as if he'd written it himself, and not George Meredith," observed Cyril, but with more affection than malice. "I shall venture forth and hoick out Lou from the mess of nippers."

"Mr. Lyngstrand, I'm sure you have a beautiful home of your own in Norway," Edmund said.

"Bergen, the city I come from, is *very* beautiful," said Hans, "and my patron, Herr Strømme, has a fine house there, an old merchant's house with Hanseatic connections. But it is nothing like this. Nor was my childhood home."

Edmund didn't quite know how to take this. He had met Hans only once before, when as editor of *The Advertiser* he had visited the Royal Hospital. "That childhood home has gone now, I take it?" he asked awkwardly.

"Yes, completely. My father lives now with his second wife on the French Riviera. Near Mentone." If Hans had told me this fact before, I had forgotten it. "On my return to Norway, it is in my godfather's house that I shall be staying," he went on.

On my return . . . But of course! In the not distant future Hans would be leaving Dengate and going back to Norway. And how would that leave my life here?

"Here they come!" announced Edmund proudly. "Now you both can meet my eldest daughter, Lucinda."

Cyril preceded his sister, with the boy infant in one hand and the girl infant in the other. And then, ducking the boughs of the crabapple tree and with three pinafore-clad, long-haired children of, at first glance, indeterminate gender clinging to her, followed an agile-limbed girl in navy blue linen skirt and blue-and-white-striped cotton blouse, the two fetching garments united by a brass-buckled leather belt around her slim waist.

Not till she raised her head after successfully avoiding contact with the lower apple-branches was I able to see the burnished chestnut of her tresses. My pulse raced, my whole body tingled. She was yesterday afternoon's girl of the Royal Gardens, she who had kept the assembled street-urchins spellbound.

"Lucinda, my dear," said Edmund, "I want you to meet Mr. Lyngstrand from Norway, staying now at Beatrice Fuller's as I have told you."

Lucinda Hough was all charming welcome, and Hans all grateful delight, and while this exchange—how appallingly long it lasted!—my ridiculous, childish habit of blushing got the better of me, and the fire in my cheeks speedily fanned itself to an uncomfortable heat.

Eventually her father guided his daughter on from Hans to myself. "And this is my promising new reporter of whom you have heard me talk such a lot." *Promising reporter, eh?* "Mr. Martin Bridges."

Miss Hough did just what I was dreading, looked me unflinchingly in the eyes to say: "Oh, but Mr. Bridges and I met yesterday, without exchanging any words. I was busy telling a few children in the Royal Gardens about flowers and trees. But I do wish, Mr. Bridges, you'd been bold enough to join us. Often I have the most unlikely taggers-on to my nature study groups. Last Wednesday, I had a nice old man almost blind but with a heightened sense of smell. And after him came a young woman on crutches with her nurse; she put her lameness to good advantage by studying insects."

I was hardly flattered by the company into which she'd straightaway put me, but this was better than having incurred her anger.

"I didn't think you'd want any further additions to your pupils," I managed. "You seemed to have rather more than 'a few' as it was."

"But the more the better," said Lucinda. My eyes were now absorbing her clearness of skin, her freshness of complexion, and her hazel eyes. "I believe, you see, that so many of the less well-off—even in a small and prosperous town like Dengate, barely eight thousand souls—live their lives in total ignorance of nature. They don't realize its pleasures cost them nothing and make them incomparably the richer."

Edmund looked on and listened to this homily with a look of such pride that he revealed a major, probably *the* major, aspect of his whole existence: he considered his eldest daughter united all the virtues plus some special ones of her very own.

A compliment was surely now called for from myself so, my face still clownishly a-flame, I stumbled through the following sentence: "I'm sure that with a teacher like yourself the kids from Farthing Lane," I was pleased with myself for getting the name right, "will learn all the better."

If my blushes were clownish, so was this attempt at chivalry which didn't suit a contemporary, probably "advanced" girl like Lucinda or, for that matter, a lively-minded, cynical reporter such as myself. I knew this as soon as I'd spoken, possibly even before.

But Cyril Hough came to my rescue: "I'd warn you to tread a bit carefully if you go on one of Lou's nature-walks. She's apt to carry with her a supply of pencils and paper, and then set little tests. That's not any man's idea of fun."

Everybody laughed now, and my gaucherie evaporated into the fragrant noonday air. A few decidedly pleasant minutes later our little band was broken into by Elsie tripping girlishly despite her age and weight out onto the lawn with an announcement that we could all go into luncheon now, grown-ups in the dining-room, children in the kitchen. This prompted a noise of protest from the last category. Elsie put out a hand to touch Hans Lyngstrand's head.

"I had a beau once with hair like yours," she said in a soft, sad, musical voice, "and he died. But your hair is more golden-like than his, and even lovelier."

Hans too proved himself capable of gallantry, though with happier consequence than mine. "Your beau must have been a very fortunate man," he said, "to have you as his girl." And endeared himself to everybody forthwith; I would never have said anything so gracefully complimentary—nor so soppy.

The long table in the dining-room made a—that word again!—cheerful sight, and an impressively orderly one considering the chaos out of which it had been, really quite quickly, created. Three lustre-jugs of cowslips and cow-parsley had been placed so their sweet scents could drift over us as we ate and drank. To eat, two substantial courses—roast lamb with new potatoes and peas and a mint-sauce from freshly picked leaves, and afterwards apple-pie with custard. To drink, cider in flagons for the males, an elder-flower concoction for the women.

"Come on then, stop thinking about all those old facts and figures you been poring over all morning, and do the carving like a proper old head of the household," Mrs. Hough called out to Edmund from her end of the table (nearest the kitchen door) to the other (nearest the garden window). Then turning to Hans on her right she said: "My father, Mr. Robert Woodison, he was a *beautiful* carver. All the other farmers here—from the Isle of Thanet to Romney Marshes—used to like to watch him carve the joint. Wonderful it was, he would just put the knife on the meat and away it'd come, like melted butter." Her husband by contrast was hacking away inelegantly and noisily at the lamb. Yet almost the moment the meat arrived on my plate it gratified the senses, delicious in aroma and juicy and tender to the tongue. In the years that have passed since this repast I have become all too conscious of the animals who provide such fare; I am, in spirit and, when I have the courage, in practice, a vegetarian.

In the next room the children made a noise like a menagerie granted the powers of speech, laughter, and tears. Elsie's control had severe limitations. For a good portion of lunch-time the children kept up a progressive chant:

"One and one is TWO,
Two and two is FOUR,
Four and four is NINETY,
Ninety and two is a MILLION . . ."

All this was periodically broken into by a scuffle, as when Annie Woodison hit Grantley Hough on the head with a spoon, and the terriers barked and snarled accordingly.

Not that those at the grown-ups' dining table were precisely inhibited. Edmund had no belief at all in that maxim "children should be seen and not heard." Cyril—something of a hero, I noted, to his younger brother, George (who that afternoon, though barely fourteen, announced to me his intention of "going into Mincing Lane like him over there")—thought nothing of bringing up subjects or opinions with which his father might at the very least be uneasy. And of crying: "You're talking nonsense again, Pater!" when Edmund voiced even quite gentle opposition. For example:

"How can a man like you, editor of the biggest newspaper in the region, be so blind, so deaf, to what's happening now in Burma?"

"Burma's not the first thought in the heads of my readers, Cyril."

"I don't know why not. It's your readers' neighbors, the lovable Froggies across the Strait who are causing this damned trouble," Cyril waved a hand to indicate where they operated from, almost knocking over a flagon of cider from which he'd already drunk quite a bit. "Pater, do you realize there's a French consul over in Mandalay right now doing his sinister little best to woo the poor deluded Burmans with concessions, in ordinary parlance 'bribes'? And what territory borders Upper Burma?"

"You're going to tell us whether we know the answer or not," chipped in Lucinda, sitting, to my pleasure, on my right.

"Assam!" cried the flushed Cyril triumphantly. "From which Britain now takes more tea than from anywhere else! Do you imagine we in Mincing Lane want the French to encourage Burmans to make forays over the border? We most certainly do not, even if the old *Advertiser* is pleased to turn a blind eye. Stands should be taken by any principled government."

"I get tired of all this stand-taking against people so much worse-off and worse-equipped than ourselves," sighed Edmund, as he did in the office whenever he heard of harsh measures being taken. The father and son, as they tossed their differing opinions toward each other, along an invisible diagonal of tabletop, looked, I thought, absurdly alike. If you closed one eye, and let the other filter what it saw through a stream of light from the window, you could see Edmund as the younger man, for all that he looked tired and put-upon today, and Cyril for all his boyish impetuousness as the older, drink-flushed man of the world.

I swivelled myself to my right, to Lucinda. "May I ask," I said, knowing that I sounded absurdly stiff but not minding so very terribly if I did, "whether natural history has been an interest of yours for a long time?"

Lucinda seemed glad to leave the public affairs that animated her brother. "Since before I can properly remember," she answered. "And how could it not be? My mother's father was a farmer, like his son, my uncle, who now runs the farm, and I was always over there as a small child, often without my brothers and sisters. And though my father grew up in Dengate, it was a smaller town then and you could get out of the place in two shakes of a lamb's tail, and his favorite pastime as a youth was to walk over the downs and along the cliff-tops, making close observations of everything around him. He became an excellent amateur botanist before he was twenty. It was at the end of a long day's flower-collecting expedition that he called at Grandfather Woodison's farm and there met my mother."

"That sounds quite romantic," I said, swiftly entertaining a picture of a vigorous idealistic young man turning up at a Kent farmhouse and seeing a pretty country girl with russet hair like Lucinda's own. "I like the idea of that."

"Do you now?" and she gave me a slightly but detectably sarcastic smile. "Well, a lot of things have happened since. Babies and children, in a word. Perhaps 'romantic' would not be the best choice of word for the present day." Nor—looking down the table at petulant, pregnant Mrs. Hough—was it.

A fresh burst of chanting broke in from the kitchen as if to prove Lucinda right.

"George Hough," said his mother loudly, momentarily stopping all table-talk, "will you be so good as to get up from your chair—and by the way you shouldn't of taken a second glass of cider; *I* saw you!—and go into the kitchen and tell those stupid children there to stop that dratted nonsense. Your father's not up to dealing with it seemingly, and Cyril's talking his head off as usual, so it's left to you."

George, with notably bad grace, did as he was bidden.

"You see what I mean," said Lucinda. "But to go back to what you asked me—though I have always loved the natural world, it's only this last year I've come to see just how important knowledge of it is for us all. For the sake of our humanity," she added, with a suitably expansive movement of her noticeably charming hands.

"I'd like to have such knowledge too," I told her, "though until March this year—that was when I moved down here from London—I hardly took in the very existence of flowers. Trees a bit more maybe. The good old London planes!"

Lucinda fastened the gaze of her brown eyes on me. She began to speak of the need for children not just in Dengate but in overwhelmingly urban London to be educated in the ways of animals and the "behavior" ("for it's nothing less than that") of plants, "and so restored to the wonderful fullness of existence."

What could I do but agree, especially as I feasted my eyes on the copper tints of her hair, the crisp white of her blouse and the strong dark blue of her linen skirt?

Eventually but abruptly, she switched from her vision, her hopes, to a purely personal subject touching on myself. "And are you happy here in Dengate, Mr. Bridges?"

"Martin, if you please!"

"*Are* you happy here?" She did not insert my name into my repetition. "The Pater has given us such a glowing account of . . ."—it seemed to me she had to spend a brief moment or so deciding how much to let me know of that account—"of your capacity for work, your interest in many subjects. But—" Well, there would have to be a "but," wouldn't there? She lowered her voice to a husky whisper so that her father could not hear her break confidence easily, "He's not sure you're happy in Dengate. He doesn't think you're *cheerful* enough, though having the nice Norwegian living at Mrs. Fuller's has changed things for the better a little, in his view."

I was impressed, and a bit taken aback too, by Edmund's power of understanding. "Having the nice Norwegian living at Mrs. Fuller's has changed things," I assented. Well, that was a truth. Then—"Your father's a good man to work for," I said, meaning it.

"You don't deny you're not cheerful, I notice," commented Lucinda fixing her brown gaze on me. "And you haven't said you're happy either. Is it Castelaniene that you don't like? When the Pater told us his newest recruit might board there, Cyril and I protested. But then we didn't know you, and we thought, well, it'll be a comfortable enough house, nice views of the sea and so on."

My pause, which might have continued for far longer, brought a knowing light into Lucinda's eyes, before she came up with: "I see. Silence speaks louder than words. Well, Beatrice Fuller has had more than her share of problems, and I do not suppose that makes her an easy landlady."

Why not say something of the truth? "There's too often," I ventured awkwardly, "an 'atmosphere' between us. If you know what I mean."

"Oh, yes, I know all right. My mother doesn't find her easy to get on with but the Pater feels sorry for her and in his usual way—he props up half the Channel Ports, I sometimes think—he performs all sorts of kindly offices for her. Like finding her a lodger because he knows sometimes money is a bit tight."

"I see!"

"The Pater was an old school chum of George Fuller's," said Lucinda, obviously realizing that I did not know this major fact. "George Fuller (my brother George is named after him) was even as a boy an enthusiast for the classics, for the beauties of Latin poets."

"And," I added artfully, "the Fullers named their son after a Latin poet, didn't they?" My mind's eye held again that forlorn expression I'd seen on Beatrice Fuller's face when I caught her alone in the Mercy Room. "Horace!"

"Yes, and much good it did him," said Lucinda.

"You knew their son?"

"How could I not? *My* father's *his* godfather, and, besides, we're much of an age, he and I!"

Well, that all tallied, and I felt somewhat put in my place. I was a newcomer, a stranger in this community, this provincial Channel Port, to which I lacked any knowledgeable guide—except Barton Cunningham—with the result that, wherever I went, I was liable to make a gaffe.

"So, you were a friend of Horace Fuller's?" I persevered.

"Friend?" Lucinda's brown eyes seemed to expand with surprise at the word. "Oh, no! Not at all! *He* wouldn't have wanted it, even if *I* had. Horace Fuller did not have friends." She seemed aware of a somewhat reproving coolness in her tone, because she amended it and went on to say, "Unlike yourself, I feel sure. I expect you have lots and lots of friends. You and Hans look already like a pair of brothers."

I was only too plainly disconcerted when Lotty, whose golden-fair hair, this Sunday kept in place in the front by a broad blue ribbon, distinguished her from all her siblings, called across the table a question she had been clearly itching to ask for some while: "Mr. Bridge," she asked, "did you go to church this morning?"

Honesty the best policy here, surely. "No, I did not!" I told her plainly, and unrepentantly. "Why, did you?"

Lotty seemed not just surprised but somewhat affronted at the question. "But of course! We all went except lazy Cyril. And the Pater of course. And, needless to say, George tried not to go, too, but the Mater said he was turning into a young heathen, and should have his face forcibly scrubbed and his hair forcibly combed, and then be dragged into church if need be."

If looks could kill! George had to be content with growling at his sister: "You talk a lot of nonsense, spiteful little missy, and much of it ain't true."

Lotty was not to be deterred: "Why didn't *you* go to church, Mr. Bridge? I want to know."

The whole table had heard her question, and both her parents were,

I could tell at once, interested to hear my answer. But I was spared having to make one, thanks to George's feeling aggressively superior to his sister.

"His name is Mr. *Bridges*, ignorant miss," he told her. "Bridgezzzz! I've never met a girl who got so many things so wrong." He smiled across at me in male complicity.

"We go to St. Luke's," said Lucinda at my side, in a quiet, confiding voice, "and not because it's the nearest church—though it's just at the end of Hillcrest Road—or because it's the newest—completed only eight years ago, and we all went to the consecration—but because Father Richardson (as he likes to be called) is such a very nice man, and a good man too, and his services are the most *beautiful* in the whole neighborhood. When Nature can boast the beauty She does, doesn't man have a duty, Father Richardson asks, to make worship of her Creator as beautiful as possible, he says, with flowers before the altar marking every stage of the Church Year, and garments for the clergy—vestments, they call them at St. Luke's—changing their colors with the seasons too."

I had nothing to say here, but Lucinda was moved to continue: "I'm sure you'd like St. Luke's, Martin." There, she had used my Christian name! "And the—what shall I say?—the *state-of-mind* behind it. We believe in Joy, you see. No dismal sabbatarianism for us!"

"Well, thank heavens for *that*!" interpolated Edmund. "Any God worth worshipping would detest all the misery many churchmen still inflict on society, and on the only day when so many hard workers are able to relax. Anyhow," it was me he was addressing, "you can count on their being no sabbatarian practices here. After lunch we'll be playing croquet on the lawn."

Lucinda gave me a smile that made her face suddenly resemble her father's. "Yes, and I hope you like the game, Martin. A friend of yours will be joining us."

"Oh?"

"Barton Cunningham. I met him yesterday evening at the Parish Jumble Sale, and he said he would love to come up and play."

I wasn't wholly pleased at this news, which surely confirmed the "understanding" Barton had spoken of for I found it hard to imagine him interested in parish affairs. As it turned out, my young colleague at *The Advertiser* was not the only friend of mine who participated in the afternoon croquet.

THE STRANGER FROM THE SEA

• • •

Though back in Norway Hans had never played croquet, he was sure a game very similar to it had been extemporized on the deck of one of his ships, and that it had been great fun. But Edmund proved adamant here; Hans must just sit in the garden and take it easy.

"You're not out of the wood yet, young man!" he told him. "You can be our judge-and-jury. There are bound to be little disputes of the finer points of the game. You can sort 'em out!"

He'd only just given this injunction when onto the croquet lawn stepped Barton Cunningham, enviably debonair: red-and-black-striped blazer, cricket shirt open at the neck, and dark flannels. The smile he flashed at me was casual yet just a mite gloating.

"I just couldn't resist the prospect of a good game when Lou gave me the invitation!" he told me. So, it was "Lou" with him, was it? The name her own brother called her. "Ever played croquet before, Bridges?"

"I have!" True, though I had never before been to a house with its own croquet lawn before.

"Something of a champion, are you?"

"I'm not so dusty!" I replied. "Hans, this is Barton Cunningham who works like me on *The Advertiser*."

Let me not bore readers with how many times I "ran" a hoop or achieved roquets (the striking of another's ball with one's own) before the impressed eyes of all participants and the referee Hans. Never in my life had I played so well; my strokes showed the requisite union of mind and muscle, and I was pronounced a real asset not only to my team but to Furzebank House as a center of the sport. The teams, with their different colored balls, were as follows:

THE BLACK AND BLUE TEAM: Cyril Hough, Martin Bridges, and (after an argument because her younger brother wanted to play alongside Cyril) Lotty Hough;

THE RED AND YELLOW TEAM: Lucinda Hough, Barton Cunningham, and George Hough.

Honesty compels me to say that Barton, after an initial overrating of himself and a few signs of impatience when what he strove for didn't come off, was sporting enough to cheer some of my best efforts, while boyishly

142

exclaiming "Darn it!" and even "Damn!" when his own proved less than brilliant. As for Lucinda, I realized in the very first few minutes of the game that her concentration, so admirably in evidence when talking to ragged children about trees and flowers, frequently strayed when it came to hoops and mallet-strikes, thus bringing out a teasing chivalry in Barton and a barely disguised impatience in George.

At about four o'clock Elsie emerged from the house with a tray bearing a large jug of a pressed lemon drink, but Cyril made it clear that this was merely an interval; more hard play (with a look at his sister here) was to follow. He and Barton then began a conversation which became quite animated on some issue of scoring, and both George and, a little to my surprise, Hans joined in (showing the knack he must have developed as a sailor for getting on quickly with, and even pleasing, the company he found himself in). Edmund went back into the house. All this gave me the opportunity to go up to Lucinda seated on a tump of grass beside her sister Lotty and strike up my second reasonably communicative conversation between us.

"You're obviously a seasoned croquet-player, Martin. It's good for us to have you here at Furzebank."

"I'm not really that, I'm afraid; in fact, I don't think I've had a game of croquet for over a year."

"That says even more for your performance today. You've certainly got yourself an admirer in my second brother, George. '*He* should have been in *our* team!' he kept on whispering to me. George doesn't think that I take the game earnestly enough."

"But do you?" I was bold enough to ask.

Lucinda smiling shook her head. "I can never think of sport in the way you men all do. Games don't deserve the huge importance you attach to them. To hear Cyril and Barton talk now, you'd think the fate of England depended on the rules of croquet."

I felt this combination of irony and reproof in her voice somewhat undermined my own recent display of proficiency, and, even more importantly, that this proficiency hadn't quite served its desired purpose of winning her esteem.

"I don't really care about such things either," I said. "For me a game is just a game. Other things matter far more."

"What things?"

This was hard to answer since what mattered to me most was my newspaper career, and I could hardly say that to Edmund Hough's daughter. So I ventured: "Other living beings—I don't want to stay as ignorant of them as I am at present."

"Isn't the remedy in your own hands? Why haven't you done anything about it a long time ago?"

"Because I was leading the wrong kind of life. A London life." As at the Gateway what came out of my mouth next took me by surprise. "I'd like to join your classes in the Royal Gardens—my work permitting, of course. Monday, Wednesday, and Saturday afternoons, isn't it?"

It was now Lucinda's turn to blush, if only very slightly. "However do you know that?"

"One of your"—I was about to put little "Martin" from Farthing Lane into a facetious category: "acolytes," "disciples," even "beaux," but have happily changed in mid-course—"*pupils* told me. He had to leave for home before you'd finished, and we collided by the park gates. He seemed to have profited a lot from your instruction."

"I'm so glad!" And she sincerely sounded it. "Well, I don't see why you shouldn't come, though the class isn't intended for the likes of you. Someone who till only recently has been a Young-Man-About-Town."

"Hardly!" I said, though I didn't dislike this description of myself. I was just wondering what brief account of my previous life and self I could now give her, by her side as I was, when I became aware that the attention of all the others on the lawn had been aroused by a new arrival.

I turned around to see no lesser person than—Will Postgate himself.

How could I have forgotten that Will was due in Dengate this very day, Will my greatest friend, the one who had given me so splendid a send-off in Soho, and written me so flamboyant an announcement of his imminent visit? Well, of course I hadn't forgotten; in point of fact, waking up at half past six at Hans's side before he slipped back into the Mercy Room, I had thought: "Today Will is coming!" But from the moment Cyril had collected Hans and me in his dog-cart to this moment now poor Will had vanished from my thoughts.

Actually no adjective could be less appropriate than "poor" for Will as he presented himself to the garden of Furzebank House. His stride and stance made Barton and Cyril seem almost schoolboys, though in plain fact he was their senior by only a short margin. As for Hans, his precarious health—revealed in his pallor, thinness, and involuntary stoop, in all of which I was coming to detect gentle improvements—was thrown into immediate somber relief by Will's vigorous masculine body.

"So this is where you're hiding yourself, Martin, my old chum," he said, in a loud, ringing voice, "and a darned good choice on your part, I don't mind saying."

No sooner had he said this than I appreciated what I had never noticed: how strongly Will's voice was redolent of London streets, more so than my own, especially as I was now doing my best to trim it to harmonize with Edmund's lightly mellow tones. No question of Will trimming anything. And his exterior appearance? If Barton's striped blazer was dashing, Will's scarlet one was nothing short of dazzling, going with his well-waxed moustache, flowing hair, and immaculately pressed cream-colored flannels. He was carrying in his large strong-fingered hands a straw boater and an artist's drawing-pad. If all that sounds unlikely garb for a man at the end of a long walking-tour of Hampshire, the South Downs, and the Cinque Ports, then he accounted for it in his next remarks—addressed to me but received (as he intended) by the entire croquet party turned silent on his advent.

"It was Mrs. Fuller of course who told me where you were, and Martin my lad, why ever didn't you tell me what a good friendly soul that excellent lady is? She wouldn't have me staying at the dismal hostelry you'd gone and put me up at. Oh no, I must stay in her house, in her best spare room, which she and her faithful old minion would get ready for me forthwith. All this was decided, I'll have you know, within minutes, *minutes*, of meeting me. But then I do seem to have this lightning effect on people. So I am now ensconced in Castle Aneen itself, antiquities on my bedroom walls and a spacious wardrobe for my togs. In this room, after a due interval, I duly made a change of apparel, and then set out for here, and a goodish uphill walk it's proved. And *voilà* as they say in Frogland.

"Moreover," and he turned his handsome head to indicate Edmund standing a few paces behind him, "I've just been granted the great honor and the immense pleasure of meeting the famous editor of *The Channel Ports Advertiser* at long last. As I've already had the pleasure of informing him, I suspect we'll be seeing a bit of each other in the months, nay years, to come, holding as we both do important positions in the same newspaper group. I haven't yet told you, Martin, that just before I left for my holiday, I was made a Deputy Editor, nothing less, of the old rag."

This obviously was the news he had tantalized me with hints of in his letter.

Everybody, from Lotty and George right up through to the broker of Mincing Lane himself was given a chance to absorb this impressive promotion and to let the jaw suitably drop. For a reason that eluded me I was not as glad to hear it as I would at one time have imagined I'd be.

The London Martin Bridges would not just have thought but would have promptly declared: "They couldn't have made a better choice than you, Will, old man! Heartiest congratulations!" Whereas now . . . could this odd dull sensation in the Dengate Martin Bridges's stomach be a symptom of some dishonorable jealousy? Surely not! I was nowhere near being appointed a Dep Ed anywhere, though secretly I had high hopes of attaining this rank (if not an even higher one) before the age of thirty, W. T. Stead still constantly in my mind. But however less than whole-heartedly pleased I was by Will's barging into the Houghs' home with breezy grandiloquent announcements of his own good fortune, I did succeed in saying aloud, "That's the most splendid news, Will! Well done!"

Will gave me a nod as if these words were no more than his due (and possibly somewhat less), and then insisted on knowing who everybody was. To Cyril he said: "Oh Mincing Lane, I'm often over there myself. Next time I go there you can give me a few scoops of your best dried char!" On hearing Barton's brief self-introduction he commented: "I suppose you've been showing the ropes to this young shaver!" (Myself!) "Well, that thankless task fell to my lot a few years back, but 'Give 'im time!' is what I say to you!" I was not best pleased by this. To Lucinda he said: "I never knew so distinguished an editor would have so distinguished-looking a daughter!"—which I thought decidedly brazen.

After all this, like some newly-dispatched general interesting himself in the pastimes of the common soldier, he gestured toward the croquet hoops and to the mallets lying abandoned on the grass, saying: "And was a battle of croquet about to commence when I so rudely made my entrance? And if so, can I atone for my intrusion by taking part? I'll be an asset to any side I join, I promise you. I'm something of a dab hand after so many games on the lawn at the back of The Crooked Billet, Lewisham. Don't you remember, Martin? Second Saturday in June last year, if I'm not mistaken. Crikey, if our team's fortunes had been left to *you* . . ." He chuckled at this dire possibility. "But happily, they weren't. One William Postgate was at hand to do the necessary."

So soon we were reorganizing ourselves for another match. But Will's brand of male panache scared off the girls, for first Lucinda, then Lotty, declared they'd rather watch than play.

"Oh, I'm sorry to hear this, Miss Hough," said Will to Lucinda. "You would have been a team's greatest adornment."

"I shouldn't have thought teams wanted adornments, only good players!" riposted Lucinda. Which made Will laugh and say: "*Touché*! . . . You and my friend Martin seemed locked in a very serious conversation when I burst in on the scene here. Putting the world to rights, were you?"

He so patently didn't think that was what we were doing that I piped up: "In a way, yes! Lucinda was expressing her belief that children everywhere, but particularly in the poorer areas of towns, should be in touch with nature, should know the names and features of the plants and animals all 'round them." *Well, if that doesn't sound like a "serious conversation", I thought, I don't know what does.*

Oh, if only I had never said all that! Will, slapping his right thigh, now exclaimed: "A woman after my own heart. I'm forever saying how London kids should be made more aware of nature, which affects them all the time without their realizing it. Expanding children's knowledge of the world is quite a little hobby-horse of mine." Was it? First time I was aware of it, but then Will's certainly was an active mind and doubtless he had many hobby-horses he hadn't seen fit to let me in on. "We must talk about this more, swap ideas . . . Anyway, back to really important business. To whit, croquet. And after we're done, I shall make sketches of you all. Brought my block of artist's sheets along for no other purpose."

The two new teams were as follows:

THE BLACK AND BLUE TEAM: Cyril Hough, George Hough, and Martin Bridges;

THE RED AND YELLOW TEAM: Edmund Hough, Barton Cunningham, and William Postgate.

The Red and Yellow team won handsomely, though not before a fit of temper from George who claimed that Mr. Postgate had cheated, and threw his mallet down in outrage at this. Only after I had taken George aside behind the largest hawthorn, and flattered him while decrying this intruding friend of mine, was peace restored.

Restored? Not exactly. Will's presence had changed something in the quality of the afternoon. Both Barton Cunningham and Lucinda Hough seemed magnetized by him, listening to him as though—well, as though he were W. T. Stead himself!

Then, as if to bring me back to the reality of my Kent life, to my job on *The Advertiser*, Edmund said to me: "I haven't yet spoken to you, Martin, about tomorrow morning. A bit of a treat for you, you might say, a contrast to the daily round, the common task."

"Oh, it's a treat and a half all right!" put in Barton, once again implying distinct ambiguity toward his alma mater.

"Mr. Whittington is expecting you at ten o'clock tomorrow morning in his Headmaster's study in School House, to tell you about all his plans for the Founder's Day ceremonies on the First of June. I suggest you take the train leaving Dengate for Kingsbarrow at ten minutes to nine—it's a mere forty-five-minute journey—with a five-minute walk to St. Stephen's the other end."

Well, St. Stephen's had played such a part in so many interconnected lives that I was now aware of, it was surely high time I saw the establishment for myself?

Now attention focused on Will—again! His quick-fire sketches of the assembled company were a huge success. George, Lotty, Edmund, Hans, and even Elsie came in for the rapid attentions of his pencils, and praises were soon being poured on him for both the accuracy and the humor of his work.

It *was* rather good, too, I have to admit. But ungenerously I could have done without having to see, and gasp over, so many dazzling examples of his proficiency. They helped to make me feel a sudden irrelevance, a mere addendum to a lively enough party, a wallflower, even a gooseberry. For—I could scarcely credit my ears—Edmund declared himself so impressed by Will's efforts as to give him, on the spot, a commission. *The Advertiser*, as I have explained, used illustrations fairly sparingly at this period for reasons of reproduction costs, but Edmund, as I knew, was already a true enthusiast for the pictorial "as more than just a re-enforcement of the verbal," (and greatly looked forward to being able to use photographs in the paper). So, on his own lawn, the happy idea came to him that his article-in-progress should be accompanied by drawings showing not just the deficiencies of Dengate's Church Steps that had spelled such disaster for Mr. Betterton but the merits of their counterparts in neighboring places, some of which he now knew to be thoughtfully equipped with handrails. The first sketches would have to be in by late Tuesday afternoon to meet the printers' requirements, the second lot (of places outside Dengate) could be done a bit later. Would Will be able to take two or three days out of his precious time to carry out this task out-of-the-blue?

Of course, Will would be glad and proud to do so. As it happened he didn't have to be back in The Smoke till the end of the week when he took up his new duties.

Like a sulky schoolboy whose desk mate has just got higher marks than himself in some test that really counts toward the final order-of-class, I was not particularly glad to learn this. Not glad at all, to tell the truth.

While the discussion of the drawings was to do was in full progress, Hans and I found ourselves isolated from the others, standing in the shadow of a white lilac tree. He turned to me and said, in a low, somehow urgent voice: "This new friend of yours, are you glad he is here?"

"Of course," I said, "Will's my oldest friend, from my London days."

Hans's face had a pale gravity that made me turn away from it. "He does not treat you as I treat you," he insisted.

And how would you describe that? I found myself inwardly inquiring. So much about my dealings with Hans had, I thought, an almost painful incompleteness about it.

Then Hans said: "He does not share things with you. I do!"

149

CHAPTER TEN

Peregrine Falcon and a Rite of Passage

*C*yril drove us back to Castelaniene; quite a squeeze, with three passengers in the dog-cart. Will talked to Cyril all downhill journey long. Though calling himself "a good Socialist, for all that a hero of mine, Charlie Bradlaugh, deplores that term," he seemed nearly as familiar with the ups-and-downs of the commodity market as the driver himself. He also told him of the many "fair damsels" he'd encountered on his walking-tour. He spoke of the importance of the countryside to him, townsman though he was, praised his own recent sketches of Hampshire and Sussex, and then was pleased to remark: "I take my hat off to your sister, Lucinda. She really understands how important it is for all Britons to know nature properly— a woman after my own heart." And this to her own brother! Crikey! "These out-of-doors classes she gives to the kids of the town—I bet they'll remember 'em all their lives." So now *he* knew about them too.

Once back in St. Ethelberga's Road, Hans felt he needed to rest. This enabled Will and me to be by ourselves. We went for a walk through the Royal Gardens, where he was much impressed by the emergent bandstand ("jolly good design, that," he remarked knowledgeably, "there's one pretty similar in Lewisham, and it earned the builders no end of compliments"), and then out onto the Esplanade. There was no lull in our conversation— was there ever a lull in talk with Will?—but it didn't, I thought, flow with its former strong current. I'd changed (or been changed) since last in his company, and he had not recognized that yet. Yet I managed to assert myself for a moment by saying:

"I shouldn't mention to my—our landlady where I am going tomorrow morning."

"Why ever not? From the way Edmund spoke of it"—Edmund already, eh!—"it was a proper commission he was giving you." Will smiled ironically at his own observation. "A visit to the breeding-ground of an entire tribe of young imperialist snobs. Is that what you left the Smoke to be doing?"

I controlled my irritation for the same notion was bothering me. "Whatever *we* might think of it, it's best not to mention St. Stephen's College to Mrs. Fuller. The place has bad associations for her."

"To do with the pretty little widow's late lamented husband?"

For all my own difficulties with her I didn't like hearing Mrs. Fuller spoken of in these breezy terms. "Something like that!" I said. "And it may not be quite what it seems, my visit to the school. St. Stephen's." For I was now determined to ferret into the pasts of George and Horace Fuller.

"Anarchy is stirring down in the goodly Isle of Thanet, eh?" smiled Will, his mind naturally going to the political and public.

I thought this jocular response intolerable, especially when looking ahead to the chalk cliffs gleaming in early evening sunshine with a refreshed whiteness and with little waves curling stealthily over the pebbles below them.

"And you," I said, "about to assume the role of Second-in-Command on our old paper, and now all set to draw sketches of Dengate for *The Advertiser*, how's *your* radicalism these days?"

Will stopped in his tracks and turned the searchlights of his dark eyes on me. And when Will did that, I was lost, yes, lost to his charm, as I had been the very first time he'd looked at me in that way, at the end of the first week of our acquaintance, so long ago now.

"Martin, there is radicalism afoot in London as never before, I promise you. The majority of our good burghers never bothers to pay attention to what might be stirring in the Engineers' Union or the Gas Workers' Union, organizations they'd probably deride as soon as they heard 'em mentioned. But the time is coming when the names of men in these organizations will be on all thinking lips—to use a phrase I coined in our paper a while back. And let me tell you that the scenes of activity that will bring these blokes their deserved fame won't be the factory or the tool-shop you might expect, but right down there in the good old London docks."

The words "good old London docks" could not but remind me of our expedition to Limehouse, and this—today of all days, in the bosom of a happy, virtuous family where a beautiful, virtuous girl was its principal jewel—was a direction in which I emphatically did not want my mind to travel.

The "light collation" Mrs. Fuller was pleased to serve up to her enlarged household was not so very "light"; in truth a deal more than I wanted after the huge luncheon at the Houghs': a generous selection of cold meats, potato, and beetroot salads, and then treacle tart with junket. And my judgment of people and their mutual reactions one to another proved, with every minute of the supper, rather less than acute. Even before he had burst upon us, all bright and brash, on the Furzebank lawn, it had occurred to me that Mrs. Fuller, that chilly paragon of refinement, would find my visitor too "common" and too confident. Not at all!—he seemed positively to delight her, even to command her respect, with his unstoppable flow of strong opinions and jokiness. His political affinities she would appear sympathetic to also, receiving stories of his and his friends' radical antics almost eagerly.

It was after one of these anecdotes we all had a surprise. Hans, who up till this moment had remained silent (understandably, thought I), suddenly piped up: "This is all very interesting to me. You see in Norway we have a Left party actually in government—*Venstre*. It addresses itself to working-people, particularly workers on the land. Our leader, Johan Sverdrup is himself a lawyer and gets great support from lawyers. He wants our country to become a real democracy uniting all different factions. My patron, Herr Strømme—he's a shipping magnate, and you might expect him to belong to the Høyre, the Right—but he is very proud of what we are trying to achieve in Norway, the only country in Europe with no nobility. He has met Herr Sverdrup on many occasions. Already the man has widened the—what do you call it?—the franchise."

Had one of the two cats in the room, Ham and Japheth, delivered himself of a brief taxonomic guide to mice, rats, and voles, Hans's fellow collation-partakers could scarcely have been more surprised.

Mrs. Fuller's response was: "Interesting! It's really so good of you to tell us about it, Hans. I sometimes think we in England do not know enough about other European societies."

Hans smiled as he received her tribute; the cliché of a smile "lighting a face up" really applied. I had, begrudgingly, to admit to myself that it was kind of Mrs. Fuller to respond to him as she had. And not only kind! Why, she sounded as if the information meant something to her. Will, on the other hand, was not going to admit he was hearing anything new to him.

"What's going on in your country," he said airily, somehow making it sound even further away than it geographically was, "is a matter of congratulation. But Britain is so much more complicated a case than all other societies except perhaps France; we're industrial, mercantile, colonial, agricultural, with the biggest cities in the world and a complex traditional caste system, so it has problems and solutions to 'em all its own. But," he then conceded gallantly, "I'm sure we could cast a glance elsewhere and profit by doing so."

I rather wished Herr—what was it?—Sverdrup could appear as if by magic at our dining table. He would surely be able to take Will down a necessary peg or two. For all his many talents my old friend was not going to become Prime Minister of anywhere.

In bed I lay ceaselessly asking myself: *Will he? Won't he? Perhaps the crowded day we've all had will have so exhausted him he's already sound asleep? Or perhaps old Will's presence in the house will deter him.* The grandfather clock on the landing below struck eleven—surely more slowly than it usually did!—and every boom proclaimed: *No, Hans will not appear.* What a day it had been!—Cyril Hough, Susan Hough, Elsie Woodison, Lucinda turning out the girl I'd so admiringly observed in the Royal Gardens, the croquet game, the appearance of both Barton and Will, like peacocks advancing toward me, tails raised to show their full colors. But shouldn't I be thinking about my assignment tomorrow? A bright idea came to me: I would take an earlier train to Kingsbarrow than that recommended me by Edmund; I knew one left every hour. I would therefore go up to St. Stephen's on the ten minutes to eight. This would give me time for some "snooping" around the precincts of the College, or at any rate a soaking up of atmosphere. *Good thinking, young man!* I told myself.

And then I saw—though I didn't hear—the bedroom door opening. Hans was always stealthy like some nocturnal animal. My heart beat the faster for his appearance, and a warming gratitude suffused me. I spoke not a word, but shifted over in the bed to make more room for him.

If Hans Lyngstrand were by inclination more talkative than most of his countryfolk, with their reputation for taciturnity, he still had the Norwegian preference for simple statements or presentations. He was no chatterbox like Will, no gossip like Barton. Having shot his bolt, his doubt about Will Postgate, he showed, as he eased himself beside me, no inclination to go over the eventful day past, to chat about Edmund or his family or my old London friend. His very action of lying reposeful under the same sheets as me was a wordless speech in itself.

After a long immeasurable silence Hans leaned his head toward me and in a half-whisper asked: "Why don't we tell each other a story, Martin?"

Well, the stories Hans had told me so far I had taken so deeply into my own self they had become virtually personal experiences of my own.

"Yes, but you must begin!"

"The story I'd like to tell is not about myself but about another sailor-boy who served on a ship in the Mediterranean."

"You've never served there?"

"No, I've not yet seen the South, the Midi, the Mezzogiorno. But I'd like to do so, very much, and I believe that one day I will . . . Anyway, one day down in those parts this sailor-boy saw a bird caught in the tackle-yard of the ship's mast. He was pretty sure it was a peregrine falcon, a female because of the size, and after watching her struggles, he knew he had to rescue her. Are you familiar with peregrine falcons?"

"Not really," I admitted. "Not at all!" should have been my answer.

"They're the fastest creatures on earth, that's what Bo'sun Johnston always said, faster even than cheetahs. They hunt on the wing, swooping down speedily on their prey. When they mate, it's for life, and the female is always quite a bit bigger than the male. They're about the size of the average duck; in fact in America, Bo'sun Johnston said, they call them 'duck hawks,' though that isn't nearly so good a name for them as 'peregrine' which means 'wanderer' in Latin. And Scandinavian peregrine falcons *do* make the most enormous journeys migrating for the winter. They have long pointed wings the color of slate, but with black tips, and the bars on their underparts are black too, and most of their faces also, but underneath each curved beak you find a white chin. Their sound is a *kek-kek-kek* which sometimes turns into a *kaark*."

"And you say one of these birds"—for I had their picture (and their sounds) now—"was tangled up in the ship's mast."

"Yes, and spent nearly an hour trying to extricate herself, the poor, brave thing, until our sailor-boy felt he had a duty to rescue her, though the rest of the crew mocked him and told him doing so wasn't worth his while. His climb up the mast was difficult and also pretty dangerous because a strong wind was blowing making it sway about violently—and, Martin, I know only too well what scaling a mast in weather conditions like that can be like! But just as difficult and dangerous was the actual business of recovering the bird herself because she didn't at first understand he was trying to *help* her. She glared fiercely at him out of her yellow eyes, she scratched at him with her talons, she even bit him with her cruel beak, on the thumb so hard it bled. In fact, to carry her down to safety inside his jacket, the sailor-boy was obliged to give her a blow on the head which temporarily knocked her out. But get her down on deck he did, and, after she'd got her senses back, and with some of the other hands still jeering at him, he released the bird into the air. Can you imagine the triumph he felt watching her fly away, rapidly soaring above the rough sea!

"Time passed, then this same boy joined another ship, a schooner, which put into the Norwegian port of Bodø."

"Is that near where you grew up? Near Bergen?"

Hans chuckled. "It's not in the least near Bergen, it's right up in the north of Norway; I have never been to the town myself but Herr Strømme has ships which call there. It's a port just inside the Arctic Circle, on a peninsula with a wilderness of mountains behind. In high summer there is no night whatever, and even in April when our young sailor went there, he was amazed at how late it was still light. He was pleased at the bustle of the town, though it was by no means an entirely safe place: so much to do, so many stalls to buy things from, and a good many Lapps and Kvens around the place, folk he hadn't encountered before. One evening our young sailor got permission from the First Mate to go ashore—"

"As it might have been you," I interpolated, "in a different port."

"As it might have been me," agreed Hans, contentedly, moving up under the bedclothes even closer to myself. "First he visited the various booths down by the harbor and bought himself some oranges—oranges seemed such strange things to see right up there in Nordland—and then he wandered 'round more or less randomly until he reached the outskirts of the town. And there he saw standing outside her own house a very pretty young girl."

As it might have been me catching sight of Lucinda Hough in the Royal Gardens.

"This girl looked at the young sailor and the young sailor looked at the girl, but when he asked her what she was looking at, she said she was trying to see the man she would marry. But it wouldn't be like him, she suggested with a laugh."

"Not very kind of her to say that."

"No, but I don't think she meant it in any way unkindly. Anyway, what she said had the effect of making the boy bold. He said he would give her one of the oranges he'd bought—she'd never tasted one before, and they smelled wonderful!—in exchange for a kiss. She thought for a moment and then said yes, she would give him a kiss as payment."

And promptly I had an image of myself exchanging a kiss with the girl of the afternoon—Lucinda.

"So—?"

"So obviously the sailor-boy handed the girl the orange. But at that moment, as ill luck would have it, the voice of some grown man (probably her father) came from the house ordering her to come inside. She attempted to give him back the orange, but he wasn't having this. Then she told him that if he came back the next day, she would be as good as her word and give him the kiss he'd asked for.

"That was something really to look forward to, but next day when it became evening, the sailor-boy found himself quite content to spend the time on board the schooner while his mates went ashore. He had the dear old ship's dog for company (Balthasar was his name), and, like my shipmate, Niels, whom I told you about, this lad was a good concertina-player, and liked to entertain himself making music. But now, as he was doing so, he was filled by a strange, strong, wild emotion, and he knew that he'd have no peace whatever until he was back on land in the town, where he'd have the kiss promised him for this very night. By good fortune there was a Russian boat moored right alongside our Norwegian boy's, and her crew signalled to him that they'd take him ashore in their dinghy, which they did. But they wanted him to go on the town with them, and out of sheer politeness, he agreed to, just for a short while.

"Well, one of these Russians fell for our sailor-boy; he hugged him and kissed him, and gave him a present of a watch-chain, and told him how handsome he was, and how he was already in love with him. And all this when there was a swarm of people about, not always respectable folk. And the sailor-boy felt he really *had* to get away and find the pretty girl and have his kiss, which he was sure would be a thousand times sweeter than even the best of oranges. So he escaped and off he went, in some desperation, in the direction he thought he'd taken the previous night. But somehow or other he went wrong—he after all was a stranger to Bodø—and, like in some bad dream, he found himself back at the harbor-front again. This was terrible! He swung 'round, and took another turn, deciding on it almost on whim, and began to run as fast as he could (and he was quite a sprinter) down a little passage. And then he saw, blocking his way—why, who else but that Russian who had taken such a fancy to him.

"'I've been looking for you all over this damned place,' this great bear-like man, smelling of drink, told him, 'and I've been crying my eyes out because I couldn't find you. I like you so, so much! More than you can possibly imagine—yet.' And he seized him in his great arms—as strong as any bear's—and gave him a hug so mighty our sailor didn't think he would be ever free again.

"Well, being kept captive against this huge male body odorous with sweat and drink when what he wanted was to go and claim his kiss from that nice girl on the outskirts of this town was more than our young hero could bear.

"'Don't hold me any longer! I have to be somewhere else!' he implored, to get the answer: 'Oh, but I must hold on to you, I *love* you, love you so much!'

"'You have to let me go!' the boy pleaded passionately, only to get a little lover's laugh in reply. So, after a rush of wilder frustration and impatience than he'd ever experienced before, the sailor-boy took out his knife, the kind of knife every sailor carries with him, and ran it into this human obstacle as hard as he could. Out gushed the blood, the man relaxed his grip, swung backwards and forwards and then—toppled over, dead.

"Panic followed—imagine it! He had hardly time to be sorry for the dreadful deed he had done. Before many more minutes the Russian's comrades would be coming along and would stumble on his body. They would then start searching for his killer, and how, with the spattered blood on him, could he not be found? Our sailor-boy ran hither and thither, terrified out of his wits, not knowing where he would be able to conceal himself, but can you believe it, Martin?—*this* time he did arrive on the edge of the town, and right beside the very house of the girl. And here she was, as beautiful as she'd been in his thoughts.

"She told him she had eaten his orange with great enjoyment; he told her he had just killed a man; she asked him why; he told her it was because the man in question had tried to prevent him coming to see her and have the promise she'd made him fulfilled. But then he went on to say what was only the truth, that the man he'd killed had fallen in love with him. This was such a terrible truth that the boy began to cry and cry.

"The girl gave the sailor-boy the kiss he had come all this way for, and for the sake of which he had robbed another human being of his life. And the kiss was more delicious than anything he'd ever dreamed of. But there was nothing she could do directly to help him, in a situation getting worse by the minute, for the search-party for the Russian's killer must surely now be underway. But she did tell him to keep his blood-stained hands out of view, and then assured him she would never want to marry anybody else. Back the boy sped toward the harbor, but of course every street, every alleyway was now a-stir with people looking out for a murderer, and he was obliged to take refuge in a very crowded waterside dive full of boozers and wenchers. To his great surprise an old woman strode into this highly unsuitable place loudly proclaiming that he—he, trying so hard not to be noticed—was her son. She simply wouldn't take his no for an answer either, but seized hold of him with a strong scrawny hand and arm. All the folk there laughed, thinking she had come to haul away her innocent lad out of the temptations of such bad company! Then—'There's nothing for it but to come with me!' she whispered to him, 'it's the only way after what you've done that you can be safe.'

"She was a Kven, one of the mysteriously gifted Finnish folk you find in the north of Norway. She tugged him down the street, pulled him into her little cabin, a humble place covered in reindeer skins and the skins of other animals from the wilderness, and made him first wipe the blood off his hands onto her skirts. Only minutes had passed before—*knock-knock-knock*!—two Russians were banging on her door demanding to know if she'd seen any young man who probably knifed their mate. She told our sailor to remain still, answered the door and told her callers in no uncertain terms to be off with their bother.

"Finally, when the coast was again clear, this old lady personally gave the young sailor the good washing he needed so there was no longer any blood on his person and made some swift changes to his appearance and his attire, saying that, looking as he now did, he could get away to safety easily enough. Down at the harbor a young relative of hers had a little skiff that could take him to his own ship; she explained how he was to find him. But one thing first—she must remove his knife. He was never to use it again! What could our sailor do but consent? Anyway, he did not want ever to use it; one killing was more than enough for him. So he sat there and let her remove the knife, but, when she'd got it from him, she proceeded to perform the strangest act imaginable. This old Kvennish woman hacked at her own thumb, so violently that the blood quite spurted up.

"And have you guessed the secret I'm coming to, Martin? Do you see the point of this story?"

"Nnnn!" I shook my head, unsure I was even here in Castelaniene and not in the remote Norwegian port of—what was it called?—Bodø?

"Well, the old woman asked our sailor-boy: 'Do you not recognize me? Not even after what I've just done? I am that peregrine falcon you helped down from the mast, and who struggled and then ungratefully bit you on the thumb. I have now just hacked my own thumb in repayment and so am able to give you that same freedom *you* gave *me* and which you've otherwise forfeited through your misdeed.'"

"And did he go free after all that, your sailor-boy?" I felt curiously agitated, and yet the tale was even more remote in happenings as it was in setting.

"Of course! In fact, all cleaned up as he was, he found the old lady's relative with the skiff in next to no time, and was able to catch up with his mates coming back from their carousals. The dog Balthasar was pleased to see him, in fact everyone on board was in a good mood, and they all went on to make an evening of it—and I won't say that our hero wasn't playing the concertina again before they decided at last to turn in."

"But did he not think of the Russian? If not that evening, then later? He'd taken his life."

Hans's eyes played on me in the darkness of bed and bedroom. "What do *you* think?" he asked.

I felt tiredness about to break over me like ocean waves. "I expect . . . Well, that he did." I finally got out.

"Of course he did," said Hans. And then it was that he leaned over me, and his tongue entered my mouth like a strong sweet-flavored fish intent on finding its mate.

Was I surprised? I don't think I was, though perhaps I should have been. His tongue was the sailor-boy setting out from that ship for the town where there was so much to do and to find. In his story there'd been a peregrine falcon tangled up in a mast and then gloriously liberated, there'd been oranges, those fruits of the south, and the sweetest of kisses that these had brought about. And there'd been knives—dangerous and disaster-bringing—but also fierce conductors to happiness.

And I myself had a knife—oh, yes I had a knife all right, and it was between my legs and, I could feel it increasing itself, expanding to that point when it was more master than possession, more owner than owned. But then the other chap, him with the intent tongue, had, I appreciated, a knife too, also getting larger, preparing itself . . . The sea-blue of his eyes, so intimately close to mine my distance from them could not be measured, shone even in the small-hours darkness of my bedroom.

Was there really any likely alternative to what now took place? My own tongue found its fish-like strength, my own knife wanted to go to its work. The Russian's hug had seemed everlasting, and the sailor-boy had grieved at the way he'd broken it, the kiss the girl gave the boy, a whole day after she had eaten the orange he'd handed her, had been so delicious that estimation of the time it lasted defied the human brain. There were

moments, with Hans, when I felt our limbs were those of one animal, possibly with a single heart, that we had some time ago passed out of our separate identities and beyond the control of the clock. Even of the sun, into
some only half-suspected realm where calendar and hourglass were as impossible as separation—or even separateness.

Well, in the end, Time did establish itself again; it always does so long as
we remain alive on this earth, and we found ourselves, a little reluctantly,
drawing apart, second-by-second accepting that this return to normal had
to be. But still we lay there with only a notional space between us, and I felt
a peace which could again be envisaged in terms of Hans's story (already,
it now seemed, part of the past, *our* past, his and mine)—the vast quiet of
the sky into which the freed peregrine had flown, and of the sea onto which
the sailor-boy, despite being guilty of so heinous an offense, had been
permitted to return.

Then I said: "Hans, you were wanting me to tell you a story before . . ."
Before we came together, I meant to say but didn't. "Then I didn't feel like
it. Now I do, if you want to hear it."

"Of course I would like to hear it, Martin," said Hans, "very much!"

I told him how at the Thomas Middleton School, Camberwell, that
big, dreary block of bricks, I was sitting one wet February afternoon as a
member of the Fifth Form, as it ground a slow way through Shakespeare's
The Tempest, under the guidance of one of the few masters I in any degree
liked, Mr. Grayson, a tall, stooping man in early middle age, with an apologetic manner but a capacity for enthusiasm rare among those paid (pretty
dismally) to teach us. We were reading Miranda's lines which surely could
have applied to circumstances in which Hans Lyngstrand had found himself on the English Channel:

> *The sky it seems would pour down stinking pitch,*
> *But that the sea, mounting to th' welkin's cheek,*
> *Dashes the fire out. O, I have suffered*
> *With those that I saw suffer! A brave vessel,*
> *Who had, no doubt, some noble creature in her,*
> *Dashed all to pieces. O, the cry did knock*

Against my very heart! Poor souls, they perished.
Had I been god of power, I would
Have sunk the sea within the earth, or ere
It should the good ship so have swallowed and
The fraughting souls within her.

I told how at the end of this evocative speech into our class walked our Headmaster. Though I beheld him every day, as the embodiment of authority, and heard him every day in morning assembly as the voice of moral power, he had never once yet so much as spoken to me nor I to him. He did not even know me by sight, as my story makes plain. He was a tall, thin man who often held his head in the air so that his gray-black beard was upward-tilted. I scarcely thought of him as a human being at all, and after the events of that particular rainy day had even less reason to believe him one.

I told Hans how the whole room fell silent with awe and wonder. None of us could remember this having happened—or even being *said* to have happened—before. Those three boys—Fenwick, Marsden, and Stiles—who amused themselves in Mr. Grayson's excellent periods by playing Consequences—that is to say, by passing under the desk pieces of paper with sentences on them for the others to complete, invariably on the subject of female anatomy—straightened themselves out immediately and sat attentively upright as though Shakespeare's last play was what interested them most in life. The Headmaster surveyed us all with petrifying eyes, and poor Mr. Grayson looked as uncomfortable as any schoolboy caught surreptitiously munching an apple during a religious service.

"I believe you have here, sir," Authority boomed, "a boy by the name of Bridges." He did not deliver these words very amiably; there was menace in them, and the beard went up even further into the air.

"I have indeed, sir," said Mr. Grayson as if admitting such an unfortunate truth might spare him—and indeed the whole class—all manner of further trouble. "Please to stand up, Bridges."

What could I do but what I was bidden. Twenty-five pairs of eyes in that classroom were on me now, as if already I'd been found guilty of something so terrible it had brought Justice Made Flesh to drag me out of the room. I myself, if completely taken aback, did not feel quite as fearful as you might imagine, for I knew that I'd been leading a completely blameless life, outwardly at any rate, and I was perhaps too innocent and inexperienced to imagine one could ever be held responsible for another's wrongdoing.

"So *you* are Bridges!" the Headmaster maintained his boom, though by now he was barely a foot away from me. He spoke as if he had very recently been wondering what I looked like and now he'd found out, didn't much care for the reality. "Bridges M., the focal point of so much grief. Sir, I beg leave to take this boy with me out of your doubtless highly instructive class."

"Mr. Grayson, possibly embarrassed by being called "sir" in public by the most august figure in his existence, had reddened as thoroughly as any junior boys, and now made inarticulate murmurs of assent (but what other course did he have?). I could feel the communal sigh of relief (in which curiosity was also audible) to which he himself contributed after I'd followed the Headmaster out of the room, and the latter had turned 'round and decisively, grimly, shut the door behind us.

The Headmaster's first words were astonishing. "I take it you have such a thing as a 'locker'!" He pronounced the last word as if it were foreign, and not the name of an item integral to the system over which he presided.

"Yes, sir," I said. "It's in Wing C."

"Please be so good as to lead me to it. I shall be watching you pack all your effects into your satchel, to be sure we have seen the last of you and your belongings."

I made no demurral whatever, felt myself in no position to. Doubtless an explanation would be forthcoming sooner or later—and I could put matters right. I therefore led him (as he'd asked) through his own school, to those dismal quarters which contained my locker (along with those of other boys with surnames in the group A to M). And when I got there, this lofty human being was pleased to stand over me, his beard now virtually grazing my neck, while I packed every item of school stuff—from Latin dictionary to a tennis ball for impromptu playground games, from a wodge of blotting-paper to, heaven knows why, a spare cuff-link—making impatient humming noises the while, as if I could not perform my task too rapidly for his satisfaction.

"Every item disposed of then," the Headmaster at last was able to say. "Just as well because Bridges, you will not be darkening our doors again."

"Sir? Why is that?"

"You should by rights ask your *father*," said the headmaster. "But perhaps you do have a right to an explanation, too. Mr. Bridges has defaulted on payments to this establishment. We exercised clemency last term, to him and by extension to yourself, so that you have had your tuition here from September to the present, to this very day, free. FREE, do you understand, sir? FREE. Not only has the outstanding amount not been made up, but we have received no fees for *this* term either. And when we requested them, we met only with insolence and fiscal incompetence. Therefore, there can be no place at the Thomas Middleton School for you, Bridges, nor is it good for your fellow pupils to keep company with one who has not been paid for, with no moneys forthcoming, who has been attending the classes FREE. And lest you think I am being hard-hearted"— it was difficult, both then and later, not to think this of him—"I will add that we do have certain benevolent schemes for parents in temporary distress. We notified Mr. Bridges of them, and encountered exactly that insolence and that fiscal incompetence"—how proud he was of finding these, I must admit apt, terms!—"of which I have already spoken. Take your satchel then, sir, and leave the school premises as unostentatiously as you can."

I now told Hans with whom I'd shared more than I had with anybody—about Walter Bridges himself, about the puritan household in East Anglia he came from and his own rebellion against their Bible-readings, their total abjuring of alcohol or tobacco, their Sabbatarianism, all of which had encouraged him to think of himself as "destined to preserve the full-blooded freedom of the Regency in the strait-laced culture of Victoria's mid-century." Certainly he unfailingly put his own pleasures— "needs" he called them—well before duties, whether to those companies unwise enough to employ him as a pay clerk (later, senior pay clerk) or to his family.

I told Hans about how I taxed this man that selfsame evening with what had happened to me in the afternoon.

"Father, you have lost me my education!" I cried, more impassioned and full-throated than I usually was with my sire. I could already smell the gin on his breath. He tumbled unsteadily sideways and had to prop himself by leaning on the mantelpiece against the mirror, to keep on his feet at all. And then . . . and then he began to laugh—such laughter as I never wish to hear again in my life.

"Excuse me, Martin," he said, "I just cannot help finding the whole thing so exceedingly comical. I am, you see, a man born out of his time, who would have thriven in the Regency with its glorious opportunities for amusement, with its golden frivolity. I was not born, you see, for our present age of canting ushers and the cash nexus."

That was all I wanted to tell for now.

Hans's reaction? He lifted his left arm and slid the hand underneath my neck. He had proved himself, prone on his back, turning his head from time to time to play the beams of his eyes feelingly on my speaking face, the best audience, the best confessor, I could ever have asked for. If I'd been then the sculptor he himself had determined to become, then this is how I would have commemorated him, in repose, his face, which only minutes back had been suffused with amorous feeling for me, showing that he was absorbing my revelations not just into his head but into his heart.

He left the bedroom that morning only ten minutes or so before it was time for me to get up for breakfast.

CHAPTER ELEVEN

I Visit the Old Hole

*F*or all the raptures and intimate revelations of the night, my spirits rose that morning in something not unlike relief the moment I turned the corner of St. Ethelberga's Road. Think of it—this was the first time I'd left Dengate since my arrival here, and it felt really good to be doing so even if only for a few hours—and on such a lovely flowering morning too. Away from Mrs. Fuller, away from *The Advertiser* (even though bound on a commission from it), away from Hans and both his tribulations and his emotional gifts. I arrived at the town's handsome station in as cheerful a mood as Edmund could have wished for me. I purchased my ticket, then walked over to the platform for the Canterbury train which stopped at Kingsbarrow.

Here I found gathered a band of twenty to thirty boys all in uniform: dark blue crested blazer, white shirt, charcoal-gray trousers, and straw boaters with blue-and-black striped hat-bands. The boys were not scuffling and shoving each other like so many schoolboys off-premises, nor did the platform echo with raucous laughter or shouts. Almost arbitrarily selecting two older boys with amiable facial expressions, I asked them: "This *is* the right platform for Kingsbarrow?"

The taller of the pair gave me a little well-bred nod. "It is indeed, sir. Kingsbarrow is where St. Stephen's College is situated, and that is where we ourselves are bound."

His friend, a fair, curly-headed boy with small bright eyes like currants in pastry, added: "This train, sir, is the famous 'Eight O'clock,' or 'Swots' Express,' as it's generally known."

Initiative rewarded, inside information about the establishment ahead coming my way already, what a journalist I was showing myself! "Oh?" I said. "And why's it called that?"

The crinkle-top boy's eyes glinted with humor: "Why? Because we day-bugs are so much cleverer than the boarders they feel obliged to put our successes down to us swotting and not to our natural genius. Anyway, if they want to call this the Swots' Express, it's only fair of us to christen the boardinghouses the Slowcoaches' Stables, *n'est-ce pas?*"

His graver taller friend gave me another courteous nod. "Dayboys comprise a mere twenty percent of the college," he explained, "so you can call us an egregious and distinguished minority." *I doubt I'd want to call you any such thing*, I thought, while recalling the coarser-grained, coarser-mannered creature I'd been at this boy's age. "But the train also has its name because in truth we do all use the journey-time for conning our texts, and often arrive at classes better prepared than any boarder can hope to be."

When the train drew into the station with ear-splitting hisses and roars, I decided not to let this obliging, potentially useful duo disappear. With studied casualness, I followed them into an empty compartment, followed by four younger boys, of whom, for the entire journey, the first pair were to take no notice whatever. When the guard blew his whistle, its shrill loudness penetrated my head like a reveille, reminding me that I had a task to perform this morning, and a double-task at that (for I absolutely must come away with some information about the Fullers!). Nevertheless, I let myself sink back into the deep, dusty, plum-colored upholstery. Before long orchards, rather than the terraced houses belonging to *Advertiser* readers, were stretching away on either side of me, dressed in the white or pale pink of apple blossom, while on the banks above the railway track the broom showed a yellow whose early morning brilliance I now would never mistake for Juggling Jerry's gorse.

Four stations between Dengate and my destination—Monksley, Plumcroft Halt, Little Amchurch, from which a branch line opened northward to Faversham, and Stodbourne. While through the walls of our compartment on both sides came sounds of laughter and lively talk, the occupants of mine maintained a self-conscious sobriety. Three of the four junior boys were living up to their train's tradition by going through an exercise demanding correct "quantities" in Latin verse, while the fourth, a chubby boy, who had pushed his boater so far forward it shadowed his eyes, was engrossed in some calculation causing him to speak figures aloud: "No, three hundred and twenty . . . *Four* hundred—four hundred and twenty-seven!"

As for my duo, sixteen years of age, I would say, and both fair-haired and somewhat spotty-complexioned, they were surreptitiously intrigued by my presence. For all their pride in the train's sobriquet, they were not swotting themselves, but relaxing before the day proper began, though the one on my immediate right, the more solemn one with the formal vocabulary, had taken an edition of Horace's *Odes* out of his schoolbag, resting it on his left knee.

I decided that I should take advantage of their presence—and apparent leisure:

"And are you looking forward to the First of June?" I asked.

They turned amazed, impressed faces on me. "But of course!" they answered in seeming unison. "It's the greatest event of the year." (Not "our year," I noted.)

"I am interviewing the Headmaster about the events for that day," I said, his name suddenly escaping me except for the monosyllabic nickname "Dick." "On behalf of the local newspaper, *The Advertiser*."

Had I announced I was covering Russian events for *The Times* the expressions on their faces could hardly have expressed more awe. "The Latin and Greek verses you will hear recited that day!—you'll never have heard the like, Mr. Whittington is a genius for picking out the best quotes and getting the best fellows to deliver them to our public. You won't forget it in a hurry!"

Perhaps it wasn't so hard to imagine someone as dedicated to the Classics as George Fuller having been a "beak" here.

I could think of little else to say, not wishing to reveal my ignorance of both the Reverend Whittington and his taste in verse. Before too long the train was puffing into Plumcroft Halt, on the left-hand wooden platform of which I could spy more boys in the St. Stephen's uniform. And as some of these climbed into our very compartment, "my" pair of older boys decided to engage themselves in a bit of swotting after all and to live up to the image they'd given me of a college of classicists. Crinkle-top got his own edition of Horace out of his satchel and put it on his left knee, whereupon his taller friend bent forward so that soon the two friends' engrossed heads appeared virtually a single physical entity.

"Book 3, Ode 5, it's a positive demon," my neighbor opined. "Regulus was a real Roman, but I haven't found it easy—minus crib—to work out from this quite what he did. But Dick"—so they too called the Rev Alfred Whittington this!—"will doubtless explain all that for us. I value so much his explanations."

I certainly couldn't have said that about my frightful Headmaster whose essentially unkind character I had revealed to Hans last night . . . Meanwhile a conversation about cricket was in progress between two of the recent entrants.

"Bennett is useless as a bowler, bally useless; he never should have been considered for the team *at all*, and as for Eardley-Kinnaston . . .!"

"Eardley-Kinnaston, my *God*!" exclaimed his friend, "if a blooming mouse was at the wicket, I doubt he could bowl him out!"

"My" pair, however, had other matters to preoccupy them. (NB, I have checked the relevant texts for writing this chapter!)

"*Caelo tonantem credidimus Iovem regnare*," the boy on my right was intently muttering, "that's clear enough: 'We used to believe in thundering Jove in heaven.'"

"Don't 'we' believe in him anymore, then?" came Crinkle-Top's voice from under the as-good-as-locked heads, "I thought Horace accepted Jove. Went and poured libations in his honor."

"He did. But I suppose there were times when he doubted. And then he'd hear the thunder and know that he still held power. In the same way—well, do you see—

'. . . *praesens divus habebitur,*
Augustus adiectis Britannis
Imperio gravibusque Persis.'

. . . Augustus Caesar's recent conquest of the Britons and the Persians makes the poet believe in *him* and *his* power."

"Wouldn't Jove mind that? Feel Augustus had stolen a march on him?"

"Of course not!" the boy sounded gently reproving of his friend's facetiousness. "Horace knew full well that Jove approved of Augustus Caesar just as *our* God approves of *our* Empire."

Strange that I should be visiting a school the very day after I had confessed to somebody—to Hans, as I could to nobody else!—the humiliating end to my own school days? If Father had managed to pay the bills and the Thomas Middleton School, Camberwell, had kept me on, would I have developed into a boy who could read Horace along with these friends? Would I then have gone on to try for Oxford or Cambridge? But perhaps I wasn't brainy enough to do so! Or not brainy in the right way!

The boys went on tearing at the lines like dogs with heads lowered over a bone, discussing what words agreed with what others, however far separated from one another in any line they might be. Leaning back again in the dusty upholstery, I let my eyes absorb the passing view, all the delicate colors of the orchards of apple, cherry, plum, and the increasingly numerous farm buildings and oast-houses. These, with their round towers and conical roofs culminating in narrow tilted cowls, made me think of the many South Londoners I'd known—at the stationer's, at the printers', around and about the various lodgings I'd ended up at—who'd come down to Kent for the hop-picking. Where would I rather be, among those Cockney lads whose tasks, however bucolic the setting, were back-breaking and ill-paid, but more often than not included a certain camaraderie, or among my present fellow-passengers on the Swots' Express, racking my brains over Horace?

But such speculations came to an abrupt stop with a loud burst of unanimous activity both inside the compartment, and, as I could hear only too well, on either side of it. As if obeying the call of some regimental cornet, these hitherto exemplarily composed boys bounced up from their seats and made for the door as though their very lives depended on making a quick exit some enemy might try to prevent.

We were pulling into Kingsbarrow.

I don't know how many passengers remained on the train to be borne further down the line toward Canterbury, but the general disgorging onto the platform seemed so prodigious it amounted to an emptying of the carriages. The modest little station with its geranium tubs was all but obscured by the arrival of so many boys, with here and there a grown man whose very gait and attitude told of a relationship to them at once deferential and resentful. Twice a day in term-time it would have to endure this overflow, that's to say for nine months of the year. Perhaps, it occurred to me, the station-master and porter, the men who looked after the adjacent allotment garden where KINGSBARROW was picked out in white pebbles, were as glad as any St. Stephen's pupils when the holidays began.

But as I mingled with these, a trifle self-consciously, what I had confided in Hans last night came back to me yet again, including details I had not lingered on. I could all but hear again my heavy footsteps ringing through the empty hallway of my school's central building, as pathetically holding on to my satchel, I walked toward its main gateway and so out into Camberwell Green, knowing that I had said farewell forever to higher education, to taking my place among those I'd surely been born to associate with, and was now obliged to lift myself up effortfully from the army of the ignorant and indigent. But who might become the W. T. Stead of his particular generation.

Northeast from the station, for just under a mile, across almost disconcertingly flat land, the main street of Kingsbarrow marches toward the tall, red buildings of St. Stephen's, which dominate everything else whether natural or manmade, and are overwhelmingly incongruous with the rest of this unremarkable, unpretentious Kent village: two opposing rows of half-timbered or clapboarded cottages and houses, a small, squat parish church, a tiny Primitive Methodist chapel, a public house ("The Red Lion") and one gentleman's residence (which a well-polished brass plaque proclaims to be the doctor's). And down this relentlessly straight line the released train-travelers in their summer uniforms advanced like a regiment.

I took quick steps—a half-run really—to get further to the vanguard and found myself more or less alongside a tall man in late middle-age— plainly, from the comportment of the boys nearest him, a St. Stephen's beak. I was reminded at once of the White Knight in Lewis Carroll's *Through the Looking Glass*, a book I still never tire of reading: high forehead from which untidy white hair streamed backwards, shaggy eyebrows and walrus moustache, and an attaché case so bulging with exercise books that its clasp had given way and an accident seemed not just inevitable but imminent. He had an imperturbable gentleness of aura which emboldened me to step still closer to him and say: "A very good morning to you, sir! I'd like to introduce myself. I am Martin Bridges and your Headmaster has asked me as a reporter on *The Channel Ports Advertiser* to come and learn what you are all planning to celebrate Founder's Day on June 1."

Startled out of his own thoughts, the man turned weak bespectacled eyes on me with difficulty in focusing them. "And I am sure," he said in a voice suggesting a habitual undiscriminating charity, "he will be most pleased to tell you about them."

Well, pleasing Mr. Whittington was not really my intention in coming to Kingsbarrow. Or was it? Edmund undoubtedly wanted him pleased, in fact had probably privately agreed with Barton Cunningham that he wasn't quite up to the job of doing so, Victor Ludorum or no. I have to confess to a rush of timidity at this White Knight's words. Here was I, a new recruit to my paper, a resident in Kent for a mere six weeks, and a young man with only the scantiest of educations being dispatched to a prestigious college completely unfamiliar to me and where everyone seemed of a superior caste to myself. Yet Edmund had thought me worthy of coming here—and actually confronting its eminent head whose explanations his pupils so liked listening to.

The White Knight's next comment made me feel, if anything, worse still: "I probably should not say so, but after chapel yesterday evening, Mr. Whittington told me of the intended visit here from a representative of *The Channel Ports Advertiser*, and the prospect delighted him for he believes so strongly in cultivating good relationships with the whole vicinity. Of course he has had many dealings with Mr. Hough over the years, and thinks extremely highly of him."

An interior queasiness—attributable to a number of causes, not least the activities of the past night—was now making for the pit of my stomach, and I raised my head toward the near distance as if seeking help there. The spire of St. Stephen's Chapel was shining in gilded metal against the blue of the clear sky, the large brick buildings, as red as meat or congealed blood, loomed, with every step we took, ever more bulkily and intimidatingly at the end of the long grass-verged street, yet there were several hundred yards to go, and having gone out of my way to join the White Knight, it might be impolite—as well as unresourceful—not to talk to him a bit longer.

"Might I," I ventured, "have the pleasure of knowing whom I am now speaking to, sir?"

After a jerk of his limbs, such as a marionette gives when the strings are pulled, he moved his plain, walrus-mustached, benevolent face to meet mine, and said: "Indeed you might, young man. I am Azariah Welbeck, and I teach mathematics at the college you are paying us the compliment of visiting."

For a moment I could not place the name, a distinctive enough one in all truth, but then I had learned so many new ones in the short time I'd been in Dengate. Almost every day presented two or three more with which it was assumed I ought to be familiar. Then it came to me. Azariah Welbeck had been the "beak" from whom the hapless Horace Fuller had stolen money. Indeed Barton Cunningham's very words, as, rather too gleefully he'd delivered them while we walked up the Esplanade, returned to me: "He stole from one of Old Fulsome's fellow-beaks—a distinguished chap, writer of a famous mathematics textbook, Mr. Azariah Welbeck. As Azzy is the very nicest of men, he tried to hush it up . . ."

"Honored to meet you, Mr. Welbeck. My colleague on the newspaper, Barton Cunningham has said such warm things about you," said I, "that I feel I know you already." This was rather more than the truth, but never mind!

Mr. Welbeck jolted his attaché case to stop two or three renegade exercise books from falling out, then observed: "Barton Cunningham. A talented young mathematician in his way, especially in the more practical aspects of the subject. Please send him my regards when you next see him."

He obviously hadn't taken in his being a colleague of mine whom I would see that very day, indeed would sit beside for three or four unbroken hours.

"He spoke well of your textbook," I said. I had of course now determined to raise the subject of the Fullers but thought I should do in the gentlest way.

"How very kind of him. Of which one in particular?"

I couldn't very well reply that Barton had spoken in the singular only, but fortunately Azariah Welbeck—who had now swiveled his head back and was looking straight before him with unswerving eyes, so that addressing him was rather like parleying with a horse—exclaimed: "Oh, how forgetful I have become! My second book—the one on the *non*-Euclidean geometers—principally Russians, believe it or not—didn't appear until sometime after he had left the Coll."

I had no difficulty in believing that Russia might produce non-Euclidian geometers, since up till this moment I was unaware of these folk's very existence.

"Yes," I risked, "it was the other one of yours that Barton likes so much." Then fearing that our exchanges might turn too particular and mathematical, I went on, "And then I think we have other people in common, sir. The Fullers. I am a lodger at Castelaniene."

At these words Mr. Welbeck came to a stop. Had he actually been a cab-horse, you would have thought his driver had tugged hard at his reins. He swung his head 'round to look at me, making his white mane shake. "Are you really, Mr., er—"

"Bridges," I supplied, maybe a bit too hastily.

"Bridges. I had indeed heard that Beatrice Fuller was now taking in paying guests, but I live here in Kingsbarrow not Dengate, you see, so I do not always hear all that town's news."

"You did not come on the Swots' Express then?"

Mr. Welbeck gave a little rattling laugh. "So you even know our local train's nickname. What a tenacious young journalist you must be! No, every day in term-time I wait for it to pull into Kingsbarrow Station, whereupon I leave my own house—and my wife and daughter and three Airedale dogs—and then join this happy band all the way to the Coll."

This admission warmed me to him. "Yes," I went on, "I am one of those paying guests, you see, and a very pleasant household it is."

Now Mr. Welbeck swung his head away from me, and resumed walking. "I am glad to hear that, for your sake," he said, "I cannot judge whether the household would or would not be pleasant, for I have never visited it, I am afraid." Something—could it be described as a chill?—had entered his cultured, gentle, gravelly voice to make me think that he was not in truth "afraid" of this last fact at all, that he had no intention of going to Castelaniene, no more than Susan Hough had, and that, like my editor's wife, he did not like the owner of the house. Had the matter of Horace Fuller's crime created an irreparable chasm between Mr. Welbeck and the boy's parents?

"Mrs. Fuller tends to keep herself to herself," I said, though I wasn't sure that this remark was accurate, for after all she was a member of the Gateway, to which any amount of solitude would, in my view, be preferable. "What with her husband's tragic death, and her son's . . ." I didn't quite know what noun would be most appropriate here, especially as I wanted to avoid at all costs the word "disappearance," and had just wondered whether "absence" might be the best choice, when Mr. Welbeck spared me further pains by saying:

"That was a sad business, that was. Very sad!"

"Well, theft is usually a sad—" I began, to be brought up short before I'd come to the end of my little platitude.

"*Theft*?" The schoolmaster spoke the word sharply and loudly, so much so that a number of boys looked in his direction. "Who called it that? Cunningham, I suppose."

I could have bitten my tongue out. Mr. Welbeck's eyes peering through the thick lenses were perfectly focused now, and on my own self, and their interrogative glare made me suddenly see him for what in fact he was: a figure of authority with the power and ability to reprove any erring or lazy boy.

"No, no," I assured him hastily, anxious not to calumniate my colleague, "it's probably me who's misunderstood."

"There were malicious tongues a-plenty only too pleased to brand the boy's action as precisely that, but I didn't know they were still at their foul work. *Borrow* money from me the boy did, even if without asking me. He left in my wallet a note explaining and apologizing for his deed and promising to repay me every farthing. As I am sure he would have done, I wasn't in the least worried, but then—*then* his own father got him into trouble for doing precisely the same thing to himself—removing cash but declaring his good honest intentions! Why my late colleague chose to treat his son as he did is quite beyond my comprehension, and always has been."

Feeling and indignation were not just apparent, they had momentarily taken over this gentle individual, whose sentences, so unexpected in content and emotion, assailed me like darts hurled at a board.

I was moved to say, "I am truly sorry, sir; I spoke completely out of turn. I probably was not attending properly to the little history Barton told me."

Mr. Welbeck sighed, then smiled, and was, I think, about to pat me on the back before thinking better of it; I was a stranger to him when all was said and done.

"I don't suppose you did misunderstand or mishear," he said. "The whole Cunningham family is addicted to gossip, I'm afraid. But because you are living at Mrs. Fuller's, whither Horace may return, one still hopes, I felt I ought to put the record right for you. I always liked young Fuller, you see, a most unusual boy. He is one of Nature's democrats, I do honestly believe"—that phrase again! Barton's own!—"and there are few enough of those around, in all truth. Always had a kind word for those who worked here, no matter in how humble a capacity. There was one little maid— Mary, her name was—whom he always stopped to talk to, even made things out of little odds-and-ends so she could put them in her room or on her person, threaded empty bird-shells or acorns on pieces of colored string. That sort of thing! And he never got praised for all his thoughtfulness."

So far today Mary's connection with St. Stephen's had clean gone out of my head. It was perhaps rather crass of me never to have wondered whether she had known Horace before his mysterious disappearance, for how could she not have done? Other people, other events in the past and present had somehow occluded Horace in my mind. The decidedly disconcerting picture of Mrs. Fuller sitting in the Mercy Room on Friday afternoon surrounded by objects bought for her son's delectation but rejected by him came to mind: "He wasn't contented here," she'd said, "in fact he was discontented, in the end nearly all the time. Many a boy would have given his eye-teeth to have only a fraction of what you can find in this room, but not Horace. He cared for none of it."

And now the buildings of St. Stephen's College, where Horace Fuller had prospered so ill, but of which so many members past and present were so vocally proud, were toweringly upon us. So commanding are these that I think any visitor to Kingsbarrow would feel himself a dull failure had he not ended his walk up the village High Street with passing under the tiled lych-gate into its front quadrangle, the first of a consecutive sequence of three. Not to do this would be to put yourself in the ranks of the lowly, the uneducated, even the unworthy. The solemn, geometric, red-brick domain ahead was daunting and compelling in about equal measures, and

I have to add that members of the boatered, blazered throng entered their destination in a happy enough spirit, as though it were one they were proud to be part of, and happy enough, too.

"A charming sight on a morning such as this," said the weak-eyed mathematics master, though, for all my reactions to the place indicated above, this would not have been my own epithet. Charming was Lucinda teaching the ragamuffins about flowers and trees, was the Houghs playing croquet, was idlers on the sea-front, was—yes, admit it—Hans coming into my bed at night. This place was too hard, too dominant, not to say domineering.

"What time, may I ask," Mr. Welbeck was inquiring, "is your assignment with Mr. Whittington?"

"Ten o'clock, sir!"

Was it my uneasy conscience or did Mr. Welbeck's face express surprise that I had chosen to come on the Swots' Express rather than later?

"Then you have plenty of time on your hands, and as a keen young journalist you would surely wish to get acquainted with the establishment which will be the subject of your pen. I am sure *The Advertiser* would expect you to do so, and now I come to think about it, I think our headmaster himself, speaking to me after chapel yesterday, expressed the hope that you could have a good look 'round before seeing him."

"That was most gracious of him!" I didn't care for the word I'd just used; horribly, it just slipped out of me. But it produced the kindliest of smiles on my White Knight's creased, pleasant, blurry-eyed countenance.

"Then allow me to find one of the older and abler boys—a Sixth-Former, a Prefect—to show you 'round. So proud are we at the college of our architecture," and he gestured toward the unhomely red piles, once again nearly causing exercise books to topple out of his attaché case, "that we exempt certain of our seniors from chapel or assembly or even from classes *if* they can make themselves useful as guides to interested visitors, whose presence means a lot to us."

"I would like that, sir!" I said. Well, it might help a bit with my article, mightn't it?

"Please then to stay where you are, and I will bring a Prefect to you just as soon as I can find one for the task."

"Azzy is the very nicest of men." Barton's laudatory statement was indubitably being confirmed. There he was, an unworldly man living quietly with his family and dogs, giving himself to the education of the young at a highly prestigious school, and writing important educational books (for so I thought they must be), who was prepared to bestir himself on behalf of a stranger. Besides his niceness had also been displayed to strange-sounding Horace Fuller, and was exercised to this day on his memory and reputation. He'd even recalled him stringing acorns, to form a kind of necklace, presumably, for the benefit of—the vehicle Mary. How that girl popped up in the most seemingly incongruous places! Connecting death and life, you might say—and there were those I'd met who would use that very phrase of her!

And here came back Azzy with my guide to St. Stephen's College in tow. Making the older man look even more like Tenniel's drawing come to life, white untidy hair still whiter and untidier, thick specs thicker, awkward gait more lumbering, this St. Stephen's prefect moved toward me with an ease of movement which also suggested a young soldier's disciplined straightness of body. His blazer and boater, though clearly designating the same establishment as those of other boys, were readily distinguishable from theirs. On his boater-band the stripes were narrower and the blue of a different, lighter hue, this variant of blue repeated in the trimming of the otherwise dark-blue blazer. Obviously here was a very superior being indeed!

"I have brought a very well-informed young Virgil to meet the requirements of your almost equally young Dante," said Mr. Wellbeck, "and, Mr.—" but he'd already forgotten my name. "I have made, I may say, a first-class choice. But let neither of you compare the place you walk through with Dante's original. That would not do at all." He emitted a rattle-like chuckle, and, uneducated as I was, only later did I understand he had jocularly referred to the *Inferno*. "So leaving you in these capable hands I bid you farewell." And awkwardly he turned on his ill-shod heels and left the prefect and me, a little shyly, to confront each other.

It was the St. Stephensite, of course, who spoke first. His immediately palpable physical self-possession was disconcerting, as was his particular brand of good looks besides which Will Postgate would have looked flashy, if not vulgar. "Well, Mr.—?"

"Bridges!"

"Mr. Bridges, Azzy—that is, Mr. Welbeck—says you have to see our Headmaster at ten o'clock, and that I should escort you in person to his study. Therefore, we have a fair bit of time in front of us, but I doubt it will be long enough to do justice to all the Coll has to offer. Are there any sights you particularly wish to be shown?"

"No, I leave things entirely to you," I said. In addition to being an important member of this community, he seemed, thanks to his pervasive self-confidence, rather older than myself, even though he also had much of the classical golden youth about him: fair hair springing back from the forehead, aquiline nose, long-lashed scabious-blue eyes, cupid's bow mouth, pink-and-white hairless facial skin (though I came to see two tiny tufts of fair stubble, one to the right of his upper lip, another at the base of his chin), broad shoulders, long, strong arms. Compared with him, I couldn't help thinking, what a sandy, scrubby little chap I must appear!

"The most important place in the entire Coll is, of course, the Chapel," announced the prefect in a suitably prefectorial voice, clear, firm, already deep-broken, but quiet-toned. "On Mondays the Headmaster starts the day with an Assembly through which he outlines the Coll's activities for the week ahead; otherwise we commence each day with a full service, a fuller one still, it goes without saying, on Sundays or feast days. So you are fortunate in having elected to come today on behalf of your paper if you want an undisturbed view of the heart of St. Stephen's."

Was I now! I was distinctly nonplussed by this little speech (for it surely was that) but replied to it breezily enough: "Right ho, then! Let's go there."

My guide did not budge, however. "Our visitors generally think it best to have the Chapel as the culmination of their tour. They can then avail themselves for a few minutes of its consecrated peace." A roundabout way presumably of saying that they could *pray* there? "I recommend we follow this course. I just wanted you to take in the Chapel before we proceed elsewhere. It was completed fifteen years ago to designs by the eminent architect, William Butterfield, though of course we used a local firm of builders for the greater part of the task, Messrs. Robinson and Forsyth of Dengate. Mr. Butterworth's patron, and our own too, Mr. Beresford

Hope found the result eminently satisfying."

It will not produce any astonishment in my readers that these names, so proudly uttered by this youth, were no more familiar to me than the Norwegian ones I have given earlier. Had I been interested in church matters (or known anybody well who was), had I been a real resident of Kent where he wielded such influence (even though he was Independent Conservative MP for Cambridge University), I would certainly have known about Beresford Hope (then living near Canterbury to die two years later), irrepressible parliamentary voice on religious affairs, often on behalf of his own Ecclesiastical Society and taking in their legal, architectural, and educational aspects, and the eminence behind the chain of Woodard Schools of Anglo-Catholic persuasion to which St. Stephen's itself belonged. But all this meant no more to me than the strange gods of the Kvens whom bo'sun Alfred Johnston had spoken of to Hans. So what could I say to my present guide but "That's good to hear"? The prefect looked mildly surprised (and disapproving?) at this, and doubtless at once got the measure of my educational and cultural level.

Anyway, he displayed little stronger than indifference to me as a person (even when I brought up the name of *The Advertiser*, which I did several times), masking, I thought, a certain (mild) disdain. Was it my clothes? My voice, my intonation, my way of walking? These ignominious doubts punctuated my whole time in his company until its strange conclusion, when my attitude changed, as readers will see. And that uncomfortable queasiness stayed in my intestines, shifting its precise location every so often, to send nausea rippling through me anew. And this on a fine morning in an atmosphere promoting and bespeaking vigorous health, for as my "inspection" (to use his curiously technical word) progressed, I saw many groups of boys making their orderly ways to appointed places, a number of whom inclined their heads deferentially to my guide, and how well set-up they all appeared, but how he eclipsed even the best-looking of them!

The tour began right in the very quad in which we were standing, with the old oak tree there. Planted apparently in 1701, it is encircled by a bench attached by iron-work to its vast, knobby bole.

"Only those of us who have earned School Colors can sit on it," the prefect said, with dignified pride. "We find it pleasant to be seated on a summer afternoon conning our books or talking over the finer points of a match with the leafy branches shading our heads. The sight of us can be quite an inspiration, I like to think, to younger boys like my own frater who will want in their turn to try for *their* colors."

Oddly this remark didn't sound as conceited as it does when I write it down. The oak tree—it features in many a book on Kent—stood in the quad dominated by the one old building in the complex; School House, originally Kingsbarrow Manor, built in 1578 in the then fashionable shape of an E (after Queen Elizabeth) and of a darker red than its neighbors, deepened by the centuries. Here I was shown the Refectory-cum-Prep Room, with long trestle-tables and a hammer-beam roof, and the School Colors' Den, whose name perhaps explains itself.

In the Library where we went next he asked me to admire sets of Gibbon and Samuel Johnson bestowed on the College by a "nameless benefactor."

"That benefactor is my father," the prefect told me in a subdued but matter-of-fact manner, "but he naturally does not wish this to be known. The library also has a quiet corner, to the back of the dictionaries section, which, like the bench 'round the oak, is reserved for those who have School Colors. The Corner, as we call it quite simply, can again act as an example to others. Also"—and here he could not restrain from a little smile of undisguised pleasure, which revealed, for a second, even in the hushed, shady gravity of this well-stocked library, something quite animal in him— "*also* we can keep an eye from it on anyone misbehaving, and deal with him—or them—accordingly."

And so on to—but I really mustn't weary my readers—to the gymnasium, the fives court, the tennis courts, the cricket pavilion, all scenes of many personal triumphs which my Virgil recounted to me so lightly that each might have been part of another boy's history, and a school museum, to the treasures of which—Roman pottery, flints, a few miscellaneous weapons of medieval warfare—the youth's father, yet again, had been an anonymous major contributor. Whoever could this Maecenas possibly be . . .?

I cannot pretend I wasn't relieved—while fearing imminent boredom —when my Virgil said: "And now for the Chapel."

Well, we approached this culmination of any proper St. Stephens tour from the second quadrangle one entire side of which was flanked by the cloisters. Above these "please note the fine row of Y-tracery plain-glass lancet windows . . ." Then after I'd duly noted them, and we were standing on the tiles of the cloisters floor, "There are two distinct doors into the Chapel, the one nearest the altar for the beaks and us prefects, the other for the rest of the school."

"Prefects stand a little nearer to God than the rest of 'em?" I suggested humorously, but my companion was obviously not amused. "Beresford Hope himself approved the scheme," he said, "because he thought it gave men here a due sense of the different stations proper to any society and how these should be properly respected."

With a reverential movement of his young sportsman's hands he now lifted the heavy bronze latch of the first of these two doors and motioned me inside. To the right lay the body of the chapel, the nave filled with rows of chairs but with pews on either side for seniors, perhaps those not yet elevated to prefectorial status, perhaps indeed of the rank of crinkle-top and his Horace-conning friend. To the left a flight of wide stone steps led up in a series of decreasing arcs to the altar. On reaching the communion table and the lofty Italianate crucifix presiding above it, the favored had two directions they could take—the one to choir-stalls and a grandiose pulpit, its sides carved with a pattern of lions and roses, and the other to further choir-stalls, the organ and some larger pews with something of the aspect of boxes at a theatre.

"That is where we fellows sit to pray," my informant told me.

"You fellows?" I queried. But I should have guessed.

"Yes, those of us with the School Colors." And just perceptibly he touched with his refined-shaped, neat-nailed fingers the light blue hem of his blazer. "As under the oak tree; as in that corner of the library."

I had of course got the point. I did not really like my guide, he was not my kind of person; after almost an hour in his company I could say this quite definitely. And I did not like the Chapel either, being unaccustomed to such places. I felt a need to turn the talk between us in as secular a direction as could be managed.

"For which sport did you get your colors?" I asked, in perhaps an inappropriately loud voice for this hushed place.

The prefect looked a little pained at both my matter and my manner, but he answered me nonetheless: "For almost all of 'em, actually. Footer, squash, Eton fives, and—naturally—cricket. I have represented the Coll in every one of those, at the highest level."

I remembered Barton Cunningham. "They might make you Victor Ludorum one day."

It was an impercipient remark. "But they did that last year. And from the point of view of the records, they should this year, too, for I have broken earlier achievements. But they may not want to make the same chap victor two years in succession. And I may not want to accept it, for the same reason."

"No, I can see that!" Personally, I didn't care one way or the other whether he got the cup; why indeed should I? Another nauseous current had sped through me. And the clammy adherent to my inside—that would surely vanish when my interview with the mighty Mr. Whittington was over and done with, but maybe not till then. I didn't want to stay in this Chapel much longer, so stuffily damp in this nice warm spring weather, and shuffled my feet as if in impatience.

But how was it that this red-brick building with its clear glass windows, not so unlike the great salon at Banstead Lodge, was penetrated on this clear sunny morning by shafts of deep emerald green and topaz blue which splashed the steps up to the altar? I raised my head and saw, high above the crucifix, a circular window set high above the window and depicting—even at casual glance this was clear enough—Jesus Christ walking on water. The now almost painfully bright emerald green was the banks of Lake Galilee, the painfully bright blue the waves on which He was treading.

My guide had noted my gaze: "Nothing is dearer to us than our rose window," he told me, though his tone was no more emotional than when he'd told me that naturally he'd got colors for cricket. "Mr. Beresford Hope of the Ecclesiastical Society wanted this to be one of the few school chapels distinguished by one, he felt it was in key with both the principles and practices of the place, the rose being so important to our religion, and so—as is often the case with Mr. Beresford Hope's ideas—it came to pass. Three of our leading artists working in unison designed it, and its execution was,

to a good extent, made possible"—I quickly guessed what was to come—
"by the generosity, once more, of my father." Perhaps I shouldn't keep my
eyes on this brilliantly-colored circle, that looked as it if were turning into
an orb, but the window *was* unusually magnetic. So much on it appeared
as if in motion; Jesus was surely coming a bit further toward me, and as for
the waves of the sea, were they not actually rippling?

"It was installed only last year, in a service conducted by the Arch-
bishop of Canterbury himself. Some four hundred people were present.
One lady looking at the figure of Our Lord asked, 'Who is that handsome
Boy from the Sea?'"

This remark—for who was *my* Boy from the Sea but Hans of last
night's intimacy?—made me for a matter of seconds so giddy I was obliged
to clutch on to the front of one of the pews. I had to avert my eyes from
the window now lest this Holy Boy approach me still more closely. Yet
wish to leave this place though I did, I did not feel just at that moment
steady enough to do so. Perhaps I should never have caught the Swots' Express, perhaps I should have had a longer, more leisurely breakfast, and
traveled straight to my interview with no conversations touching on the
Fullers, invaluable though I felt it had been, and no prefectorial tour guide.
Too late to think all that now. But to keep myself just a few moments longer
where I was, and not to disturb my inner clamminess any further, I found
myself saying—what indeed I'd been rather irreverently and irrelevantly
thinking: "Whatever do you School Colors chaps *think* about when you're
praying up there in those stalls?"

No sign whatever he thought me impertinent or offensive. On the
contrary, out the answer came as lightly, as effortlessly as if I had asked
him his name: "I can only speak for myself, obviously. What a fellow prays
about is very much his own concern. But I try to think about the Coll and
how I can best serve her, and I try also to put my mind to this great country of ours, and what I can do for *her* both at home and overseas. And I
pray for the happiness and prosperity of my own family who are so good
to me." This was so overwhelmingly different from the movements of my
own mind in almost any situation that I felt an intensification, more, a
worsening, of my physical unease, could feel too the blood draining away
from me . . .

"Here, are you all right? No, you're not, sir. I can see that. Come we better get you out of here!" All the youth's leadership qualities were in those words, given out, I should add, with instantly palpable concern, and in the action he suited to them. Seconds later I was, almost without knowing I was doing so, entrusting myself to him and being led out of the Chapel and into the cloisters outside which the whole quadrangle, with its huge velvet-green lawn, might just as well have been swaying upon the disturbed waters of Galilee so unstable was it to my gaze.

The prefect gripped my arm with muscular tightness. Then, "You going to chuck?" he asked.

And as he spoke that one vernacular word, all his snooty coolness, all his tendency to sanctimony, all his assumption of the airs of a "man" of rank, and all his dubious relish in exercising his allotted power fell away, and he became—well, a boy speaking to a boy. And I felt, surprising myself even amid my chagrin, greatly comforted.

"Mmm!" I made such noises, one, because I couldn't trust myself to speak, and two, I was sure that this was exactly what I was about to do.

"Trust me!" The prefect spoke to me as an intimate might, as old Will Postgate himself might do, and it was impossible not to acknowledge the kindness in his voice. "I know the place for the job, and it's not far. Between these Cloisters and the Library there's a little Garden of Remembrance, planted to honor Old St. Stephensites who joined the Services and fell for their country. Only beaks and those with School Colors are permitted to tread there. I'll lead you and you just concentrate on putting one foot in front of the other."

What a company-leader in India or West Africa he will make, I couldn't but think (rightly, as it's turned out!).

In this little garden sandwiched between the two largest structures of the school, grew bushes of lavender and rosemary, deliciously, cleansingly fragrant, and here, supported by the prefect who seemed to entertain for me and my malady no hint of that disdain I'd earlier found in him, I threw up copiously. The coffee I'd drunk, the kippers and the toast reluctantly served by Sarah at so early an hour and hastily bolted—out of me, in stinking little jets they all issued.

And confirming my feeling that my guide had changed radically in approach to me, "You poor chap!" he said. "It's the worst feeling in the world, isn't it?"

At that moment it was certainly hard not to assent. The "chucking" was not over until I'd given about five irregularly spaced heaves.

Then came the blessed moment when I could take a deep breath, and then another, and draw myself up into normal posture again. I accepted his offer of a handkerchief to augment my own for the wiping of mouth and face. And then thanked him for being my guide with a hearty sincerity I would not have envisaged possible a quarter of an hour before.

"I never caught your name," I apologized.

"I don't think I ever gave it you. Prefects don't usually do that when showing a visitor 'round; we prefer to be thought of as mere representatives of the greater whole, The Coll. But since you ask—it's Donaldson. Donaldson Major, or Ma as school usage has it."

Sometimes now I wonder if I hadn't already guessed. Nevertheless, weak as I was still feeling, I stepped back from him in recoil. And—just my luck! I thought—just as I was beginning to, well, *like* him. For I couldn't but remember that Barton Cunningham had said all the adulation at The Old Hole of the Donaldson family was enough to make one "chuck."

At this point bells began to ring out; the roast-meat-red walls of the symmetrically arranged blocks made them reverberate, while their peals swung up, as it seemed, to bounce against the blue panoply of the sky.

"That means five to ten, sir," my guide-and-helper told me, "and you're expected at the Headmaster's study—in School House—at ten. He is a very busy man, and appointments with him must be kept promptly."

"You best start leading me to him then!" I said. After vomiting, your whole bodily frame aches, as after cruel abuse. And what a state for a young reporter eager to be thought well of to find himself! Why, it might be thought that he'd spent the previous evening "on the ale"! Could have been true of some of Will's pals, could have been true of Will himself— occasionally—but never true of myself.

We walked slowly across the Old Quad, past the aged oak tree. I liked the former manor that was School House more than any of the buildings put up in more recent times for educational purposes, the Chapel included, and admired its line of mullioned windows now catching the sun, and the shape of its many tall old chimneys erect against the bright sky.

"You reacted to my name as if you knew it already," Donaldson remarked, "but it was doubtless the Pater of whom you'd heard. Sir Greeley Donaldson."

"But, of course!" I said. Barton should never hear of this encounter if I could help it!

"Here is the door to the Headmaster's study. I shall knock on it myself, and do whatever explanation I deem necessary, for in truth we are only two minutes late of the appointed hour . . ." My heart was thumping with agitation, more like a schoolboy's than that of an already fledged if still young man-of-the-world, while, to my disconcertion, another wave of giddiness, similar to what I'd just experienced in the Chapel, broke over me. "And may I thank you, sir," Donaldson was continuing, "for being so receptive and interested a visitor to the Coll, and may I express the hope that you will favor us some day soon with more of your time."

Readers, is this the point at which I should confess that I did actually attend the First of June Founder's Day which I was now to hear about, and with a seat reserved me in one of the front rows for that part of the ceremony (which included the Headmaster's speech) in Chapel Quad itself? For this day was to prove a turning-point in my Dengate life; of that I am now sure.

No sooner had Donaldson got out the first half of his sentence—"Here is your visitor, sir, and I am sorry to tell you that he has been in—" (*indisposed*, presumably)—than the tall, tonsured, clerical-garbed personage he was addressing cut in decisively with:

"The poor fellow! No need to say any more, Donaldson. He is clearly in need of ministrations!" His voice was loud, resonant, commanding, and kindly. "You may now leave everything to me, but once again very many thanks!"

Before I almost realized what was happening to me, I was asked to sit in a deep, soft armchair covered in dark green silk. It enveloped me, most welcomingly, as if made out of some miraculous soothing unction, and as it did so, I shut my eyes and tried to rectify my whole position to the world outside my body. Now at least I knew what Hans had experienced when he'd fainted at the Gateway. But I was *not* going to faint. I opened my eyes and looked up to see the ecclesiastical giant who was St. Stephen's Headmaster standing close beside me, smiling away.

"I wouldn't mind betting I know what's up with you, my dear Mr. Bridges," he said. "You got out of bed and did your ablutions too quickly this morning; you bolted your breakfast; you hastened to catch the train, up at an earlier hour than that usual for you as employee of *The Advertiser*; and, then—our fault perhaps, though we meant well—you went around sightseeing instead of quietly preparing for this meeting of ours."

"How—do—you—know—that?" I gasped out, impressed, because emotional factors apart, was he not right in his assumptions?

Mr. Whittington smiled yet more broadly: "I've been a young parish priest in my time who didn't look after himself sufficiently, have I not? And who thought he could dispense with doing so. When I'd given early morning communion, I'd rush back to my presbytery, and gobble my breakfast so fast it's a wonder any of it went down at all. However—I have made time for you, so let's have you sitting composedly a while and drinking some good hot tea—and then to business!"

Mr. Whittington had the sleeves of his soutane rolled up on this warm morning so that I could see that they were egregiously muscular, those of a formidable spin-bowler perhaps, an impression not contradicted by his disproportionately large, and equally muscular, hands. (I was later to learn that he was an ardent gardener.) Barton Cunningham had spoken, a little bit contemptuously, of "Dick" as being abbot-like, "monkish," and his noticeably round head did rather endorse this adjective. His hair proceeded in very straight strands from his tonsured crown, and in the morning light looked white, if surely not with age (I put the man at forty-five at the most). On scrutiny its color was shown to be the palest possible yellow, as though the sun had bleached it when he was performing his outdoor manual tasks.

The room that was his study Edmund Hough could well have called "cheerful," and it was far tidier than any of my Editor's. Bookshelves full of leather-bound volumes covered two walls, rugs soft to the feet and bright to the eye (Bokhara? Shiraz?) lay on the well-polished old boards of the floor; French windows, this morning about a quarter open, let in the aromas of the walled garden beyond, larger than that of Castelaniene, and full of lilacs, ornamental cherries, and in the borders, stocks and Sweet Williams. Near them, so that the sweet air could drift over him, stood the Headmaster's handsome rosewood desk. This was of the type, made in the earlier years of our century, called a Register Desk—a sloping writing surface above a fitted well on the top, with, on either side of it, a small band of drawers so convenient for the lighter tools of the writer's trade, and complementing the larger, more capacious drawers below. I coveted it at once, and my respect for the individual who owned it and kept it in such excellent and appetizing order (again, unlike Edmund back at the paper) increased.

There's further admission to come. When we eventually and unhurriedly got down to the matter of our meeting, I was—I can find no other expression!—won over by the man's enthusiasm for what had been arranged for Founder's Day in every corner of the College: friendly matches, contests in which members of boys' families could join in, instrumentalists' performances, readings of extracts from the gems of English Literature, and so on. As the Head expatiated on all the many and various festivities for the First of June, I was able to envisage the setting for each one, to see its intrinsic advantages and perceive how it would relate (either by attractive contrast or by naturally blending in) to what was going on in adjacent parts of the Coll. I was still engaged in doing this when the "great man" broke off, leaned forward and said:

"Donaldson Ma has, I can see, done a very good morning's work, your knowledge of the College—which to my absolutely certain knowledge you had never visited before—is absolutely exemplary. But I will go one further. Donaldson Ma had an egregiously good student. In fact, I will say that I have never met someone who has picked up the features of our establishment so quickly, so interestedly and been so tenacious of detail. You are truly to be congratulated."

Well, how could this not please me? How could not it incline me to a favorable picture of "Dick" Whittington, me always so responsive to praise, not least from a headmaster after having been so badly treated by my own? So when the man went on to say that he believed St. Stephen's met the great Beresford Hope's desiderata for every community, that it should strive to be a secular Sancta Civitas with every citizen, be he senior classics master or under-gardener, honoring God by cheerfully fulfilling his duties, I smiled, nodded my affirmation, and jotted down this lofty vision of the establishment, virtually word-for-word, in shorthand.

How different a return journey always is from the outward one! Those very orchards which only two hours earlier had announced liberation from the scene of my daily round, my entrance into the boundless-seeming fertility of the interior, of the Garden of England itself, now more and more presaged the Channel Port that already had absorbed the London boy I was. I had brought out sympathy—and, I dared to think, respect—in two of St. Stephen's most important "citizens," three if you counted Mr. Azariah Welbeck. What I had learned about the Founder's Day celebrations would make not just a decent piece, but an appealing one. And yet I could not say to myself in all honesty—but perhaps in all dishonesty I did do so that morning—that I either cared or approved of the institution I had visited and all that it entailed and all that I meant.

Come to that, what had my real reactions been to Furzebank Ho?

I can't answer these last questions, not fully, not satisfactorily, even as I write now.

Too satiated with recent impressions, and still trying to settle my recalcitrant system down, I leaned back in my dusty plum-colored compartment seat and began to review what I had taken in of the regime and values of St. Stephen's. And then—belatedly, it may seem to my readers—it occurred to me of all the information gleaned, none was more extraordinary, none deserved further analysis, than the (half-) statement by Mr. Welbeck that Mr. Fuller had drawn attention to his son's misdeed, even had it labeled as a far worse offense than it was—for Horace Fuller had explained to his father that he was borrowing the money and would endeavor to pay it back in full. And he'd always been so tenderly kind to young Mary.

That evening, after really very little thought on the matter, I slipped a note under the door of the Mercy Room:

Dear Hans,
After returning from this morning's visit to St. Stephen's College, I found that my activities on The Advertiser *have undergone a significantly increase. Good for me in most ways, though a little daunting also. I hope I'll be up to their expectations of me, but I will really need uninterrupted nights if I am to do all this new work as well as I can. I am sure you will understand this, and for your own health I believe that quiet nights will be the best thing too.*

    Yours very sincerely,
    Martin

CHAPTER TWELVE

Friendship's Changing Faces

*N*ever earlier would I have believed that Will's presence, and in the same house as myself, could prove bane rather than blessing. In South London I had cherished every moment I spent with him out of the office. But down here in Dengate he wasn't the old Will of London. Or— terrible, disloyal thought, perhaps he was! Could it simply be that, back then, I had been so patently his junior, so unabashedly in need of an elder-brother guide and protector, and he too vain and lazily good-natured to refuse the role, that I hadn't been able to see the extent of his indifference to almost all feelings of other people except their admiration, actual or potential, for himself? I should, I now told myself, have recalled more often our visit to Limehouse, that second dark event I still needed to confess to somebody but had, out of self-protection, suppressed so that it returned only in the occasional bad dream or involuntary twinge-like thought.

Now I see that my resentment of Will—from (to be truthful) Sunday night's supper to the Saturday morning he left Dengate (to be in time for a cricket match in Streatham on Saturday afternoon)—was inseparable from my severance from Hans. Fear of Will's finding out about our intimacies had beyond doubt played a huge part in my determining on this. But it would be incorrect—as well as dishonest—to blame him for what I myself had set in train.

But Will's own behavior was in itself vexing. Take his dealings with Mrs. Fuller herself, *my* landlady, *his* hostess. I ought to have known from his very appearance on the Furzebank lawn—togged up in his nattiest— that he had charmed the mistress of Castelaniene, for how else to explain that she had, almost on sight, offered him her private visitor's bedroom (her late husband's dressing-room). And Sunday's "light collation," during

193

which he'd told stories of himself as a man well-known in both worldly and radical circles, was the first of no fewer than five other evening meals. Mrs. Fuller no longer absented herself from her own table, but attired herself specially to grace it, sticking an absurdly large comb into her Grecian hair and draping over her shoulders a shawl I had not seen before—and I thought I knew them all. Sitting there I allowed my attention to stray— I had plenty, too much indeed, to think about, including the to me reproachful absence on Tuesday and Thursday evenings of Hans Lyngstrand, apparently feeling unwell again, and having his meal brought up to the Mercy Room by Sarah. That suited Mrs. Fuller and Mr. Postgate just fine, they could indulge in sophisticated badinage to their heart's content. And this young man who had so persistently mocked all forms of snobbery now encouraged Beatrice Fuller to talk about herself and her stupid petted early life, early visits to France, including a trip to Monte Carlo itself, her girlhood friendship with fascinating old Lady Winchelsea, and one never-to-be-forgotten experience the two of them had had in a small half-ruined old church on the edge of Romney Marsh where, indisputably alone one winter's afternoon, they had most definitely heard a monk singing a medieval chant through the shadowy chancel. At this point, I have to admit, that Will did turn to me and give me a surreptitious, unmistakably amused wink, but by this time (it was Wednesday, so the *fourth* damned dinner), I was too fed up to do anything but pointedly, unsmilingly, ignore it.

And Will's ways about the house—had I not noticed how he made Mrs. Fuller's usually pretty low spirits rise, had I not been fully aware that in any choice between the two of us, she would have straightway plumped for him—I would have been embarrassed by them. Why my very own parents—neither of them of Mrs. Fuller's lofty circle—would have considered him socially unacceptable. He walked around without his jacket or waistcoat, baring vulgarly bright braces and shirts with the sleeves rolled-up; he whistled as he performed his ablutions, shrilly and loudly, and even sang snatches of music-hall songs in that careless manner I'd formerly found endearing.

"Let me introduce a fellah,
Lardy dah, Lardy dah!
He wears a penny flower on his coat,

Lardy dah! . . ."

But he could (and did) vary that kind of thing with "*La ci darem la mano*," or "La *donna è mobile*" (sung in cockney Italian).

Yet had Hans Lyngstrand and I not been avoiding each other, had he not absented himself from two out of the five weekday meals, had he not kept the door of the Mercy Room more often shut than open, I would probably—despite all the above—have been less intolerant of Will. All Hans ever said about the letter I'd slipped under the door of the Mercy Room was "I agree with you, Martin! We both need a good night's sleep." And as if to demonstrate this need he was consumed by a terrible cough, rendering his face first alarmingly red, then alarmingly pale.

Mrs. Fuller was not the only female whose path Will crossed at Caste-laniene—and I am not thinking of poor Irish Sarah either with her "Roman" devotions. There was, of course, Mary, who came to the house every day except Sunday, the very day on which Will had arrived there. For obvious reasons "the little vehicle" and I could not exactly do as Hans and I were doing, keep out of each other's way. But, ever since the meeting at the Gateway we had tended not to look each other in the face when, as we were bound to do, we met—in hall, on landing, on embarrassingly nar-row staircase—though I gave the attic floor a wide berth when I knew there was any likelihood of her "doing" it. But the sly not to say furtive glances she regularly gave me out of sore eyes set in puffy cheeks repeatedly im-plied some disreputable secret between us (as there surely was; I did not feel that I came out of the evening at Banstead Lodge well). How in the world had it come about that this daughter of Dengate's Farthing Lane had discovered her ability to get in touch with the next world? And what had she thought of my acting on behalf of Hans Lyngstrand? Had she won-dered at a bond between us?

And I more than suspected she had. Whether her intuitive powers really extended beyond the tomb I was from the first sceptical, but just from observing her I felt they were quite formidable when exercised on the still living. And now I could add to myself—though probably wasn't candid enough to do so—that she was perfectly capable of telling the dif-ference between a bed slept in by a single person and one slept in by two! Will however had no such recollection or suspicion to impose itself between his appreciative eyes and Mary's ubiquitous body. I knew only too well that before long he would make a jaunty remark about her to me when we were alone together. And he did. It was late on Tuesday afternoon—Will's drawings had now gone over to our printers' to be readied for Wednesday's issue of *The Advertiser*—and the two of us were sauntering homewards to St. Ethelberga's Road.

And, out of the blue, he remarked: "I'm quite surprised, my friend, you've never spoken to me of Mary, a nice little wench fair to outward view, that is if she could get over her summer cold, or whatever it is that's the matter with her."

Needless to say, I blushed at this, deeply, hotly, but hoping Will would not notice. However he did.

"Oho, so you *have* taken her in," he crowed, grinning. "If she could get her flesh a little more evenly distributed and a spot of color into her face—which we won't call 'pasty,' will we, Martin?—then the old poetic word 'buxom' might be applied to her, *n'est-ce-pas*?"

"I wouldn't have thought so," I mumbled. "That suggests quite a different sort of—character." Buxomness surely went with Edmund's prized quality of "cheerfulness." It would be hard to think of anybody with less of this attribute than Mary Poulton.

"So you've given the lass a bit of thought," he said, grin staying on his face like the Cheshire Cat's in *Alice*. "Glad to hear it. I'm relieved your only preoccupation isn't Our Sensitive Sailor from across the German Ocean."

I didn't like the tone of this, and a current of decided resentment of, if not downright hostility to, Will ran through me. "Since Mary appeals to you so much, even though not yet buxom," I said tartly, "you could do worse, I suggest, than find out a bit more about her."

"I've found out quite a lot about her, thank you very much, Martin. I am rarely slow or silent (or deaf for that matter—sometimes to my peril) when it comes to girls."

"Oh?" And I could hear aggression in my voice, but I must keep it low. Every bow-windowed façade in the residential street might have ears. "So what things about her do you now know?"

Will tossed the sketch-pad he'd been carrying up in the air and deftly caught it; as a sportsman he relished such displays of his prowess, however trivial. "What do I *not* know, soldier? The dear thing can be quite a little chatterbox at times. I know that Mr. Poulton senior (who may well, she fears, not be her father) is a bricklayer by trade who has fallen on hard times—like so many men in this glorious decade of English history in which we are privileged to be living. That her mother was ill after the birth of her last child, and still has to drink porter daily. That the late Mr. Fuller—clearly a most admirable individual; it'll be a brave man who walks in his shoes!—took pity on her when she was working at your horrible St. Stephen's College and, out of the goodness of his heart, found her a place in his own household. And I have in fact come across a very interesting confirmation of his feelings for Mary . . ."

"Come across?" I couldn't keep the interest out of my voice. And felt they boded badly.

"Yes, up in my room I have been giving the Dear Departed's impressive array of books a looking-over. Impressive in *number* that is, I'm not much of a one for the classics, as you should know by now. In my opinion the allegedly magnificent classical education accorded to our upper crust is more a curse than a blessing. Anyway in between the pages of a volume of Odes by a chap named Pindar—one of those books full of footnotes in tiny print—I found four little samples of Mary's hair, each labeled."

"Of Mary's *hair*!" I clapped my hand over my mouth for I feared I'd spoken too loudly in the polite quietness of this street. It was possibly—outside Hans's stories—the most extraordinary thing I'd ever heard!

"Yes, Mary Grace Poulton, aged 10—Mary Grace Poulton, aged 12—Mary Grace Poulton, aged—"

For some reason I didn't want to hear any more. "Yes, I get the point!" I cut in impatiently. But only in a literal sense did I do this. Why, at the ages Will had cited, Mary wasn't even skivvying at St. Stephen's. Just romping about Farthing Lane, presumably, dodging or minding her numerous baby brothers and sisters.

And then into my head came old Azzy Welbeck's words defending Horace Fuller: "I always liked young Horace, a most unusual boy, one of Nature's democrats. Always had a kind word for those who worked here, no matter in how humble a capacity. There was one little maid—Mary, her name was—whom he always stopped to talk to, even made things out of little odds-and-ends so she could put them in her room or on her person, threaded empty bird-shells or acorns on pieces of colored string. That sort of thing!"

Yet at the time he was engaged in such charming acts of kindness to a small girl, she was already so well known to his father that he was taking samples of her hair, docketing them and slipping them into a volume of Pindar (of whom I *had* in fact heard, if no more than that).

Will himself had not apparently noted this discrepancy, though he had in his possession all the facts needed to do so. "And she is a keen reader," he continued. "She likes the Brontë sisters. She can write a beautiful hand, thanks to Beatrice Fuller, and she's even taught herself shorthand into the bargain. One day she hopes to rise above the servant-class—even her position in a cultured household like Castelaniene—and become someone's private secretary. That'll be the day!"

Annoyed as well as more than a little surprised by my friend's boastful account of his knowledge of Mary which so outshone my own, I said: "Well, Will, there is still more you could learn about her, I think."

"You have in mind . . .?" There was a lubricious twang to Will's voice.

"The fact that she regularly relays messages from the dead."

"You don't say!" He sounded, as I'd both hoped and expected, incredulous.

"Hasn't she told you about it?"

"Relays . . .? The dead . . .?" I had shot a successful bolt here all right. Will was the most stalwart of skeptics. "I don't believe you, Martin. It isn't true."

I suppose it is a sign of the fashion of our times—where séances of one sort or another continue still to be quite the thing, and in a variety of circles, including those eminent ones graced by the great W. T. Stead himself—that his dismissal of my information did not sound as whole-hearted as it might have been on some other topic.

"There's only one way to find out—ask her!" I retorted and quickened my pace toward Castelaniene with the monkey-puzzle tree in its garden and the conspicuously many-colored fanlight over its door.

I am pretty sure he never did. Perhaps I'd set up doubts enough in him to nip for once a little underhand dalliance in the bud. It would have appealed to him, enjoying the favors of a skivvy employed by a woman to whom he was being the attentive young gallant; it had happened before after all. Maybe he had already snatched a kiss, indulged in a little deft pawing on the stairs—or am I extrapolating here from my own buried store of carnal fantasies? But to have a liaison, however brief, with a practicing medium was quite another matter.

Practicing medium? To say this phrase to myself was to arouse questions I had not quite allowed to occupy me; they were surely worth asking. How had Mary discovered her strange powers? How had Mrs. Fuller known that she possessed them? What had led them, singly or in duo, to the Gateway, and how had others there—a haughty, educated crew—come to be so impressed that they had agreed to make Mary (for all I could see) their only conductor to the road trodden by the dead?

At *The Advertiser* they all took to Will, damn him!—well, he did not meet Mr. Betterton, as Dep Ed his own coeval, until Thursday. But with that exclusive duo, Philip Goodenough and Archie Percy, he was on joking terms within (as it seemed to me) a matter of seconds. They were amused by the sight of his artist's block, and asked him if he would like them to pose for a portrait, and told him it was like having Leonardo or Raphael about the place. Will beamed in response from ear to ear. To Terence Hathaway, soft-spoken, bushy-bearded king of layout, Will as illustrator was directly answerable, and he addressed him with a lightly borne but patently sincere respect that would have melted a far less warm heart than that exemplary one. Before long too Will was swapping and sharing very specific financial details with Mr. Forrester, our business manager. (I can't say whether Will gave him genuine quotations of affairs at my former newspaper or whether he just plucked them out of the air—something he would even nowadays be capable of doing.)

When he saw the Bible beside the balance-sheets on Mr. Forrester's desk, Will—usually a proselytizing unbeliever—commented (the hypocrite!): "Ah, there's such practical wisdom between those covers—even for those coping with the money problems every newspaper in the country poses!" And Mr. Forrester's thin, severe, Primitive Baptist's face lit up, so unaccustomed was he to hearing from his colleagues good words about the Good Book.

Waggling his chin so his wispy beard so like a painted Chinaman's wriggled in the air, he said: "It's a real pleasure hearing a man as young as yourself say that."

With the man who was as young as himself, to whit Barton Cunningham, Will was markedly less friendly; indeed without being rude he was not friendly at all. Despite the fact that they had been on the same (winning) side in the croquet game, no bond had been forged between them, and Will, whenever, between sketching bouts, he was hanging about the offices, did not once go over to Barton's corner. But though he did not overdo it, he made himself very much at home with Edmund himself. In fact, to hear the laughter that punctured their talk, and the names of the amazing number of chaps they knew in common, you would have fancied that here were two old friends, and that Will, though youthful in mien and manner, was essentially of Edmund's ilk, rather than Barton's or mine.

When his drawings appeared in Wednesday's edition of our paper, they were universally commended. In fact the whole issue (which contained some advance notices for Founder's Day at St. Stephen's College) gave general satisfaction. Edmund had really gone to town in his piece on the Church Steps, which was not only given pride of place but took up the best part of two pages. Nobody reading it could possibly attribute the Deputy Editor's accident to his having been tight; on the contrary it made it clear that proper civic action had not been taken over a spot that had spelled danger for Dengaters for a long while. Will's drawings—which had come out well, our printers had excelled themselves—emphasized all Edmund's points in easily assimilable form.

Talented though I had long believed Will, causing me to treat him at times with something like awe, I now realized I was capable also of underestimating him. Amusing caricatures passed around in an office or a Soho restaurant were one thing, helpful but intrinsically satisfying illustrations to a serious article that nevertheless could stand up for themselves, quite another, and I had not appreciated that he had either the gifts and the know-how to achieve them. He would, it was generally agreed, be the perfect choice to illustrate the grand opening of the Bandstand itself. What could be higher praise then that?

• • •

The weather was both fresh and pleasantly warm, a combination that distinguishes May at its best. Windows in offices were open to admit the day's light breeze, indoors men and boys took off their jackets and rolled up sleeves. But the temperature was energizing rather than enervating; one's thoughts went to lambs bounding about in fields outside the town boundaries, or to birds with twigs in their beaks finding new trees for nests, and you felt you could easily match such liveliness with activities of your own. Were Hans Lyngstrand in the good health he deserved, then he and I would be setting off late afternoon/early evening for some long cliff-top ramble—or else we'd go down together to the nets of the local cricket club, where we'd find Peter Frobisher and sometimes Barton Cunningham practicing. As it was the two of us could express our needs, our yearnings, our increase of spirits only in the quiet of night, in the confines of a bed, and this communication I had now jettisoned. Forever!

"Does us all good, doesn't it?" Philip Goodenough was pleased drawlingly to remark, sticking a pencil behind his ear and preparing to give what he'd been working on a good read-through, "to be free from Him-with-the-Gold-Watch-and-Chain."

No doubt who he was referring to, no doubt too that his sentiment was shared by everybody within earshot, and probably (thinking of Edmund in his office) by those out of it as well.

"There's loyal, there's respectful," grinned Archie Penry, while even the virtuous Arthur Forrester couldn't quite find it in himself to disagree, though the hour of the morning was upon him when he liked to exchange advertisements for the Good Book. But we were later to think it unfortunate that Philip had said what he had; sailors are not the only men who are superstitious. For which of us could not feel when we heard the unmistakable sounds from the stairwell of a stick being thudded purposefully on step after step, and a middle-aged man's heavy breathing and equally heavy gait coming closer and closer to our open door that this unwisely slighting reference to him, this articulation of continuing pleasure at his absence had conjured the Dep Ed out of the fragrance of the May air, and brought him into the premises, there to shatter our calm?

"Thomas," Edmund, who also had heard these betokening sounds, stepped vigorously (but a little apprehensively too, I thought), "how good to see you! And how brave of you, when you're still merely on the mend, to venture forth to visit us on publication-day!"

Never had the contrast between the two men seemed greater, and obviously my own perception was heightened by what Barton had told me about his godfather earlier, his career in Bengal, his hopes for himself on *The Advertiser,* his bitterness that these had been disappointed. Mr. Betterton's accident, and the walking-stick it had forced on him, made him look rather old, a bit older indeed than his fifty-five or fifty-six years. He was out of breath, in patent discomfort, and the whites of his eyes were heavily veined. His stomach, protected from the world though it was by garments of which the waistcoat was the uppermost, looked today more uncomfortably bulky than ever, by contrast with which Edmund's portliness appeared merely the comfortable layers of a man who liked to live as well and easily as he could and believed so much in instinctual good health that he was prepared to leave questions of weight and diet to Nature herself. Mr. Betterton suggested in his movements and the suspicious play of his eyes discontent with life, a grudging conviction that he was being cheated of his rightful due, whereas Edmund gave off contentment, a (modestly proportioned) pleasure in himself and his place in the world, even if he were, as at this moment, worried or uncertain about something.

Mr. Betterton by way of reply to his superior's somewhat over-effusive greeting thumped his stick on the floorboards.

"I have read today's issue," he said, in so ringing a voice that the whole newspaper team went silent. "I have read it from cover to cover." Philip and Archie's mouths dropped open, I swear, in unison; they could scarcely believe their luck that a scene (what else?) was to take place for which they had front seats.

"I think—well, to tell the truth, I know already," said Edmund, "that the powers-that-be will get their skates on where the Church Steps are concerned—and several comparable places, all pointed out in my article."

Mr. Betterton, to our united surprise, gave a sarcastic little half-bow here, an inclination of the head in mock-gratitude, unfortunately causing his dewlaps to shake. "I thank you, Edmund Hough," he said, "as a result of your words that idler, our mayor, should be stirred into some civic-minded action at long last! In that sense, you can say—you *will* doubtless say, to satisfy your conscience—that the latest *Advertiser* has given a senior figure in the community, to whit myself, sadly brought low by physical mishap, some necessary consolation, some hope that justice will be dispensed and that in future others will go safely where, alas, I did not."

Philip stifled a snort of laughter here, which mercifully Mr. Betterton, intent on his duet with the Editor did not notice. For of course if Mr. Betterton had drunk less at his Masonic "do" that evening, then, for all the failings of the steps, he surely would *not* have fallen over and injured himself. And, all of a sudden, I appreciated that the Dep Ed was himself perfectly aware of this fact, and, neither fool nor innocent, knew that many other Dengaters would also be. Therefore, he would have preferred there to be no piece at all on the subject in his town's one paper. Yes, of course, he was exonerated by what Edmund had said, the blame for his accident had been laid elsewhere sufficiently plainly and with enough documentation to quieten all malicious wagging tongues. But they might have quietened even faster had Edmund simply written nothing.

"But there are other features of the issue with which I am rather less satisfied," Mr. Betterton, resting his considerable weight on his stick, turned himself slowly around to see that we were all taking his words in. "I am a journalist, a newspaperman of experience, Edmund Hough, with very many years' hard, and—dare I say it?—distinguished experience behind me."

"Indeed you are, I would be the first to proclaim it," said Edmund. "I don't know what we would all do without you."

His was not the most judicious choice of words.

"I can tell you what you would do without me; indeed, I will *tell* you." Awkwardly, one might almost say precariously, Mr. Betterton moved his free arm so that he could point to the most recent copy of our paper. "*That* is how you would fare. A paper that sets at nought my plans and hard-earned practices as a thoroughgoing professional who has worked in offices from Dakar to Dengate."

It was at this moment, I now think, that I knew for sure that I myself would not be spared the Dep Ed's spoken displeasure. I saw Barton Cunningham and myself truculently busying ourselves on the man's portly Remington. How could we defend ourselves?

"What, might I be so bold as to ask, happened to the account of the celebration of Judge Pettifer's sixtieth birthday?"

Edmund did not look embarrassed, let alone guilty, as he answered: "Oh, we had to hold that over, I'm afraid." And this, though I had with my own ears heard him say to Archie: "Oh, I think that can go the way of all flesh—if not the Judge's just yet. But you'd better hold on to the article just in case." So, I knew that I was not the only person who did not tell the entire truth when it suited him; the estimable, the virtuous Edmund did not.

"Hold it over, pray? Until an issue even more unsuitably further away from the good Judge's natal anniversary than this week's?"

"Well, always better late than never!" said Edmund cheerily, and I have to admit that he didn't sound as if he meant what he was saying, nor that he cared that he didn't.

This was surely what Mr. Betterton himself thought. "As you say, Edmund, as you say," he said, in a significant voice. "Always provided—this goes without saying—it is preceded by an editorial note to the effect that the paper humbly apologizes for its tardiness in its publication."

"I don't know about *humbly*," said Edmund, "but an apology of some sort might not come amiss, I do agree. It was all the Church Steps material that left us so cramped for space for other subjects."

Touché, I would have thought, and for a moment the wind did appear to be taken from Mr. Betterton's full sails. Reprieve for Barton and me perhaps? But in fact the man was preparing to air his next grievance, and to air it so that it went home to the malefactors.

"I have not finished. Not by any means. I next come to the Higginson and Busby affair."

Higginson and Busby? I had all but forgotten the names in the case that Barton and I had used as a means of showing the beauties of the W. T. Stead–like new journalism. This was the name of the firm that had gone bankrupt in circumstances that had led its directors to impugn other firms with whom they been dealing.

"When I relate a history, sir," said Mr. Betterton principally to Edmund, "I relate it in logical, not to say chronological stages, so that step by step the incidents, the events, call them what you will, are clear to our readers.

I obey in short the laws of Cause and Effect. But when I turn to the account in this week's *Advertiser*, what do I find?"

Bang-bang went his stout stick on the floor, while *wriggle-wriggle* went my innards, like an invasion of worms. "I find, sir, a flouting of these laws, that it begins at the end and works backwards and then forwards again, a whole lot of modern nonsense that I ABHOR." This time he really did shout—no two ways about it. "Yes, *abhor*. That method is here today but will be gone tomorrow, when the time-tested, indeed time-hallowed ones will return."

I looked across at Barton Cunningham as at a partner-in-crime who must be having the same uncomfortable sensations as myself. And saw him staring down at his shoes as if that were the only place he wanted to look.

"Perhaps, Mr. Bridges, you could tell me the name of the process by which this time-hallowed structure is—shall we say—overthrown?"

Yes, I was actually being addressed; this was not one of those moments of embarrassment that the imagination feels so often compelled to construct, but the real thing.

"Name?" I idiotically stalled.

"Yes, I believe this new, this Eighties way of doing things has a name."

Then it was that I knew Barton Cunningham and his godfather had had a conversation prior to the dramatic entrance and angry harangue by the latter, and that the younger man had, reluctantly, enforcedly, admitted what we had done, and in doing so was obliged to mention my name.

"Come sir. I'm waiting for your answer," continued the Dep Ed. "I'm all impatience, you see, to learn the correct, the *London*, the metropolitan, term for this wondrous journalistic innovation."

So many eyes burned their intent mocking gaze on me it's a wonder the skin of my face wasn't completely scorched off. And Barton Cunningham's head was bowed so low I wondered it didn't fall off his trunk and bump onto the floor. All I could see of him was his carrot-top.

"Inverted pyramid," I managed to say.

"Come again, how much?" Very nearly toppling his heftiness over, Mr. Betterton was pleased comically to cock an ear forward to catch the low-spoken syllables of my answer.

"Inverted pyramid." The phrase sounded irredeemably pretentious spoken as it now was, by a self-conscious neophyte, into a deadly silent room of hostile ears.

"Oh, that explains everything, and I thank you kindly for your invaluable assistance in bringing me up to date." And Mr. Betterton made me the same parodic bow he'd proffered Edmund. "As I now understand it, the process entails beginning with the rear and ending with the prick—oh yes, it's all so clear now." Coarse language I had heard from schoolboys, soldiers, and East End stevedores, and neither I nor anybody else could be completely sure whether the Dep Ed had made a deliberate anatomical *double entendre* or not; Archie winked at Philip who winked back, Peter Frobisher, amazed at hearing the word "prick" spoken by a man he regarded as a veritable ancient, giggled into the hand he hastily put over his mouth.

Edmund, who (as I now know) had so elevated and Meredithean a view of natural functions that he thought verbal obscenities little short of blasphemous, and who was clearly anxious to get his staff back to their duties, now stepped in—literally at that; he advanced toward us—to bring to a close the scene his Number Two had decided to stage.

"Well, well, well, this is not the end of the world, we're talking about," he said, and then seeing the frown he'd brought to Mr. Betterton's red-eyed, red-flushed face, went on: "All the same we do owe you an apology. Since the article in question does not bear your name, no one, Thomas, will ever ascribe its stylistic peculiarities to yourself." It then occurred to me what I'd best keep to myself: that Edmund, knowing Barton and me to have worked on the piece, had himself read and approved it, for likely his view of his senior employee's work was pretty much the same as my own, stoked by (I saw more clearly than ever) a strong personal antipathy. "But I do remember, Bridges, your employing the term 'inverted' . . ." —he couldn't bring himself to go on, possibly, it later occurred to me, because it tickled him, made him want to laugh aloud—"whatever-it-is and maybe you should bear in mind that however interesting a method of presentation it is you should reserve it only for those pieces you yourself have been commissioned to write."

If Mr. Betterton thought over these words from his chief, as I'm sure he did, he would have realized that there was precious little of rebuke to me in them, or of support of himself. But Edmund's tone was suitably emollient, and besides he added: "Bridges, I think perhaps you could express your regrets to Mr. Betterton—and forthwith. And then we can bring the whole wretched business to a close."

With blazing face and awkward tongue I said, in a voice that all had to strain to hear: "No offense was intended, Mr. Betterton, and I am sorry if it were taken."

Mr. Betterton nodded his huge head once again, as if in receipt of this, and I have to say right here that he never referred to the matter again, at least not to my face, though he did not trouble to disguise that he did not much like me. In his position I might myself, I now think, have been angrier, even more vindictive. While he was not (for me anyway) a sympathetic or appealing man, or even a tolerably admirable one, he had principles, and it was these that guided him to working hard for an editor younger than himself, promoted above him, and representing uncongenial political and social views as well as being temperamentally incompatible.

Why, my readers may be asking, did I not get up on the spot, and cry out: "This is unfair, this is intolerable! I'd never so much as heard of 'inverted pyramids' before Barton Cunningham told me about them, and started applying the principle, quite off his own bat but urging that I assist him, to his godfather's uncompleted article." Surely readers can supply the answer themselves. "Thou shalt not sneak" is the schoolboy's first commandment, and woe betide him who breaks it; he will find it hard to live with himself afterwards, and, perhaps more importantly, others will find it hard, and probably impossible, to live with *him*.

And Barton Cunningham, for his part, who was sitting near me, now shuffled himself along, and, raising his head so that I saw his pale face as well as his red hair, and speaking according to our code, said: "You were a brick just now not to say more than you did. About—about the I.P., you know. It's made me decide—when we're alone together, to let you into my confidence."

And this he did, out in the sun-drenched Dengate street: "The thing is, Bridges, I have this damned wanderlust thing I just can't cure myself of—however hard I try. I want to go back to Bengal—no matter how much it rains there, no matter how terrible the climate is and how far away from everything. You never know—I might even make a little pile out there, like

Godfather Betterton, and come back home to England to live in style. There's only one other person I've confided this to—and, this won't surprise you, I think, that's Lucinda Hough. She was very understanding; I think she knows what it's like to feel cooped up. And that, by the bye, is the only understanding we *do* have."

The day being Wednesday I decided to walk the long way home for the obvious reason. The turquoise stretches of the sea to my left rippled in the breeze, down on the beach two boys were trying to push out a rowing-boat. Then before me the Royal Gardens presented themselves, the Bandstand glinting in the sun, that edifice which Will before so very long would be honoring with his artistry. I passed through their gilded wrought-iron gates, keeping myself hidden from full view by the avenue trees.

And see them I did, as I thought I would, from behind the larger horse-chestnut—saw first, rather as if they were further growths of the full-flowered magnolia, their two straw hats first, in such proximity as to resemble a single statue of a happy pair on a grassy plinth. The children from Farthing Lane and its like had scattered rather diffusely on the lawns; clearly their demands could not compete with Will's panache. As so little could.

Lucinda was wearing purple gingham that afternoon, and when she removed her straw bonnet, the sun made her copper hair shine in a hundred different tints of gold and red.

I pass now to Friday, the last complete day of Will Postgate's present Dengate stay.

That day, back from work earlier than usual, I had no sooner entered Castelaniene than I heard a loud *rat-tat-tat* on the front door which, no immediate response to it coming from any quarter of the house (Sarah, down in the basement, was anyway, I now realized, a little deaf) it surely fell to me to answer. *Rat-tat-tat, rat-tat-tat* again!—this was someone with a sense of his or her own urgency and even importance. But there on the doorstep I discovered a boy, thirteen at the very most, whose eager, happy, polished-looking face announced no kind of calamity. I took one look at his grinning rosebud mouth, at his brown eyes and the little snub nose on a face as freckled as my own, and even before he'd told me his purpose, heard in my head that idiotic music-hall song:

> "Mary Ellen at the church turned up,
> Her mother turned up, and her dad turned up,
> Her auntie Gert and her rich uncle Bert,
> And the parson with his long white shirt turned up,
> But no bridegroom with the ring turned up,
> But a telegraph boy with his nose turned up
> Brought a telegram which said he didn't want to wed,
> And they'd find him in the river with his toes turned up."

I'd always felt sorry for the boy in these lines who brought such dreadful news to Mary Ellen who would be hurt, offended, and shamed by it. I hope she treated him decently, but who could blame her if she didn't? Shooting the messenger is an ancient tradition after all.

This Friday afternoon's little telegraph boy said with perky pride: "Got *two* telegrams, sir. One's for the lady of the house, and other one for someone with ever such a funny name! Never had to deliver *two* 'grams to the one place before, and both to different persons, and I been doing this job ever since Jem Hackston gave up." (Clearly, in his estimation a long time ago!)

"I'll take 'em both," I said, a little apprehensively because I was far from sure that the persons being addressed would want me to see the contents. But there was the boy waiting to see whether there was any answer, and nobody had come into the hall, so I had no alternative to taking the matter into my own hands and reading the 'grams, now did I?

The one for Beatrice Fuller herself read: "ACCEPT THE DISAPPEARED'S OFFER FORTHWITH. YOUR TRUSTY ADVISER." The provenance was Canterbury, where I knew Mrs. Fuller's lawyer to live.

I felt a trembling throughout my body at the word "disappeared" with its associations with the Gateway. But giving a direct answer to the telegraph boy was easy enough.

"No reply!" I told him, "Mrs. Fuller will be dealing with it herself in her own time." (And this despite the word "forthwith"!)

"My boss," said the boy, "says the other 'gram's not English. Thinks it must be to do with that Norwegian ship what capsized in the Channel."

And indeed MR. HANS LYNGSTRAND was the addressee of the other telegram. My pulse quickened to the point of discomfort. I unfolded it with a sense that I might be trespassing on territory as foreign to me as that revealed in Hans's stories of life on *Dronning Margrete*.

"TIRSDAG KOMMER JEG TIL MAJESTIC HOTEL, DENGATE. VI SES! KARSTEN STRØMME," it read. Karsten Strømme, Hans's patron, that man of influence and power, was surely announcing his arrival in Dengate, to escort back to Norway a Hans now judged suitably rested and restored.

Aloud I said: "Yes, your boss was right, it *is* to do with the ship that sank. One of the survivors is at present living in this house, you see."

"Coo!" said the boy, and his eyes widened in appreciative interest, as if I'd been telling him I had personally rescued this particular survivor. "Coo, you don't say!"

"The words here are Norwegian, of course!" I told him further. "There's nothing to say in return." Then, remembering the question of payment, I fumbled in my pocket to find a coin or two. In fact I pulled out more than I'd intended but felt I could hardly put them back. "Here, take these, soldier," I said, feeling it was good for my own self-respect to use Will's big-brotherly term for me to somebody unmistakably younger than myself. "I bet you were wanting to knock off for the day rather than traipse up here to St. Ethelberga's Road."

"Oh, I never mind when I have work to do," the boy told me, his eyes shining with patent sincerity. "A deliverer of telegrams is indispensable to the whole community is what Mr. Pritchett always says."

"Mr. Pritchett?"

"He's my boss in the telegraph room, isn't he? I'm his favorite 'gram-boy, the one what he can always trust to do a job properly. Anyway, thanks you for the tin, sir, it'll come in handy. I'm saving up for a dictionary for my very own personal use. I've got ambitions, you see." He gave me a salute and stepped neatly backwards off the doorstep. "I trust what I brought was good news."

I didn't in truth think either telegram could be so described. There was an ominous quality emanating from the one sent by the "trusty adviser," with its implication that time was of the very essence. As for the other, well, Tuesday, May 19, lay not at all far ahead. It might well be the date when I parted from Hans forever.

And yet hadn't we parted already? There was something within myself that did find the second telegram "good news": it would be a relief to have Hans removed from the daily scene. The breach between us was unbearable, each passing day made it worse. And yet did I want to mend it?

But I must be a man and take Hans what after all was his.

I took his telegram upstairs to Hans himself, after placing that for Mrs. Fuller prominently on the hall table. It seems to me now that I knocked on the Mercy Room door like a somnambulist.

After his muffled "come in!" I entered to see him sitting in his chair which he'd now arranged directly below the gap between the two dangling Spanish galleons, perhaps thinking doing so was the best way of coping with the strong aura imparted by all the room's cluster of objects. On his knees I saw what else but that book on Thorvaldsen—he must know the text as well as the images off by heart by now! When he saw me standing before him, no smile lightened his face as it would have done any day before Monday, May 11, but he did not scowl or turn his head aside or tell me to go away. I suppose he must have realized that I had come up on some serious errand independent of the issues between us, and of course it's possible that from the very first moment of my appearance he saw that it was a telegram I was holding in my hand.

"Hullo, Martin," he spoke with a disconcerting formality, but then he often did. "It's a beautiful afternoon and I have been spending a good part of it outside in the garden. So lovely. But then I felt a bit tired, a bit of the old trouble though not too much," and he patted his chest, "so I came to my room for a rest. But I am feeling all right now."

"I am pleased to hear that, Hans. I've come to bring you *this*—it just arrived for you!" and I waved the 'gram, for which, after all, I had paid out of my own money. "I had to read it, I'm afraid, because the boy who brought it needed to know if there was an answer. It's in Norwegian, but I think I understood its import."

It goes without saying it took him but a few seconds to read. Nor did its contents in any degree surprise him! "So Karsten is arriving just as he said."

"As he said—" I repeated wretchedly for I had known nothing of his patron's imminence, a fact surely of the greatest significance to our friendship, that is if I had not prevented its development.

"Yes, I received a letter from him on Monday saying that he would be in Dengate on Monday the eighteenth or Tuesday the nineteenth. He had some shipping business to attend to in London first. I suppose it must be taking slightly more time than he had thought. '*Tirsdag*' is Norwegian for Tuesday, you know."

"That's what I supposed," I answered, "but why did you not tell me about all this, Hans?"

"I was going to, but—I did not know that you wanted to hear things from me."

"But of course I want to—want to hear things from you, Hans."

"We are friends still?"

The plea is his voice was unmistakable and tore at my heart.

"How can you doubt that?" I told him.

Hans looked up at me with brighter eyes than ever, and very deliberately laid his volume of Thorvaldsen on the floor.

"No. I do not doubt it. Not now, not at all. But I have done. Doubted."

I was incapable of referring to the events of that night, to the appearance, if you like, of the Peregrine Falcon and the Sailor-Boy in my life. Perhaps he too was unable to talk about what had passed between us, what we had expressed to one another.

"I will always be your friend," I told him.

He nodded with a glowing solemnity I never forgot. "And I will always be yours!"

And on hearing that I made for the door. Then I asked him: "I think I understood your telegram, but what does '*Vi ses*' mean?"

"Just 'We'll be seeing each other!' It's a phrase I hope we can use to one another our lives long, Martin."

I had, believe it or not, completely forgotten about the first telegram that the snub-nosed boy had bought. I was now to be somewhat more than reminded of it. I descended the lower staircase to see Mrs. Fuller, very obviously waiting for me, at its base, with the missive in her hand.

The set of her mouth, the icy glow in her eyes did not bode well for me. Nevertheless—

"Oh, so you found it?" I remarked disingenuously.

"Oh, so I found it!" Three other precedents in my life with landladies presented themselves in my mind to tell me that this sarcastically spoken sentence was the Start of a Real Row. "I did indeed find it—on the hall table for all the world to view."

I was my unfortunate schoolboy self again, or the youth I had been in my very first digs. "Well, you wouldn't have wanted me to put it where you couldn't have seen it, would you now?"

"I wouldn't have wanted you to put it anywhere at all!"

By this time I had reached the bottom of the stairs. "What should I have done with it then?"

"Mr. Bridges." It was hard to believe that I was actually taller than the woman addressing me so haughtily had she drawn herself up. "I do not intend to parry questions and answers with you when I have a point of the utmost seriousness to make. Who is the mistress of the house?"

I was tempted to say that this sounded jolly like just such a parrying as she'd just derided, but luckily for my head at which she might possibly have aimed blows, I did not. "Yourself, obviously."

"Then when a telegram comes addressed to her what is the correct procedure for a third party?"

"Receiving it is not the correct one, I take it?"

"If the master or the mistress to whom the telegram is addressed is not available—and as it happens I was at the far end of the garden at the time of its arrival, and did not hear the door, while all other occupants of the house save yourself were out—then there is but one course: *To ask the telegraph boy to return with it on another occasion. That is what the telegraph office itself would expect.*"

"But if a suitable member of the household is to hand," I began, whereupon Mrs. Fuller stepped an inch or so nearer me to hiss out at me:

"Suitable. You suitable? A nosy, manner-less, *very limited* young man"—and it would surely have been hard for her to come up with a more damning description of me—"*suitable* to receiving a private communication concerning affairs he has already shown himself perfectly incapable of understanding—what delusions about yourself are you suffering from? I wouldn't trust you with a laundry list let alone a telegram from a distinguished legal figure."

Well, after all this I need never at least wonder again where I stand with Mrs. Fuller, I thought. Her long musical fingers were busy playing scales on the folds of her dress. "I'll continue if I may. It truly amazes me, is almost beyond my powers of belief, that I should be standing here having to teach a young man of twenty-two—"

"Twenty-three," I said, almost automatically.

"Your pert little correction only emphasizes the sadness of your situation, Mr. Bridges. Having not done the appropriate thing, that is, inform the bringer of the telegram that the lady of the house was not in to receive it, I have no doubt whatsoever that you did the equally inappropriate one of reading it—with the hypocritical excuse that you needed to know whether it required an answer or not. Though why you should feel yourself equipped in any way to give one on my behalf is beyond my comprehension? Might I make my disapproval of your management of the whole thing clear enough by insisting you tell nobody else—nobody at all—what my telegram said, a point I clearly need to establish because you had left it on the hall table so for everybody to read."

I did not offer an apology, did not feel I had anything in the least to apologize for. On the other hand, even in the face of her declared lack of trust of me, I did feel virtually obliged to propose: "I will take your reply to the telegraph office if it is still open, and you can put your reply in a sealed envelope so I can't read it."

This offer, my readers will immediately perceive for themselves, was as impertinent, if not more so, as anything else I'd done or said (though I do not think I quite understood this). Turkey-cock red in the face, Mrs. Fuller looked as if she were about to strike me.

"You will do no such thing, and anyway the office is bound to be shut by now. Just for your information, I have no reply to make the telegram. I had already dealt with the matter it referred to."

Had accepted the offer of the Disappeared, I could have rejoined here, but did not.

"Well, if you're content to leave it like that . . ." I hardly knew what

I was saying anymore. I'd only come downstairs anyway because, in all the fuss of the telegrams, I had left two folders from work behind in the hall. All I wanted to do now was to get away from Mrs. Fuller and her wrath as speedily as I could, and now I knew that the Mercy Room door was no longer shut against me, I could at least relax in my own bedroom, and amuse myself with a book. At this notion a pleasant possibility occurred to me: "Perhaps in light of our conversation just now, when I seem to have offended you without meaning to, it would be best if I stayed upstairs during our evening meal."

Mrs. Fuller's eyes blazed anew, and if she didn't literally stamp her foot, she so much metaphorically did so that she might as well have done. "It would *not* be best, Mr. Bridges. You will come down. I am tired of all this playing fast-and-loose with mealtimes, which is not at all fair on my poor dear Sarah." At this point I could have told her that—unlike herself, unlike Will Postgate, unlike Hans Lyngstrand—I had sat down at the supper table every single day that week. But I judged it best not do so. "And anyway, have you forgotten it is *your* friend's last evening in Dengate. Surely even you would not be so impolite as to skip it because you feel like sulking after being told a few home-truths."

My readers are probably expecting to be now told what a tense, unpleasant affair supper was that night, and certainly I descended to the basement with trepidation and a resentment only made endurable by Hans's returned and friendly presence. But what curious tricks life plays on us— or rather what curious ones we play on ourselves. Will, who arrived back at Castelaniene soon after the disagreeable colloquy I've just recorded, was in a state of such high self-satisfaction (more drawings by him praised, yet more commissioned) that he spilled it over on all of us seated at the table with him (or close to him, for his mood affected the three cats also). We rejoiced (and knew ourselves to be doing so) in his evident pleasure in the way he was going about his life, and he rejoiced in our rejoicing. Being Friday, we ate fish, delicious Dover sole with new potatoes. Beatrice Fuller asked interested questions about what duties Will's new post would demand, Hans appeared impressively and maybe surprisingly well-up in the affairs of *Bergens Arbeiderbladet*, of whose "left" political stance and appeal to the workers Will at once smilingly approved (his smile seemed to guarantee it eternal prosperity and readership), and I myself had some little stories to tell which nobody else there knew about those south-coast newspapers with whom *The Advertiser* as a member of the same group enjoyed a certain (mildly competitive) relationship. Everybody appeared interested in what everyone else had to say, while relishing every mouthful of the food, and really can you ask (particularly in those circumstances) for anything much better than that?

And at the end of the meal, after Mrs. Fuller had proposed that, the occasion being what it was, we should all adjourn for coffee into a garden still awash with warm sunlight, Will said: "But first I shall sing to you. In Oakeshott's this afternoon"—Mrs. Fuller nodded for she had known this piano and musical instrument–dealer all her life—"I found the banjo I've been looking for quite a while. I'll show you, put it to use."

As he did, sitting in a dining chair near the window, bathed in soft sunshine, the strong fingers of his left hand flying over the fretted, mother-of-pearl neck of the instrument, and the even stronger fingers of his right energetically plucking all the five shining strings above the parchment-covered "drum," while he sang in his warm tenor voice:

"I wandered today to the hill, Maggie,
To watch the scene below,
The creek and the rusty old mill, Maggie,
Where we sat in the long, long ago.
The green grove is gone from the hill, Maggie,
Where first the daisies sprung,
The old rusty mill is still, Maggie,
Since you and I were young."

The nostalgic lilt of the tune by the time Will had embarked on the second verse paradoxically brought me unasked-for pictures of a time, an all but unbelievable one, when everybody assembled in the kitchen of Castelaniene would be old and likely to address a loved partner to remind him or her of those irrecoverable days long gone by, would be thinking of 1885 in, say, the year 1925 when I would be sixty-three or 1945 when I would be a preposterously unimaginable eighty-three. Somehow the very idea that we all, whatever our dispositions, shared the frightening but somehow also wonderful inevitability of being thrust forward into time and age—and aging, and beyond even that into the measureless unknown (think of the Gateway and the lustrous path it proposed for us here) made me wonder why we were not as nice as possible to each other all day long—or, at any rate, a lot nicer than most of us managed to be.

Speak for yourself, said an inner voice.

The song and its encore came to an end, and Will was sincerely, even humbly thanked (as indeed he deserved to be). After that my friend put his new banjo away into its black case, and stowed this in the hallway, ready to be taken by him with his other bags when he left in the morning. And then he and Hans exchanged house for garden, Sarah waddling behind with the coffee-tray.

Mrs. Fuller and I were therefore left in the hall, she standing in fact in the very spot from which she had harangued me so sternly and so shrilly only two hours before.

I must say something to her, said I to myself, but whatever can I find that would be remotely fitting, that would not earn me another moral rebuke?

"Mrs. Fuller," I began. But I was rendered incapable of going on any further. For Beatrice Fuller moved toward me, and half-taking me into her arms laid her head on my shoulder. And wept. And wept and wept.

I could feel my own body relaxing to receive her overwrought one. And what could I do better than stand there, permitting not dismissing, accepting rather than spurning.

"I'm sorry," I think I managed, but through her sobs she said: "One tries so hard, so desperately hard, to make life good, but—but I don't think one succeeds. I don't think it's possible for one *ever* properly to do so."

A minute, perhaps two, passed before she bade me go into the garden for my coffee. She would be following as soon as she had dried her eyes. She was as good as her word, emerged without a trace of her outburst on her fine classical face, and there in the long shadows on the lawn talked with particular vivacity about former times in Dengate and the great blessing it had received when Auguste Pugin created for the town so many fine and God-honoring buildings. But never fear, she continued, brushing back an errant spray of white lilac, Pugin's spirit lived on. Think of the influence

Beresford Hope was having, yes, here in Kent, from Canterbury where he had restored a priory to St. Stephen's School . . . Will, passing me the sugar bowl, gave me a wink just as Mrs. Fuller's usually rather low voice soared on the very word Hope. Yes, my friend and I—largely anyway—still saw life eye-to-eye.

The barometer rose the next day. The sea, very calm, and still offering up to a virtually cloudless sky those extraordinarily deeper blue streaks in its blueness caused by plankton, looked as though it were positively inviting the visiting hordes from London, the gaudy regiments of bathing machines, the pulsation of the marina down to which a bit later on a little train would run from the main station. Mid-morning Will, having, I imagined, taken an affectionate leave of Beatrice Fuller (did she lay her head on *his* shoulder?), looked in on *The Advertiser* and everybody there sped him on his way back to The Smoke with a warmth of regard extraordinary considering they'd first met the man only on Monday! And he was coming back, oh yes, he was coming back all right! He'd be doing the opening of the Bandstand proud!

After he'd left Mr. Forrester turned to me, tears in his usually inexpressive eyes, to say: "A thoroughly nice fellow that friend of yours, Bridges. How rare and how welcome to meet someone of his—of your— generation with a natural, lightly worn regard for the Bible, who isn't all cynicism and Mr. Huxley!" And he gave that thin beard of his an extra hard tug as if by doing so he could explain that wateriness of the eyes which, in truth, embarrassed me, especially as I knew Will and he did not.

And later Mr. Betterton—wonder of wonders!—was pleased to say to me: "Enterprising fellow that friend of yours, Bridges, even though he does think a shade too well of himself. But he combines enterprise with judgment, with a prudent assessment of matters, and you could well take a leaf out of his book. They're damned fine drawings he has done of our town—he has respect for it, you see, Bridges, and I am truly pleased to hear we're going to have many more of 'em."

Ironically the fact that I had introduced Will to Dengate (and vice versa) had raised the community's regard for me to an extent that no efforts on my own part had done—or probably could ever have done . . .

What would they all have thought, had I been able to tell them, about Will's taking me to Limehouse, years ago it now seemed. He'd led me through a wilderness of dark warehouses and tenement buildings, to a house with a virtually windowless front, and in its rotting interior an older mulatto woman ensconced on a throne-like chair smoking a pipe with a strangely powerful sickly-sweet smell. She had, under her charge, several girls, some of them clearly many years younger than myself (I was twenty-one) and not one of them speaking the Queen's English, indeed only two of them actually were English. I was then asked to choose one of these; she would then take me to a little back-room I could already glimpse off the landing, with dirty tattered muslin curtains. I was rendered wordless, was absolutely incapable of making this choice for myself (and not out of *embarras de richesse* either). Instead I turned to my omniscient friend and worldly guide who alighted for my delectation on a girl slightly older than the rest with golden-colored skin (I believe she came from Ceylon, that mysterious Island of Spicy Breezes). She proceeded to lead me into that designated little room, but so horrified me there with her depraved and utterly loveless gestures and her crude verbal obscenities (which came out of her like imperatives on behalf of vileness itself) that I turned tail, and fled to Will now waiting for me in the cheerless hall chatting (but doing nothing more) with a couple of the other girls. I clung to him (in a not dissimilar way, truth to tell, to how Mrs. Fuller had clung to me on Friday night; we human beings do not have available to us so many other physical modes of expressing our feelings), begging him to release me from this trial of manhood.

A little perplexed but quite genuinely concerned, he said, "I made a mistake, soldier. I'll get you out of here." And he did.

After supper on Tuesday evening, a Buttons arrived at Castelaniene from the Majestic Hotel. In his braided, brass-buttoned, bandbox-neat uniform the little lad seemed hardly made of flesh-and-blood but when he spoke, he did so, of course, with the accent of "Martin" from the Royal Gardens and the telegraph boy. His voice was one of squeaky excitement.

"A great rich foreign gentleman wants you to meet him in the west conservatory in an hour and a half's time," he informed me. "He is Herr

Strømme from Bergen in Norway. He is something big in shipping. He has at this moment his ward, Mr. Lyngstrand, also from Norway but not a hotel resident, dining with him. Am I to tell him that you accept?"

"Yes, of course," I said, "with pleasure!" But these last two words were inappropriate surely.

"And he begs to be allowed," bowing here to Mrs. Fuller, "to call on Madame at her house at eleven o'clock tomorrow morning, an occasion he looks forward to with the most enormous pleasure. Will I be able to take back to him Madame's confirmation that this designated time is suitable?"

I had passed by the Majestic Hotel almost daily but had never yet gone inside. Entering the hotel's palatial foyer, I was to be assailed immediately by uncomfortable boyish shyness and a sense of my own social obscurity. Scarlet and gold lavishly complemented each other everywhere: on the double staircase; in the vast dining-room even now very full, in the uniforms of all the many flunkeys who, on being addressed, spoke as Buttons had done, as if they were birds (or captive natives) who'd been taught a great many sentences of our speech but were not completely certain of their meaning. Even on this balmy night, so suitable for loose clothing and such casual delights as a quick swim in the sea, men of only-too-obvious importance were parading about in evening dress, their shirts so well-starched they could have stood up unaided, while their wives, often proudly on their arms, swished long-trained dresses behind them and darted the beams of their eyes suspiciously about, as though on the lookout for the multiple signs of conspiracy. I didn't care for the place at all, but the more I registered its lack of amiable qualities, the more I felt I would never make the grade appropriate to one of my ambitions unless I were considerably more acclimatized to it than now.

The Majestic presents to the Esplanade a front of glass conservatory broken only by the grandiose entrance. The conservatory is a captive jungle of potted palms and of other plants all too exotic for me to identify (having in some cases never seen their like before): scarlet flares emanating from fleshy dark-green leaves, long prickly stalks with white flowers on their spikes like little severed heads. Among this riot of tropical flora tables were placed—bamboo, or was it that fashionable thing, *mock*-bamboo?—at which people, couples of a certain age for the most part, were sitting, re-

ceiving and enjoying from the panes of the glass roof above them an am-
plification of the day's waning sunshine while sipping those drinks proper
to the rich. I did not relish the prospect of passing time among these fine
folk, of possibly crashing into some rare thorny plant or knocking over
somebody's bottle of vintage champagne. But happily the pair I had come
to see were sitting, I now made out, not far from the door: Hans himself
and an older man surely nearer sixty than fifty. Neither had seen me come
in, so I was obliged to present myself, something which can make me feel
awkward even to this day.

"Good evening!" I said, positioning myself in front of their table.
"Allow me to introduce myself, Herr Strømme; I am Martin Bridges."

"And very pleased to meet you I am indeed," said the older man getting up. "You have—I have heard many times including today—made my
Hans very happy during his time in Dengate."

And just how happy you can have no idea, and never will have, I could not
help irreverently saying to myself.

"It is kind of him—and you—to say so!" And the little inclination of
my head I almost automatically gave this "great rich foreign gentleman"
was more appropriate to a Norwegian, or indeed to most young men from
a European country, than to someone like myself used to the mores of
South London streets.

"Please to sit down with us!" Herr Strømme beckoned to a flunkey
and asked him to bring me a chair. "We are refreshing ourselves with hock-
and-seltzer and we will be glad if you join us."

Well, I could hardly ask for porter, could I?

Herr Strømme was gray in hair and gray in his beard too which ran
from earlobe to earlobe but was not long. His complexion was a weathered one suggesting much exposure to wind, rain, and sun, though he
must have spent a good deal of his time in offices and counting-houses
rather than on the high seas on board his own ships. His close-set eyes
were even bluer than his ward's; repeatedly in the hour that followed my
own eyes traveled to them, so fascinated was I by the sheer intensity of
their color. Even more than in the case of my dear friend, I thought it
like glimpsing fragments of sky or sea at their very best as they peeped
out between skin and bone. His voice was a remarkably deep one, which

sank to an unusually low level when he was wanting to emphasize a point. For all that his English sounded like an educated Englishman's, he became at such moments quite hard to follow, and I had to lean right across the table, in danger of knocking over a glass as I did so, to catch all of his steady, serious, kindly but not unintimidating conversation. Of which I shall give the gist.

But before I do so it is important for me to record that Hans remained noticeably and (as far as I was concerned) uncharacteristically unanimated throughout my visit to the Majestic. No doubt his reunion with his patron had moved him greatly, had overwhelmed him with its reminders of experiences and emotions temporarily put to one side whilst he had been in England. He sat there, from time to time lifting his glass to his lips, attending to the shipping magnate half as though he were in his employ (as in a manner of speaking he still was), and therefore eager to do the respectful and grateful thing, yet at the same time, in some private but palpable part of himself at a distance from his situation, even detached from it. While it was more obvious to me than for some days past that Hans had only quite recently recovered from an extremely serious illness, he also looked—dressed in comparatively formal clothes Mrs. Fuller had acquired for him—far more ordinary than I would have imagined possible, than surely was the case. He held himself very straight and rather stiff, and any person casually observing him would have put him down as a well-bred young man, not English, but from one of those northern countries we are pleased to acknowledge as cousins; a bit conventional-ridden, a little afraid of social spontaneity, but with a natural dignified decorum.

If this person had been able to take in all Herr Strømme's comments, he or she would have had some of the above confirmed (the patience of Hans's reception), others a little confused, because the picture that emerged of his ward suggested a certain amount of willfulness, even caprice rather than of sustained circumspect behavior.

"Hans here has always been a young man keen to learn, it is one of his qualities his many friends like him for. And learn he has—many, many things, and very diligently and quickly—but always they come, I think, from enthusiasm, from having his imagination fired. At school, classes in mathematics did not appeal to him—with the result, he has deficiencies even to this day in that intrinsically important domain. Were he been sitting the examinations essential for becoming a Second Mate, we should have to attend to that.

"But now he has other ambitions for himself, and for reasons of health—after the terrible shock to his system following the accident in the Dover Straits—we should, I believe, respect these. But one does not become a sculptor"—he gave a kindly but not altogether uncritical, let alone approving smile here—"simply from the wish to make a statue, or even from the thought of what pleasure it would be to have clay in your hands. Even those artists who have their Christiania studios in Pultosten—the renowned "Cream Cheese" to translate into English—the very center of our city's Bohemians, of experimentation with style and subject—study all day and all night to perfect their art. They bother with the most exacting and perhaps tedious studies of both calculation and measurement, be they ever so wild. They have the closest knowledge of human anatomy, fit to rival if not eclipse a medical student's, they understand the chemical components of the material they work in and the problems of its strength and durability as thoroughly as any builder or engineer. I know that some of our most audacious artists in Norway—Christian Krohg or Erik Werenskiold—would say precisely what I am saying now were they to encounter Hans here in a conservatory of the Majestic Hotel, Dengate"— and he smiled again, perhaps at the absurdity of this notion—"and would, I fancy, say it in terms of far greater technical detail than unfortunately I— a mere man of ships and accounting offices—can ever hope to do.

"I therefore insist, if I am to help Hans some way toward achieving what is, at the moment, his ambition"—his very intonation suggested the possibility (the probability?) of what was true of *this* moment, on this lovely May evening by the Channel when Hans was still virtually a convalescent, not being at all true of later moments, even, say, a couple of months hence—"that he applies himself to every aspect of mastering his chosen mediums, learns—as we are speaking of sculpture—of the arts of Greece and Rome, and for aught I know, of Egypt and Assyria as well, that he allows dates and numbers into his brain, and teaches his hands how to accomplish the most precise and demanding tasks. It will be a training—and I use the word advisedly, just as I might of someone starting work on one of my ships or in a counting-house I respect—demanding at least three years of his life, and possibly four."

I bowed my head before this. The man who had spoken had a kind heart and a morally discriminating conscience; that much was clear for all the pedantic Puritanism an easier-going person such as myself was bound to be irritated by in his little speech. I did think, however, letting the seltzer fizz in my mouth, that if ever Hans was to do anything in the world as a sculptor, it would owe immeasurably to this man here, who had such energy behind the dignified composure of his exterior.

"And now we must talk about yourself," Herr Strømme said, but his knowledge of the newspaper world from Christiania and Bergen to Berlin and London was such that I felt I would cut a figure little more impressive than that of some glorified errand-boy, so concentrated in my replies entirely on the composition of the area my paper served—the Channel Ports of Kent and Sussex—a subject on which I was now pretty thoroughly informed, with many (probably not very interesting) facts and figures to give.

Then the great shock. "I think Hans and I must bid you good night now, Martin. We need to retire a little earlier than usual, as we have much to do in the morning."

I must have positively gasped out my next sentence: "But isn't Hans coming back to Castelaniene?"

Herr Strømme was rising from the table. "Oh, no, we would not presume on Mrs. Fuller's wonderful hospitality any longer. Guardian and ward are reunited now, praises be. We shall of course be visiting Castelaniene tomorrow morning. At eleven o'clock."

"But I shall not be there," I protested, hearing an unwanted squeak of indignation in my voice. "I shall be at work. I shall be busy all morning at *The Advertiser*. Perhaps of course you could both look in . . ."

Hans's guardian's smile was all benevolence. "Regrettably we will not have the time for that. Our train for London departs at half past twelve. I fear then, since you will not be at your place of residence tomorrow morning, we shall have to do our leave-takings here. May I thank you for all the friendliness you have shown Hans, and may I hope to see you in Norway some time where you will surely be welcome."

And he shook my hand, and then—what else?—I shook the hand of

Hans. We did not—I am pretty certain of this—look one another in the face.

"Goodbye, Hans!"

"Goodbye, Martin. Thank you. Thank you very much!"

"I hadn't expected, you see . . ." I began.

"I shall write to you," Hans said, "if I may!"

If he may!

I walked westwards along the Esplanade hardly able to see the Royal Gardens and the poles and paraphernalia of the emerging Bandstand for tears.

Even remembering the nights after my parents' deaths, I do not think I have spent hours more desolate than that in which May 19 turned into May 20. Whether I slept at all is immaterial so great was the feeling of loss that prevailed hour after dark hour.

It was indeed as if I had once crossed a threshold between death and life for Hans's sake, and then made a calculated retreat from it. Had taken myself off the great shining pathway for a room behind a closed door.

CHAPTER THIRTEEN

Summer's Long Strong Spell

*M*ay had been warm, with spectacular blooms—the Clematis Montana in the garden of Castelaniene was a vast pink galaxy in its sky of green leaves—but June brought warmer weather still, and as June moved toward July each day seemed—often in contradiction of actual barometer readings—hotter than its predecessor. At *The Advertiser* we opened the sash windows on opposite walls so that a current of air, even if slighter than what we wished for, passed through the room, tempering the sweaty heat of our bodies. All of us, even pompous old Betters who repeatedly described himself as a "stickler for etiquette," worked with jackets off and shirt-sleeves rolled up. Back in Bengal he'd had to adapt to a far more inclement climate! Visits to the printers now seemed like sorties to the mouth of an inferno, from which the poor compositors would emerge, moisture dripping down from their foreheads and huge damp patches at the armpits. Nor could you turn your eyes out toward the Channel for refreshment without almost immediately averting them so strong and smarting was the glare of sun on sea; the sky was so cloudless that the baked blue of its inverted bowl mocked you with its apparent unbreakability. At times we would have given anything for a sight of just such small fluffy nimbuses as had drifted overhead that Saturday afternoon when I sat out in the garden of Castelaniene interviewing Hans Lyngstrand. A long time ago that seemed—I was still the new member of a leading local newspaper's staff, with a lot to do and a lot to learn, and uncertain security or status. I felt the need for both!

Trains regularly brought down day-trippers from London to revel in the sun on Dengate Sands, and just such bunches of spirited lads with loud laughs, ostentatious appetites, and lubricious winks as Will and his mates in other summers. Once I couldn't help myself from remarking as the sounds of one of these floated up from the street below: "That was *me* and *my* pals this time last year!" Couldn't help, too, the sadness in my voice, for truly the coolness I felt from all the people around me, except Barton, the only kind of coolness there was these days, was—especially when added to the cool formality of my adieu to Hans—making me very despondent. Within a few minutes these young men sauntering along the street would be swaggering onto the beach; they would make for spots close to gaudy umbrellas with the prettiest girls beneath them, and then show off to them, with a ball-game or with the pantomime that follows casting off shoes and dipping bare feet into the still surprisingly chilly seawater.

At first, I wondered whether I'd spoken my words aloud so long was the silence that followed them.

Then, "Is our cockney sparrow getting a little homesick for his nest?" said Barton Cunningham, and though it was meant as a jest, denoting acceptance of rather than anything else, it jarred on me rather. I suppose, truth to tell, all of us were feeling out of sorts, with the sun so strong on us (no curtains, no blinds) and our perspiration so continuous and pungent.

Thomas Betterton was pleased to reply: "They come and then they *go*, my good Barton, they never stay and settle, as you surely by now have noticed." Ostensibly the trite observation could apply to trippers in the streets beneath us rather than sparrows; even so I felt sure I was the main butt of his wit. True, he had, quite sportingly, never made any allusion (at least in my hearing) to the Case of the Inverted Pyramid, and had indeed, on the First of June Founder's Day, even publicly acknowledged me among all the smartly dressed guests at St. Stephen's but at the same time no word or look from him had ever suggested that he accepted me as a permanent addition to the team.

At night when I found it hard to fall asleep in the intense stuffiness of my attic-room which even an opened window could not relieve, I'd go over little scenes, such less than welcome remarks as above, so trivial when set down on paper, so near-momentous when experienced or relived. Strange that it was these that occupied my mind rather than the more extraordinary episodes of Hans's embraces, so unprecedented in my life. (But these did return to me in the form of strong surges of desire in the very early morning when the mind is so dependent on the condition and concurrent demands of the body.) I would frequently re-enact happenings at the office according to the French notion of *esprit d'escalier*, when, too late, you come up with the truly witty retort that eluded you at the time. I convinced myself there were few young men anywhere in the United Kingdom less popular in the workplace than myself, and naturally the more convinced I became, then the harder it was to act in any way to change that regrettable situation. Would it be such a very stupid thing, I asked myself, to do as I'd half-suggested to my colleagues, follow a homeward-bound band of young visitors back to London, and stay there?

Stay there, yes, but where, and doing what? Could I turn up to my old newspaper and say to its editor (a genial enough man who, when letting me go, had demonstrated a certain paternal regard for me): "Sir, now I've seen what it's like down in the provinces, I realize that I'm far happier working back here, nearer the pulse of things under the direction of your good self and of senior members of your team. And I won't even mind trotting along to the bloody printers like before. I have matured, I see now that in all jobs you've got always to take the rough with the smooth."

But one of those "seniors" with whom I would have to curry favor, was now none other than Will Postgate, one of the newspaper's two Deputy Editors. I doubted he would be particularly pleased to see me back. He could no longer be the brightest star in my firmament nor I to him the flattering hero-worshipping younger brother. His second visit to Dengate—busy though he undoubtedly was with his sketches of the Bandstand as it neared completion—had, if anything, undermined our friendship more than the first. He had given me almost insultingly little of his time, and Mrs. Fuller's pathetic anxiety to cater to all his whims and to listen to him talk as if he were a true metropolitan celebrity was even more trying than before. But she was conscientiously polite to myself, and inclusive of me in all her conversation whenever Will and I were there together, so I was given no grounds for complaint. But my friend had not brought his new banjo down with him, so there was no restorative song to bathe wounds and improve the state of the soul.

Indeed, just as the temperature on the barometer never went satisfactorily down, so my spirits never satisfactorily rose, and on the last evening of June, a Tuesday, after my day's work was over, I did indeed take myself to Dengate Station (though significantly I had no bag with me). It was, I now see, something of a dare to myself, such as I used to make as a schoolboy wanting to run away and join an actor's troupe or when I was bored at the stationer's (which was not seldom). Prove yourself a free man by boarding the next London train, an inner voice tauntingly directed.

And I had a more-than-usually-strong good reason for doing so. An incident that morning had greatly upset me.

Normally—and it is as true of now as of then—I can be relied on to have the right books, stationery, documents, etcetera for any given occasion. I say, when praised for this, that it is part of the (perhaps unexpected) tidiness of my mind. But this particular Tuesday (the day we went to press), I had just reached the western gates of the Royal Gardens when I realized I had left behind a newly drawn-up list of localities—background for an article compiled by three of us, Archie, Barton and myself, about plant-nurseries—behind in my bedroom. So back to Castelaniene I went.

I turned the key in the lock of the front door with the dexterity of impatience, and ran breathlessly up the two flights of stairs, onto the landing and into my room, the door of which was open, and in which stood—Mary.

She had a duster in her hand and resting on the surface nearest her a dustpan-and-brush, so she presumably was up here to clean. But the surface in question was the top of my desk, on which also reposed a pile of papers topped by that list of nursery-gardens which I'd come to retrieve. From the startled way in which she drew back I knew she'd been peeking at it. And why not, you might say, isn't that what every housemaid would do, to alleviate the boredom of her common round. Anyway, a fat lot of good it would do her, learning what places between Dengate and Deal are best for buying interesting breeds of roses. But I still didn't like her nosing 'round my things, any more indeed than I liked *her*.

"I'll thank you to let me get to my own papers on my own desk," I said sharply, though my heavy breathings made my remark sound less cutting than I'd intended. And all but pushed her aside.

Brushing against her as I did this was not, disconcertingly, an unpleasant experience. My body had registered, even if for split seconds, the edge of her left breast and had instinctually responded to it. She had anyway these last weeks been looking a good deal better; whatever ailment had been inflicting her had virtually cleared up. Her nose was no longer sore, her eyes no longer plagued with sties, and somehow or other, and somewhere or other, for I always tried not to look at the specifics of her person, she had lost quite a few pounds. Beneath the dark-hued cotton frock her shape was far from displeasing. Almost crossly I snatched up the required sheets of paper with an aggressive gesture that could have been intended as a rebuke to herself.

"On the whole," I said with a sarcastic little smile, "it is best not to peer at other people's papers that are no concern of yours whatsoever."

Mary's answer to me was immediate and deadly: "On the whole," she said, "it is best not to leave your linen in a disgusting state after two persons have been sharing a bed."

I was so caught out, and so horrified that she had said at last what I had most dreaded her saying, I all but dropped what was in my hand, the object of my return walk, onto the floor. *After two persons* . . . Nobody had ever made such an appalling remark to me, but then of course I had never made myself vulnerable to anyone's doing so. From the triumphant glimpse in her small (if now sty-free) eyes I knew her to be referring, quite unambivalently to—issue.

Fear of the most unadulterated and unmanning variety assailed me. Though she had not said so, she was perfectly aware who the two persons had been; indeed how could she not have been?

Incomprehension and dudgeon were my only possible resort.

"I would keep a clean tongue in your head, Mary!" I said. All the way to the newspaper I pondered whether indeed there could be such stains on bedclothes as to proclaim a dual rather than a single presence?

One thing was certain, however. I had, by my reactions, confirmed Mary's nasty suspicions. (Why "nasty" where something so joyful was concerned?) What a curious creature she was—object of Mr. Fuller's solicitous tenderness, receiver of charming little presents from the younger Horace Fuller, Mrs. Fuller's treasured vehicle and Colonel Walton's too as conveyer of messages from the next world able to take in the missing crew of a Norwegian ship and the inhabitants of suburban Kentish villas alike! Furthermore, I noticed, she had delivered her last horrible sentence to me in a very different accent from that she often employed—and had used for her communications to the Gateway. Hearing her almost copy-book articulation now made it no longer surprising that she had read a novel by one of the Brontë sisters nor that she had added to her many practical skills various other more intellectual accomplishments (with the hopes perhaps of becoming that most modern thing, a Perfect Private Secretary). She was somebody it was advisable for me to treat with caution. What might she not say to or about me, especially after my un-wisdom of this morning? Maybe I would be doing myself an immense personal favor by parting company with Dengate, its tight, smug community—this very evening.

Nobody here would miss me. Perhaps of course it could truthfully be said I had done nothing to engender that emotion. I was not right for this Channel Port, and it was not right for me.

It was not clear from the one letter I had received from Norway that Hans Lyngstrand missed me either. That he didn't suffer for *me* the dull ache of felt absence that daily I entertained for *him*. His letter had been disappointingly short and matter-of-fact though he did say he had all but forgotten how beautiful his own country was and how glad he was once more to be reunited with the granite mountains, the long fjords cutting into them, the rocky islets off the coast, though he still hoped to travel south to see where the masters of sculpture had lived and worked. Not a word about Dengate, not a word about myself either, except to say he hoped I was well. Why, Barton Cunningham would have hoped as much, and he'd have done so in a brighter, well more "cheerful" letter!

Before the temple-like portals of Dengate Station I stood dithering internally. As I'd found toward the end of fervid boyish daydreams, running away is far easier thought than done. Where, for example, would I sleep tonight? I could turn up at my old lodgings, I could throw myself on old Will's mercies, but . . . Then think of the trouble I would be causing Edmund who had taken me under his wing so enthusiastically and whose decision to do so I still properly had to vindicate. To give myself time I entered the branch of W. H. Smith's adjacent to the station. Here I bought myself the most recent copy of *Tit-Bits*, and at once there came back to me all the brilliant journalistic ideas I had had before I came down to this . . . stupid old Channel Port. But had they altogether left me? Had my Dengate experiences from de facto social ostracism to sexual unorthodoxy really banished them from my mind so thoroughly that I could not reanimate them—and to the advantage of my present life?

Leaving the shop, I saw a poster on the advertisement hoarding opposite the entrance to the station. In bold letters imitating some street-fair handbill of the previous century (a pastiche our printers, Barrett Brothers excelled in) all could read:

SATURDAY JULY THE FOURTH EIGHTEEN EIGHTY-FIVE

THREE O'CLOCK

IN THE ROYAL GARDENS, DENGATE

GRAND CEREMONIAL OPENING OF THE NEW BANDSTAND

BY SIR GREELEY DONALDSON OF HARLAND COURT

AND

MR. GEORGE BARLEY, HIS WORSHIP THE MAYOR OF DENGATE

Beneath this lay the particulars of the concert with which the Bandstand would be inaugurated, to be played by the Invicta Orchestra. I had them by heart already as I did the words above them; I'd sub-edited them enough times:

J. Strauss: The Blue Danube (waltz)
A. Sullivan: H.M.S. Pinafore (medley)
J. Sousa: Congress Hall (march)
E. Grieg: Symphonic Dance No 2

A ten-page program—published under the auspices of the paper and printed by (again, of course!) Barrett Brothers, and available only on the day itself—would explain more about these items and about the players that would render them. But, standing there gawping at the proclamation and with approximately one half of me spiritually already being chugged toward London, I appreciated I knew a good deal already. That the conductor, James Millbank, was uncle to the boy Peter Frobisher in our office. That the oboe solo, important for the Grieg dance, would be played by Herbert Danwell, a young dentist who lived next door but one to Castelaniene. The name for the whole proud, but inevitably, somewhat scratch orchestra had its origins in county history—"Invicta" was the unconquerable horse who'd carried into victory King Vortigern, the great Kentish king.

Why then, with all this knowledge of the components of the scene, did I not remain in Dengate till at least the Bandstand's inauguration? Further intimate details of the occasion occurred to me. His Worship the Mayor was a distant cousin of Mr. Betterton himself, while Sir Greeley Donaldson, of whose munificence to St. Stephen's his son had made me fully aware on my visit to the establishment, was a man whose hand I had actually shaken at the school's Founder's Day; Donaldson Ma had introduced us, the boy clearly thinking (though obviously not saying) that my "chucking" had formed an indissoluble bond between us. Sir Greeley, I was now aware (as who in Dengate was not?), had made an extremely handsome donation to the erection of the Bandstand, and furthermore had persuaded an American bank with which he was connected to do the same: this indeed accounted for the precise date of the opening (America's national day) and the inclusion in the program of a march by an American composer making quite a name for himself in his own country.

To a Londoner such as myself all this might, you would think, appear parish-pump stuff, and often I tried to dismiss it as this, but I could not disguise from myself my pleasure in amassing facts and figures and my pride in my almost effortless retention of them. And *this* gift, to call it that, unlike my quick wit of which I was more proud, did not go unacknowledged by the other members of the newspaper teams; on the contrary it was looked on with favor. On not a few occasions—if I'd been happier, I would have felt the more gratified—long-standing members of the team had turned to me, *me*, for information or clarification.

So—*Oh well*, I said to myself, as if yielding to external persuasion, *I might as well stay on for the blessed July the Fourth do. Then when all the fuss is over, I can decide how best to spend my life. As for Mary, I shall just have to go very carefully—not throw my weight about as I've tended to . . .*

What, I asked myself as I trudged up St. Ethelberga's Road, *if Hans Lyngstrand were still there on my return? What if I went up to my room and virtually stripped myself bare of clothes—as the hot weather demanded I should— and the door stealthily opened, and* he *came in, at once gentle and strong. And shedding his own garments, he once again flung himself upon me, and we became two united youthful summertime bodies whom Bertel Thorvaldsen himself might have wanted to honor in his art on account of their mutual joy and satisfaction?*

But all that was almost as much a part of the past as the great gale which had brought Hans to the Kent coast in the first place.

And how sad it was to think like this! While some episodes in one's life—my parents' deaths, for example—are so painful that little could be more terrifying than the possibility of their recurrence, there are others one would like to hold on to forever. And to be aware that they are receding further and further from easy recovery is as painful as the literal watching, after departure, of a dear friend dwindling until he has reached complete invisibility.

Later that day, after such dark as the June night could muster, still far from sure that I had done the right thing earlier in not boarding a London train, I took that mile-long, mostly uphill cliff-top walk which starts with a stile at the southernmost bend of St. Ethelberga's Road and culminates in what is known locally simply as the View, a knoll marked by a compass stone indicating the directions and distance of a variety of places in relation to this eminence, some of them on the other, the continental side of the Channel.

Tonight, and by no means for the first time, all three Castelaniene cats were pleased to accompany me, the stile and its three successors presenting no obstacle whatever for them. For the most part they walked some yards behind me, in the order Japheth, Ham, and, preserving a strict distance from her sons, Mrs. Noah, but every now and again one of the two toms would flatten his ears, turn himself suddenly into some squirrel or rabbit startled by a gunshot, and bolt ahead, whereupon his brother felt honor-bound to follow suit and overtake him. At such moments, to make sure she was of the party, I would look 'round to see that the sharp triangular ears of Mrs. Noah were still visible above the tufts of the grass with her yellow eyes bright beneath them, and still maintaining exactly that number of yards from myself she had decided on at the outset. But when we came near to the compass-stone itself, she did what she usually did—leap onto the top of it, obscuring with her body many of the place-names, and survey—as if with accompanying reflections—the terrain around her. It was easy on such occasions to believe her capable of the strange powers the Gateway ascribed to her. She allowed me to stroke her head, but never lowered it so as she received my attentions she appeared to be at the same time absorbing the whole famous eponymous view into her quiet, mysterious being.

And what a vista it was, almost better at night than by day, with ribbons of lights unfurling below, northeastwards down to the harbor, and then becoming tauter, stretching up the opposite hillside toward downland now engulfed in blackness. Moving my head to my left I beheld a sea like a sheet of dark, lightly creased watered-silk. I thought yet again of how different its smooth surface was from the tempestuous roiling waters of the spring equinox that had thrown Hans into my life, and which I had never so much as glimpsed yet. A gentle breath seemed tonight to rise up from the Channel, without significantly stirring it, like a gentle, involuntary sigh from a sleeping body that refuses to be disturbed by it, and naturally I couldn't but think here of Hans and his slumbers at my side. Now he was lying alone in some different bed far, far away—far beyond the Channel, indeed at a point so far up the German Ocean that it was making room for the Norwegian Sea, the sea that would carry all who embarked on it to the polar regions themselves. It would still be light at Hans's latitude, his was as near the land of the Midnight Sun as, from down here, scarcely mattered. Perhaps he too could not sleep and was taking a strand-side stroll. Would he, just as I was thinking of *him*, be traveling in his mind back to Dengate and myself?

But even as I write that sentence, I remember my resolution to be as honest in these memoirs as I can be. I have written to no purpose if readers have not understood that in these weeks of June when—*when*!—I permitted my mind to dwell on the matter of Hans-and-myself, I was as changeable in both feelings and attitudes alike (the two being far from the same) as the little night-moths now flitting above the turf in front of me, or as the light of the glow-worms behind those little molehills, so prone to abrupt self-extinction. I simply did not know what I should make of what had happened between the two of us, mostly dismissing any recollections of what either medical science or religious morality would have to say on the matter. But tonight, the image of his young body, at once sailor-strong and invalid-vulnerable, bathed in the soft light of the Norwegian white night was an appealing one as I leaned against the compass-stone. If I could have conjured it into proximity I would have done, I believe.

All of a sudden Mrs. Noah gave a loud *miaow* puncturing the audible, almost tangible quietness enveloping us, and then jetted her head forward in a sharp sudden action reminiscent of a snake. And then she started purring, the kind of warm, rich purr cats emit while rubbing themselves against human legs, invitations to stroke. But Mrs. Noah was seemingly rubbing herself against night air. Her sons, who had sat themselves down at the foot of the stone, looked up at her in wondering surprise, but did not change their own postures. That their mother was pleased about something, they and I could both tell, but it was a moment or two before I saw the cause, not a something but a somebody: a man coming up toward the View out of the darkness below, wearing—not inappropriately considering the temperature—a panama hat and loose fawn-colored tropical suit and carrying a walking-cane. I knew him, didn't I? My host at Banstead Lodge—Colonel—whatever *was* his damned name?

"Mrs. Noah, I'll stake my life on it!" he said. "And who better to stake one's life on than you, you dear and wise old thing?" And now Mrs. Noah did have an object to rub her head against, the old colonel's palm. "And if I mistake not, my feline friend has a companion. The young man who had the courage to ask a question of our treasured vehicle on his very first visit to our Gathering."

So that was how he saw it, was it? Be grateful for small mercies, I told myself. Your behavior and its consequences could be quite otherwise interpreted.

"Good evening, Colonel!" I said, hoping this address would be socially acceptable. Then his surname came to me, and after a pause that must have been only too easily discernible for what it was, I said aloud, "Walton!"

If Colonel Walton minded my having forgotten his full identity, he did not show it. "And you have two other cats with you!" he commented. "May I be introduced?"

"They're Japheth and Ham, Mrs. Noah's sons," I said. "They like to come on a good-night walk with me."

"Greetings, Japheth and Ham. Nocturnal strolls are, I find excellent for the soul," said Colonel Walton, still fondling Mrs. Noah who, looked at closer to, still retained at night her distinctive lavender-gray hue. "And there are times—perhaps you have arrived at one such yourself—when the soul has particular need of feeling the essential benign mystery behind our earthly life."

Remembering my temptation to quit Dengate only a few hours back I could hardly disagree with his observation.

"Perhaps," I conceded.

"How old are Japheth and Ham?" the Colonel—who looked in the moonlight with his topping of white hair rather like a newly sharpened pencil—made the question sound oddly urgent.

"I don't know, sir, a couple of years each, I suppose. They're brothers."

"So George Fuller never saw them. They post-date his—"

Please don't say "disappearance," I begged him. *I don't think I could bear to hear that stupid word again.* But to my slight surprise he finished his sentence with "departure."

"Certainly!" I said.

Colonel Walton—to whom Mrs. Noah was continuing to be affectionately attentive—went on to say: "Of course whenever I think of Mrs. Noah—which, like all of us at Banstead Lodge, I frequently do with gratitude and admiration—I think of George Fuller. It was he, after all, who found the cat—on a boat in the harbor—and brought her home, named her, and tended her. He must have missed her when he was over in Italy before his—" (and obviously he was now obliged to use the baleful word) "his disappearance."

Disappearance. The Disappeared, The Disappeared's Offer. (To be accepted if you listened to a trusty adviser in Canterbury!) In the vastness of the night these words had a different ring from how they sounded indoors, in the confinement of one's head. In a somewhat bumbling way I spoke this last sentiment aloud, looking Colonel Walton in the eyes as if indeed he had stepped from off the Golden Pathway and had news to tell me. I swear he turned his head away from my look, as if—yes, embarrassed.

Our goodbyes were both perfunctory and conventional.

I entered Castelaniene by the basement backdoor to which I now had a key, given to me by Mrs. Fuller expressly on account of my new habit of nocturnal rambles. The relations between the two of us were (at least superficially) more amiable than at any point since my arrival. It was as though her fury with me for reading her telegram had purged her of her many resentments of me. And that subsequent strange burst of tears had been an offering of real sorrow on her part that things had not been as they should have between us. My acceptance of her weeping (but how could I have pushed her away?) was also an acceptance of her solemn unspoken intention that henceforward our dealings with one another should be courteous, considerate, completely unexceptionable. And so they had been, though probably not without a certain strain on both our parts, not least during Will's second visit, when she nervously and unceasingly catered to my friend's inordinate conceit.

"There the four of yous are!" Sarah exclaimed in her usual cross tone which, I was beginning to realize, didn't, as far as I was concerned, mean anything very much. "I was after havin' the bellman after yous at this god-forsaken hour."

The cats now padded in toward the kitchen proper in the expectation even at this late hour, of being given more scraps of food.

"It was nice having the three of them on my walk," I said. "I walked as far as the View," (but she probably did not even know where that fine spot was) "and who do you think I met? Colonel Walton."

"Oh him!" Sarah did not sound impressed. "Glad to get out of that horrible great mansion of his, I shouldn't wonder."

"He certainly talked about the beauties of being out at night," I agreed, "but he wanted to talk about Mrs. Noah and Japheth and Ham more than anything else."

"Well, you don't have to go out on the clifftops to think about *them*," rejoined Sarah.

"We also," I added, "talked about Mr. Fuller."

The unease in Sarah's curiously flat and wall-eyed face was so unmistakable I could not do other than take my chance:

"Sarah, did they bring back his body all the way from Italy for the funeral? I gather it was a pretty big affair."

We were both speaking in whispers, which the subject itself seemed to demand though at this late hour Mrs. Fuller was certain not only to be up in her bedroom but most likely asleep. Even so Sarah looked quite wildly all around her before answering me in a yet lower voice, "No, how could they do that, Mr. Bridges? With the poor man crushed to a pulp in a climbin' accident in them mountains near the village he loved so. Only his heart could be found, and that the Eye-talians sent back. In a casket. Terrible sad it was, but Madam said, we mustn't be all sad, Sarah, it is beautiful also, to think of part of him there in Castel-aneen until this old world of ours comes to an end. And them at the Gateway—thanks to your friend Colonel Walton—have messages regular about Eye-talians he is with now, and all the beautiful things he loved on his journeys to their country he now has around him for all eternity."

Her words—which for all their grotesquerie touched a nerve in me I scarcely knew was there—brought home to me one of the oddities in what believers say about the dead; on the one hand they are, they tell us at peace, at one with places they loved, on the other they are in some antechamber waiting for the terrifying moment, aeons ahead, when every single human being will have died, and the world will be declared at an end, and judgment can occur, and paradise proper begin. The two ideas, often uttered in the same speech by the same person, seem to me utterly to contradict one another. But probably I have not understood the thinking of the religious here. From boyhood on I have never been much of a one for the abstract, the pursuit of the absolute as some of them call it.

"I see," I said, a little awed by what Sarah had just told me. "So there was no kind of wake for him. Just the laying to rest here in Dengate of his heart . . ."

"I should think it's workin' you are tomorrow, and if so, you'll be needin' your bed!" said Sarah sternly, "and I can hear that Japheth mewin' away for more bits o' fish." She must have very acute hearing, I thought, for I had not caught this noise from my old feline friend. "It's all 'cos of yous, Mr. Bridges, you've given him that much food he can now never have enough. He's your favorite, an' you've fair spoiled him."

Up in the mugginess of my attic bedroom I had too much to think about for sleep to arrive with its usual promptness; indeed I held it off for, I would say, an hour and a half with thoughts that at times alarmed and excited me so much I wanted to bound up and down on the bed like a rubber ball, or to bang walls and doors as expressions of a tumult I felt at once mental and moral, of both the head and the heart. Suppose that "disappeared" were indeed the correct word for what had happened to Mr. Fuller? Suppose that Barton Cunningham, and all the other many mourners at his Dengate funeral, had walked behind a coffin containing some old Italian villager's heart while his owner's body, heart completely intact, was over in Castelaniene, breathing, feeding, taking in with senses and brain all the multiple sensations that simply being alive entails. The Headmaster of St. Stephen's College, Alfred Whittington himself, did not preach the address at the funeral service, I recalled, and the task fell to Edmund Hough, always so protective of his widow, to do so. Had he discharged it because he in fact believed, or even knew the man not to be dead, and, naturally eloquent, would be able to find the best words with which to establish the fiction? Perhaps my mind was running away with me, but in one direction I was pretty sure it was not. The telegram spoke—or rather could be taken to speak—of a monetary arrangement that still pertained between "the disappeared" (George) and Beatrice Fuller. Which made it—according to my more orthodox way of looking at things—more likely the man was alive than deceased.

But everything I knew about Mr. Fuller was strange and incomprehensible: the devotion to Latin poets that won him a grudging respect but little liking from Barton Cunningham; his belief that the village of Castelaniene in the Abruzzi was *un antícipo di paradiso*; his preservation of locks of Mary's hair; his attitude toward his son when he was in trouble . . .

Come, I told myself, *going on like this will not do; I shall never calm down enough for even a few minutes of sleep, and tomorrow, Wednesday our paper comes, and we will have the usual business of facing down our reading public.* A change of mental occupation was called for. But how? Of what kind? And then it came to me. I re-lit my lamp and picked up *Tit-Bits*. It was a judicious decision; clearly I knew myself reasonably well. What a treat its Puzzles and Conundrums page was this issue! As ever! And, it suddenly came to me at past one o'clock, why shouldn't *The Advertiser* have a similar feature? To which you could add (*I* would add—for I saw all this as a coup in which I reclaimed my rightful position on the paper) such related items as amusing games and conjuring tricks (at which, I'd like to boast, I'd been a bit of a dab-hand at school).

My brain was kind to me now, its fertility soothing rather than a stimulant. I would include among conundrums not just those well-known and often distinctly unfair old chestnuts like "How many horse's tails would it take to reach the moon?" (answer: one, if it were long enough!" which is an answer that satisfies nobody), but the more elaborate and intellectually exacting ones, like that a one-time favorite of mine cast in verse and beginning:

> *Twice nine of us are eight of us,*
> *And six of us are three,*
> *And seven of us are five of us—*
> *Oh, dear! What can we be . . .?*

Only too characteristically the next time (the following day, of course!) that I went into (burst into, more likely) Edmund's office, I could not refrain from telling him my new plan for the paper. And, after a slight but suitably loaded pause (during which I imagined a whole swarm of contradictory responses emanating from him) he responded not just with pleasure but with a detectable enthusiasm. *As well he might*, I feel obliged on my own behalf to add. The eventual implementation of my proposal gave rise to what has been steadily one of *The Advertiser*'s most popular features. I can't tell you how many folk have said to me what a gap it filled—"How come the paper didn't have these columns before!"—and I suspect there are boys who read this part of the newspaper only, together with the sports pages of course. But for now—"It will all have to be thought about most carefully!" said Edmund cautiously, again mopping his brow. (He seemed to respond to the heat more badly than any of us, perhaps because he weighed more, perhaps because he was having to work harder in the teeth of it than anybody else!) Egotist though I was (and sadly still am), even I realized that this was a coded way of informing me that, where a proposal involving myself in any active role was concerned, he would have to proceed very cautiously with the others. Had I not turned an experienced journalist's article into an Inverted Pyramid?

On the fourth of July itself, a night troubled, like its predecessors, by reflections disruptive of peace of mind, I woke up to a morning already pretty hot and, as I looked out of my dormer window, possessed by a curious thick whiteness in which—somehow matching my first thoughts—all the usual components of the scene appeared to be stranded. Some kind of summer sea-fret, I supposed, that nobody had yet told me about. After all, even though I sometimes felt I'd been living here for a century at least, I hadn't yet experienced the full course of one Dengate summer. However, another look out of the window before descending for a breakfast that I, for once, scarcely felt like consuming made me see that it was the roof of the sky itself that was white. On the ground, the walls, roofs, trees, and houses were clear enough in all their outlines, but once I moved my gaze to the Channel I saw it was hung with haze; not the merest suggestion of France or French-bound ships today!

"None of us feels like eatin' in this, so we don't," said Sarah, when after stumbling down to the kitchen, I tried to explain my rare want of appetite this morning, "'Tis the devil's own heat. And we have that Mr. Postbox friend of your comin' at lunch-time, and a right pity it is, I'm thinkin'."

Well, I am not sure that I didn't think the same. Will had been decidedly cavalier about informing me of his movements—and in a place more mine than his!—but naturally I knew he was to be here, attending all events, hobnobbing with everybody great and small, particularly the former, a conspicuous and ubiquitous presence with his busy pencil and natty sketchbook, doing drawings of the Great Day that would elicit all the cooing cries of admiration so apparently necessary to his well-being, and the success of which, in both newly executed and newly published forms, would swell his already swollen head even more. If that were possible!

"I shouldn't think a spot of sun will take your Mr. Postbox's appetite away," said Sarah with the sourest of smiles, as she brought in the milk-jug for the coffee. She had shown an unexpected ingenuity in finding variations

243

on old Will's surname: "Postman," "Postchaise," "Posthorn," "Postcard," the most derisive being "Postboy."

"I doubt it will," I agreed, thinking a little disloyalty might do me good, for, the more I let the imminence of this third visit of his sink in, the less pleased I felt. "My friend Will is, not to mince matters, distinctly greedy."

And he will be flirting with not a pretty little widow, as he thinks but a wife who denies her true status, just as she has her widowhood. Whatever would Will make of that? True, my knowledge of my friend's relations with the opposite sex sprang from his own boastful talk of his exploits or from casual sauciness delivered to pretty passing girls. Of his real taste in women, let alone his intimate dealings with them, I knew considerably less.

This important Saturday morning was surely even hotter than any of its predecessors that week. Above the stillness, above the white nebulous layers high in the sky, there was, one felt, a tug-o'-war of some kind going on—a vast sheet of white paper perhaps about to be torn in two by an invisible warring pair. Back in the offices of the newspaper even the draught from those two opened windows—the *courant d'air*, Barton always called it, remarking rightly that the French term was far better than our one English word—failed to do its needed work. It was airless almost to the point of suffocation. However, it had a unifying effect on the whole team; the others quite forgot to look askance at yours truly, but included him in the general exchange of commiserating glances: fancy us having to work in all *this*, and on this day of days too.

The Advertiser's involvement in the Grand Opening was, readers will already have surmised, extensive, having given it advance publicity every week for the past month and a half. Only right then that both Edmund Hough and Thomas Betterton had seats actually *inside* the bandstand itself, would be, in other words, elevated as town worthies above the rest of the audience, alongside the borough's official dignitaries, the mayor, and the six aldermen and eighteen councillors who had chosen him, and such eminences as Sir Greeley Donaldson (of course!), the Vicar of the Dengate's Parish Church of St. Peter's, the Vicar of St. Luke's (Lucinda Hough's church), the Methodist and Congregationalist ministers, Father Mahoney from Sarah's church, the director of the Royal Hospital, the harbor-master, the captain of the lifeboat service, a local admiral, the headmasters of Dengate Grammar School and of St. Stephen's, Kingsbarrow, the curator of the Royal Gardens, the chief architect of the Bandstand, and the head of the local building firm responsible for its construction.

"And Old Uncle Tom Cobbley and All," remarked Philip Goodenough predictably, with a sour smile, after yet another discussion of the placement for the afternoon, but in truth his jest was inapt. Who sat where told you a great deal about the values of a society which took the keenest and most palpable pleasure in bestowing trappings and doling out rewards such as the best seats at a ceremonial concert. It was himself and his like (me, for instance) who fell into the proverbial category of Old Uncle Tom Cobbley and all, yet were we not given chances, every day, to raise ourselves up? Wasn't this the late nineteenth century, so different from any other epoch in history? Hadn't I myself, coming from obscurity, been given such a chance and wasn't I muffing it pretty thoroughly?

Edmund came out of his own office into the main one, sweating and sighing: "Oh dear, oh *dear!*" he exclaimed to the room at large, making even the imperturbable Terence Hathaway look up startled. "Even the best laid plans can falter, and sometimes through the very person who most wants to be of help."

He then explained. Each luminary seated up on the Bandstand was to receive, gratis, both a booklet-style explanatory program of the inaugurating concert and a handbill listing other activities taking place in the Royal Gardens after it was over; indeed the second publication would be slipped between pages 5 and 6 of the first. But owing to a misunderstanding (by Leslie Midgeley at Barrett Brothers—"the nicest, the most Christian of men who thought he was doing me a good turn") separate parcels of both items had been delivered that morning to Furzebank House itself. Edmund ran his fingers through his hair in gentle despair at this unnecessary well-intentioned mishap.

"The best that could be done now, as I see it, is for those programs and those handbills to be collated, and then sent down to Mr. Higginson at the Bandstand ready for distribution on the allocated seats. But who up at my own house could carry out that task? My wife is not feeling at all well in this appalling heat—her condition, you know!"—meaningful looks all 'round here; nobody had officially been told of Susan Hough's latest pregnancy—"my eldest son and daughter are not due in Dengate till later on, my son George is at school this morning (where else?), and my daughter Lotty has taken the Little Ones over to their cousins, and so there remains in sole charge of the household only our faithful relative, Miss Woodison but she . . . well . . ."

Well indeed! Having met the woman in question I could see exactly why Edmund would not want to trust that job, simple as it might sound, to so dithery an individual. "I was wondering if—well, Peter, I know the good Thomas has got you checking that report from the Marina Railway about its finances, and Barton, you are occupied with the captions for Will Postgate's perfectly splendid drawings"—I had rather felt that should have been *my* task, but was glad that it wasn't—"so that leaves you, I'm afraid, Martin. I shall go and dig into our coffers to find you money for a cab, which will have to wait up there and then take the stuff (and you with it) down to the Royal Gardens. Anyway I am sure Miss Woodison will make you most welcome at Furzebank."

I had no doubt of it, and a talkative welcome it would be, probably getting in the way of my discharging my (easy enough) duties.

Two cabbies were out at the entrance to Dengate Station waiting for fares, their lovely chestnut horses perspiring miserably with the sheer exertion of just standing stock-still in harness in such sweltering, thirsty-making conditions.

"Furzebank House," I gasped out, "that's right up at the top of—"

"I know where Furzebank House is, young feller-me-lad, no help required, thank you very much," said the cabbie whom I chose out of the two apparent equals. "Been goin' up there when you was crawlin' about on the floor, and couldn't string two words together."

I had not been up to Edmund's house since that May Sunday when, emotionally, so many, too many things had happened. For what reason would I have done so? I had fallen into his Dep Ed's bad books, and therefore it would not really have been politic for its owner to have invited such a person as me back, though once or twice, in rather unspecific terms, he (Edmund) had hinted that he would like to do so. On my first visit the residential roads and lanes climbing up to the bare, open down-land it stands beneath had been adorned with lilac, laburnum, hawthorn and—need I remind readers?—Edmund's and George Meredith's beloved gorse, the bloom which had given the place its name. Today, July 4, all these were gone, the green of leaves was darker, duller, the color of the copper beeches a somber brown not the luminous pink-tinged hue that makes them so appealing at the start of a season, and in the gardens there now flourished lupins, delphiniums, peonies, campanula, and roses, roses, everywhere roses, their united scent becoming an element as palpable as air or water the nearer we were to the land adjacent to the house. Incongruously this aroused in me a memory of physical passion—and there was only one person in the world with whom I had experienced *that*, and he was far away by a fjord looking up at granite mountains! Passing that signpost worded TO FURZEBANK HO I recalled that the one and only time a conveyance had taken me down this narrow lane (now lined with tea-roses) Hans indeed had been sitting beside me, soon to be charming his hosts with his combination of sweetness, resoluteness, adaptability, and complete lack of affectation. And it had been on the very night following this visit that we had expressed our delight in each other . . .

Well, for today (maybe forever!) best to concentrate on the lane and on the nut-orchards beyond (same old geese in them sensibly keeping now to the shade of the trees). And here we were turning into that untidily cluttered yard, and here, on hearing the clopping of the horse and the scrape of wheels, coming out of a door in the side-wall at this time of year covered in rambler roses, was—no, *not* Miss Woodison, though for a split-second, the gait and attitude of the head made me think her that good, dependable eccentric but—Lucinda Hough herself.

Though I had obviously counted on seeing her at some point during the day, had indeed prepared some gallantries for when we coincided during the afternoon's pageantry, I was wholly unprepared for the sight of her at this moment. She was wearing green gingham, which became her marvelously, making her through its contrasting checks appear a Dryad dressed in different leaves.

I was all self-consciousness as I clambered out of the cab. Edmund had suggested I might ask the driver to wait for me till I had finished my task; I felt at a loss as to what I should now do about this, Lucinda's presence not having been bargained for. And I hated to look indecisive.

"There are some programs and handbills which have been sent up here by mistake and need sorting out. That's why I've come! At your father's request!" I sounded almost apologetic as I delivered these sentences, for the principal expression on Lucinda's face was bewilderment tinged with apprehension. I was aware too of my cabbie grinning sarcastically to himself, as though at my obvious ineptitude in the face of a very pretty girl so much my superior in composure of manner.

"Oh, yes, Elsie did mention two large packets had arrived here; they're standing in the kitchen now. Cyril and I arrived a bit earlier from London than we'd originally planned. He's upstairs with my mother at this moment; she's not feeling at all well. But I'm not doing anything much myself at the moment, so I could probably give you a hand with things."

No need whatever then for the cabbie to wait. Cyril would take both me and the sorted-out publications down to the Royal Gardens.

"It's strange yet to me, as a student of human nature, very interesting," said Lucinda in a warm, confiding voice that, paradoxically, needless to say, rendered me self-exasperatingly shy, "of all her children Cyril is undoubtedly the one who irritates our mother the most, with whom she gets crossest and finds most fault. Yet when she's upset or ill, he's always the one she wants to see, and who proves the greatest comfort to her. Today, for example, she felt better almost as soon as he stepped into her room—especially as she wasn't expecting to see him in the morning at all."

"I hope your mother will recover soon!" I said lamely, awkwardly.

"Not much chance of that," said Lucinda a touch breezily (sounding her father's daughter). "'Never be heavily pregnant when it's eighty in the shade!' is all one can say on the matter."

I had never heard any girl—or indeed any female of Lucinda Hough's class and education—speak on this difficult, delicate, infinitely fascinating subject this way, which took the mind into so many mysterious yet vital, and everyday, regions. For once my embarrassment was such that I did not outwardly blush, rather felt—as I followed Lucinda into the comparative cool of Furzebank House with its thick, white-washed walls and flagged floors—suffused by an inward disquiet, a sense of being almost culpably ignorant of essentials of life, that took my conversational powers away—or all but.

"It isn't as if the Mater hasn't been in this predicament before," said Lucinda, compounding her own unexpected earthiness, and, with it, my own unease, "and it may well not be the last time either. No question of her being present at all the junketings this afternoon, though . . ."

"I suppose if she felt better, she might . . ."

"Do you know, even if she did, she wouldn't want to come along. She hates people seeing her waddling about with all that extra baggage on her. She has her vanities, our mother, I'm afraid. She was the beauty of her neighborhood, and never forgets it." There was, I noted, real affection in her laugh which I found endearing but also socially disconcerting, I was as unattuned to these domestic surroundings as some scarecrow might feel, brought in from a field and not sure what to do with his unwieldy broom-stick limbs.

But just then a high-pitched cannonade of yaps broke into my gaucherie, followed by an advance of cold, wet noses, and a voice to the back of me declaring: "This poor young man, so hot and bothered, who *can* he be? And why not think of his well-being, Lou, and offer him some of my lemonade. I have never made better." The arrivals were, of course, the two Cairn terriers and Elsie Woodison who (a little to my chagrin) had forgotten who I was. But then, as she brought forth out of the cool of the larder a jug of a perfectly delicious drink of lemon, honey and mint, she recalled the circumstances of my one visit here even if I myself eluded her. "There was a boy from Norway on that occasion, was there not? Such beautiful hair, so wondrously gold. It reminded me of a beau I had who died. I should have so loved to have taken hold of his head, and caressed it."

Now I did well and truly blush, but Lucinda would surely put this down to a healthy dislike of hearing women cooing over the charms of another male. At any rate she said rather briskly: "Elsie, Martin Bridges has come here to work—on the Pater's behalf—on the stuff in those two packets there. Why don't the two of us go into the garden-room, and set to on them together. When Cyril comes down from the Mater's room, he can join us, if he's a mind to."

The garden-room was essentially a conservatory, with glass doors today open onto the garden, but, thank heavens, it was pleasantly most unlike those surroundings at the Majestic Hotel in which Herr Strømme, Hans, and I had, somewhat too formally, drunk hock-and-seltzer and bidden each other farewell. The place was untidy for a start, with children's toys—a humming-top, two skipping-ropes, even a toy violin, all of them spelling peril to the careless foot—strewn between the basketwork chairs and occasional tables. Hibiscus, oleander, and St. John's Wort abounded, and many tobacco-plants whose flowers provided the heady fragrance in which as it seemed, we proceeded to take our seats.

"All these," I remarked, looking around me, "must take some looking-after!" I found it difficult to envisage either of the older Houghs, for different reasons, doing this, but of course people of their status would have a full-time gardener and the conservatory would be his responsibility.

"I enjoy doing it though. I don't think the Pater and Mater would have bothered with *any* of these beautiful blooms if it hadn't been for me. And when I'm away—as I have been quite extendedly this past month"— she shot me an almost apprehensive glance here, as though to ascertain whether I'd been aware of this fact or not (I had, of course, noticed, with a dull kind of relief, that she had not been there with her ragged handful in the Gardens!)—"then there's always Elsie naturally—but she doesn't always remember what to do to which, if you understand me—and there's also my young brother, George, who, believe it or not, has got quite a feeling for plants."

Did I know then the hours beyond counting of deepest satisfaction that Lucinda and I have been privileged to share since, tending just such plants as these, some of them having originated indeed as cuttings from the very growths all about us that July morning? Sometimes I believe that I did know, though how hard it would be to argue the case to, say, a skeptic like Will Postgate or a cynic like Cyril!

I now ripped open with my pocket-knife first the packet of concert programs, then that of handbills. "And let's hope and pray that the quantities match!" I said. "And it'll be a finicky task putting them together."

"Finicky, but couldn't it be just a little enjoyable?" riposted Lucinda. For a happy moment I thought she was actually flirting with me.

And enjoyable enough it turned out, but our time together did not flow past easily. Our conversation got off to an awkward start. For a reason that defies my understanding I began it by deliberately commenting on the very feature of the matter with which we were dealing about which I least wanted to talk and which most irked me.

"These are pretty good drawings old Will did of the Gardens and Bandstand, are they not? They absolutely *make* the booklet and have come out on the page jolly well. Barrett brothers did 'em proud."

"Will?" queried Lucinda, "Will?"

Odd not to grasp immediately who I was talking about, especially considering the gallantry he had shown to her a month back, indeed in these very Royal Gardens he had now honored in pen-and-ink. Did she, friendly in manner though she was, believe herself to reside on such a different social plane from the likes of Will and myself, who carried the tang of London streets wherever we went, that she could banish from her head a few meetings with him as of no consequence and need her memory jogging?

"Will Postgate. You must remember him." It was still impossible for me to imagine anybody forgetting my exuberant, magnetic friend. "Edmund—your dad . . . your father—commissioned drawings from him first of the Church Steps that were Mr. Betterton's undoing and then of the Bandstand."

Lucinda gave a little laugh which I would have considered artificial coming from anybody else. "I don't think Thomas Betterton *had* an undoing. Just short-lived discomposure and a few days of hobbling 'round, a little dramatically (dare we say?) with a stick! And anyway, it wasn't the steps themselves that brought about his accident, they were merely the means, the catalyst. What was responsible was the Demon Drink, I fancy." And she laughed again, a little more naturally this time.

But if she remembered all this, I pressed, she surely must also remember Edmund's asking Will for drawings.

"Oh yes, of course!" she said. "It's just that, having been away from here for such a while, I have had other things to think about than the Bandstand and all the fuss that it's been attracting. But yes," and she applied her gaze to a page which showed the structure from the south, as if taking it in for the first time, "he really has caught it well, your friend. I can't remember: did he study art ever?"

"No, he's been a common-or-garden journalist all his working life. But, like Mr. Betterton except at a far earlier age, he is a Deputy Editor on his paper now."

"And is that *your* ambition, Martin, may I ask?"

"My—?" I was speaking, after all, to the Editor's daughter! How could I possibly tell her of all people about my plans for myself, let alone those concerning my place on *The Advertiser* itself?

"I don't know that I have ambitions of that sort," I fenced. "I just want to be a good journalist."

We by now were about a quarter of our way through our work. A simple enough task yes, but one second's slip might result in a distinguished person, in his eminence of a Bandstand seat, lacking a sheet of important information. I couldn't afford to take any risk of botching our job (nor, I hasten to add, did we do so!) but the chance of talking about myself to the prettiest and most charming girl I had met in my entire life was scarcely one I could pass by.

"I suppose," I went on, "it's different for you. Girls are not expected to have ambitions and then to live up to them. Or not live up, as the case may be." I could not keep out a wistful note from my voice. I had set myself the goal of succeeding where my father had failed—who had realized such ambitions as he must have had only in grandiloquent, drunken talk—and yet there were days when I felt it must be nice to be, say, a whistling post-boy content (seemingly) with his daily round.

Lucinda paused on these last words of mine, handbill fluttering from her hand in mid-air. "Whether they are expected to or not, girls should have ambitions," she said. "I'm a New Woman, at least, I think I am. We can't just spend our entire time on earth ministering to the needs of the masculine or to the House Beautiful."

"No," I said, taken aback, jolted into some thought, if of a momentary and minuscule kind on the subject. "I can see that." A life devoted, day in day out, to the House Beautiful would, it suddenly occurred to me, be so deadly dull as to be unendurable, at any rate to any woman remotely like myself (a being hard, if not impossible, to construct). Wouldn't I rather be a soldier in the blood and burning dust of Khartoum or a sailor having to jump into a longboat to avoid being dashed against the hull of his sinking ship than a girl in such a situation? "But nobody talks to you about rungs of ladders or spiritual mountains to be climbed to the cry of 'Excelsior! Excelsior!' which is the lot of almost every young man."

Lucinda laughed again, but it struck me that there was no mirth in it. "I suppose one idea for us women now—the idea that I try to make my own—is to find things that you believe in, free from all the paraphernalia of jobs and positions and payment and pensions and so on, and do it. But that's easier said than done, let me assure you! (Martin, will you pass me another booklet, please?)"

"Do you know," I spoke my words aloud when I should, I thought, have kept them to myself, "do you know something? I have never once given a thought to what a girl—particularly a girl like you—thinks about what's she's going to do with her life. That's strange, isn't it? Maybe it's because I had no sister—no sister who survived, that is—and my mother was unwell a lot of her life, and died, when I was seventeen, in a Fever Hospital near Epping only two days after my father's death in South London of very different causes. So I never really had the chance of talking over how women should think of their futures." Heaven knows why I felt it necessary to insert all those details of my own life, except first, that I am (and was even more so seven years back) an egotist, and second, that I divined it would interest her. Divined rightly; her eyes shone with sympathetic curiosity.

"I am sad to hear about all that," she said, "but perhaps circumstances aren't ever explanation enough for anything. Cyril and George have sisters, me first in years among them, but I doubt they have given the subject of women and the opportunities they should have for a fuller life any sustained thought whatever. I honestly believe that if there was some measuring instrument—or a barometer or a divining rod—for the human brain, you would find that Cyril has thought a hundred—possible a hundred thousand—more times about the changing price of tea than he ever has about the inner life of any female. Except the Mater when she's upset, and he can do his male, humorous, cheering-up act."

I could well believe this to be true.

"So, don't be too hard on yourself for not having been thoughtful enough in the past. What's important, Martin, is that you have done so now. It's like starting a language—once you have realized, say, there are two definite articles and two major auxiliary verbs—I've been learning Italian so I can take examples from that: articles '*il*' and '*la*,' and verbs '*essere*' and '*avere*'—then you have the key, and once you've got that, you just have to apply it to the door or the chest or whatever it is you're wanting to open. Now you've understood that certain questions you ask every day about yourself and your friends equally apply to the women of your acquaintance, you'll never be able to think of life in the same way again."

It seemed ungainsayable, so much so that there was little else for either of us to do but to resume the task until it was—triumphantly—finished. A whole pile of booklets quite unmistakably containing handbills lay on the little glass-topped table before us. The temperature in the conservatory (and outside, doubtless) had become higher, the scent of tobacco-flowers stronger, the white of the sky whiter and even more pervasive, for the canopy had descended so that it appeared to be almost touching the thirsty-looking ground, and Elsie brought us more delectable and needed lemonade.

Time for me to go—for Cyril to be summoned to get out the dog-cart, and take me down into Dengate. But Lucinda waved a hand as I said this.

"Drink more of Elsie's concoction first," she said, "and it's nice for me to have a bit of a chat before the day gets underway . . . I am glad to be back in Dengate, I suppose, because things didn't—well didn't really work out in London. I had an introduction, you see, from Father Richardson of St. Luke's—where I worship, as I think you know—to Father Marwood in an East End parish, Poplar, and I thought of doing the same for the children of his neighborhood that I did for ours. Tell them, show them the delights of the natural world as it reveals itself in the city, all the birds to be seen, and the plants growing in waste-ground or peeping out from behind cracks in walls, and some surprising sights in unlikely places—wild strawberries, for example; *fraises du bois* really thrive in soot. But they were not interested; they were *uninterested*—and worse."

Worse I interpreted as hostile, even belligerent. Poor Lucinda. I could see that for all her ardor and apparent confidence, she was vulnerable, indeed easy to hurt.

"I suppose the truth is that there is a lot more to do for the poor in society than just take them on a few nature walks, and that—like you and women, at your own confession—I simply, culpably, haven't given it proper sustained thought."

Such a look of dejection came over her face when she had said this that I was given the chance to say: "It's you who shouldn't be too hard on yourself, I think, Lucinda."

She could not bring herself to agree. "And instead return to a life of taking a handful of Farthing Lane kids 'round the Royal Gardens," she said, with an unamused, in fact positively rueful smile. A pause followed in which neither of us felt comfortable and I got up onto my feet but without making for either door, but it was she who broke it. "Anyway," she said, "my father thinks you are a bit happier in Dengate than when we last met"—*was I?*—"but still not happy *enough* in his view. I listen to Barton Cunningham often—we have an understanding, but I know he would like you to be told, because he has said so—all about his constantly itching feet, his desire to be off and away somewhere adventurous, so I am used to hearing the secrets of restless dissatisfied young men. Aren't you both those things?"

How could I not think here of Hans Lyngstrand with his enforced sea-voyages and his ambition to be a sculptor? And how could I not think also of Barton Cunningham, and in his case with a sudden unadulterated warmth. He had indeed taken me into his confidence, as much as he had Lucinda, and it had been such a relief to know that Lucinda and he were not a semi-affianced pair that I'd felt a rush of generosity toward him for that reason alone. But I didn't want him to leave Dengate either; he was my best friend here.

"Restless?" I remembered my abortive visit to Dengate Railway Station. "Perhaps not literally. And dissatisfied—well, maybe not now I have had this Big Idea."

Lucinda's eyes opened wide in (just) perceptibly ironic curiosity.

"A Big Idea. Whatever might that be?"

I told her about my plan for puzzles, conundrums, and jokes. And while I was doing so somebody else came, through the door from the house proper, into the garden-room. George Hough, liberated from Saturday's schooling for the rest of the day because of the town festivities. He nodded his head in a pally sort of way at me (he clearly remembered my croquet prowess) and then seizing the jug of lemonade, tilted the contents (quite expertly) into his mouth.

"A puzzles page! A jokes page! Cripes, that's an idea and a half! Go on—give us some samples," he cried after his rough-and-ready self-refreshment.

"Well, here is a puzzle," I said.

Reciting its lines formed a little island of pleasure in what was to be a charged and hateful day, because I could see that listening was going to bring Lucinda a necessary, if short-lived, freedom from care:

> "Twice nine of us are eight of us,
> And six of us are three,
> And seven of us are five of us—
> Oh, dear! What can we be?
> If you've not had enough of us,
> And still would like some more,
> Then eight of us are five of us,
> And five of us are four."

This baffled both Lucinda and George, as it would myself had I not known the answer already.

"Try letters," I advised them, and then not unhappily seeing the continuing blankness on their faces, explained. "Take the first line. How many letters are in the word 'nine'? Four, are there not? So twice four accounts for the 'eight of us' in the verse. Then apply that reckoning all through."

Both of them did. I saw now that sister and brother could look very alike, and that what united them was a capacity for intent enthusiasm.

"Yes, yes," George all but shouted, "'And five of us are four.' 'Five' has four letters! Bravo! . . . And now I want to hear a joke."

"A joke?" I echoed, stalling. "Well, I'll try to do my best. See if this tickles you. A man went to a dinner party, and when the vegetables were passed 'round, he took hold of the dish and turned it upside down on his head. You can imagine what a mess he made doing that, and what a clearing-up there had to be. But the hostess kept her best society manner throughout, and simply asked him: 'Why ever did you do that with the spinach?'

'*Spinach*? My God!' exclaimed the guest heatedly. 'How absolutely dreadful! I thought it was cabbage!'"

See if it tickled George Hough indeed! Becoming more and more helpless with laughter, he threw himself for support against a large potted oleander, and so slight was his control of himself that he came pretty near to knocking the whole thing over. "'I thought it was cabbage! I thought it was cabbage,'" he repeated, red in the face with his breathless delight, "that's absolutely priceless, that is. Tell the story again!"

"Well," said Lucinda—hard to deduce, after so overwhelmingly hearty a reaction from her younger brother, how much, if truly at all, it had amused her!—"if, Martin, you're in any doubt about the success of your New Page for our paper, George is giving you your answer."

After we had deposited the programs-containing-handbills with the overseer of the ceremonies in the Royal Gardens, Cyril—who did not appear much impressed either by the Bandstand itself or the festivities in its honor—insisted on taking me back all the way to Castelaniene. I didn't refuse; it was almost too hot to walk anywhere, even to the nearest letterbox, and that uncomfortable sensation that the sky was bearing heavily down on us all was steadily getting more oppressive. I had no need to return to the paper; all the offices, shops, and businesses which could were closing at lunchtime, for the whole town was *en fête*.

"Denners is an excellent place, one of the excellent-est, and we all love her," observed Cyril. "as I remember telling you before, I need to come down here from The Smoke pretty often, to do my poor old soul a bit of good after so much erosion by tea and tin. But when the town puts on airs, well, then it becomes bloody parochial, and I get embarrassed witnessing it. The Invicta Orchestra scraping its way through a few dull pieces and that bookshop poet reciting some sententious doggerel he's written for the occasion—what man with a ha'p'orth of gumption would want to waste his time listening to stuff like that?"

It was hard to disagree with this dismissive question, not that Cyril gave me much time to do so. "Of course Denners suits some people more than others. It suits my sister Lou, for instance. She would like to think it didn't. But it does."

After what was coming already to seem like an extraordinarily intimate talk between his sister and me in the Conservatory, I could not desist from asking: "Why? I mean, why does she want to think Dengate doesn't suit her when it does?"

Cyril emitted two or three staccato laughs of ironic amusement, but took a moment actually to reply to me, so busy was he guiding his obstinate and already rather tired horse around the corner into the street where I lived.

"She wants to do good, Lou does, feels she was born to do so. I say, just get on doing the good you can, don't go seeking opportunities all over the bally globe. But she feels she should be working on behalf of democracy and freedom of the spirit—that sort of business—for which talking to a few ragamuffins in the Royal Gardens isn't quite enough. So she betook herself to The Smoke—where I saw surprisingly little of her so otherwise engaged was she—and she has returned—well, pretty darned miserable. For Lou anyway. I mean, I see the picture clearly enough. The daft old cleric, to whom her incense-swinger at St. Luke's introduced her, went and put her up in some little mausoleum of a clergy-house in Poplar, and off she went each day, trying to introduce the rough kids of his parish to the joys of ferns sprouting in factory yards and Red Admirals hovering on sprays of buddleia, when what they really like is fights with knives and kicking each other in the unmentionables and getting pally with shady adults so they can join their desperate gangs sooner rather than later, and all that sort of jolly stuff. Lucinda, you see, is something of a New Woman, desperately committed to thinking the best of humanity—and I don't say that there might not also have been a man somewhere in London who let her down almost as badly as those wretched Poplar brats. Anyway she has come back pretty despondent, but she loves her native town, and will gradually improve."

"She was happy enough helping me with all these concert programs," I could not forebear observing, "and she was amused by one of my jokes for our new Entertainments page." ("New Entertainments page" indeed!— it was still two or three months off!—besides, *had* she really found it amusing? I was not convinced.) "Though not nearly as much so as your brother George. He was beside himself."

"Oh, my brother George!" said Cyril, and I could hear the real affection in his lazy voice. "He's a huge one for laughing when something appeals to him. Tell me the joke that got him going this morning."

We were now clopping along slowly past the row of houses in which Castelaniene stands. Somewhat shamefacedly I told him the story of the man and the dish of spinach prefacing it with the rider that it was intended for the unsophisticated. But Cyril laughed fully and genuinely.

"Well, that had better be the lead in your new page. I doubt the Pater will chuckle, the poor man's got no sense of humor at all as you must have realized. Too busy finding divine laughter in the Cosmos and merriment in Nature to have time for foolish human antics and incongruities . . . Well, here you are at 'Castle Aneen,' as I delight in calling it. Don't give any superfluous regards to Mrs. Fuller; she wouldn't want 'em. And since you seem to have had such a benign effect on some of my nearest and dearest, why don't you start coming 'round to Furzebank Ho more often?"

It was one of the more happily prescient statements of the day which had more misery in store for me than, even at that advanced point (not far off one o'clock), I could have supposed.

Even if I had not known that Will was expected—even if I hadn't been told, nervously, defensively, by Beatrice Fuller herself—I'd have learned as much from the obsessive way she fussed about the house on Friday evening, arranging vases of fresh roses here and little bowls of potpourri there, when I could have told her that Will was largely oblivious to pretty objects.

But there on the hall table was a letter for me. From Hans. (Well, who else wrote me letters?) Considering the lively vernacular he had listened to and employed every working day on board ship, and his familiarity, as I knew from first-hand, with a wide range of English intimate terms not used in polite company, his epistolary style was one of unalloyed formality, not to say stiffness, matching the immaculate copper-plate which served it. It was three pages long, and a good part of it surprisingly (for me) uninteresting and therefore not worth quoting, about living arrangements made on his behalf by—well, of course—Herr Strømme, and involving details of prices which I was surprised to find interested him. Though "my patron believes it's important to live on a small budget. Only that way can you appreciate the big and important things in life." *I wonder, I felt like saying here, in my experience some of thrift's most ardent advocates have never known a day's financial worry in their lives, and exercising it is a kind of vicarious satisfaction for them.* (After all, someone who believed very much in small budgets would not have put himself up at the Majestic.) The letter continued:

I have now been accepted for, and indeed registered at, Bergen's Vestlandetskunstakademi, *a fine institution founded in the last century. (The name means "The West Country Art Academy," as you've probably worked out.) However, for certain sculpture classes it may be necessary to go to the capital, if only for a few days every now and again, and my patron has written to the celebrated sculptor, Julius Middelthun at the Christiania School of Design to see whether he can be of help to me. You may wonder why—personal ties to Bergen apart—Karsten does not want me to be actually enrolled in that school. Well, he is fearful of certain influences from the bohemian circles in the capital who are powerful in the art world, and becoming more so with each passing month. Karsten, though in no sense an artist or even like one, is very open to the arts, as you will have realized from your meeting at the Majestic Hotel.* (Had I realized this? I was not at all sure that I had. In fact, I'd thought him quite the opposite.) *He thinks that Christian Krohg and Erik Werenskiold, perhaps the two most celebrated members of the younger generation, are men of the most enormous gifts, who will put Norway well and truly on the map artistically. Nevertheless, he is a little anxious about the values that are promoted by the suite of studios known as Pultosten (the Cream Cheese) where they work and spend much of their leisure. Their radicalism extends to every aspect of living, overthrowing what a great many people—as Karsten puts it—think essential to keep a decent society going. There have been certain rather dreadful scenes and incidents, scandals in other words—most of them happening whilst I was away from Norway and on the high seas—which have made some people suffer and distressed many, many more, and it may be that an impressionable young man (Karsten's words about myself) needing to come to grips with disciplines to which he is still a stranger, is better at a distance from them, though, from the point of view of his work, he should certainly acquaint himself with both their ideas and their practice.*

"For here is the funny thing, Martin, and it excites me because it suggests that Fate has played a kindly hand in my life. Christian Krohg and Erik Werenskiold are intimates of the most eminent Parisian artists and proponents of all the theories that make their work so impressive and challenging. Many of these they have brought into their own canvases. But more and more they are saying to themselves and the world; "If you are Norwegian, you should not neglect Norway. Do not give us French scenes in a French style, give us Norwegian scenes —and, if you are a portraitist or a sculptor, Norwegian individuals— and find the manner appropriate to your country, your weather, and your race. Only then will you make living art." Well, that rings true, as I believe the expression is, does it not, Martin, and does it not suggest that I have come back to Norway from afar precisely when it is expected of the truthful artist that he does so? But I still feel, like many of my compatriots, those who make up the Scandinavian Colony in Rome, that sooner or later every artist should go to the Mediterranean countries which saw the birth of western art . . .

There was, for a comparatively short letter, quite a bit more in this vein. I had an uneasy feeling that, essentially, Hans was repeating what Karsten and his fellow high-ups had said to him, their warnings about the dubious ways of certain apparently well-known artists. I could sadly only catch the very faintest echoes of all the confidences that had passed between the writer and myself, and I couldn't be sure that even these weren't an illusion.

Anyway at that moment, down the stairs, into the hall, came Will Postgate, who obviously had not only arrived but changed for the great event ahead.

"You have a curious aroma, Will?" I said. He did too; it was like new-mown hay.

"'Curious aroma,' soldier! I have put on my body—'splashed' would be a more appropriate word—'coumarin,' a new and fashionable man's fragrance from France, deriving from the tonka bean tree."

"You don't say!"

"Everybody who's everybody uses it now."

"Not me! But I suppose you're now going to make the obvious retort. I'm nobody."

"But I would never have dreamed of saying so," smiled Will. He could hardly have appeared more of a summer season masher if he'd tried, as of course he very much had: bright-red-and-black-striped blazer, same-striped straw boater (at present in his hand) ribboned to match, and white trousers. In the hand that was not carrying the boater was a rolled-up paper.

"Well, I suppose I have to say you *do* look a somebody," I conceded. "I am surprised you are not sitting up on the Bandstand the way you're togged up . . ."

Will flushed slightly as, after a detectable little pause, he admitted: "Well, I *was* invited to do so, as it happens. Because of having done all the marvellous drawings for the program. But you know me, Modesty Personified. Similarly Edmund asked me to a dinner up at the Houghs, at Furze-bank House, with other Bandstand grandees. But I felt—no, that wouldn't be right either, that would be gate-crashing Dengate society, and if there's anything I dislike, it's being a gate-crasher . . . Anyway Beatrice Fuller had already said she would prepare a delightful dinner for me tonight. So I shall shortly be just mingling with the happy throng in the Gardens, cheerfully receiving, needless to say, the compliments I am offered (and I daresay there will be many), but in the evening I shall be a positive sybarite behind the closed doors of Castelaniene."

What I was being told did not consort with the picture of Will that I had built up over the years, thanks to his general propensity to talk about himself. Indeed the whole announcement—which begged the tiresome question of whether or not I was expected to be present at Beatrice Fuller's delicious dinner—did not ring quite true, to use the idiom Hans had so proudly employed in his letter. Why it did not, I could not define.

And was Will aware that in all likelihood Mrs. Fuller was not a widow at all?

"I've brought you a little present from The Smoke," Will said.

"Present?"

"*This*, old bean," grinned Will, and he released from his left hand the latest number of *The Pall Mall Gazette*, "this is really 'something.' An A1 issue."

Even at the quickest glance W. T. Stead's now famous, not to say notorious bold, tantalizing, and carefully chosen words leaped out at me. I had the immediate sensation, before absorbing them, that, sooner or later, they were to have some personal significance for my life.

"Notice to Our Readers: A Frank Warning"

Who could fail to read on, after that? Standing in the hall, under my stylishly dressed old friend's amused, knowing gaze, I now did so:

Therefore we say quite frankly that all who are squeamish, and all who are prudish, and all those who prefer to live in a fool's paradise of imaginary innocence and purity, selfishly oblivious to the horrible realities which torment those whose lives are passed in the London Inferno, will do well not to read the Pall Mall Gazette *of Monday and the three following days.*

"Crikey-Moses, Will!" I exclaimed almost involuntarily. "Whatever can Monday—this coming Monday!—be going to bring us?"

"Isn't it for us merely to guess?" said Will. "We are being confronted here with one of the nation's masters of publicity—and suspense."

"You must have heard *some* rumors," I said. "I thought you were on nodding terms with old W. T. S."

"Even if I were—which is a bit less than the truth, though I have exchanged the odd sentence or two with our Great Man, it's true—it would hardly make him tell me his carefully laid master-plan for his next four issues. But," and he turned to face me full frontally, and his eyes were twinkling with fun as he said: "Limehouse."

Ever since my last night with Hans, the horror of the name had yielded to disgust pure and simple (to use a highly unsuitable phrase).

"Oh, dear!" I said. "Well, I must get myself kitted up for the afternoon now; the ceremony will soon be upon us. I take it I can keep the *PMG* awhile?"

"It's a gift, soldier!"

And even as I performed my ablutions and chose my attire I read further into W. T. Stead's proclamation of the sensational contents to be found in the next few editions of his *PMG*:

"The story of an actual pilgrimage," he warned in preacher-like tones, "into a real hell is not pleasant reading, and is not meant to be. It is, however, an authentic record of unimpeachable facts, 'abominable, unutterable, and worse than fables yet have feigned or fear conceived.' But it is true, and its publication is necessary . . ."

"Necessary"? Necessary for what? How or why was anything to do with "Limehouse" necessary?

The ceremonies of the afternoon—my readers will probably have sat through a hundred, nay two hundred such, each unique in the minds of its organizers, and for a while, in the eyes and ears of those present, until, probably at halfway point, the tedious familiarity of them breaks through. And then one has to combat the feeling that the sooner they are over and done with, the happier one will be. Home beckons more alluringly than one can almost stand. So . . . Dengate, July 4, 1885.

It was hard to know, either at the time or afterwards, which of the two men actually opened the "Bandstand," Sir Greeley Donaldson of Harland Court or Mr. George Barley, the town mayor, an ambiguity already present in the wording of the poster, despite the "and" linking their distinguished names. Had it been a question of who was dressed the more impressively for the making of the great pronouncement, then the palm would undoubtedly be awarded to Mr. Barley, who gleamed and clanked with his copious mayoral chains, from which small metal porpoises and anchors hung down, with every step he took, nay, with every gesture he made. But Sir Greeley Donaldson delivered from a loftier eminence still, quite literally for he was extremely tall, like some great wading bird, a species of heron encountered only in remote parts but not so shy of humans that he refrained from exhibiting his natural powers. And truly the baronet did have a habit of suddenly lowering his head on its long neck as if he'd just spied a fish way below him and must gulp it up quickly. His height apart, he was very much his son's father, clearly a sportsman, of a physique surpassing most middle-aged men's, his complexion weathered enough to suggest that recently, his deals done and his estate running to his command, he had been relaxing on board some yacht to receive sunshine from the sea and reflections on the waves.

"I am come among you," he told us, "as one who, while he rarely has time for music himself, greatly values its importance in the lives of *others*." On this last word he made another of his strange pouncing movements of the head as if he'd seen, somewhere in the very row in which I was sitting, a fleetly moving salmon-trout. "Those who have more hours to spare than I, alas, have," he went on, somewhat belaboring his point, "will doubtless find much enjoyment in years to come listening here to sweet strains from the incomparable Invicta Orchestra. But never let us forget the *purpose* of music." I had not known music *had* a purpose and shuffled in my hard, uncomfortable seat to find out what it was. I was soon to be left in no doubt. "Its purpose is, I will venture to say, a simple one. To strengthen the spirit. To oversee the banishment from the common mind of all its usual dross, of all that is base and demeaning, all that is impure and ignoble, sybaritic and idle, or even"—and here I was quite sure that Barton Cunningham and I were the targets of the arrows of his eyes—"downright *foolish*! Music can, and should, lift you up, so that you can discard what is worst and weakest in you, and, thus cleansed, become nobler subjects of Her Britannic Majesty, and more diligent servants of the Lord our God."

Heavens, I thought, a bit taken aback, while Barton whispered to me: "He says 'you,' doesn't he? Doesn't put himself in the category of the lowly rest of us."

"Therefore," continued Sir Greeley, "it is positively the discharging of a duty"—and he briefly surveyed us all as if defying us to deny that it was this—"to declare the bandstand in Dengate's Royal Gardens . . . open!"

The sycophantic and, to my mind, disproportionate applause that followed was broken into by the mayor stepping into the stand's gap between the pillars from which Sir Greeley had been addressing us, and indicating that he now desired to mount the extemporized dais and address the crowd himself. Clearly the opening of the Bandstand had *not* been yet made. The sound of chains rattling thus preceded the mayor's own speech, which, unlike the baronet's, demanded the regular consultation of notes. Mr. Barley's

Kentish vowels, mild as they were, contrasted only too obviously, as far as most members of the audience were concerned, with Sir Greeley's patrician sounds, high-pitched yet virile, slow yet energetic.

The mayor—as befitted his position—was pleased to give us a history of Dengate from the Celtic tribes who apparently had made it a most delightful and thriving port "even before the Romans were so bold as to cross the Channel," through the Dark Ages—"but who can say they were dark? I have no doubt Dengaters then were as full of light as they are now!"—right through to our own times, stopping once he'd reached these only too frequently at the various mayoralties he had known before his own.

"Who can forget dear John Bannerman?" he apostrophized, "with his three bull-terriers and his meerschaum pipe and his habit of whistling 'Sweet Lass of Richmond Hill' whenever bothersome arithmetical details were mentioned. Or Samuel Etherington-Burgess."

"Not Samuel Etherington-Burgess!" groaned Barton but still maintaining his whisper. "If ever there was a crashing bore, it was him!"

"Samuel, bless him, could match any event, be it ever so humble, with a quotation from Shakespeare. And so, in declaring as I officially do, our bandstand well and truly open"—and he turned clinkingly 'round to Sir Greeley to give him a look that was at once reproachful and gloating— "and seeing the Invicta players ready to perform for us"—and here he smiled as he delivered the orchestra's name as one, who unlike Somebody Present, had got it right first time—"I will emulate old Samuel and remind you of the Bard's immortal words: 'If music be the food of love play on!'"

And while these overfamiliar words were being uttered, I turned my head to observe Mrs. Fuller, looking her most Grecian, seated beside Will several rows in front of me. There was an odd but unmistakable air of pride about her.

But perhaps it was pride in Dengate itself. Its girls and women looked lovely in their dresses, and their men-folk so pleased to be with them.

And Barton said to me: "I have told you myself, and I know Lucinda Hough has told you, too, Martin, how often I get longings for a more adventurous life—to go to Bengal as my old man did—but when something as damned nice as this afternoon happens, then I want to stay put."

Tragically, as it turned out, he did not. Barton Cunningham died of fever, holding down a petty post in Bengal, without any of his nearest to hand to offer him the last comforts. I hate, deeply hate, thinking about this. For I have to record that, by the time he left Dengate, we had drawn very close, for reasons that will be apparent at the end of this chapter.

Donaldson Ma from St. Stephen's was in the throng—how could he not be?—and, in the interval before the music began, came up to me and asked if I were going to write about this occasion for "my" paper.

"Oh, it will be a joint effort, I expect!" I said, modestly—and correctly.

"But I expect *your* contribution will be the best part of it," said the noble prefect flatteringly. That is"—and here he leaned toward my ear almost roguishly—"if you don't 'chuck' before writing it." Then, resuming his normal dignity of stance and manner, he continued: "I would like to introduce you to my pater, but regrettably, as you can observe with your own eyes, he is parleying with all the bigwigs who are present. You see, if there is a bigwig around, then the pater will not only know him but have something on the man!"

This I could well believe. At this moment however, someone who most certainly could be termed a bigwig appeared at our side: Mr. Whittington.

"What fine speech your father's was, and how truly proud you must feel at being his son!" he enthused to Donaldson Ma. "I myself rejoiced in his every syllable. Did you not do so, too, Mr. Bridges?"

"But of course, sir!" I said.

Mr. Whittington beamed at me as if, on this happy day, he had chosen quite deliberately to believe I was telling the truth. "And, Mr. Bridges, I am looking forward to an account of this day as splendid in prose as that you penned about St. Stephen's Glorious First of June."

Well, I had arrived, hadn't I? It endorsed the moment in Mr. Whittington's comfortable study in School House.

Lucinda seemed always to be on the furthest edge of any group of people I approached, protectively escorted—I nearly wrote chaperoned—by her brother, Cyril. I wondered that Will, who was nodding and smiling away at a great many folk, did not go make his way up to her and start his usual flirtatious banter, but he scarcely left Beatrice Fuller's side, so was reserving his gift all for her, I supposed.

As for the music provided, the Invicta Orchestra played, in my then ill-informed opinion, extremely well, their firmly marshalled sounds floating up toward the tightening white of the sky joyously and at times splendidly. But it was the Grieg Symphonic Dance that took me out of myself most completely. It had a wistfulness that was yet positive and spoke of love of life, a charm that was enveloping but not too sweet, an infectious lilt of melody and a liveliness of rhythm that carried the listener forward to a realm that was, I felt, right there—somewhere—in this real world. I glanced at the program notes and saw that Edvard Grieg's ambition was "to paint Norwegian nature, Norwegian folk-life, Norwegian history, and Norwegian folk-poetry in music."

I thought of Hans again. Hans from Norway, Hans now *in* Norway. I regretted the distancing formalities of his letter. He should be here as a presence, kind in body as in soul, right beside me in Dengate.

But all during the ceremonies, and the social exchanges of both the interval and afterwards, meteorology was asserting itself formidably. The heat was less and less bearable—too many of those proudly printed programs were being used as fans by hands working them with something like desperation—and yet, strangely, the sun itself was obscured by the thickness of that all-consuming white sky canopy. The sensation became inescapable that this was aerial material being pulled tauter, and yet tauter, by the minute, until tearing-point was reached. Then the anxious looker-up saw that into the whiteness black clouds, heavily laden it would seem, were moving, more and more obtrusively. Thus the last items of the concert and the later exchanges of social intercourse were strangely illuminated, in some hybrid of day and night when you could still see as clearly as in the first but had the unease, the feeling of being out of one's natural element that one can have on a nocturnal walk (such as mine to the View a short while back) when surroundings well-known in ordinary circumstances turn foreign, and almost menacing.

Back in Castelaniene, how to disport myself? It was even more socially difficult for me this evening than it had been on Will's last visit. Beatrice was so much his gladsome hostess, catering and anxiously observant, I so very much a lodger (even if my situation had improved somewhat) in the way of things. And the weather was now easy—and alarming enough—to read. The heat was breaking; we were in for a real storm. *Given the relationship flourishing in the body of the house, I would be perfectly willing*, said I to myself, *to spend the evening alone in my attic-bedroom*. The eruption of thunderstorm we all knew now to be an inevitability would be a dramatic accompaniment that could add to the pleasures of whatever travel-book or adventure-novel I chose.

But that solitary consolatory occupation was not to be permitted me.

Will and I coincided in the hall while Mrs. Fuller was down in the basement with Sarah discussing particulars of the delicious dinner ahead.

"I'm very much afraid, old Will," I said as decisively as I could, "that my good landlady thinks I am playing gooseberry."

"Steady on, soldier," said Will, and the somewhat over-deliberate smile he'd worn all day left his face at last. "I'd say it's poor Beatrice who's feeling she is the gooseberry!" He repeated the word with detectable dry amusement as though he didn't think it quite appropriate to such sophisticated circumstances. "And can you blame her? When the three of us are together, you say everything to *me*, never even shifting your glance in her direction."

"I do not!" I said.

"Old man, you do, and you know that you do! Like this!" And on the spot he gave a grotesque parody of what my movement had looked like twenty minutes back, head swivelled to one side so that I could barely see where I was going.

"Very funny!" I said. "Quite a Dan Leno turn! Does Beatrice Fuller like you best for your incomparable humor, or does she prefer you in the role of Don Juan?"

"Come off it, old man, you're spoiling for a fight, I can tell, and that isn't like you," said Will softly. "Why do you mind so much me being friends with Beatrice—"

"Being *friends*!" I echoed scornfully. "That's the right phrase for it, is it?"

"Acting the beau with," said Will, flushing ever so slightly. "It's the way of the world, *n'est-ce pas*?"

A headache that had begun after the Invicta Orchestra's last musical offering was now irrefutably worse, its ball of pain enlarging, and surely gyrating behind my forehead, disturbing who knew what areas of my brain, itself aware of imminent conflict in the sky beyond the house.

"But," Will was continuing, "I do accept now that you think I shouldn't be pursuing intimacy with your own landlady."

The idea behind his last words was so comically mistaken I couldn't resist a sarcastic laugh, one louder than I'd intended.

"What rot, what utter rot you talk," I said.

"Well, if that side of things doesn't trouble you," said Will coolly, standing with his feet firmly placed wide apart on the floor, like a young bull about to charge, "what the devil does, might I ask?"

I could still hear, some way below, the voices of Sarah and Beatrice, but not the words they were actually saying. Even so I stepped more closely to my best friend from London to say what now I simply had to say but that she mustn't hear—at least not yet.

"What troubles me, Will, is . . . she isn't worthy of you."

For at least a minute I thought he couldn't have heard what I'd said and was about to repeat myself when: "You know everything about worth, do you, old man?" spoken with a quizzical smile.

"Of course I don't; how, knowing me, could you believe I'd claim that of myself?" I said. "But I do know *you*, and I do know *her*, and I know the difference between you."

"Well, with so much knowledge perhaps you'd be so good as to hand it on!" The teasing formality of his language had about it more of the throwing down of a gauntlet than of entreaty, and I realized this at once, but what could I do now but expand on my statement?

"She doesn't tell the truth." I whispered these words in his ear, but I felt as though I were shouting them.

"Strong words, old chap," Will stroked his splendidly black and bristly moustache. "I can't believe a lawyer would let you get away with saying them, and I'm not sure that I should either."

"Hear me out, Will, please. Her husband is not dead. I'm now pretty sure of what, somewhere inside me, I suspected all along. And—worse still!—she has cast out their son."

Will stepped back in something like shock. Afterwards I was to think that really a self-appointed Lothario like my old pal, my former mentor, wasn't much concerned about a husband whether living or dead, and had perhaps himself detected certain ambiguities, even contradictions in Beatrice Fuller's accounts of hers. But a *son!*—this he had not bargained for.

"She has no son," he said as definitely as he could manage, "as she has informed more than once." I could tell that, to his consternation and chagrin, I had scored a point, and that whatever he'd just chosen to say in reply, he believed what I'd just informed him was true.

"That's what I meant by 'not honest,'" I made myself elaborate, for what I now could feel in my stomach was that unmistakable jellifying motion of sheer fear which comes about when you've truly offended someone you care for and cannot extricate yourself. "She said that to you because she knows it can have two meanings, and that if you challenged her, she'd say she doesn't have a son she any longer recognizes. But she does have."

There was much more I could say here, but at that point, through the window of the door to the garden, we saw a flash of lightning, followed at once by another, like a brief dazzling image of a two-legged skeleton. Then came the growling tumble of still far-off thunder.

These gave Will the time he needed to deal with me and my revelations. Once more he came a few paces closer to me, once more he resembled the image of a young bull lowering his head with only aggressive purpose.

"Don't you say another thing about her, do you hear," he said, "you evil-minded little—*virgin*. Do you think I've forgotten the pathetic exhibition you made of yourself at Limehouse? Charles Bradlaugh and Mrs. Annie Besant are absolutely right; the male who shuns the flesh, the normal sexual instinct is . . . sick. The very word 'chaste' is eunuchs' cant. The sickness gets into the head, and there it bloody well stays."

What I could say in retort to this cruel judgment? But the voices in the basement stopped, and in the horrid silence we heard Beatrice ascending the stairs.

"I had had fantasies of a dinner *al fresco* tonight. But it cannot be," she said, "so we shall have to have our repast in the usual dull place. Martin"—I was surprised she called me this and not "Mr. Bridges"—"we are of course expecting you to join us."

271

Good of you, when I pay for all my food here, I felt like saying. But what *should* I say? "Oh, thank you, Mrs. Fuller that is really so generous and hospitable of you"?

But I was forestalled by Will who, in a brisk no-nonsense voice, said: "Oh, but Martin's just been telling me how he has an invitation for this evening he simply can't get out of. Quite the society man he's becoming these days, don't you think, Beatrice? A young-man-about-Dengate if not about-town!"

Beatrice Fuller looked at me with virtually the first natural expression on her face with regard to myself that I had as yet seen. I might have been her son. And when she spoke it was in a low, almost anxious tone:

"But, Martin, it seems just a little foolish to be going out now when—when there's a real storm not just brewing up but actually beginning. I'm sure whoever's expecting you will quite understand. Nobody would want any guest to go braving thunder-and-lightning purely to be polite."

I rose to the occasion. The old actor in me again!

"Oh but you know me, Mrs. Fuller," I came up with a jocular voice that positively amazed me, for I absolutely wasn't going to set myself against Will Postgate, Will my *former* friend. "My word is always my word. Besides when—if—I get there, I shall be enjoying myself tonight. And no young man can resist an opportunity for enjoyment."

So there was nothing for it now but to accept the sou'wester and umbrella Mrs. Fuller proceeded positively to press on me, to supplement my mackintosh, and leave the house.

By the time I had passed the Royal Gardens day had given way to night—and it was not yet eight o'clock. Above the clustered alleys that lie to the back of the harbor I saw lightning zigzagging like some luminous whip being flicked, then cracked; its movement made this premature darkness seem darker still. Then, from somewhere over to the West I heard bangs and thumps of thunder. What schoolboy in our land has not had to learn by heart our Laureate's "Charge of the Light Brigade": "Cannon to right of them,/Cannon to left of them,/Cannon in front of them/Volley'd and thunder'd." I was not in this situation yet, but as I walked toward the Esplanade I was approaching it. The storm was certainly moving westwards, while I myself was walking eastwards; sooner or later our paths could not do other than converge. This meeting was, I felt, what the whole tense, white day had been tending toward.

As the Majestic with its line of lighted conservatories came into fuller view, the rain came down. Came down as suddenly and as overwhelmingly as though its descent was the result of a switch being turned by some resourceful theatre producer in some cunning modern device. Its fall was very straight and very fast, for there still was next to no wind.

Wherever to take myself in these conditions? I had been a rash fool to turn myself out of doors. More bangs, more thumps now, and no longer just over the west, the marina itself seemed the target of this aerial bombardment, and when I heard a heavy crashing in the near distance, like the ejection of a positive avalanche of boulders from some quarry in the sky, I looked ahead of me surprised that the marina hadn't been blown up. In fact it was standing strong as ever in all its gaudiness, as the flashes of lightning revealed. Perhaps, I thought with a bitter inward smile, I should take myself into the lighted luxury of The Majestic, but even in this storm I could not bring myself to dare to do this; I doubted any of its stuck-up uniformed staff would let me in. Instead I must head, like the Six Hundred in Tennyson's poem, into the "Jaws of Hell." But angry and unhappy though I was, I did not think I wanted this destination, not just yet, indeed never at all. I surely didn't deserve hell, in which I'd never been able to believe.

Lowering my head, though, in this breezeless air, that made little difference to the soaking the skies were giving me, I walked on until I appreciated—two short bright swishes of lightning enabling me to do so—that I had now arrived at that point of the Esplanade at which two months back, walking in the other direction, Barton Cunningham and I had spotted the two pretty girls and had simultaneously turned 'round to have another look at them. On my right side the sea, as yet smooth as a roll of fabric, was blacker than the sky and receiving, without demur, the downpour it was releasing, but only yards away was that little piece of municipal chinoiserie, the little shelter erected on the Esplanade's seaward side. Beneath its pointed shingled roof and seated on its wooden bench—which had space enough for at least four people—I would at least be out of the rain, and comparatively less vulnerable to any ground-aiming forks of lightning than in any other possible place in the immediate vicinity.

Virtually the moment I stepped inside it, the rain increased in velocity. Before long its vertical lines were battering the roof so fiercely I feared for its survival; the timbers might well come splintering down onto my head. The shelter was open on both the landward and the sea-facing side, so, for all the continuing lack of wind, blasts of rain issued in from the Esplanade to deposit rapidly expanding puddles on the uneven ground. Hopes of keeping dry soon faded, and any enterprising streak of lightning could have struck at me without much difficulty. Nevertheless, I thought, here I'd better stay, and who knew for how long? Dante and Beatrice, as I sarcastically called the pair in Castelaniene, were doubtless now billing and cooing indoors. For all the latter's words of affected concern for me, I wondered if either of them were giving me a thought. I imagined their sportive frolics interrupted by a knock on the door. Four men (policemen? St. John's Ambulance?) stood on the porch carrying a stretcher. On it lay the body—was it alive, or was it burned-out shell?—of a young man struck by lightning: one Martin Bridges late of *The Advertiser*.

Such thoughts, embellished to induce further self-pity and dark gratification, occupied me so thoroughly that it's a wonder I became aware at all of another person availing himself of the shelter. Afterwards, going over the encounter (as time and again I would obsessively do), I thought it distinctly possible I neither saw nor heard him make his actual entrance into it. He was, as I was to note presently, stealthy in movements. But at this moment, as I strive to bring the scene back for my readers' sake, I now believe, obscured though he was by all the resentful images of Will and Beatrice playing inside my head as in some perverted puppet-theatre, that the burly but bent figure of a man did impinge on me even as it came in from the rain, shaggy hair dripping water just as the roof-ledges were so noisily doing, and clasping in his rough chapped hands a brandy-bottle.

Even so his addressing me—and after how many minutes I cannot say—in that low, harsh huskiness so characteristic of both heavy drinkers and sufferers from bad colds made me, quite literally, jump in my seat. And this despite the fact that I had been just roused from my gloomiest broodings by the loudest explosion of thunder so far, surely detonated a mere matter of yards above the Esplanade and this more-and-more fragile-seeming shelter.

"*That*," my fellow-occupant gasped, tilting his chin upwards toward the blackly bruised sky beyond, "is *his* only way of speaking to us. He has just the one language for expressing what he thinks, for giving us warnings."

And he heaved his bottle to his lips through which he proceeded to let fall a few drops of its dark-golden liquid. He smelt powerfully of this stuff; he must have been swigging away for some time. He'd perched himself on the edge of the bench as though he didn't intend to stay in the shelter any longer than he could help, it being a mark of weakness to be there in the first place.

His remark didn't seem to admit of a reply. Besides I, Martin Bridges, product of the nineteenth century and employee of *The Advertiser*, felt physically, nervously jolted by this latest clap from the heavens, and, if I spoke, might well betray this reaction. I still had some pride.

"I was talking to you, young man!" said my fellow refugee. "And when I choose to speak, why, shucks, I expect other people to listen. If I wanted to talk to myself, I'd have done so, and if I wanted to talk just to *him*"—again the tilt of the chin, which, I could see in the dim light, sprouted only a short beard, of what color I couldn't discern—"then I'd have done so aloud without bothering to say anything in *your* damned direction. And I still might do, you know, 'specially if we hear his voice again. Because I respect *him*, you see, I'm not frightened of *him*, though he *is* frightening, for he is *mighty* and there's none able to challenge him."

Even without "shucks" and that adverb "mighty" I had decided from the rhythm of his sentences and his burred *r*'s (and also, I might add, his spitting to punctuate certain phrases) that the sharer of my shelter was an American—of some variety or other, for he didn't much speak like the other few (very few) Americans I'd met, nor even like the many imitations of them I'd heard.

"Quite a storm!" I said in that jaunty way I had with intrusive strangers. "Still I suppose it had to come, didn't it? And of course, it's made everything cooler."

The relief of this was something I hadn't fully done justice to, what with the overhead tumult and my own equally tumultuous feelings. Perhaps I should have been more inwardly grateful—to *him* perhaps?

"'Made it cooler,'" growled the man, "made it a darned *sight* cooler,

I'd say! But . . . well, if that isn't England for you! Always so practical, always thinking of itself and its damned comforts, and blind—blind and deaf both—to what this world really means. Shucks!" As if to illustrate his contempt for the country where he now was, he tilted the brandy to his mouth with vicious jerks of elbow and forearm, as if he were already engaged in some sort of fight. "Did you hear what I said to you, young fool who's said in his heart there ain't a God? I've told you, clear enough, I'd have thought: '*That* is his only way of speaking to us meaningfully. He has just the one language for expressing what he thinks . . .'"

I reverted, I knew it, to my Thomas Middleton School self, one in truth I'd never left for long: "I heard you the first time," I replied.

Then, as if to complement this American's repetition there came another boom of thunder, though perhaps slightly less loud, and perhaps a fraction (to be welcomed) less directly overhead.

"So you did, did you? Now I know—as I could have done just by looking at you—that you're some very cheeky as well as some very *stupid* English kid," the man spat the insulting adjectives out at me. "No wonder Ukko utters what he utters when the land beneath him is crawling with idiots like yourself, godless little wretches all of you."

Surely he was—well, did I really need to say it, even to myself, stinking high to heaven as he was?—pretty half-seas over. Then—*Ukko*, I wondered, *whoever is Ukko and what can it be that he's uttering?*

"*Ukko?*" I asked, half in protest that he could expect me to understand such an outlandish name. But I'd heard it before, had I not? A Kvennish name, if my memory served me right.

"Ukko," another spit, right into the spreading puddle at his feet. "Ukko, Old Man—*Ylijumala* as my ancestors and kin would call him, the over-God, the Captain of the Heavenly Crew. Thunder came into the world because Ukko mated with Akka, yes Ukko actually *fucked* Akka, and every one of us, Yankee, Britisher, or Kven should remember that truth— or else . . ." And here he gave another upward jerk of his arm, the bottle still in his hand, and pointed this time not at his own mouth but in my direction, as if in a hostile toast, or as though to see me off with an obscene gesture from his phallus. "Yes, those who know no better call thunderstorms 'natural disasters.' Goddam fools!"

Heavens, I didn't care for this man at all, noxious and *obnoxious*, with his incomprehensible drunken talk, and but for the remorseless *swoosh-swoosh* of the rain, and the likelihood of further lightning I would have moved away from him at once. But the continuing bad weather beyond the shelter held me captive beside him. Not as he talked on, it was me he was really addressing: "Gee, when in March he made himself heard and seen, in such an awesome way as even a traveler like myself had never seen before, then I told him square, said to him straight out: 'Ukko, Old Man, *Ukko*, it is not just your right, but the nature of your being, that you manifest yourself like this, and don't think I don't know it! I would never be so foolish as to make lamentations, not like the poor-witted creatures all around me, with their complaints and their silly prayers and their crying out loud like goddam babies. I shall go down if that is what you want. I shall make for your arms and if you stretch out your hammer I'll be ready to take it. Always ready, always!'"

This strange little speech was every bit as alarming to me as anything in the outer world (which had after all inspired it). Oddly the man didn't slur or even trip over his last words as you might have expected in one who'd consumed as much brandy as the state of his bottle indicated. But there was something alien about his delivery all the same, almost as if he were not employing the language he was most deeply intimate with. *Ylijumala*, "my ancestors and kin" . . . for all that he'd used the exclamations "shucks" and "gee," maybe he was not an American at all.

I glanced at him as full-eyedly as I thought wise. He was dressed—like myself—for a summer's day, with loose blue trousers of that strong twill cotton known as "jeans," and a short-sleeved shirt, also blue, of some towelling material or other. The arm nearest me was pretty thoroughly tattooed; I could just, before turning my eyes back to the view of the Esplanade pavement immediately in front of me, catch a mermaid and an anchor. A nautical man, therefore. A nautical man who was and was not an American. Who talked of Ukko and Akka and had actually used the word Kven . . .

The stab of fear I experienced as his identity broke in on me was violent enough to make me jump and cry out. And though I did not *precisely* do these things, I am pretty sure some noise not quite normal, and by civilized standards not natural, emerged from my throat and that I made an involuntary movement which rocked the wooden bench.

At any rate he turned around, and I could see a look of aggressive challenge in his dark, almost black eyes.

"Something wrong?" he growled. "Some goddam thing you want to say?"

And this time he didn't sound like a Yankee at all.

One thing I was absolutely certain of. The man—the sheer reek of him was confirmation enough—was not dead. No revenant. Only too alive, and possibly dangerous to boot.

"I was just thinking," I spluttered, hoping to hear some footsteps coming along the promenade through the wet evening, but no such luck, not yet. "That the rain's let up a bit at last. And we haven't heard any thunder-claps for—"

"Get yourself out in the storm then!" As if he had the authority in this shelter when it was me who had entered it first. "Doesn't show you're brave if you do so, if that's what you're thinking. The man who respects Ukko—who wants to find out what he's trying to tell us in his power—doesn't desert him and go rushing through rain like some spoilt brat."

And truly, whatever the degree in its intensity compared with before, the rain was still splashing heavily down, and wasn't that—further off, ad-mittedly—another sky-sent rumble?

"When he rages for day after day, then that's another matter, pal, and when that happens, you may well think the time has come to submit to his will."

Well, I would take a risk. I could not do otherwise, however far from brave I was.

"As you did in March?" I ventured, my pulse quickening as soon as I'd spoken, and the saliva forsaking my mouth. I was feeling less steady even than at the Gateway, and yet—wasn't I, in an important sense, back at the Gateway a second time?

"In March, Ukko was hard even for me to understand. Such vengeance he took then, who the hell, I thought, was I to be spared his wrath. But"—and just as I felt I was getting somewhere, even if it were somewhere he (and I with him) dreaded, he swung his head to meet me, his action making the brandy shake in the bottle—"hell, what's an English boy like you doing knowing about Ukko? I thought the English had turned their back on gods of every kind."

This was something I hadn't heard before, though, recalling my own antipathy to church-going and scripture lessons, maybe he had a point. But any defense of myself as representative Englishman that I might have liked to make was wiped out by the shock of confirmation I now received. I saw that the man was red-haired.

In my head I could hear Hans Lyngstrand saying, *He was clean-shaven.* Well, that was no longer true, though his beard, I could see was of recent growth. *And a redhead. A darkish sort of red. And then there were his eyes. Black but their blackness changed—and I wasn't the only chap on board to notice this—with the weather. Clear when the skies were clear, clouded when the skies were overcast.*

Certainly in each eye pupil and iris were one—as black as coal. And the weather, which this union of color denoted, could scarcely be more inclement.

Again Hans's voice echoed internally: *But Alfred Johnston talked about things that didn't belong to natural history or any branch of science we'd ever been taught.*

I said his name aloud. This seemed to amuse him.

"Say it again, English boy!" he ordered, and when he did, gave a deep laugh of such phlegm-ridden wheeziness it scarcely deserved so innocent a name. "Yes, I've called myself Johnston. On more than one ship. Friman's another favorite of mine. But neither is my real name, any more than the others I took on simply for the sake of being a respectable member of a crew. My real name I shan't divulge to anybody. Certainly not to a shivering little English boy who talks about the ancient gods without understanding them . . . But how come you know about them at all?"

For the time being, I decided, I shall not speak Hans's name aloud. I felt afraid to do so, and largely because everything about this bo'sun come back from the missing seemed fearful, and dislocated from any life where there were persons and things to depend on.

"Friends have told me. One friend in particular. Who once served with you."

THE STRANGER FROM THE SEA

"Well, a darned many have done that."

"On *Dronning Margrete.*"

Alfred Johnston sighed, "Oh, that was a bad business that truly was. A beautiful ship, but Ukko knew that he had to treat her with savagery. He dashed her to pieces in the very Channel to the back of us and showed little mercy. But he favored *me*, did Ukko, because I am his loyal servant, and know his power. Can't remember everything that happened, though. When the mast split, I was able to get into some kind of dinghy . . ." Just as in Hans's case in our early conversations, the dreadful experience the man was trying to recapture in words was suddenly so vivid it banished the speaker's actual surroundings. "Yes, and then—then I had the fortune to be picked up by a Belgian boat. She took me to Antwerp and safety, and there they put me in some sort of seamen's hostel. They were all good enough to me, doctors, nurses, fellow-sailors, probably couldn't have survived without 'em, but it was like—like being a dog, a proper dog, German shepherd or an elkhound, shut up in a damned human kennel. Then they went and found for me—would you believe it?—another position as bo'sun, on an Antwerp boat ship going to Santander. We put in to Dengate to pick up some cargo, but then"—he grimaced, but his narrative—probably for the most part true—had steadied him a little, his speech was more coherent, his face a little more composed—"but then Ukko showed his temper yet again, and so the Captain wisely decided not to put out to sea again till the morning. So I decided to hit this town. I hadn't had much fun this year, and bad weather brings back bad memories, and those have to be dealt with. But I didn't get so very far from our berth in this port."

"But far enough"—I knew it was now or never; my suspicious reluctance to pronounce my friend's name in his company must be resisted—"for you to encounter somebody who knew Hans Lyngstrand from *Dronning Margrete.*"

"Knew who?"

"Hans Lyngstrand."

The man edged nearer to me, and I thought: *If he doesn't strike me unconscious with his fists, then he will through the sheer dirt and stink and ill temper of him.*

"Alive?"

"Yes. But he was in the cold sea a long time and got a severe pulmonary infection. He . . . he recuperated here in Dengate awhile, and now is back in Norway."

"And you're a friend of *his*, you say?" The words were not spoken in the least nicely, in fact were spat out, with foul-smelling spittle at my face.

"Yes, I am."

"Well, be so good as to tell him when you next see him—in England, Norway, or at the bottom of the sea—that in my view, and in Ukko's, too, of that I have no doubt—that he, the good little Hans Lyngstrand, was the true cause of the storms we suffered—that sent the beautiful *Dronning* under—not the low depression or whatever else learned Norwegian First Mates like to talk so grandly about. Disgusting piece of shit! That's what he was! Offering his bum to all and sundry, by day and by night, sucking the cocks of any one who asked—and Ukko knows there were a damned sight too many sailors who did just that—and all the time the sweetest innocent smile on his face, the most obliging offer to be helpful to everybody in just whatever way he could. As though butter couldn't melt." His voice assumed a strange high tone here, presumably in mimicry of Hans's effete desire to be helpful. "'I'm Hans and I hope you like me!' And you—you probably fell for him, too. You look the kind of fool who would! I'm a *man* with a man's rule. When I love a woman—as I did her up in Molde in Norway—I expect from her faithfulness, obedience unto death—and way beyond even that. That is how a true Kven, a true server of Ukko thinks. He doesn't like stupid girls, silly women who run off with other men just because it appeals to them to do so. He thinks they're filthy tarts, and wants them to pay. And even less he likes boys who do women's work with their bodies, and then pretend that it's natural. Damn them all to hell, I say. Ukko won't be sending the likes of little Hans to the great peace of beyond with his flying spray, I can tell you that much. No! He'll gladly let them sink to the far depths of the sea from which he'll cast them for ever into the fires of the underworld . . ."

These appalling last words were the last I heard from the bo'sun. In my revulsion, two sentences earlier, I had hauled myself up off the bench, left the shelter and was now running—for dear life, even if that literally meant death—back in the direction of Castelaniene. Better to face Will and Beatrice than to hear one syllable more from this Kven's violent, evil mouth.

By the time I gained St. Ethelberga's Road, with my mind so stunned it could surely receive no further impressions, and with my body painfully pierced by stitches such was the desperate ferocity of my speed, the storm had virtually passed over our particular Channel port and was making for the next one.

I remembered what old Doris had told me when I was a small boy: "Always cast off wet clothing the moment you get inside, and then give every inch of yourself a thorough rub-down till your skin tingles." (My poor mother was too engrossed in the sorrow that was her married life, and my father too little interested in anybody's welfare, his own included, to worry about such things.) So now, many years after my home life had come to an end—and, if truth were to be told, scarcely happier than then—I entered Castelaniene with the intention of doing precisely this. All corners of all my garments, all inches of my body beneath them, had been attacked or invaded by the vicious summer rain. But before I could even begin to attend to these necessary and restorative attentions to my person, I saw Mrs. Fuller coming through the hall toward me with vigorous, agitated, dramatic strides. She clearly didn't expect the person to be entering Castelaniene to be myself.

"You're not Will!" she said, in a tone of reproachful accusation. "I thought you might be Will coming back—I didn't see how he'd make the London train he wanted to get—but perhaps, after all, he did! Anyway, you're not him. And he's taken his door-key with him!"

"Will went out—in all this?" I said, shaking the sopping hairs of my head. "Why ever . . .? What about the nice dinner you'd got for him?"

"Never eaten," said Mrs. Fuller, "on account of things *you* were pleased to tell him about me, Mr. Bridges."

"The things weren't *about* you," I said, never imagining my long over-due confrontation with Mrs. Fuller would take this particular impromptu shape (and I could still hear rain beating on the porch behind me). "They were facts of your situation which I thought"—though what exactly had I thought as I imparted my incomplete knowledge to Will—and hadn't it been a matter of feeling rather than of thinking?—"that he ought to know in light of the . . ." But what was it? "The growing friendship between you!" was what I decided on.

"You told him about George and Horace," Mrs. Fuller spoke the words quite flatly, and sounded more injured than angry, and more sorrowful than either.

"I told him what I'd worked out, quite carefully, for myself. Together with things I'd gathered from other people." I shook my saturated head again, like a retriever dog. "But my knowledge wasn't very complete. I'm sure it could be a lot completer. But you had after all given me to understand that your husband was *dead*, as indeed you had made the whole town think, considering you organized a public funeral for him. Not true, I am pretty certain. As for Horace you never mentioned him until I stumbled on you in the Mercy Room."

Mrs. Fuller bowed her head as if at last submitting to a judgment from me. *I must take advantage of these charged moments, I told myself, a beneficial towel can wait, and if I get the mother-and-father of all bad colds, well, so be it! I shall suffer—but I shall survive, I'm strong enough.*

"Mrs. Fuller," I went on, "I met someone just now—in the little shelter on the Esplanade, quite by chance—and he turned out to be Bo'sun Johnston from the Norwegian ship, the very man your Mary, that excellent little vehicle, brought Hans Lyngstrand and me a message from—from the Great Pathway beyond the Gateway. The man is no more out there in the land of the dead than you or I are at this very minute. What Mary said was a lie from beginning to end, and it wasn't for the first time she was guilty of one, was it?"

"Mary acts under the influence of the spirits who govern existence without our always realizing it," said Mrs. Fuller, more to the floor than to myself, "and into the bargain she has remarkable, prodigious talents."

"I've no doubt of it. *Among* her talents are the writing and reading of shorthand, I now know. I put two and two together just now, as I walked fast through the rain to this house: Mary read, on my bedroom table, those notes I'd made for my interview with Hans Lyngstrand about his experiences at sea. Not all of what he told me was suitable for the newspaper, you see. That's how she knew the story I'd told nobody else of Bo'sun

Johnston and how Hans had heard him venting his rage and distress to the elements when the ship was caught in a storm."

Mrs. Fuller said, but her subdued, near-apologetic voice had something girl-like, indeed almost waif-like about it: "I did not know this. I did not know it was a . . . lie. How could I? I don't read shorthand myself. I was always—am always—impressed by the things Mary says at our sessions. Shows such imagination and ability to identify with others."

"How about the many messages from George Fuller? Another person whom the Gathering assumed was dead, but who was in fact alive and well in Italy, in the real Castelaniene, I have no doubt. As nobody knew better than you."

"I suppose," said Mrs. Fuller in the same curiously pathetic vocal register, "that she exercised her intelligence at such times just as she did in the case of—of your Norwegian's bo'sun. Also, she'd known George personally, ever since she was little, and obviously later listened to me talking about him, and . . . and besides . . . Well, I suppose that's yet another thing you, the ever-snooping journalist, know?"

At least she hasn't called me a Mr. Peter Pry! I thought.

"I don't know what you're now referring to, Mrs. Fuller." And then suddenly—well, of course!—I did!

"Mary is my husband's daughter. She doesn't know this herself, but I suspect she has guessed by now. Her mother was a woman from Farthing Lane who also used to work in the kitchens at St. Stephen's College. An easy enough friendship to form if you've a roving eye for vulnerable lower-class women like my unfortunate husband. He was always terrified that Horace would feel the same kind of attraction to Mary as the boy grew older; that was one reason he was so keen to get him out of this country, that and his own infatuation with that stupid old Italy and all its many *treasures* . . ." She hissed out the last words, and hadn't she a right to her anger? Her husband had, I now knew, masterminded her son's expulsion from school so that he could leave the country and lead an Italian life, free from any danger of being attracted sexually to his half-sister.

Readers, please believe me when I tell you that for the first time (even counting that occasion when she broke down and wept on my shoulders) I felt unmitigated sympathetic sorrow go out from my own self to Mrs.

Fuller. To the woman who, to my real embarrassment, had got herself into a crouching posture on the hall-floor, a reduced personage indeed.

"Mrs. Fuller," I said, as softly, as warmly as I could, "you don't *need* to tell me everything you've been through. You've suffered, really suffered, I see that now. For some years. Far more than you should have done." Then, "I am sorry that's been so!"

Mrs. Fuller said, equally softly, "I do believe you are, Mr. Bridges, I've always suspected you of a kind heart somewhere, which you largely preferred to keep hidden . . . Yes, imagine how awful it was having your husband and son both leaving you, of their own volition, how tongues clacked spitefully and reprovingly here in Dengate, Edmund Hough's alone excepted. It was George Fuller's own idea that we should make out he was dead. He's living another life under another name with another— shall I call her *wife?*—in Italy. And I decided once we'd come to that arrangement to take up Mary—seriously take her up—teach her a little of literature and the arts, while paying her to do work in this house"—*pay her for skivvying*, I added privately, for wasn't that what it had been?—"and also encouraging her to make the most of her truly amazing gifts for improvisation by introducing her to the Gateway. Of course, that was a very good place also to ensure everyone in this community thought George had died. You do realize, I hope, that if I hadn't helped Mary as I did, she'd have— well, gone the way of many a girl in Farthing Lane and entered the oldest profession in the world. There were definite temptations in that direction. There was one terrible old woman in Farthing Lane who was ready with contacts for Mary in Dover. I ask you!"

She didn't altogether need to. Limehouse, I could not but remind myself here, perhaps all along Mary had induced in me thoughts of Limehouse and its activities, to my shame, to my reluctant, guilty enjoyment and my confusion.

"I suspect your opinion of me must be a very low one," said Mrs. Fuller, from her discomfiting physical lowness of attitude, "but I want to tell you something, Mr. Bridges. That telegram I was so angry with you for seeing, and leaving about for others to read, concerned new arrangements between George and me. I am now as his full legal widow in complete command of his former British property. I shall sell Castelaniene

—which has brought me misery rather than happiness—and move somewhere out of Dengate, probably abroad, and take Mary with me. She shall work in a menial capacity no more. I shall raise her to that station in life which will bring out all that is best in her."

And as if to prove that she was robust enough to do this, she raised her own body up from the hall-floor. Somewhat incongruously she then said: "Mr. Bridges, how very terribly you got caught in the rainstorm. You must now rub yourself down, very hard, very thoroughly; it's not too late to do this. We don't want you catching your death of cold. I shall go and get you a large towel from the kitchen."

"That's very kind of you," I said, "and I'll avail myself of your offer. But I'd best tell you that after this conversation, I'd prefer not to stay here in this house. Even for tonight. I shall go, despite the hour and the weather, 'round to my friend, Barton Cunningham. He has always said the Cunningham house is a very large one, with several bedrooms vacant, one of which I could rent from his parents. It'd be a happier arrangement for me. Though I shall miss the cats here! I'll collect my stuff and pay you any arrears of rent tomorrow afternoon."

And that's what I did, though—a point in my favor, I think—I was to go 'round to see Mrs. Fuller and the three cats repeatedly and not without pleasure on all sides, until Mrs. Fuller did sell Castelaniene and move away. My first night not in her house—but in the comfortable bedroom at the Cunninghams'—I slept but little. I lay there on my new bed listening to the still continuing sounds of rain falling off roofs and guttering and dropping from walls and trees—*whoosh*, *splash*, *drip-drop-drip*—and to the sea rustling and shivering after so much liquid disturbance of its orderly surface, unable to decide what of all the dark histories I'd heard tonight—about Hans on board *Dronning Margrete*, about George and Beatrice Fuller, about Mary—was the hardest, the most painful, to accommodate in mind and morality.

That much-heralded issue of the *Pall Mall Gazette* for Monday, July 6, and for the three following days, exposed the scandalous extent of prostitution in our country, the netting and caging of young (often extremely young) girls for commercial purposes in London's ill-regulated stews. (Like the one in Limehouse.) It shocked the whole British nation, and brought further fame to W. T. Stead himself. Well, there by the grace of Mrs. Fuller went Mary the vehicle from Farthing Lane. Perhaps such matters—Hans's bestowal of favors to his shipmates was another among them—were best left to the intrepid, the buccaneer journalists like Stead himself. I wasn't like him, was I? I wanted life to be serene, harmonious.

But if in relating my departure from Castelaniene I have reached what seems like (and in so many important ways is) an ending to the story of my induction into Dengate, then I must affirm unequivocally that it also marks a beginning—the beginning of a new life which, as the calendar moved on, made the previous months' experiences seem not just remote but worth jettisoning from the mind. Anyway they got crowded out by other concerns. Living with the Cunninghams made me into a Dengater. In their hospitable household I saw not only Barton's friends but members of his parents' large, self-confident, lively circle, with whose interests—and gossip—I became familiar. I got to know (I am sharp in such matters) who was on the rise in the town, who was in difficulties (or even trouble), who was going out with whom, who was about to come into good fortune. All this knowledge, all this identification with other people affected my engagement with *The Advertiser* where increasingly I felt it was my own town whose affairs I was dealing with as young editor and reporter. So involved was I indeed that the longing to be adventurously out-and-about rather left me. Hadn't all that culminated in my ghastly meeting with Johnston in the Chinese/Japanese shelter on the Esplanade? Whoever in his right mind would want to take the risk of such a thing again? Besides, major changes in my personal life were compelling and demanding enough for me not to seek factitious dramas (as, in my security, they now seemed) elsewhere.

I wonder if I ever would have been even tempted to write a memoir of my arrival in Dengate and what followed if, six years later, I hadn't been jolted into confrontation of what I had both witnessed and been through. I had quite abandoned dreams of being a writer (perhaps all the time I had deep-down been in search of the mundane, the domestic?) but—after I had recovered from the shock—to confront was to feel anew the urge to write. Anyway, I now take my readers to events nearly six years later, to the afternoon of May 11, 1891.

PART *Two*

CHAPTER ONE

"*I'm Going to be a Sculptor*"

W ill Postgate and I are sitting in the stalls of Terry's Theatre, just off
 The Strand, with the curtain shortly to go up on the first English
performance of *The Lady from the Sea* by Henrik Ibsen (in a translation
from the Norwegian by Eleanor Marx-Aveling). Will, having now added
theatre-going and play-reviewing to all his other Dep Ed activities, has invited me to come with him as his guest to the opening matinee.

"I seem to remember your being interested in Norway, and Norway's
Mr. Ibsen seems all set to be the big man of the coming decade in the English theatre. If we want him!" As it happened, I had an appointment of my
own in town that morning—a discussion with a solicitor in Southampton
Row about a possible infringement of the libel laws, Edmund increasingly
entrusting me with such commissions—and so I accepted. I scarcely ever
went to the theatre and almost never read the notices in the national papers, so I had no idea about who its big men should or should not be,
though the name rang a bell—one I would prefer not to hear.

Suddenly old Will gives me a sharp nudge with his powerful elbow.
"Take a look at your program, Martin," he says.

He's surely rebuking me for spending these anticipatory moments
just looking around me. But why not? This theatre is only four years old
and impressive. The outside is in the Flemish style, patterned brickwork,
crow-stepped gables, and the inside, from the curtains and hangings to the
enamelled iron-framed seats, is a pleasing blend of colors—perhaps Flemish
too?—deep brownish-pink, apple-green and gold. The audience this afternoon is not large, in truth it's rather sparse, but it has a sophisticated
feel, some being what Will calls "true worshippers at the Ibsen shrine,
ready to sing hymns of praise to their master at every touch and turn."

Will digs me in the ribs again. "Why the devil don't you do what I say, old chap? One of the names in the Dramatis Personae will interest you."

Will it? I said: "I doubt it'll mean much to me, Will, I know so little about actors."

"'Dramatis Personae' doesn't mean actors, it means the characters in the play, you juggins." Will says this loud enough for two men behind to laugh. "So, go on—*look*! Well, *now* do you see it?"

How could I not? "*Lyngstrand*." I keep my head lowered so Will can't see my blushes—at twenty-nine I still blush as I did when readers last met me—and of course, my heart quickens its beat. Lyngstrand—well, well, well. I wonder how long it is since I have given Hans sustained thought—how could I, with pressure at work and at home too: three children now, with little Arthur born only last November, and another child on the way?

"Lyngstrand *was* the name of that Norwegian boy at Castelaniene, was it not?"

"Yes, that's right," I say, "but I know even less about Norwegian names than I do about the London stage. The surname may be a very common one."

But now I see from the program that the action takes place in "a small fjord-town in Northern Norway." Well, couldn't Molde, from where Hans had written to me, be so described, the town where the appalling Johnston had (as he'd told me) betrothed himself to his woman? Hans's words—from a letter I'd skimmed and had never replied to—came back to me with vexing clarity: *If you think, as people from Christiania are apt to, that anywhere many hours northward from Bergen is "north," then Molde is a northern town, though for many tourists it's just the start of boat-trips going a lot further north still.* But probably many a place in Norway could be similarly described.

Anyway why come to a play by Ibsen in the first place, I say to myself sternly, *if I cannot take reminders of the one, the only Norwegian I have known well. Too well, but also not as well as he deserved!*

Do my readers find it strange that after events of July 4, 1885, Will Postgate and I have—outwardly—returned to how we were with each other in South London when he was both mentor and pal? Readers will be the more surprised at the lack of change, I warrant, when I acquaint them more fully with what has happened in the intervening period.

When I tell them that Will is the father of my eldest son, Eddie [Edmund], and is unaware of this fact, or has chosen to be. When I refer them to a certain afternoon in early September of that same year when Lucinda, with whom I was now on the best of terms, invited me to take tea at Dengate's Blue Bird Cafe, and there, at a table overlooking bright beds of nasturtium and fuchsia, said: "Martin, I am expecting a child. And the child is your friend, Will's."

And then go on to relate that, without blinking, as they say, I responded with: "In that case I can find the courage to say what I never believed I'd ever be able to. Dearest Lucinda, marry me. Marry me, and tell the world the child is mine."

I have no rancor against Will, not a drop really. Without him I should not have what happiness I do. And I can't envy him—or only in patches. Yes, he has his precious freedom, I grant, but it is he of the two of us who is the restless, dissatisfied one, though maybe he never tastes that melancholy I am so regularly familiar with. He is now beau-ing, he has told me earlier this afternoon, a "most enchanting young creature, a wonder of nature really." He will doubtless lose interest in her soon enough, just as he did with Beatrice Fuller (now a resident with Mary in Arcachon in France in a small villa bought from the sale of Castelaniene), just as he did with my dear Lou after only a few weeks, to his great loss and my even greater gain. That he has never spoken or written about his love-affair with her, to either of us, might irredeemably have tarnished that early respect I held him in, I suppose, but respect isn't the only emotion behind a friendship— and I have a whole heap of warm memories of him. Despite everything I am fond of him.

When trying to persuade me to join him at this Ibsen performance, Will said he had something he greatly wanted to talk over with me. But when I reminded him of this over luncheon just now, over his favorite steak-and-kidney pie, he said, oh, yes, that's right, he had indeed—but he must wait till *after* the play, for which he needed to be on his mettle. As a reviewer!

"Anyway I should tell you something, ignoramus that you are, about where I'm taking you to. Interesting place, Martin, Terry's Theatre." I found myself assuming the kind of face I used to in times gone by, when I was so anxious to absorb any information he imparted and worried that my lack of knowledge showed even as I did so. "Terry's is run by a pretty interesting old cove, Terry Edward O'Connor, a capital comedian—though now he has one Mr. Edward Terry, a shrewd mind if ever there was one, to assist him in his management. Had a few memorable words myself with both of 'em not so long ago, and mentioned 'em in a little piece of mine. Terry's great success came with Mr. Pinero's *Sweet Lavender*, couple of years back, as you won't need to be told." I nodded here, but did need telling, I'm afraid. "But I bet you didn't know it ran to 684 performances, making a profit of £20,000." Twenty-thousand quid! Stupendous indeed! The old Will, the radical determined to lift up Peckham and Tooting from social penury, might have thought such a sum should be ploughed back straightaway into slum clearance. But if this were the present Will's opinion, he gave no hint. A part of me longed to remind him also, that, with everything else on my hands, the commercial triumph of *Sweet Lavender* passed me by. "I suppose Terry's have high hopes that this new Ibsen lark of theirs will have the same sort of ride as the Pinero. Well, we'll see. I'm not at all sure we Britishers *need* the sort of goings-on you find in old Mr. Ibsen's plays: people throwing themselves to their deaths into mill-races or shooting themselves in the privates." Put like that it was hard to disagree, but I didn't catch the references.

Now, fortified by lunch and looking every inch the half-casual, half-smart professional writer, Will has got his writing-pad out and is resting it on his knees to jot notes about the show. But at this early point he's reluctant to let the point about names drop.

"It certainly seems a coincidence to *me*," Will says, "and I'm surprised you're not more surprised. Imagine going to a theatre in Christiania and seeing in the program there's a character called Bridges or Postgate."

Once again, I can't disagree. But at that moment the lights begin to dim, and, as always at some cultural occasion, I feel a sort of agitation—neither pleasing nor altogether *displeasing*—in the stomach, stronger than the proverbial "butterflies," but less strong than the sensation that you have before the dentist decides you need chloroform for that particular bit of tooth-work. Besides—perhaps because I've been to plays comparatively seldom—I have never quite lost the sense that the theatre is not just illusion, but another reality, established by an invisible power and progressing toward an end which must therefore be inevitable but may upset, and even horrify one. Sometimes I fear I might suddenly act as small children are supposed to do and shout out that *this* should not happen or that *that* simply must. The deep brownish-pink, apple-green, and gold of the curtain as it lifts up is swallowed by the darkness that descends from the ceiling and walls, and then by the blaze of light from the stage.

And on this stage I see—or am transported to—a garden, framed on one side by a veranda and on the other by a hedge with a small gate, and containing a flagstaff and an arbor. Beyond the garden runs a tree-lined road and between the trees you can glimpse a great stretch of water (the fjord, obviously); beyond that soar mountain-peaks. I am in Norway at last!

In the garden a middle-aged man in an old velvet jacket (rather like one of Edmund's) and a wide-awake hat attends to the flagstaff ropes, the flag itself sprawling on the ground beside him. Some feet away from him stand an easel holding a canvas and also a camp-stool on which lie brushes and paints ready for use. A pleasant-looking young woman—well, young-*ish*; she's probably my own age, and I'm a husband, father, and a newspaper's "daily manager"—comes into this garden from a room on the interior side of the veranda, carrying a large vase of flowers. I almost always have difficulty picking up the real drift of the opening lines of any play, mostly (I suppose) because I am anxious I won't grasp it, and so not properly follow what's to come. I also notice that actors usually shout at the beginning of a play and exaggerate everything, whether solemn or amusing, dramatic or trivial (or do they, in truth, do this all the way through, and one simply gets used to it?). At any rate I have to fight between my awareness of being taken into a real place at a real time, and my resistance to such artificialities of voice and gesture.

This first exchange isn't very interesting. Not to me anyhow. A visitor who hasn't been back in the town for some years is due, here at the Wangels' house, this very morning, and this painter-fellow, Ballested, who seems also to be a kind of odd-jobs man, must get the flag hoisted before he arrives. The pleasant woman of the same age as myself then goes out, Ballested reapplies himself to the flag-ropes, but then, walking along behind the hedge and stopping near its gate appears a youth, clearly intrigued by the easel and the painting equipment. He is very thin, his face well-scrubbed, his clothes neat and nicely ironed and pressed, but oh so shabby, so indomitably shabby. Ballested, after a few false starts, gets the flag up as required, and then turns to greet the newcomer, who says in an amiable innocent sort of voice that he knows he must be addressing a painter. Ballested is pleased by his saying this, and so, when the youth asks if he could come into the garden for a moment, invites him to take a peek at his canvas. This turns out to be a picture of a mermaid dying in the brackish water of the fjord, unable to get out into the open sea again. The youth is no end impressed; he opines it's going to be a very fine work when finished. In his place I wouldn't have been so confident, but then Hans was always so much kinder, so much more generous in his responses than I. *But then Hans*, did I just say? Is this third member of the Dramatis Personae *my* Hans Lyngstrand?

Well, who else? A lean, poor, artistic young man, friendly and polite almost to a fault! I lean forward in my iron-framed chair, not caring how this sudden rush of attentiveness strikes Will. Ballested now observes of the visitor, that, from his appreciative observations, he must surely be "in the profession" himself—i.e. a painter. And the reply?

"No, I'm not that; but I'm going to be a sculptor. My name is Hans Lyngstrand."

This is exactly, but exactly, how Hans would introduce himself, at once eager and bumbling, sure of his judgment but touchingly, comically naïve. I squint at the program and see that the young man's name is in fact Mr. Herbert Sparling, but I know this to be a disguise. Here is the Hans Lyngstrand I knew. In person. With whom I shared what I had never to that date shared with anybody else. Will's—or his paper's—gift of a 10/6 seat in a theatre off the Strand has united me with my friend again, at a period of his life three years later than when I last saw him, when he was moved to write me a letter to which I didn't deign to reply, any more than I had to its predecessors. How could I after what Bo'sun Johnston had told me?

Concentration on Ibsen's play ceases to be an effort now. I am drawn right into the action, would find it impossible to extricate myself.

BALLESTED: So you're to be a sculptor? Yes, yes; the art of
sculpture is a nice, pretty art in its way. I fancy I've seen you
in the street once or twice. Have you been staying here long?

LYNGSTRAND: No; I've only been here a fortnight. But I shall
try to stop till the end of the summer.

BALLESTED: For the bathing?

LYNGSTRAND: Yes; I wanted to see if I could get a little stronger.

BALLESTED: Not delicate, surely?

LYNGSTRAND: Yes, perhaps I am a little delicate; but it's nothing
dangerous. Just a little tightness on the chest.

Readers, imagine my feelings on hearing this, especially that last
poignant sentence. I who know, none better, exactly how dangerous that
"little tightness" is—or rather was. Alone (I imagine) of all the members
of this audience I know what the end of this would-be-sculptor will be,
how soon in stark fact it would come. For Hans Lyngstrand died in the
spring of 1889, just short of his twenty-fourth birthday. I give a quick
glance to my right at Will, who had already flashed me a quick grin on
hearing Lyngstrand utter his own name. And "Right age, too!" he murmurs. But I don't think I have anything else to fear from him; if Will had
suspicions about our friendship, Hans's and mine, they never went beyond
a kind of office-mate's light lubriciousness of fancy, never penetrated to
any reality of mutual feelings, and almost certainly by now he had probably
forgotten he ever entertained them.

It is myself, Martin Bridges, who should be fearful of what lies
ahead—and what will befall Hans—on these boards which represent the
Norway of three summers ago. (The play, I see from my program, was
written in 1888.)

And the explanation of this strange, never-anticipated situation? Well,
is it so difficult to find? Norwegian Mr. Henrik Ibsen could easily have visited Molde at the same time as Hans, and shamelessly used him and those
he came into contact with. Used them for his own purposes, without bothering so much as to change the names. (In the case of somebody as obscure
as Hans, he probably told himself there was no need to worry—no possible
libel trouble of the kind I had come up to London to discuss.) That shows,

I'm afraid, what so many writers really are like, even the "big men," the famous like Mr. Ibsen: bloodsuckers, carrion, living off the feelings, experiences, and sufferings of others. Newspaper-men have a cleaner trade, I think, because they never pretend that they are dealing with people of their own invention.

But back to the play, and concentrate, Bridges, concentrate! For even if I did not have the special reason for absorption in it that I do, I would find keeping hold of the threads of its story far from easy. Ibsen relies such a devilish lot on hints and implications to tell you important stuff—sometimes the most important stuff—and they're even less easy to recognize, let alone seize on, in a theatre than in the social encounters and gatherings of normal life—and there they can be pretty damned difficult, as any honest man will tell you. Also such a lot has happened to Mr. Ibsen's people before we actually meet them, you have to be something of a human archaeologist accustomed to excavating under many layers of deposits, to do them proper justice. But for the story of what happened to Hans Lyngstrand before he appears in the Wangels' garden I am, I hardly need say, in an unusually, maybe uniquely advantaged position. Come to think of it, I am a part of Hans's past myself.

Of course I am riveted by other people than Hans, by Ellida, the Lady from the Sea herself, (played by Rose Meller as lovely as the eponymous Lady is meant to be); by Dr. Wangel, her husband, bluff, kindly, but a mite too easy-going, who loves her, his second wife, and is baffled by her long—on the face of it inexplicable—estrangement from him; by his two daughters, Bolette, who runs the household and is in danger of becoming "an old maid" and Hilde, young, beautiful, almost demonically capricious; by Arnholm who once loved Ellida when she lived out at her father's lighthouse in Skjoldviken, but who now is drawn to Bolette whom he once tutored. But my real engagement—how can it not be?—is with the young sculptor, who embarrasses me sometimes with his blunders, his gaucherie, his invalid's clumsiness, but other times wins me over (arouses something in me?)—just as, at best, he did back in Dengate.

And the dark figure in Hans's story—who is also, as it transpires, the dark figure in Ellida's—is the bo'sun, the American, Johnston (also once known as Friman, as I knew), the Stranger (as the Dramatis Personae has it). What will I think of *him* when eventually, after such nervous anticipation, he appears? I begin to sit in dread of this . . . Sometimes at night, Lucinda tells me, after I've been over-working, I have bad dreams in which I call out that Ukko is coming for me.

"Ukko? Who is he?" asks my wife. "A figment of my young imagination," I reply, half-believing myself . . .

Hans tells Ellida and Arnholm, shortly after the latter's arrival, that paradoxically he is grateful for the grim events at home (mother's death, father's cold-hearted rejection) that sent him, under his guardian's aegis, to sea, and equally for the disaster in the English Channel, for all the casualties and suffering it entailed.

LYNGSTRAND: It was in the shipwreck that I got this little weakness of the chest. I was so long in the ice-cold water before they picked me up; and so I had to give up the sea. Yes, that was very fortunate.

ARNHOLM: Indeed! Do you think so?

LYNGSTRAND: Yes, for the weakness isn't dangerous; and now I can be a sculptor, as I dearly want to be. Just think—to model in that delicious clay, that yields so caressingly to your fingers!

ELLIDA: And what are you going to model? Is it to be mermen and mermaids? Or is to be old Vikings?

LYNGSTRAND: No, not that. As soon as I can set about it, I am going to try if I can produce a great work—a group, as they call it.

ELLIDA: Yes, but what's that group to be?

LYNGSTRAND: Oh! Something I've experienced myself.

ARNHOLM: Yes, yes; always stick to that.

ELLIDA: But what's it to be?

LYNGSTRAND: Well, I thought it should be the young wife of a sailor, who lies sleeping in strange unrest, and she is dreaming. I fancy I shall do it so that you will see she is dreaming.

ARNHOLM: Is there anything else?

LYNGSTRAND: Yes, there's to be another figure—a sort of ap-

> parition as they say. It's her husband, to whom she has been
> faithless while he was away, and he is drowned at sea.
> ARNHOLM: What?
> ELLIDA: Drowned?
> LYNGSTRAND: Yes, he was drowned on a sea voyage. But that's
> the wonderful part of it—he comes home all the same. It is
> nighttime. And he is standing by her bed looking at her. He
> is to stand there dripping wet, like one drawn from the sea.

Well, Hans had not decided precisely on that tableau even when I knew him, but it was already latent in him, already an inhabitant of his mind. (And I know something else too—as do, without being aware of it, many strollers in the Royal Gardens, Dengate, today—that the subject underwent metamorphosis, the result being a work which I was completely unable to include in my own house.) Ellida is fascinated, transfixed by this description of a sculpture which in truth the artist has as yet come nowhere near actually to making; it exists only in plans and hopes—and talk.

Arnholm, the Wangels' visitor, plainly hasn't taken to Hans at all, just as Will hadn't back in Dengate, thinks him a ninny not capable of much besides coyly and ingratiatingly presenting older women like Ellida with outsize bunches of flowers (the sort of thing, I have to agree, that the Dengate Hans might easily have done to Beatrice Fuller). So, somewhat censoriously, very much like the schoolmaster he is, he rounds on him with: "I thought you said it was to be something you had *experienced*."

But of course (and who knows this better than myself?) Hans is able to defend himself here perfectly: "Yes, I did experience that," he protests, "that is to say, to a certain extent . . ."

And then out it comes, the very story he told me as the interviewer from *The Channel Ports Advertiser* in the blossom-filled garden at Castelaniene on just such a May afternoon as this one (for outside the theatre London is today, for all its dirt and hectic bustle, a huge, warm, surprisingly fragrant, sunny miracle of blooms and leafing trees): the engagement of a new bo'sun at Halifax; the rough weather in the Atlantic, Johnston spraining his foot, and Hans feeling ill, and the two of them cooped up in the same cabin; Johnston reading of the Norwegian paper, "uttering a sort of

yell" and then crushing, crumpling, and tearing up the offending publication "into a thousand shreds." Followed by the exclamations: "Married—
to another man. While I was away!" and "But she is mine, and mine she
shall remain. And she shall follow me, if I should come home and fetch
her, as a drowned man from the dark sea." Said, apparently, in perfect Norwegian. And I, English Martin Bridges, can to this day (when I try!) remember them in that language.

This story of his truly galvanizes Ellida. We all now can see—well,
certainly *I* now can see (but does Will, with his notepad, still blank, against
his knees, do so?)—that herein lies the key to her own haunted state of
mind. And now I feel a terrible sadness sweeping through me as I recollect
sentence by sentence all the plans Hans had for his work, and yet cannot
but wonder, despite myself, whether a work-of-art that turns a situation
into such rank melodrama—as his "great group" surely would have done—
could ever really be at all a satisfying creation? Certainly, what now stands
in the Royal Garden does not satisfy me, though it must have some power
I suppose, otherwise I could not resent, and at times detest it, as I do. (And
yet I cannot destroy it either—Lucinda sees that as well as I do!)

And just as we have been given a real proof of the good qualities of
Ellida—unwittingly brought about by Hans Lyngstrand's maladroit gift of
flowers—the curtains descend on the first act. But the lights do not come
on afterwards, and I am very pleased to be granted a few minutes' dark
tranquility—even if it's not literally this, not with all the reverberant
thumps and bangs indicating a substantial change of scene being effected
on the stage. But it gives me a break long enough to come to terms with
my surely odd lack of further astonishment at what is being presented me,
the unfolding of the hitherto hidden later history of someone briefly of
immeasurable importance to me, whom I then determinedly spurned to
the point of ignoring his every letter—but who is perhaps now reclaiming
his rightful status in my life, as the human being who (I am apt to think)
taught me most about my deepest nature . . .

"Rum crew these people," Will whispers to me. "Wouldn't be *my*
choice of folk for a summer's day party."

That makes me think—it was at a summer's day party of sorts (even
if early summer, the present month) that Will first met my Lucinda and

wrought such a profound change in her. He doesn't do either wisely or well, even unthinkingly, to remind me of such occasions, otherwise I shall be forced to admit that in my still self-confident, still companionable friend there's more than a dash of the cad.

The curtain lifts a second time, and certainly the scene-shifters have done wonders; we are now somewhere quite different. The program tells me that the setting is now the "View," a shrub-covered hill high above the resort with, it soon transpires, magnificent views of fjord and mountain-peaks beyond—but of course it also reminds me of Dengate's View when I (and the three cats) encountered Colonel Walton and first truly appreciated the uncomfortable ultimately unmanageable truth behind Mrs. Fuller's life.

This Norwegian View, like our Kentish one, is famous for what it of-fers toward the sunset hour, so late in the northern latitudes as to be but a prelude to sunrise, and toward it the townsfolk (of Molde?) including courting couples, and tourists, one little posse of these last being led by the many-talented jack-of-all-trades Ballested, are wending their way from a bandstand where musicians are playing (more Dengate associations here!—and I don't suppose they'll stop coming either), up a precipitous path, to enjoy the beautiful scenery on a perfect summer's night. Dr. Wangel's two daughters hove into view, the frightening beautiful Hilde in advance of her preferable sister, Bolette. Their exchange does not strike at all a pleasing note:

> BOLETTE: But, dear, why should we run away from Lyngstrand?
> HILDE: Because I can't bear going uphill so slowly. Look—look
>   at him crawling up!
> BOLETTE: Ah! But you know how delicate he is.
> HILDE: Do you think it's very—dangerous?
> BOLETTE: I certainly do.
> HILDE: He went to consult father [Dr. Wangel] this afternoon.
>   I should like to know what father thinks about him.
> BOLETTE: Father told me it was a thickening of the lungs, or
>   something of the sort. He won't live to be old, father says.
> HILDE: No! Did he say it? Fancy—that's exactly what I thought.
> BOLETTE: For heaven's sake don't show it!

HILDE: How can you imagine such a thing? Look, here comes
  Hans crawling up. Don't you think you can see by the look
  of him that he's called Hans?
BOLETTE (*whispering*): Now do behave!

And now up onto the "View" comes Hans Lyngstrand, puffing heavily, pathetically, disablingly after too strenuous and steep an uphill walk,
and using for assistance Ellida's parasol as a walking-stick. He thus estab-
lishes himself further as a ninny in the eyes of those disposed to be unsym-
pathetic. Clearly poor old Hans—for all the costly medical treatment both
in England and in Norway that he must have received in the three years
since his exposure in the water and the consequent illness—has deterio-
rated considerably, though his spirits, his will not just to survive but to lead
an active, creative life, are possibly stronger even than earlier.

But it isn't just contempt that my poor friend's weak health brings
out in those not altogether favorably disposed to him. The dreadful if be-
witching Hilde taunts him with his inability to do this or that on account
of his health, makes fun to his face of his belief that he is getting better
(not in so many words, but we all realize this is what she is doing, though
Hans himself doesn't) and even derives an odd gloating satisfaction from
the fact that he is deceived about his (that terrible word!) mortal illness:

BOLETTE: Why are you always going about with him?
HILDE: Oh, I only do that because of the weakness.
BOLETTE: I've never noticed that you in the least pity him for it!
HILDE: No, I don't. But I think it so interesting.
BOLETTE: What is?
HILDE: To look at him and make him tell you it isn't dangerous;
  and that he's going abroad and is to be an artist. He really
  believes it all, and is so thoroughly happy about it. And yet
  nothing will ever come of it; nothing whatever. For he won't
  live long enough. I feel that's so fascinating to think of.
BOLETTE: Fascinating!
HILDE: Yes, I think it's most fascinating. I take that liberty.

A wave of loathing for this cruel child breaks over me. For a second I'm afraid I shall behave as I did on that never-to-be-forgotten evening at the Gateway and rise to my feet and speak out. But I do not. Besides Hilde is obviously totally unaware of the talents for love that the sick young would-be sculptor has inside him, which I sampled so memorably—like, if Johnston was to be believed, many another before me. But anyway, this girl's conduct only makes the spectator feel fonder of Hans, and not simply out of pity. He has just remarked that he doesn't altogether regret what he euphemistically calls his "weakness," and the reason—"I think it's because of it that everyone is so good and friendly, and kind to me."

Too much to feel here—no, honestly! That sentence will come back to me at some vulnerable hour of the night, and I shall have to face my own accusations, and confess that though the Hans I am seeing now will think of his one-time English friend as having been "good and friendly and kind"—that's indeed what he said in the letters I skimmed—I also let him down, even betrayed him, for when he was living in Norway and still needed me, I showed no goodness, friendliness, or kindness. Quite the reverse. What misery I must have caused him.

Mr. Ibsen and, with him, his audience have of course other concerns than Hans Lyngstrand and his health. Up at the View Dr. Wangel and his wife have a long and belatedly frank talk about the present failure of their marriage, inextricable from Ellida's haunted mental condition. I know nothing of all this, of course, and focus my attention on it as best I can. I try to imagine the harsh blow it would be for me if Lucinda "went away" from me in the same way the Lady from the Sea has from her good doctor, for all his kindness, for all her surely sincere love for him—and if the previous man in her life (in my case now lolling in the seat next to me) was the cause of this self-distancing.

Ellida tells Wangel of an involvement of hers ten years before, when she was still living at her father's lighthouse out at Skjoldviken, not with the teacher Arnholm (as Dr. Wangel has half-supposed) but with a man whom nobody else in local waters knew, who was Second Mate on an American ship which had put in for repairs. And of course the moment I hear this I know what man she is about to introduce, to force imaginatively on us, her spectators. Once again, my pulse increases its beat, and this time refuses to revert to its normal rate for quite a while . . . A man is imminent who to Ellida's face called himself Friman, but later, in ardent letters, signed himself Alfred Johnston—though probably wasn't entitled to either name as he was in provenance a Norwegian Finlander—a Kven, as he had indeed, and only too memorably, told me himself.

This Johnston (to call him this) fell for her so entirely, says she, that he insisted on an immediate betrothal; the current of feeling was flowing quick and fast and strong between the two of them. (Just as Johnston himself had attested to me—and earlier to Hans.) But there was another reason for the summary nature of the engagement ceremony; he would any minute be on a "wanted" list for a killing he had indeed just carried out—a crime Dr. Wangel himself knew about, as he went out to Skjoldviken personally to do a post-mortem on the dead body of the victim, the captain of that American ship—and so had to escape just as fast as possible.

WANGEL: Yes, I remember it very well. It was on board that ship that the captain was found one morning in his cabin—murdered. I myself went out to make the post-mortem.

ELLIDA: Yes, it was you.

WANGEL: It was the second mate who had murdered him.

ELLIDA: No one can say that for it was never proved.

WANGEL: There was enough against him anyhow, or why should he have drowned himself as he did?

ELLIDA: He did not drown himself. He sailed in a ship to the north.

WANGEL: How do you know?

ELLIDA: Well, Wangel—it was this second mate to whom I was betrothed . . . At that time he called himself Friman. Later in his letters he signed himself Alfred Johnston.

WANGEL: And where did he come from?

ELLIDA: From Finmark, he said. For the rest, he was born in Finland, had come to Norway there as a child with his father, I think.

WANGEL: A Finlander, then . . .?

ELLIDA: Well, then he told me he had stabbed the captain in the night.

WANGEL: He said that himself! Actually said so!

ELLIDA: Yes. But he had only acted rightly and justly, he said.

WANGEL: Rightly and justly! Why did he stab him then?

ELLIDA: He wouldn't speak out about that. He said it was not fit
for me to hear.

What acts were those so unspeakable to a woman? I knew the answer, and could not repress a shudder. Somewhere in my head I heard the rain beat against the little shelter on the Esplanade . . .

Anyway—so thoroughly had he cast his spell over poor Ellida, then little more than a girl—that she agreed to his proposal:

"He took from his pocket a keyring—and drew a ring he always wore from his finger, and he took a small ring I had. These two he put on the keyring. And then he said we should wed ourselves to the sea. And with that he threw the keyring, and our rings, with all his might, as far as he could into the deep."

No playgoer, even one as unseasoned as myself, could fail to perceive from the intensity and the specific details of this conversation between man and wife—that the seaman, the "disappeared" Johnston will soon come back to claim his woman, "his" because according to his own relentless, primitive beliefs, the two of them have actually married. But I have a different type of knowledge to back this realization up; I already know that Johnston did come back to Molde because Hans in a letter to me described his unexpected sighting of him—though there was no confrontation between them, even of the casual and merely literal kind. Below the surface of my conscious mind, I now begin to await the former bo'sun with painful tension.

Not that everything about this man is menacing or malign. Asked what the two of them would talk about, Ellida replies:

"About storms and calm. Of dark nights at sea. And of the sea in the glittering sunshiny days we spoke also. But we spoke mostly of the whales, and the dolphins, and the seals who lie out there on the rocks in the midday sun. And then we spoke of the gulls, and the eagles, and all the other sea birds. I think—isn't it wonderful?—when we talked about such things it seemed to me as if both the sea beasts and sea birds were one with him."

And yes, Hans had told me this, and in a not dissimilar tone. Lyrically admiring. An inner voice whispers to me: *And did he love the bo'sun too, your Hans? Did he offer himself to HIM?*

I hardly know how properly to respond to the Third Act—back in the Wangels' garden, but in a sequestered part of it with a carp-pond and even more splendid views of the mountain-peaks—when the Stranger makes his reappearance in Ellida's life, from the other side of the hedge, just as Hans did earlier on. Him I would not at first have recognized—he now has a bushy red beard and is no longer the drink-smelling disheveled specimen of the Esplanade shelter. Ellida does not recognize him to begin with. Then she takes a closer look, and cries out, as well she might: "The eyes! The eyes!" He has come to the town, he says, on a visiting English steamer (as a passenger, not as a working seaman), for no other purpose but to claim her, to take her. As his own. He begs her not to be frightened of him (though it's hard to see how she can't be this, given his complete assumption that she must submit to his will), and even in the presence of her husband, the long-suffering Wangel, he declares that Ellida and himself are bound to one another in a "wonderful" marriage. Just as he has faithfully kept himself for her all these years, while voyaging all the seas and visiting many lands, many continents, so she should have kept her vow to him and waited patiently for his return—which his letters promised her would one day be a reality. But he does protest that he doesn't wish to take her, as her poor husband seems afraid he might, by brute force; she must come to him of her own free will.

"I have kept the word I gave you. And so now you must think it over till tomorrow night. Now I'm going with the steamer up the fjord. Tomorrow night I will come again, and then I shall look for you here. You must wait for me in the garden . . ."

Hans, the one person who could have understood and even cast light on this meeting after so many years between the two of them, has not been present at the scene. But he has (as I uniquely in this theatre know!) caught a glimpse of him:

LYNGSTRAND (*going quickly up to Ellida*): Now, Mrs. Wangel,
   you must hear something wonderful.

WANGEL: What is it?

LYNGSTRAND: Fancy! We've seen the American.

WANGEL: The American?

HILDE: Yes, I saw him, too.

LYNGSTRAND: He was going 'round the back of the garden, and thence on board the great English steamer.

WANGEL: How do you know the man?

LYNGSTRAND: Why, I went to sea with him once. I felt so certain he'd been drowned—and now he's very much alive.

WANGEL: Do you know anything more about him?

LYNGSTRAND: No. But I'm sure he's come to revenge himself upon his faithless sailor-wife.

Is he right or wrong to say this? For making so absolute a demand on her as he just has done, imposing such a decision on somebody so vulnerable, does seem to me a kind of revenge.

Now for the interval, and I have to say I'm grateful for it. I'm grateful even for Will's hearty sociability for of course he wants to chat and smoke alongside practically everybody in the auditorium, all of them, it would seem, unimpressed by the play to the point of scorn.

"If this is the work of a great master, I'll eat my hat!" says Dan Havers, an older large-mustachioed, cynical-eyed man whose opinion Will much looks up to. "Will she or won't this Ellida woman—Rose Meller at her very best, I have to say—go off with her tramp of a Stranger? Who can make a logical prediction? But then who could care? I'm jolly glad I wasn't present when she and her inamorato had their endless conversations about nautical matters. There seems to me to have been a bally sight too much talk about the sea already as it is."

"Shh!" theatrically Will puts a finger to his lips and rolls his eyes. "I see a few members of the Ibsen Worshippers' Tribe making their way down yonder gangway, and I don't want 'em to hear us blaspheme. Come to think of it, I'm not at all sure we haven't another Tribesman, another Ibsenite in our midst. Martin, come clean. Confess!"

"I'm not confessing to anything of the kind," I say, not wholly pleased by Will's jauntily superior tone. "This is the first of his plays I've ever seen. But such a lot is yet to happen, so shouldn't we wait till the end of the play before coming to any conclusion about it?"

"Touché, my dear chap," Dan Havers replies. (I think Will is not altogether pleased with me for saying what I just have—he likes to make up his mind about a thing speedily, indeed preferably on the spot.) "Possibly I've just met someone who'll soon swell the benighted ranks of us theatre-reviewers, and do so in most distinguished fashion."

"Oh, you'd be wrong there," Will tells him officiously, and maintaining a grin but there's an edge to his voice. "Martin isn't a literary chap at all."

Well, I was asking for that! Therefore, I'm at once relieved and anxious to take my seat again, and let the deep brownish-pinks, apple-greens, and gold all fade to make way again for a Norwegian garden toward the end of summer, with fjord and mountain-peaks to remind us that they continue even when human dramas come to their end.

Hans Lyngstrand appears in a distinctly different light in the two acts that remain. Nobody wants him to talk about his past, nobody appeals to him to say any more about Johnston/Friman—something which surely could have been helpful to the Wangels. Instead he makes appeals on his own behalf, first to Bolette, then to Hilde, reminding them that he is soon to go south for the sake of both his health and his art—and where could that mean but Italy, for so long the Promised Land for so many Scandinavian artists, the more so if consumptive? He begs them to think of him in his long absence. He will be creating great works of art under a sunny sky while they stay back at home in the confines of Norway, but "it would be so delightful for me to know you were at home here thinking of me!" He says he has given marriage thought, but that it is certainly not for him at present—even assuming he could afford it, which he can't; even with his patron's help—Herr Strømme is not mentioned by name, but his presence is felt—this young artist is indigent. But he suggests that the understanding between him and each sister that he proposes it to will be in its way a *de facto* marriage.

He sounds pretty silly, I have to say, conceited and crass, when he talks to the Wangel sisters in this fashion, and the laughter from the audience suggests they think this too. Theirs is not kindly, or even indulgent laughter.

"How ridiculous he is being," proclaim these guffaws. "This young sculptor is a noddy, a spoony." Will joins in all the merriment, while I, who can't really dissent from the general opinion of which it is an expression, now begin to wish the play would move swiftly to its conclusion. Would Hans have spoken in this vain, foolish manner? I can't completely convince myself that he would not. There was, for all his many merits, some of which I have not perceived until this afternoon—at any rate until the interval—a little vanity, and a dram or two of foolishness in Hans Lyngstrand, there even when he crept into my attic-bedroom and lay himself down beside me, even possibly when he cast his body on mine and his tongue went into my mouth like a little fish after he'd spun me a preposterous tale about a peregrine falcon and a sailor-lad.

All the same it is profoundly saddening (if rather too understandable) to hear Bolette and Arnholm discussing the young man in the following terms:

ARNHOLM: What is it, dear?

BOLETTE: Oh! It's that poor [*pointing*]—see out there.

ARNHOLM: Is it your father?

BOLETTE: No. It's the young sculptor. He's down there with Hilde.

ARNHOLM: Oh, Lyngstrand! What's really the matter with him?

BOLETTE: Why, you know how weak and delicate he is.

ARNHOLM: Yes. Unless it's simply imaginary.

BOLETTE: No, it's real enough! He'll not last long. But perhaps that's best for him.

ARNHOLM: Dear, why should that be best?

BOLETTE: Because—because—nothing would come of his art anyhow.

He will die young, she says, and that's really for the good, because he has no artistic talent at all, and it would be painful for him ever to know this . . .

But nobody says that he carries with him an individual *self* (a soul, if you like!) more precious than any quantifiable talent, artistic or otherwise. And nobody says that because of that he *will* execute something. Whether good or bad I still don't think I have the ability to say, but stamped *The Sailor's Revenge* is with his own irreducible personality.

Naturally all attention now is on the choice that Ellida will make. The summer night gradually deepens over the Wangels' garden, over the whole resort too and the fjord and the great mountains beyond. The Stranger—for such I too now call him (and was he, for all those ghastly moments of physical proximity, anything else to me?)—will turn up again, true to his vow, and Ellida herself, and increasingly her husband too, would now appear to believe that the force of Nature (or something of the sort) will exert itself into ensuring her departure with him.

> BALLESTED: But you know she [the English ship] comes from between the islands. You can't see anything of her, and then she's alongside of you.
>
> WANGEL: Tonight is the last voyage, then she will not come again.
>
> BALLESTED: A sad thought, doctor . . . The glad summertime will soon be over now. Soon all ways will be barred, as they say in the tragedy. It's sad to think of. We have been the joyous children of summer for weeks and months now. It's hard to reconcile yourself to the dark days—just at first, I mean. For men can accli-a-acclimatize [sic] themselves, Mrs. Wangel. Ay, indeed they can.

But though Mrs. Wangel comes very near to leaving with Johnston on the imminently departing ship, she does not in fact do so. She decides, once and for all, not to go with him, deeply moved as she is by the demonstration of love her husband has at last given her—prepared to see her go off (and with such a man, a proven murderer!) rather than keep her a prisoner of his benevolence in his house. Her satisfaction with the outcome is profound, for never has she ceased loving the good doctor in the deepest regions of her heart, and by the time the curtains are ready to fall, she has come to a sort of evolutionary conclusion about her situation. Every Lady from the Sea must be tempted to go back to the ultimate origins of humankind, but every Lady too has the ability to adapt.

Can adapt? Is that what I have done these last years following Hans's departure to Bergen?

ELLIDA: When you have once again become a land-creature you can no longer find your way back again to the sea, nor to the sea-life either.

True? True of her, true of me? I wonder. And Hans Lyngstrand? He would shortly leave this little Norwegian fjord-town to make the long journey south that he has always wanted, and, from the point of view of health, long needed, to undertake—as in reality he did. But no personal farewell is said to him, no tribute paid to his own trust in the imagination in general, and in his own in particular.

That is a pity. When the curtains are brought down, I cannot prevent a wave of sadness breaking drenchingly over me. I dread the post-mortem in the public house now to come.

The two of us now ensconced in a tavern of his choice, Will looks up from his rapid scribbling on our tabletop with a smile of near-roguish contentment, the schoolboy who's learned a new conjuring trick he's sure will fool you or who's whipped out of his desk a naughty photograph to show you under the teacher's very gaze.

"When you think about it," he says, "no, when *I* think about it, the play we've just seen is as much a damned *farce* as it's anything else. All that talk about chucking two rings into the sea in a pagan wedding ceremony, and then the bridegroom in question, the Stranger popping up from nowhere after all those years and demanding his wife back—well, I ask you!" He throws back his head in mirth at the very idea of such things, and reaches afresh for the port he ordered, to pour himself (but not, I notice, me) some more. This "potable," in this shadowy corner in which we're now seated, has for me the look of thick blood stored in a glass container for some alchemical purpose, emphasizing that being here at such a time is quite wrong for an afternoon of such delicious late spring weather, just such spring weather in which my friendship with Hans Lyngstrand blossomed.

The play we have seen together spoke of the freedom of the elements and the freedom of the spirit. So it doesn't seem quite right to be indoors in a fug listening to Will's urbane mockery; I want already to be at nearby Charing Cross Station, taking the train from that handsome, crowded structure, back home to Dengate, where, at the end of my journey, the sea will await me with its hundred tints of blue, green and silver, and with white gulls crisscrossing each others' flights overhead.

"All those coincidences, old bean—yes, farcical is the word."

I can't have this. "I don't see *The Lady from the Sea* like that at all. And are its strange coincidences any stranger than those in absolutely *every-body*'s life?" I say this, for me, almost defiantly. "I'm sure I haven't understood it all probably yet—I mean, I haven't understood even what actually happened on stage, let alone the real meanings of all that's said and done, or the symbols." I produce the last word self-consciously.

Will guffaws: "The meanings or symbols are the easy part, my friend!" I keep my dignity by not making a riposte to this deliberate mis-understanding. "Pretty bally easy, I'll grant you. Kids' stuff. Facile."

"Well, if you say so!" I sip at my own port, which leaves a deposit, a light sediment on the tongue.

"Curiouser and curiouser," says Will, looking at me with one of his well-known quizzical expressions. "I mean I thought it curious just from squinting at you during the performance, that a fellow who never sets foot in a theatre from one year's end to another should be so rapt by this play. But now you've become a positive Counsel for the Defense. I see we really do have an Ibsenite in the making. Perhaps old Dan Havers was right, and we critics should be looking to you as a new rival."

I don't want any more talk of Ibsenites in which I can get caught out, shown up, and so on. I say, "I just found this play—well, very moving."

Will doesn't even smile. It's as if (think I) I've just described London as a provincial village or myself as one of the most important newspaper-men in the country; he's flummoxed.

"And many of the fellows in the audience were moved, too," he says, "to laughter, not to say giggles."

"Well, *I* was moved—almost to the other thing." That—in a conver-sation with Will Postgate, my long-standing guide into sophistication—counts as boldness.

"Can't for the life of me think why. That namesake of your old friend was a fair old muff, was he not? Hans Lyngstrand. Couldn't see the point of him myself."

While he speaks, I fear he has seen through me, that he does in truth know the reason (or the principal one) why I have been, so "curiously" in his view, moved: I've been witnessing the history of a once dear person unfolding before my eyes, a person he himself couldn't "see the point of" in actual life, but who brought out something deep and new in me. But then I realize this is not the case, Will hasn't a clue, not the foggiest notion. He would never have called him "that namesake of your old friend," if he had.

I can't hold back—no, not from making a proper confession—impossible! But yet: "There's very much a point to Lyngstrand. Shall I explain?"

"Well, as I'm responsible for getting you into this intellectual *pose*"—I try not to bridle at this deliberately uncomplimentary word—"I have a duty to hear you out, I suppose."

Well, let me hope some of it sticks. But I must be careful not to give myself away.

"Lyngstrand may look and sound foolish, bumbling, naïve, young for his years—though also like an old man in some other respects because he's always got to go carefully on account of his severe illness. *But,* if you sit back and think about it"—I try to appear as if I'm doing exactly that, though in truth I am feeling as tense as though screws have been tightened at my temples—"he sees more deeply and accurately than anybody else does, and nothing—absolutely nothing in the drama—would have happened without him."

Will is too much of a "seasoned" journalist not to be roused to attention by these words of mine, and, besides, as he's reviewing this damned play (and his piece will be syndicated), he doesn't want to have missed something that might be important.

So I go on:

"It was he who back on that ship three years before realized he was witnessing something very significant when closeted in the cabin in rough weather with the bo'sun, Johnston: when that man cried out when looking through the Norwegian newspaper because he'd read something that distressed him, and then ripped its pages into shreds. And vowed he'd come back for the woman who, he'd just read, had married another man, and fetch her—whether he was alive or dead."

"Something like that's always easier to do if it you're *alive*," Will cuts in, "gives a fellow no end of an advantage."

I ignore this. "This, you see, was the artist already at work in Lyngstrand. I'm talking about his ability to understand that what he'd witnessed was something telling you an important truth about how humans can and do behave, how strongly they can have an effect on the lives of others—he didn't just see it as an extraordinary incident that had happened once and couldn't be repeated. That's what artists do, I believe—see an action as more, as greater than how it appears at the time."

Will says: "I'd no idea I'd been friends with such an expert on the arts all these years." He takes another generous swilling mouthful of port.

"I'm *not* an expert on the arts, and couldn't begin to think myself one," I say with an attempt at a little laugh. "I've just been watching the play you were kind enough to take me to with the concentration it surely deserves." That damps him down a bit; Will wouldn't like to think he doesn't concentrate, though, to be honest, for all his indisputable industry and capacity for hard work, I'm coming more and more to the conclusion that he's quick rather than deep, brilliant rather than thorough, sharp-eyed rather than serious or analytical. "But Lyngstrand's insights don't end there. You see, Will, it's what he *does* with what he saw and heard that's so interesting and important. And I'm not talking about his sculpture here— that's all still in his head, or principally so; we don't even know whether he's made any of the rough sketches for it like sculptors usually do. Some inner voice tells him that the episode of three years ago and the work of art he intends to make out of it have bearing on the life of the Lady from the Sea herself, not only her past life but her present and her future. And she sees that too, otherwise why should she extract from him that account of what his sculpture will represent. So don't you follow me, Will?" No, I just can't keep out of my voice—or my gestures, or my eyes, more likely than not—the excitement I feel rising up in me, like a dolphin leaping up above the level of the waves. "Nothing, literally nothing, would have developed the way it did if it hadn't been for Lyngstrand. It's *his* story that makes Ellida realize what has been happening to her—that the onset of her illness, her terrible condition, coincided exactly with what he'd witnessed during the bad weather on the voyage. She actually tells her husband"—I find, to both my relief and my distress, that the sentences in question have already lodged themselves in my head—"'He learnt on board that I had married another while he was away. And so that very hour this came over me.' She's speaking of the malady that also ruined her poor child's life."

This is all news to Will Postgate I can see. Without my own motives for what he's called my "raptness," probably I wouldn't have noticed all the complications, the almost diabolical twists and turns of history behind the happenings enacted on Terry's boards. Will furrows his brow, as if in dissenting thought.

"You mean, if Ellida—ridiculous name, that, but I shall have to get it right for my review—if Ellida hadn't heard, through Hans Lyngstrand, all that stuff, she wouldn't have confided all she does in her poor old block-head of a husband, and therefore couldn't confront the Stranger as she eventually manages to?"

He sounds as if he's conceding to me, so I give him my most amiable smile and say: "Exactly, Will, exactly."

"But he doesn't make a damned difference to the outcome, does he, your chum?" I start at this last word, before appreciating it's only a face-tious turn-of-phrase, as per usual (to use another one Will favors).

"No, but as you have just said, by giving her his confidences, she doesn't deal with him as a sick, unhappy provincial doctor's wife, but as a woman already in possession of important aspects of her own life. And any-way, he *does* try to give her a warning about the Stranger's reappearance, though he still hasn't seen just how direct the connection between the bo'sun and Ellida is. He says he is 'sure he's come to revenge himself upon his faith-less sailor-wife,' and in a sense, I suppose that's what he has come to do."

Will's look tells me he can't really see why I'm taking Ibsen's play so seriously, but is prepared—at any rate for some minutes and some more mouthfuls of port—to indulge me in this.

"I must say, if I were that doctor chap, I wouldn't be prepared to take back a woman who very nearly walked out on me to go with that rough old tar, who'd already killed another fellow, we were told."

The whole question of Johnston the bo'sun is something I want to apply myself to even less after this afternoon's play. I am not sure I don't agree with Will here, but knowing what I do about his own behavior to the opposite sex, I can't forebear saying: "You expect complete constancy in any woman of your choice then, Will? In the past as well as in the present?"

"Pretty much!" Will, obviously enjoying our talk now, stretches out his legs under the table making the "blood" in the decanter move against the glass sides. Then I see from a sudden darkening of his eyes that the implication of what he has so unthinkingly just said breaks on him. He is after all talking to me, Lucinda's husband, and if he knows nothing about his child, he must know everything about what led to his making, what brought Eddie into the world, however overlaid in his memory it now is by his many other amorous episodes—and betrayals. "I wouldn't write that in stone though."

"Some of us don't write such a sentiment in anything at all—if we love the woman in question," I say.

And here in this smokiness, in such contrast to what we could discover by just a minute of walking out of this establishment, the communication has at last been made between us—that Will paid amorous attentions to Lucinda and then abandoned her, and that I married her in full knowledge of this.

A silence falls on our little nook, and I almost envy the other corners their chatter, their hoarse laughs. Perhaps it was risky even to say as much as I just did.

Then—"No, some of us probably don't," says Will in a low soft voice, "and there are others of us who are jolly grateful to them for that." And I know that's the best he will ever do in this matter, the best also I'm prepared to hear without going over things too painful and embarrassing to be spoken aloud.

He returns in manner to the jocose. "But this 'ere play, are we done with it? Are we to assume poor Lyngstrand won't finish that sculpture of the stranger returning to his faithless wife? He's going south, he says, for health reasons and to make his fortune as an artist. Italy, I presumed. That's the country they favor, the consumptives, isn't it?"

"I presumed that, too."

"But he won't get better?"

"Dr. Wangel doesn't seem to think so, does he? Nor his elder daughter, Bolette. And his younger, Hilde the pretty and fiendish one . . ."

"Yes, she did seem both pretty and fiendish, didn't she?"

". . . imagines herself wearing black because he has—" I do not want to finish this sentence, nor do I need to.

"Poor chap! Not able to finish the *chef d'oeuvre* he has carried about in his head so long."

"Yes, poor chap!"

Will is suddenly seized by a notion, a recollection. He bangs his hand against his forehead. "I just remembered—your Norwegian fellow, the one in Ma Fuller's house—he was pretty ill, wasn't he? Some lung trouble or other. And hadn't *he* been in some shipping accident in the Channel."

How could you have ever forgotten all that? I silently wonder. But Will, as nobody has better reason to know than myself, lives so very much in the present.

"You don't think, do you . . . that old Mr. Ibsen knows your fellow?"

I am glad he uses the present tense. It makes evasion so much easier for me.

"Who can say?" I answer, aware that he won't go on wrestling with the question for very long. After a decent pause, I say: "Well, I hope I've managed to make you see how carefully Mr. Ibsen weighs the merits of each of his characters."

"More or less. I have to say, if it won't insult you, Martin, you've surprised me a good deal by your grasp of a play on just one afternoon's performance. Mr. Clement Scott, the critic I esteem the most, had better watch out, I'm thinking. There's a certain Editor's Manager down in Dengate who might well take his place."

"Small chance of that. Anyway have I persuaded you to change your opinion of the work?" I point to the sheet of scribble.

Will grins. "Well, maybe just a bit, but honestly I think I will stand by what I composed as we were walking to this pot-house, and have now written down. I don't usually go back on a composition, you know." I do indeed. "I've trained myself not to over these many years."

"Well, am I to be honored with a hearing of it?"

"But of course." Putting his glass down and lifting up his pad, he says: "Here goes then:

"The chief impression made by the performance of Mr. Ibsen's play, *The Lady from the Sea* yesterday afternoon, was that Mr. W. S. Gilbert will have to look to his laurels. And not only Mr. Gilbert, but all our most successful writers of farcical comedy would have to tax their powers to the utmost to produce a more diverting piece than the five acts of unmitigated rubbish which were presented to a scanty audience on the first bright summer's afternoon of the season. Those who came to listen attentively remained to scoff, the ripple of laughter almost continuous during the fourth and fifth acts . . ."

Well, what more could I say than what I had already said? And a fat lot of effect that had had! I suppress a feeling of sadness.

Aloud I ask, "You said you had something else to discuss with me?"

"Yes, if things work out as they seem to be doing, my taking over the editorship—yes, THE EDITORSHIP!—of that favorite news-rag of yours and mine is pretty well in the bag. A *fait accompli*. Should become reality by August. And of course, I shall want a proper trustworthy Deputy Editor, and there's nobody in the present team with quite the nous for that, not in my very experienced view. But I do know just the man." He pointed across the table directly at my heart. "I'll move heaven and earth—or at any rate a goodly portion of 'em—to get him that job."

Tears well up in my eyes. What with this offer, and what with all the memories Terry's has brought up of poor old Hans, two years dead, I have a sudden inclination, you might say a temptation, to put my head in my hands, and break down into sobs. But I don't give way to it, naturally. What Englishman could? "Will," I said, "it's no end good of you. But I belong to Dengate now."

CHAPTER TWO

My Legacy

*M*y train takes me through all the long-familiar sprawl of South London into the well-farmed Kent countryside and toward the sea, and all the time I hear its noisy rhythm saying: "This return is forever—and ever and ever and ever!" As I sit in my compartment, the early evening outside the smoke-blotched windows benign in its warm light, I go over not the play in which I have just seen Hans reappear but the coming into my life of his statue, *The Sailor's Revenge*, proof (among other things) that he had, in the short time permitted him by his illness, lived up to his hopes, his ambitions for himself.

Imagine my feelings on getting the following letter nearly two years earlier:

29th August 1889

Dear Mr. Martin Bridges,

I write to you as a kind of envoy from our mutual friend Hans Lyngstrand who spoke of you repeatedly, and never more so than during his last week of life. I had the privilege of attending him to the very end, which he met, I may tell you, most peacefully, with his head cradled by my arms. Witnessing his passage out of life is, I believe, the greatest privilege I have yet been granted, and while I cannot believe myself worthy of it, I have the strongest wish to be proved not altogether unworthy. Please, by the way, forgive any peculiarities of English style, though it was in English that I always spoke to dear Hans.

I assisted in laying him to rest in the cemetery of the Scandinavian colony in Rome. His grave therefore now lies among those of many another Northern seeker after light, who finally succumbed to incurable sclerosis of the lungs. None of them, however, could have surpassed our friend in courage or equanimity when meeting death, though his disappointment must have been acute. He had come south, after all, less for his health than for his art, and had dreamed of creating so many meaningful works once he was here in the Mediterranean world. But it is the point of this letter to inform you that Hans's story is not primarily one of defeat. The great work gestating within him for so long, the "summa" of all his artistic aspirations, is now ready to stand where it was meant to stand—so that you yourself, Mr. Bridges, who played such an important part in its inception, can behold it every day.

Honesty compels me to admit that The Sailor's Revenge—*this was the sculpture's title from its very inception—could not have been executed without the help I myself gave Hans, and that, once again through my offices, it reached completion only after the artist had expired. That sad event occurred in March, on the twenty-first, to be precise, the date of the spring equinox which, he always liked to tell me, had four years before brought about the terrible storm in the English Channel which, among so many tragic casualties, bestowed two great blessings on him: his awareness that he had a vocation in life, to whit, be a sculptor, and—you will, I hope, have guessed—his friendship with your good self.*

March 21 seems already a long time ago, and this year of Our Lord 1889 well advanced. August is drawing to a not unwelcome close, but la vendemmia, (*the grape harvest) is to hand again, and soon the sweet-chestnuts will be ready for the gathering. For the first two months after Hans breathed his last I was too overcome by grief to undertake work on* The Sailor's Revenge, *and even when, eventually, I felt strong enough to resume, I had to combat a strong feeling of personal inadequacy, a fear that I might, simply by persevering, be doing the person I so admired more injustice than justice. But my wisest counsellor, the man I still am happy to call Father, persuaded me to put these doubts, however well-grounded, aside. High summer is a period of great, and at times unbearable, heat here in central Italy, so you can understand why it is only now that I can declare: "My task is done. Let the work travel to its rightful home." And let it not be judged too harshly, for it is doubly a labor of love. First, obviously, by Hans*

Lyngstrand himself who strove to attain the greatest heights of his chosen art when he was suffering a mortal weakening of the body and even a certain mental debilitation. And secondly, by myself, who cared so much for Hans and who believed so ardently in his contribution to sculpture that I abandoned business of my own to see to its realization.

So now, Mr. Martin Bridges, The Sailor's Revenge *can go on the long journey for which it was destined, but—thanks to the insistence of this wise counselor of mine—it will not travel alone. For I myself shall be accompanying this, in literal terms, weighty work of art all the way from its Italian place of creation to England. Both the arrival of this letter and the portage of the sculpture may well take more time than one would like, so I will not confuse or alarm you now with any statement about dates which might prove grossly inaccurate. But I am assuming the first event will precede the second, so I will merely enjoin you to await Hans's* capolavoro *with patience and a sense of pleasure to come. I hasten to assure you—are not the English a mercantile people?—that all costs are taken care of, thanks to the administration of Hans's legacy by the Wise Counselor himself—so all you have to do is to wait for the telegram I shall dispatch to you when I am actually safe and sound in London.*

But "Who is this man?" I hear you ask. "Is he somebody I should be trusting?" Well, in answer to the first I will content myself with saying that I was for many months Hans's neighbor and constant confidant, in both matters personal and artistic, though not so much a fellow artist as a fellow craftsman. That is to say, I do indeed know about clay and calculations, maquettes and measurements, the working methods of Bertel Thorvaldsen and of the greatest sculptor of the present age, M. Auguste Rodin. But I do not have any talent that the world would care to label "artistic," my abilities and achievements lying in other directions. And to address myself to the second question—what shall I say that will properly convince you? . . . Well, I know that you and Hans met when you were both living at Castelaniene on St. Ethelberga's Road in the Kentish Channel Port of Dengate. I know that you had the room on the left as you ascended the third staircase, whereas he occupied that on the right. And I know that

the editor of the newspaper, to the address of which I have taken the
liberty of writing this, goes by the name of Edmund Hough. I know,
too, that you grew up in that part of London called Camberwell, where
you attended the Thomas Middleton School. If these are not proofs of
an intimacy of information about your life bestowed on me by the de-
ceased, then I do not know what in the world would constitute them.

Yours in the friendship of Hans Lyngstrand, beloved Norwegian
sculptor who died so regrettably young,

Orazio Martello

Until this moment I had not known Hans Lyngstrand was dead. The last
letter I had received from him had come a good month before the Christmas of 1888. In common with my practice with its predecessors, I had read
it (this perhaps more thoroughly than the others) but had not replied to it,
nor contemplated doing so. I knew therefore that he had arrived at long
last in Rome, the city of his hopes and dreams, knew too that he had found
a hearty welcome at the Scandinavian Club there, a majority of members
of which were practicing artists, some as young as himself, "feeling the
need to surrender completely (for a while, at any rate) to the noble but joy-
ous achievements of the classical world." The Club had an excellent library
apparently, and organized many delightful social events, debates, parties,
excursions, picnics. Hans had supplied the names of many persons,
Norwegian, Danish, Swedish, Finnish, even Icelandic, all of which, it must
hardly need saying, meant precisely nothing to me. Hans's only complaint,
but lightly, almost casually made, was that he still felt "too tired rather
too often," but the enormous distance he had had to traverse to reach the
Eternal City was probably the principal cause of this, and when he'd rested
more often and not accepted quite so many irresistible social invitations,
then he would doubtless feel better. More himself. Himself? And involuntarily I'd seen two images of my correspondent imposed on each other, one
a pale, thin youth struggling painfully for breath, as on those first nights
at Castelaniene, the other my bed-companion I have tried to pay homage
to with my pen.

"*Only* complaint," did I just write? There'd been another. That he
hadn't heard from me "for a long time." That, of course, was euphemistic

politeness. After my first and reasonably friendly letter to him following his departure from Dengate with Herr Strømme, I had deliberately not answered any letter from Hans whether it came from Bergen in Norway, Saeby in Denmark, Molde in Norway, Hamburg and Munich in Germany (en route for Italy), and now from Rome itself. How could I after learning that what he'd given me and I had so lyrically accepted had been but a continuation of his practices he'd handed out to others, as a ship's whore, a seamen's moll. I could only wonder at his going on to write to me at such length and so comparatively often. Nor had I felt even that Christmas-tide the slightest temptation to pick up a pen and give him the asked-for reply. But I did, I know, experience a real pang when he mentioned his persistent tiredness—that much I will say in my own favor—and, if I am honest with myself, did not rate the chances of his ever putting that condition behind him very high.

So, my readers, how have you envisaged my state of mind after reading this document from Mr. (Signor) Orazio Martello? Here was I being told that (despite never getting a line from me in four years) Hans had been speaking repeatedly of me the very week he died, and in such a way that two people at least—the letter-writer himself and this mysterious "Wise Counsellor"—believed the proper home of *The Sailor's Revenge* (and just its title itself quickened my heartbeat!) would be with myself! Sorrow, guilt, shame, confusion—all of these surged to the surface of my being within a handful of minutes, together with some far less praiseworthy or morally dignified concerns which it will be my painful duty to set down.

I looked at the date at the top of the letter. August 29, 1889! What a long time it had taken to reach me; it might well now be out of date, and the writer have completed his own journey. August, which had witnessed such unrest in England as we had not known for half a century, was over and done with, and we were now over halfway through September. *The Channel Ports Advertiser* was just about to publish a detailed article on the autumn equinox, trying to assure readers of the possibility of no seasonal gales blowing up this year. I was not seated at one of the long tables in the office, at which readers last left me—oh, no! A five-foot-high green baize screen now separates me and my big desk from all the other toilers in the field providing me with a kind of extemporized study-room. Yet the screen, indispensable as a symbol, does not guarantee me true privacy, I'm afraid, and Edmund (whose idea, after all, it was) can and does come barging in on me any time he feels like it.

So though I needed time to take in the information my letter from Italy contained, its matters of life and death, I was not permitted this. Waving what looked like a positive wodge of telegrams, my editor/father-in-law burst in on me, the perspiration (of pleasure, judging by his expression) pouring down his amiable, florid face.

"It's actually happened, it's actually come about!" he exclaimed. "The 'dockers' tanner. And what I say is: Hooray, hooray! Hooray for the Cardinal, hooray for Londoners and the English spirit, hooray all 'round in fact!"

With my mind trying to image (or, more accurately, trying *not* to image) my former friend Hans Lyngstrand (whom I'd once loved not only in spirit but in physical form) drawing hourly nearer death and yet speaking of, why, of me, Martin Bridges, I needed, believe it or not, a full moment to take in what Edmund was so excited about, even though the phrase it contained had been ringing in all our ears and dancing in front of our newsprint-reading eyes these past many weeks. Three years of crowded domestic life (for I have reached this concluding chapter of my book in May 1892) can make even the public events of 1889, last year of the last decade, seem distant, gone forever. All summer long—do you recall it?— the dockers, among them some of the very poorest men in the kingdom, had marched and formed protest groups in the London streets, arousing not reluctant but lively, instinctual sympathy and support in unexpected and powerful quarters, outstandingly in Cardinal Manning, the Archbishop of Westminster himself, who soon passed from being a supporter to becoming an outright impassioned champion. Over in The Smoke, Will Postgate and, even more so, his special handful of still radical friends, had got much exercised by the affair, whipping themselves daily into fresh furies or choruses of exhortation, and had naturally tried to rope me in. Names that Will had regaled me with, that evening walk on his first ever visit to Dengate had been on all lips, together with that of Ben Tillett, the dockers' leader, "a hero in the land, a Man among men," to use Will's own words. I had been involved only superficially, I'm afraid, though I tried hard to pretend otherwise. Besides I could not say I cared for the look of certain scowling chaps hanging around the quays in Dengate, trying to get something going at the wharfs. Anyway, was I not, unlike Will and many of his best socialist cronies, "a family man" now?

As for Edmund himself, half cockerel, half schoolboy with pleasure at what had just come about, the dockers" agitations had not, in truth, made for an easy or enjoyable time for him (though he always tried to make the best of everything), and this during the season when Dengate was usually celebrating itself with genial pride, encouraging everybody to forget worries, and come down to its sands. A goodly proportion of his readers were far from friendlily-disposed toward the strikers or the attention they had attracted, especially when, on the twenty-second of August, work in the Port of London docks stopped altogether, and there were 100,000 men with time to vent grievances. Significant "friends" of *The Advertiser* had interests in Channel Ports docks and ships, and literally the last thing they wanted was any copycat activity in Dengate, Dover, Margate, or any encouragement from the region's press. Some of these august and influential men wrote letters to the paper—most of which Edmund "forgot" to publish—saying that Ben Tillett was a traitor, a latter-day Jacobin who ought to be hanged as an example to all, and that the self-styled Dock, Wharf, Riverside, and General Laborers' Union was an evil rabble, every bit as barbaric, if not more so, than the movements produced by Revolutionary France or Russia in one of its regular phases of anarchy.

By the second week in September, however, the public mood throughout the realm had so perceptibly changed that Edmund in his *Advertiser* articles could write of the respect shown at last to laborers who had "given so much and received so little" as a proof of "that great heart and that noble tradition of fairness that distinguishes" England from almost every other country—and some of those readers only recently fuming with rage wrote to the paper to say how in sympathy they felt, and how gratified they were with the generosity the Editor was displaying. And now, said the telegrams Edmund was wafting in my face, with particular thanks to the Roman Catholic Archbishop, the dockers had won their right to sixpence an hour's pay, and the whole country was prepared to rejoice with them, the Channel Ports included. Edmund indeed saw himself in the very vanguard of the celebrations and wondered that I was not similarly elated.

"Oh, but I *am* pleased," I assured him. "Dockers' tanner at last—that's tremendous. If I sounded—it's just, you see, Edmund, that . . ." But I did not want to go into the contents of Signor Martello's letter, doubted indeed that I could summarize them without fatally tripping over words. Besides Edmund would probably by now have forgotten who Hans Lyngstrand was, though he might, if prompted enough, have remembered that he was the subject of my first interview-based article for him. "Personal stuff—well, I know all about that, naturally," said the ever-kind Edmund. "There are times when I can't remember how many children I have. And talking of private matters, among these epoch-making 'grams came one addressed for yourself, reply paid."

He must have been quite surprised at the way I snatched it.

ARRIVED IN LONDON YESTERDAY. WOULD LIKE YOU TO COME AND COLLECT YOUR INHERITANCE TOMORROW AFTERNOON FROM GIORGIO FATTERINI GALLERY, BOND STREET. I SHALL EXPECT YOU ABOUT THREE O'CLOCK. PLEASE WIRE TO SAY CONVENIENT. ORAZIO MARTELLO."

My heart's missing a beat caused me to gulp alarmedly for restorative air.

"I have just become a legatee," I told an amazed and immediately curious Edmund, "and I need to go up to town tomorrow."

I did not tell Lucinda the reason for my imminent visit to London; I would have to do so in due course, unless by some happy stroke of the mind I could think of a way of evading that. At this stage the very word "legacy" was bound to beget the question "who from?"—it was not as though I came from a large or affluent family, coming indeed from the precise opposite of this—and, for reasons too obvious to need stating, I did not want just now to utter the name Hans Lyngstrand to my wife. Besides she had only met him that once, when he had made but a slight, if entirely amiable impression on her. I would, I said, like to go for a walk, after dinner, "to think over this meeting I have in London tomorrow. I'll be taking Balthasar with me, of course."

"What, to London?"

I pretended to take the question as a serious one rather than a willful misunderstanding. "A dog in the West End? In Bond Street? That'd be out of the question, Lucinda. I meant on my stroll now."

Balthasar would anyway have assumed he accompany me on any evening walk I took. Our house being situated at a convenient distance from Furzebank House itself, it was easy enough to take a path up to the very crest of the downs to look down over town and harbor. But the day had been one of seasonal sea-frets, now intensifying with the onset of dusk. No stars visible in the sky above, and the waters of the Channel showed like a slice of darkening flesh between shawls of gray mist. Tear these apart, though, and the true expanse of sea would be revealed, and, though still, indeed calm tonight, who knew what treachery it might not soon be capable of, when the equinox came around again? The assurances my newspaper was giving its public on this subject meant little! Balthasar was burrowing his nose into tufts of grass which had doubtless preserved the aroma of a rabbit or another passing dog, and I found it better for my spirits to turn to him and investigate what he was up to, for the sight of the fog and water brought today's news back into my mind in an uncomfortable new guise. Death had not taken Hans Lyngstrand here in the Strait down below, but it had caught up with him sooner rather than later, after a long cat-and-mouse game, and to what avail his body-wracking survival four years back, with all its concomitant hopes and plans? Yet, against all odds, he *had* carried out the great work born of his experiences in the ship that had gone under only a few miles from where I was now positioned. And tomorrow I would be seeing it, would be in touch again with Hans, whom I'd treated so ill.

"Come on, Bal, good dog! That's enough."

But Balthasar didn't agree but buried his long proboscis further into the matted grasses. And then he looked up to indicate that Japheth of the noticeably, beautifully pricked-up ears was walking toward us to join us for the rest of the walk. He had not accompanied Beatrice, Mary, Mrs. Noah, and Ham to France, but had chosen—I believe the active verb is the correct one—to remain in Dengate with myself.

• • •

Well, here I was in Bond Street. For all, as I was often pleased to proclaim, that I was a Londoner born and bred, I scarcely knew Mayfair, and that day felt a stranger in its elegant, symmetrical, expensive streets. During the journey up to town, remembering the gloom of my evening walk and the discomfiting dreams of the long night just past, I had done my best to banish thought altogether, and more or less succeeded. What lay beyond the train windows had greatly aided me. The mists having lifted by mid-morning, Kent, beneath sun and clear sky, stretched on either side of the rails a real feast of ripeness, apple-orchards and nut-orchards laden with fruit and peopled with pickers, hedges so full of haws they could appear as they passed by as much red as green, and cornfields like palettes of gold with blue flowers at the edges. And the month's predominant reds and golds continued into the capital itself, and I wondered—as I nearly always did on my return visits—why I had not done enough justice during my growing-up to all its many parks and gardens.

Yet Bond Street was urban enough in all truth, smart façade succeeding smart façade, many of them with uniformed flunkeys at the door, uncongenial, not to say alien to, the kind of person I was, who was finding it difficult enough getting used to living in the kind of house that was now my (and my own family's) home, under the ownership though it still was of my mother-in-law's undereducated yet fiscally shrewd and therefore well-heeled farmer-brothers. What a figure I must cut to call on an enterprise with the pretensions of Giorgio Fatterini's. The suit I was wearing, smart enough for most of the Dengate occasions to which I was thought good enough to be invited, surely looked a touch common beside the attire of the young men I was now seeing just about everywhere, coming out of grand townhouses, stepping into the offices of financial or legal firms with the elite as clientele, or standing behind the luxuriously decked windows of the street's *raison d'être*, all those galleries, jeweller's, specialists in furniture and *objets d'art*, picture-dealers.

And here was the destination, and it was exactly two minutes to three o'clock. The premises of Gregorio Fattorini and Son stand opposite the turning into Conduit Street (if you're coming down Bond Street from Oxford Street), and I could not disguise from myself what my body was, in all its components, telling me: that I was filled with a dread of such a heavy intensity as, even at the most difficult moments of the history I've been unfolding, I had not yet experienced.

I wanted to hear no details at all of Hans's dying; I have none of the morbid inclination for such things that many, including *Advertiser* readers, apparently have. More, I have the greatest possible aversion to having them inflicted on me, often by people whose business it is not. But in the case of Orazio Martello his business it indubitably *would* be. My old—well, I'll call it friend—had died with his head cradled in this man's arms, and how I wish he had not seen fit to tell me this! Typical foreigner's, typical Mediterranean's love of sensation, thought I. An Englishman would have kept such a fact (if "fact" it truly was) to himself, might have known it would prey on the mind of the letter's recipient, and, out of good taste, decided to spare him such mental discomfort. But not Signor Martello of Rome, not he! His letter I now had by heart—it had even got in the way at times of the russet splendors of the Garden of England—and I did not think I liked it, in other words that I liked the character of its writer. The way he boasted of his knowledge of me and my provenance was impertinence really, particularly as he had given me no satisfactory information about himself, not his age, not his line of work, not the circumstances in which he had drawn so close to Hans Lyngstrand as to be taken into both his personal and his artistic confidence. So much so in truth that he had applied himself, both in the sculptor's lifetime and after it, to seeing that his *capolavoro* saw light of day.

And behind these questions never more insistent than when I finally stood outside the window of the Fattorini gallery, other ones menacingly lurked.

(i) What information did Signor Martello have about Alfred Johnston, to call the man that, the real begetter of *The Sailor's Revenge*?

(ii) Did he know what intimacy there'd been between Hans and myself?

(iii) Had Hans told him that I—cruelly, disgracefully, as it now seemed—had shunned him totally?

Behind the glass of the window four large oil paintings of Italian landscapes (for such I correctly took them to be, pines and ruined temples and snow-capped mountains above inky-looking lakes) in massive, many-layered, gilded frames stood propped up on a red velvet drape that uncomfortably could not but remind me of the hangings and table-covers of Dengate's Banstead Lodge. This was not a comfortable place, but because of this entirely fitting for an interview which was not going to be comfortable either, though I was going to leave it as owner of—apparently—a *capolavoro*.

Even outside so fashionable an establishment as Fattorini's a group of cloth-capped men loitered with a collection-box and a huge placard telling the world in huge scarlet letters: "WE ARE DOCKERS. HELP US TO THANK THE GREAT CARDINAL FOR WHAT HE DID." Well, I had no spare money on me to give Cardinal Manning, despite approving of the sterling work he'd done, and, what's more, I'm ashamed to admit, I didn't want to embarrass myself—in Bond Street!—by conversing with these triumphant, strong, but still obviously indigent men. So you could say that for these moments embarrassment triumphed over dread; certainly it was on the side of inevitability. Taking an almost theatrically deep breath, and looking away from the dockers, two of whom were no older than myself and probably like me had young kids to worry about and care for, I crossed the threshold of the celebrated Mayfair concern. I tried to reduce my awe at this dark interior and at the tall bearded Levantine figure in skull-cap and dragon-patterned maroon robe worn over an impeccably tailored suit now gliding slowly over the close-carpeted floor toward me.

"Signor Giorgio Fattorini?" I inquired, in answer to the quizzically interrogative expression on this exotic individual's face.

A negative noise. An almost pitying shake of the head. "No, no! No more!" Then he gave a sigh: "Is gone. Totally gone!" Then, lest his words had suggested death, he added with a mocking smile: "Is with Royal Household. Is taking Household more beautiful things."

Difficult to know the right thing to say here. But all around me, in this shadow-land of an interior, what a profusion of Italian scenes and classical heads and busts, on shelves, tables, inside open-doored cupboards, on top of them, underneath them, and none of them, at first glimpse anyway, taking my fancy in the very least, some exposed to the gaze, some discreetly covered with cloths. All so proud, so unhomely, so reeking of high prices! But well could I understand that there could be a superfluity of such stuff here as to make its owner think of offering choicer morsels from it to Buckingham Palace or Osborne House. The man—he was about forty—was smiling at the effect his words had had upon me. What a contrast he made, in his conjuror's outfit above a suit from nearby Savile Row, to the September sunshine outside, to both the stylish young-men-about-town and the victorious dockers enjoying it as it splashed down on Bond Street.

"I am Son," the man informed me in his unrepentant un-English accent and manner, and smiling at me though he had just played me an irresistible practical joke, as, in a muted sort of way, I suppose he had. "Gregorio Fattorini." He half-bowed. "And you are young man come from country?"

I didn't feel this instant description of myself flattering. Down in Kent I was—or, rather, until taking residence in my present home, had been—thought a Londoner, whose ways smacked of coarser but livelier streets than those of Dengate burghers. But up here in town I apparently struck this sophisticate as some clodhopper stumbling into such temples of culture as these premises to better his knowledge of the arts.

"Not at all," I countered, "I have an appointment at this very hour, three o'clock—I have the telegram in my pocket to prove it—with one Signor Orazio Martello."

The man's eyes, the color of old leather, noticeably brightened. "You Mr. Martin Bridges?" He spoke as one perfectly familiar with my name. "But how not?"

"I am here to—"

But at that—"So you are Mr. Martin Bridges?" inquired a figure stepping forward from the deeper shadows of the back of the gallery. (I nearly wrote "shop" here, but that word would never do!) "Well, well! You're not a *bit* how I'd imagined you!"

But his surprise at me was nothing to mine at him—especially in the context of his surroundings and of the only other person apart from myself nearby. I could not for the first minute or so, determine his age. My eyes were first drawn to his hair, and truly amazing it was, long, longer even than was the custom of those lascars I'd glimpsed at London or at Channel Ports docks, though nearer to their style than to any other I knew. It flowed well below the shoulders in thick, dark, matted-looking lines of ringlets. A gold ring dangled from his left earring, and, caught by a shaft of sun, winked brightly and almost painfully at me through the gloom which framed its owner. But for all the cool and shade of the room this Signor Martello—for obviously it was he who had just made his appearance—suggested summer, and long, arduous but contented exposure to its fiercest sun. Not only was the face below the tangled black hair well-tanned but the arms bare from just above the elbows down and the backs of his hands were the brown of some fully ripe but entirely hard pear, of which the peel is warm with a saturated sunshine that has not yet managed to soften the flesh. Around his neck this man who had summoned me peremptorily to London was wearing a red, white-spotted handkerchief knotted in front, above the Adam's apple, and contrasting with a white satin short-sleeved shirt more like a vest than the equivalent garment young Englishmen don for cricket. His gray flannel trousers were baggy and a mite more conventional.

"Let us shake hands," he said. "This is an important moment for both of us, surely?"

"Oh, yes," I said uneasily, "it can't *not* be."

We stepped toward each other, and like a member of the chorus in a play, Gregorio Fattorini moved away from us, back toward a desk placed nearer the front window of the gallery. Signor Martello, as he came up to me—he was a little taller than myself—immediately imparted a sense of suppleness and general physical competence. And as I shook the hand he proceeded to offer me, and felt its muscularity extending to the tips of his fingers, I found it quite easy to imagine the individual it belonged to carrying out the hardest and most exacting labors a sculpture could demand.

But his eyes—interestedly scrutinizing me even during the handshake—were not, as the whole gypsy-ish appearance might have suggested, dark—but a remarkably light blue. Their color disconcerted me. Far from reminding me of the dark depths of deathbed attendance and arduous travel undertaken for altruistic reasons, they proclaimed a freedom from care, almost from responsibility itself, an insouciance. Irises like his invited, it seemed to me, a pleasant, cleansing ascent into the azure of untroubled skies, and here I was, in my dreary, inexpensive, "common" best suit, with dread still lodging in my body.

"Well, what shall we talk about?" my "envoy" from Hans Lyngstrand asked me, releasing my hand as if he found doing so—doubtless my tension was palpable—a relief. "What do you *want* to talk about? We have no lack of subjects at our disposal."

Which, I wondered after he'd spoken these sentences, would be more accurate as a description of his voice: that it sounded both Italian *and* English, or that it sounded neither Italian *nor* English. He articulated, I thought, more precisely and emphatically, particularly on the final consonant of any word, than did the normal Englishman. On the other hand, he had the roll, and the confidence of delivery, of a native speaker. And he was idiomatic in his language. I was reminded of the "part and parcel" and "safe and sound" that he'd employed in his letter to me.

I was, of course, quite thrown by his verbal invitation, so what had been preying on my mind ever since the receipt of Signor Martello's letter came to its forefront.

"What did Hans say about *me*?" I all but gabbled in response. "You wrote that he spoke about me, particularly toward the end"—I recalled the crucial and somehow troubling adverb—"*repeatedly*. But what was he actually saying?"

Yes, I was even at this very instant afraid to learn that the poor dying young Norwegian had recited to the man before me every syllable of our nocturnal exchanges. And surely it was not so very improbable that he would have done, especially when far too sick to keep a bridle on his brain let alone his tongue. And would not this signor with his wild ringlets and his fair-ground trinket winking just below the right ear seem a readier recipient for such stuff than most men?

Signor Martello shifted his stance and, doing so, indicated a low table on which stood a large, indeed monumental sculpture completely covered by a black velvet drape. Underneath it I could see the forms of two figures, and instantly knew that beneath the dark material stood *The Sailor's Revenge*, for did not two figures comprise that work? He grinned, displaying startlingly regular, startlingly white teeth, and in doing so reminded me of somebody—yes, somebody I knew reasonably well—but I could not think who it was. His changed expression made him look younger than on his initial emergence from the back. He was surely about my own age, (then) twenty-seven.

"You have a friend," he said in a slow, wry, mocking voice, "who suffered a painful illness, a distressingly painful one, and who took four whole days to give up the ghost (some doctors would say that he took 'four whole years' to do that), and who expressly asked to have his *capolavoro* sent to *you*, Mr. Martin Bridges of Dengate, a procedure which has involved great cost and great effort—and all you are interested in, when you meet the man who held him at the very last, and who has gone on faithfully to carry out his wishes, is—'What did he say about me?' *Me!*"

Who could not feel crushed and ashamed at this rebuke, to which there could be no riposte? Nevertheless—

"That isn't 'all' I'm interested in," I protested, "not by any means."

"Perhaps it was not fair of me to get you to speak first. This must be an awkward occasion for you—for me far less so, though I am a little travel-weary still. I shall not keep you any longer from dear Hans's bequest to you, *The Sailor's Revenge*." And before you could say Jack Robinson, Mr. Martello (for suddenly I was sure he was essentially English) had flicked off the black drape, and two figures on a plinth presented themselves to me.

Of their genuineness I had not a second's doubt. I recoiled.

"This is terrible!" I cried. "I can't have it. Don't want to have it!"

"But you *have* to have it!" this probably English gypsy-man said. "It is law that you do. It is a legacy."

"And legacies can't be refused?"

My interlocutor drew himself up as one offended, "I do not know about such things. But your refusal will have to be done on your own. By yourself. Mine was the legally sanctioned task to bring the sculpture to you, and that I have done. My part is over, I am free to go back to Castelaniene where I live."

"To Castelaniene?" I repeated, for a split second imagining this young man was returning to the house in St. Ethelberga's Road.

"Yes, Castelaniene where I live. The real village, not the stupid suburban house. Don't you, you poor Martin Bridges, understand who I am? What is the English of my name, Orazio? *Horace*, you surely agree? And what is the English for my surname, Martello? *Hammer*—or *Fuller*, would you not say? When my father made his move to live in the village of Castelaniene in the country of the Aniene valley that his most admired poet,

Horace had once lived in—the poet who loved both women *and* men—he was adamant that I stayed beside him. He makes a good enough living there, teaching Italians, at school and in their homes, not only the beauties of the English language but the treasures of their own ancestral one, Latin. I, for my part, have done different work, being good with my hands—with my body generally—but never tying myself down to anyone. I labor for Castelaniene itself, and the mountains beyond it, for Nature, for liberty of every kind."

Oh, how could it not make sense, little though I might want it to? Besides, the thing had an extraordinary, I might almost say a beautiful, logic to it. The last inhabitant of the Mercy Room had passed away in the company of him for whom the room had originally been designed, as a way of keeping him in his place as a young Englishman. But that scheme had not worked, and never could have done. There was always the *antícipo di paradiso* waiting, for father and son.

"Mr. Bridges," Horace was now saying, "you look so shocked. Forgive me if I add to your condition further, but I have some pages for you which our mutual friend penned with difficulty in his last weeks. When I said to him, 'What are these?' he gave an odd sort of smile, and said: 'Oh, nothing very important. You should bequeath them to Mr. Martin Bridges, along with my *capolavoro*.' And he tried to laugh, but the laugh cost him much pain."

As I now approach Dengate, my vow to write this book having been privately made at some point in this railway journey, Hans's sentences chant themselves in my now weary head. How can I do otherwise than give my readers now the document in its entirety:

> *The new April morning streams green toward me, through green slats. I leap out of bed to fling open the shutters . . . No, I don't. I can't any longer leap out of bed, and I doubt I'll ever be able to again. Instead, breathing like some wounded young elephant, I lift one slow foot after the other over the red floor-tiles to gain the window. Then, to recover myself, I lean against the wall for a moment before performing that action after which the day proper can begin. Behind me the night has been so cruel. I thought the bout of coughing just after midnight*

would smash me up, I compared myself to a little wooden boat I once saw tossed on a rock by a gale-force wind and splintered to bits. My temperature had risen also, sweats so strong I couldn't tell whether I was hot or cold, or what the difference between these states was. But I did fall asleep, and when, at four o'clock I woke up briefly, I had improved, really improved. The fever had subsided, my breaths were regular. So now, despite my labored movements across the room, I can feel my old optimism about to take hold of me again.

With a slight effort I push back the shutters, then gasp not so much with illness as with health, the health of strong sensory pleasure. Below me—I'm quartered in a second-floor apartment in a tall stone medieval house with a front-wall like a cliff-face and similar houses hanging both above and beneath—the valley lies filled with a lake which reminds me, at first glance, of certain lakes I knew on walking expeditions back in my own Norway. Except that this one isn't a reed-and-stone-fringed blue, but a heaving white, with gleaming silver waves at its eastern end. Except that it isn't composed of lapping water but of mist, and will soon break up into formless clouds that will drift upwards to disperse among the surrounding mountains. Then I can look down onto the valley floor with its serpentine river lined by poplars and water-meadows where youths collect edible snails, and then across to all the neighboring villages, which, far from dropping down to a lake-strand, as you might now suppose, perch on hillsides and crags like the nests of clever birds. I take slow steady breaths and the air tastes sweet in my mouth, laden with the scents of ripe vines and chestnuts. I say to myself: "Yes, they were probably right to bring me up here from Rome, sixty kilometers away, too sweltering by day and too steamy by night for my health to stand it." Yet every day I'm tormented by the possibility that I may never be at large again in that wonderful city, where my life began, for the second time. Mightn't it really be better to be down there, where the hopes and dreams of years can be met, letting it do its worst on my poor wracked body, than to be putting up with this banishment, this pleasant, calm, picturesque (yes, go on, say it!) tomb.

Ripples pass over the surface of the "lake"; there is the mildest of breezes, though the September day ahead will surely be very warm, very still. I turn my head to my left and a face smiles and a hand waves at me from the next-door window but one: Giulia, so kind, so hand-some, so assuring, so difficult to understand with her country dialect that doesn't fit in with any grammar I've studied, any Italian book I've tried to read. Knowing I'm not only awake but out of bed, she will now go and prepare my breakfast (just coffee and rolls), which she'll bring in along with a filled ewer and a bowl for washing. When I'm done and dressed, I shall go into the room immediately next to this bedroom, my studio (well, I'm entitled to call it that) with its comfort-ing aromas of oils, charcoal, clay, turpentine, and tinker with sketches until my model and helper, Orazio arrives.

What would the Wangel girls, Bolette and Hilde, say if they saw me here? I often ask myself that question. I was drawn to the pair of them back in Molde, spent much time with them, confided in them too, and they for their part were friendly, indeed hospitable to me. But they also laughed at me, Hilde, the younger and the prettier of them, more (and more openly) than her sister. Her mockery of me behind my back doesn't bear thinking about, even now! I'm pretty sure neither of them believed in me as an artist, ever thought I'd make it as a sculp-tor, even if my health permitted me to work. In their opinion, though they never exactly said as much (at least not to me), Herr Strømme has been supporting me out of charity, or some purely personal whim. (Was he perhaps my biological father?) Bolette and Hilde would never have anticipated the kind of acceptance I was to find in Rome, the way my enthusiasms and projects were listened to at the Scandinavian Club and even outside it. And wouldn't even Hilde be impressed by the way (this very morning, for instance) I override my complaints and apply myself to my chosen medium, how after a night of tormenting coughs and feverish sweats I busy myself getting ready for my model, and with precise knowledge of what has artistically to be done?

And wouldn't my former friend in England, Martin Bridges, be impressed also, though such (I take it) is his shame at himself for the love he accepted from me, that he has never been able to write me even the faintest note of help or inquiry?

Orazio. He's due at eleven o'clock, but punctuality isn't one of his strongest points, and he can be up to an hour and a half late, always for an excellent reason, during which time I get impatient, restless, almost annoyed. I'm eager for his visits—to be getting on with work I believe in, to have company, and that of somebody my own age and largely of my sympathies—and yet they fill me with dread, too. That's the paradox. There are times, and today, I'm afraid, is one of them, when I could almost wish he were not coming to pose for me.

First, the good things. As a model he is incredibly patient. The artist using him couldn't be more pleased with his capacity for sustaining demanding postures than he is himself. He revels in his own strength and suppleness. Though I can never be quite sure how long he will be able actually to stay with me, whatever our discussions on the matter the previous day, I know that once here he will not stint himself. Also he is genuinely interested in the whole making process—in my sketches, my calculations, my little clay figures suitable for holding in my palm to guide me toward the big work. He takes a contemporary's ambitions to be a good sculptor perfectly seriously, whereas in northern Europe, absorption in an art is apt to be taken as one further proof of a young man's idiocy. Orazio belongs, you might say, to the land of Michelangelo and Bernini and Canova (and my revered Thorvaldsen, with his "Roman birthday"), even if to an obscure corner of it. But—a paradox—he doesn't, I'm sure, come from it. His father—whom I have only spoken to in my poor Italian—is, I am pretty sure, an Englishman, fled from his native country to the warmth of this classical land, whose poets and sculptors have taught him, he once told me, to find the spirit in the flesh, and the flesh in the spirit.

Second good thing (though here, I think, the problems begin). He has a general alive-ness which communicates itself from the moment he passes through my door, possibly even before, as I hear his springy step on the stairs. It's a tonic in itself to be in the presence of somebody who gets such satisfaction simply from being himself. From existing. And then the mean inner voice whispers:

Why couldn't Hans Lyngstrand have been granted Orazio Martello's easy good fortune? Hans has had ideas, plans, which go far beyond the limits of himself, and from which humanity (is it wrong to think in such large terms?) could benefit, but which he will very probably never realize. Whereas Orazio . . .

If I break out into punishing coughs, if I have a giddy spell when my vision temporarily betrays me and the objects in the studio I've so carefully assembled threaten to merge into each other and melt, nobody could feel to me more kind than Orazio, with his arms steadying my shaking frame, his muscular hands rubbing my back. I put it like that—"could feel to me more kind"—because I'm not wholly sure that Orazio in himself is kind. I'm far from sure that (like Hilde Wangel back in the fjord-town) he doesn't despise me (well, a little, if not a lot) for my condition. I can tell him till I'm blue in the face (as I fear I often am) about that terrible shipwreck in the English Channel which I survived but which put paid to normal health for me for ever. The sly judging look that then comes into his eyes tells me his thoughts only too clearly: "If that had happened to me, *Orazio Martello, I wouldn't have turned out like you now. I'd be just as you see me today, able to tackle anything and everything I want to, I wouldn't have become weaker, not by one millimeter." And if I dare meet the pale blue gleam of his eyes, which I often avoid, I receive something even more disconcerting, the challenge, the proposition (as I sometimes think it) that to deal with my life, I should* become *him. How, you might ask? Even the possibilities of an answer brings on an increase and an irregularity of my pulse, too often quickened by fever anyway.*

Orazio can't be held at all accountable for another reason why I dread his visits. No modelling session, for all the scheme I've worked out beforehand, goes as well as I've been hoping it would, or even— poor fool that I am—been expecting, even on my best days, even on those when I've scaled down the agenda. Well, I suppose that's a situation all artists, including those in perfect health, have to face some time or other. Execution never, or only exceptionally, matches conception, especially if the conception is ambitious. Friends down in Rome have told me tales of the Michelangelo of our time, some of whom have actually called on him: Auguste Rodin. At the start of this decade he received a staggeringly handsome commission for a great work which was going to rival Ghiberti himself, more, was to match in bronze (in its scope and power) nothing less than Dante's Divine Comedy *itself. Yet though he has produced figure after figure, he has not yet been able to blend them into any kind of whole, and is already disappointing those who believed in his genius. Ridiculous, I know, to make a comparison between such a living titan and a young sick Norwegian nobody. But nevertheless I always make it—after hearing myself talking to Orazio, in my slightly theatrical Italian, about my intentions. He's perfectly aware, I know, of the discrepancy between what I've announced and what I've actually managed in any sitting (indeed in the totality of sittings), and the look in his eyes—this is what is so disquieting—suggests that he doesn't put this down entirely to my illness either. I feel he has some instinctive ability (just as pretty Hilde Wangel did) to see right through to what is weakest in my character. "There he goes again," his face, no, his whole body says, "giving his dreams too much headway. Take those dreams away from* il signor norvegese, *and what would be left? Certainly not the ability to make this tribute to his sailor-friend's tragic adventures we've heard so much about. (Rather too much, to tell the truth!)*

And that brings me to the third and maybe most important thing about Orazio which gets between me and my work and makes me sometimes wish he didn't come to my studio. Yes, like him, *Orazio's a well-built, vigorous male (with a good deal of amorous experience behind him, I would think), but in truth he has scant similarity to the original inspiration for my—well, allow me to call it, my one serious contribution to the art of sculpture. Down in Rome my friends and colleagues at the Scandinavian Club found me models who did suggest, at least to some degree—by the lines on their faces, by the alternations of brightness and cloudiness in their eyes, the involuntary gestures of their great hands—his physical versatility, his capacity for burning passion (and, as I was later to find out, for inspiring it in a woman), his brooding inability to forget any injury to his heart or his dignity,* his *knock-about life in three continents and on many seas, throughout the rough, tough varied scenes of which he ceaselessly recalled that magic he'd learned in his remote boyhood. Not so Orazio. Never, for one moment, does he suggest any of all that. But he does suggest the second figure I intend to include in my* capolavoro, *and that is how I shall use him, as the eternal foil to* Him.

Him! *As I work on my sketches or on my palm's-breadth clay models, I'm thinking of him with all the intensity I can muster, reliving our strange proximity, trying to work my mind into his powerful, bewildering person as hard as I can. I would be utterly amazed, dumbfounded indeed, if I learned that* he *were thinking of* me*! He's rarely, I would wager, given me a thought! For a long time I believed him dead, was almost certain that the English Channel in its ferocity must have carried him off. Did I not have that message at the Gateway in the summer of 1885, with all those convincing details? But some form of telepathy must have been in operation there. Because, three years later, quite unexpectedly, and in the beautiful company of the Wangel sisters, I encountered the man again. We did not speak, we did not even exchange glances. He went away from Molde on an English ship, on which he was a passenger, his passenger's ticket probably having been given him as a reward for work done for the line to which she belonged. I expect he is bo'suning for that company now.*

I don't even know how best to refer to him. Which is, of course, another way of saying I don't know what I should call my sculpture depicting his agony. I got to know him as Johnston, though even then, callow though I was, I doubted that was his real name. On our re-meeting, up in that West Norwegian fjord-town of summer sunshine, flowers and mountain vistas, I learned through Ellida, his loved one, that, before I came across him, he'd been known as Friman. Being Johnston then had been a means of escape from the troubles of being Friman—which I'm almost positive wasn't his name either.

But, despite the drama of late summer last year, Johnston is how I think of him. Though wouldn't Friman sound better, have more resonance, as the title for a major sculpture? Yet was he freer than any of the rest of us? If he had the ability to know more intimately than most men can the secret ways of Nature, of the rough seas and the whales who both ride and inhabit them, of the eagles in the mountains that sweep down to northern harbors, and the seals who brave out storms on rocks, then he had none of the abilities which a free man needs, to let gentleness prevail, and harmony be your guide.

What a life I've led! Odd, but honest, to be using the past tense about it now. At the end of my first year in Norway my patron took me to Sæby in Denmark, on the coast of Jutland, and there, among the charming, little low (usually one-story) color-washed houses, and the sand dunes and the beaches on which I loved to find glinting pieces of amber, I came across most days a distinguished frock-coated man in middle age, with fierce eyes and an immaculate white beard, muttering to himself about the life of the sea, about all the myriad forms that are sustained beneath its blue surface. How part of humankind longed to go back there to join them, but never—or only rarely—could admit this to itself. Then, two years later, when I went to Molde, that "Town of Flowers" on Romsdalsfjord, I heard of a man, a writer, who had stayed for a summer in one of the two grand hotels that have recently been erected on the sea-front, and who could never stare down long enough at the sea—often from little rowing-boats which he'd take out himself on to the fjord—and who again talked to himself about how all existence was intricately related to the ocean depths. If only we knew how to attain them again.

And other times this man (he was famous) would go—along with many another visitor to Molde—all the way up to the View. From its eminence, you see, on the opposite side of the fjord, row upon row of mountain-peaks, cones that in the sun glisten white or silver with ice and snow, 222 of them, so the locals say. And these told another truth about existence, that we were all bound up with the obstinate mineral world, whether we liked it or not, and must be received into it sooner or later.

It will be sooner, of course, that I, not yet thirty, will enter the domain of Nature's supremacy. Why pretend any longer? I'm too exhausted to do so. And nothing is stranger in my life than that I shall make my entrance from a quiet village near Rome (that Mecca for all

Scandinavian artists), whose existence I first knew about just after my shipwreck from the name of the house in the Mercy Room of which I lodged for a few weeks. Castelaniene, Castelaniene—a beautiful name for a beautiful place. And back in England it honored the scene of a beautiful love.

Martin Bridges, my Martin, if I am unable ever to offer you again my lips, my loins, my heart—and I surely am unable—then I shall give you something endurable enough to survive till the day of your own death, may it be ever so distant!

I shall revert to the past tense now for have I not reached the very evening when I wrote the first sentences of this memoir, the evening of May 11 last year, when I watched Hans Lyngstrand move again, on the boards of Terry's Theatre and when Will Postgate had made me an irresistible offer which I nevertheless whole-heartedly resisted?

I took my dog Balthasar out for his walk, and my feet took me of their own accord down to the Royal Gardens. (Where else?) There of course it stood, sturdy enough to face up to all weathers, *The Sailor's Revenge*, which I could never have in my own home or garden but which by giving to the people of Dengate I had not exactly spurned. I realize that I have not informed readers of the particularities of the two figures that constitute it. One figure is Johnston, newly emerged from the sea, irate, threatening, arm raised to strike. The other is a young man, who has clearly not yet seen him but will surely shortly turn around and, appalled, do so. I suppose the model for him was indeed Orazio, though in truth it is a generalized enough figure. But I cannot see him either as Mrs. Fuller's "disappeared son" or as a mere composite representative of youth. I know that this second figure on the plinth is none other than myself. And how do I know? Because he holds himself in the very posture in which that now-distant summer night I received Hans's love.

Publication Note

*T*he sculpture still stands in the Royal Gardens, Dengate, Kent. Martin Bridges's will specified that after his death the memoir he had written "accounting for the work" should be bequeathed in perpetuity to the Dengate Museum, which has accordingly held it since 1946. Martin Bridges's grandson, the art historian and Thorvaldsen expert, Horace Bridges (1922–2003) gave the work its present title.

Historical Note

W. T. (William Thomas) Stead (1849–1912) was an influential British editor and pioneer of investigative journalism, the "New Journalism" in Matthew Arnold's famous phrase. The *Pall Mall Gazette* under his innovative editorship was to the fore in exposing hypocrisy and injustices in British society, and a series of articles in 1885 (the main year of this novel)—all fearless, well-researched, and morally principled—shocked the reading public with its exposure of sexual exploitation of girls and young women. Stead in his working life was connected with many leading figures including politicians from William Gladstone to Cecil Rhodes. In the early 1890s he also espoused the cause of spiritualism. He died on the RMS *Titanic*, bound for a Peace Conference in the United States at the invitation of President Taft.

The story of Hans Lyngstrand appears in *Fruen fra havet* (*The Lady from the Sea*, 1888) by Henrik Ibsen (1828–1906). The first English translation of the play was that by Eleanor Marx-Aveling (1890), used for the play's first performance in May 1891 in the very circumstances described in this novel. A good modern translation of *The Lady from the Sea* is that for the *New Penguin Ibsen*, editor Tore Rem (Volume 3, Penguin Books 2019) by Deborah Dawkin and Erik Skuggerik. For the most acclaimed recent life of Ibsen, readers are referred to *Henrik Ibsen: The Man and The Mask* by Ivo de Figueiredo, translated by Robert Ferguson (Yale University Press, 2019). For a discussion of the play's character Hans Lyngstrand and its general view of creative art, see *With Vine-Leaves in His Hair: The Role of the Artist in Ibsen's Plays* by Paul Binding (Norvik Press 2006).

The story that Hans tells Martin in Chapter Ten is an early version of that which appears as "The Sailor-Boy's Tale" in *Winter's Tales* (first published by Putnam, 1942) by Isak Dinesen (Karen Blixen), (1885–1962).